TWAIN'S END

Also by Lynn Cullen

Mrs. Poe

Reign of Madness

The Creation of Eve

I Am Rembrandt's Daughter

TWAIN'S END

GALLERY BOOKS
New York London Toronto Sydney New Delhi

G

Gallery Books
An Imprint of Simon & Schuster, Inc.
1230 Avenue of the Americas
New York, NY 10020

First Gallery Books hardcover edition October 2015

Interior design by Davina Mock-Maniscalco

Manufactured in the United States of America

10 9 8 7 6 5 4 3 2 1

Library of Congress Cataloging-in-Publication Data is available.

ISBN 978-1-4767-5896-1
ISBN 978-1-4767-5898-5 (ebook)

In Memory of Tami and Jess

One gets large impressions in boyhood, sometimes, which he has to fight against all his life.

—Mark Twain, *The Innocents Abroad*

After luncheon he came gaily into my study to say that his day's work was done and to read the result. In it he reminisced, telling of his childhood. He was deeply moved for all the morning he had been living with the ghosts of long ago. And so his gaiety was assumed.

—Isabel Lyon, daily reminder, February 12, 1909

TWAIN'S END

PART ONE

The New York Times, September 8, 1908

NEW YORK LOSES MARK TWAIN

Physician Leases Fifth Avenue House and Author Will Live in Connecticut.

With the leasing of 21 Fifth Avenue for a term of years to a physician that address ceases to be the town house of Mark Twain. Mr. Clemens will spend his time principally at his Italian villa at Redding, Conn., in the future. His physicians have pointed out to him the strain of life in town during the Winter, which in his case involved attendance at many dinners given in his honor.

The author's daughter, Miss Clemens, is due to arrive on the Caronia on Thursday. She has been traveling abroad with friends. With the party is Charles Wark of New York, whose engagement to Miss Clemens has been rumored.

The New York Times, September 19, 1908

BURGLARS INVADE MARK TWAIN VILLA

Captured After a Pistol Fight on a Train in Which Prisoner and Officer Are Shot.

DANBURY, Conn., Sept. 18.—Mark Twain's home at Redding, "Innocents at Home," was visited by two professional burglars last night. The wakefulness of Miss Lyon, the humorist's private secretary, was the undoing of the bold crooks, who were captured after a fight on a New Haven train.

1.

January 8, 1909
Stormfield, Redding, Connecticut

ISABEL'S MOTHER WATCHED HER tie on her hat with the look of intense pride and suppressed doubt that is particular to the mothers of grown daughters. "But Isabel, how *will* you serve Miss Keller tea?"

Her mind on other things, Isabel returned her gaze from the snow salting down outside the frost-etched windows. She took in the snug parlor with its fringed green velvet davenport, its painting of the Pitti Palace in Florence, its rocker turned toward the fire. The King's framed portrait presided over the mantel. He was younger in the photo, roughly handsome, his tornado of hair still dark. He frowned off in the distance in a way that suggested he could see things that mere mortals couldn't. *I Am the Youthful Sage*, he seemed to say. From the opposite wall, in a more recent photograph dated not only by his white hair but by the white suit that he'd taken to wearing two years ago no matter the season, he frowned mischievously: *The Wise Maverick*. On the side table next to the sofa, in a photo snapped with Isabel and friends in Bermuda last spring, he sternly confronted the lens while the rest of them made merry: *The Lonely Genius*. When had he last looked into a camera and let himself just be Sam Clemens?

"Miss Keller," Isabel's mother repeated. "How will you serve her tea?"

Isabel stepped into her rubbers next to the door. "She's blind and deaf, Mother, not paralyzed. I'll simply hand her a cup."

"But how will you ask her what she takes in it?"

"Mrs. Macy will sign the question to her in her hand. Or I'll ask her myself. She puts her thumb on your neck, her forefinger on your tongue, and her middle finger on your nose, then listens in that way."

"With her fingers all over your face?" Mrs. Lyon pursed her own lips, accentuating the soft pouches on either side of her jaw.

She had been a handsome woman once, with a small sharp nose and large brown eyes like her daughter's. As Georgiana Van Kleek, one of the prominent Hartford Van Kleeks, she had attracted all the best men when she had come out back in '61. No one had been surprised when she won the affection of dashing widower Charles Lyon, a distinguished professor at Columbia University who was as handsome as he was prosperous.

Now she was forced to live through her daughter, who hadn't ever married and who *worked.* It might be modern times, what with people racing around in Oldsmobiles and cranking up phonographs and shouting into telephones, but for a woman of their class to *work* was still a shameful thing. At least Isabel worked for a very famous man—the *most* famous, and the most beloved, too, if you could believe the slogan on the cigar box. "Known to Everyone, Liked by All," indeed. If everyone knew his terrible temper like Mrs. Lyon did, he would not be so very liked, she could tell you that.

Better that the public didn't know. As it was, her daughter's association with him had almost restored Mrs. Lyon's bragging rights to just below the level attainable had Isabel produced a beautiful grandchild, although they fell short of what they would have been had Isabel married a gentleman professor like her own father had been.

The situation could be remedied handily if Isabel would simply *marry* Mr. Clemens. Regardless of his shortcomings, he was ripe for wedlock now that "Livy" (as he had called his sickly wife Olivia, as if she were some gay young thing) had finally succumbed to whatever it was that had kept her bound to her bed and quarantined from him for months on end. The ship had sailed for grandchildren, unfortunately—Isabel was forty-five, and Mr. Clemens was in his early seventies and looked it—but he did have an honorary degree from Oxford in England and was a friend of the English king. If the English king could overlook Mr. Clemens's crude country roots, Mrs. Lyon probably could.

As a good mother, Mrs. Lyon often reminded Isabel of the desirability of a marriage, but with no favorable results so far. Evidently, Isabel had not minded lurking behind the potted palm trees with the servants at the lavish seventieth birthday party at Delmonico's thrown for Mr. Clemens by the Harper publishing crowd, when she should have been sitting right next to him, dining on Lobster Newburg.

Such a waste of potential! Isabel had been brought up to consort with gentlemen far more educated than Mr. Clemens was. While other little girls were paging through their McGuffeys, Isabel's father had taught her to recite passages from *The Iliad*, after which he would invite her into his study and stand her on his desk so she could entertain his scholarly friends. He had delighted in broadening her mind by taking her overnight to New York to see edifying Broadway plays. It was at such a play that, as a little child, Isabel had placed her hand on Horace Greeley's knee, and the venerable editor of the *Tribune* had *not moved it*. To keep this highly cultured girl waiting by the kitchen door as if she were no better than the Clemenses' surly maid Katy was as wrong as eating roast beef with a fish knife.

"The King says that Miss Keller puts you right at ease about it." Isabel bent down to tug the rubber over the heel of her pump. "It feels quite natural to have her touching your face. And even though she can't hear herself, she has mastered answering with her own voice. I've heard her—it's remarkable."

"I wish you wouldn't call him that!"

Isabel righted herself. "What?"

"The King."

"Why not?"

"It sounds so—so *subservient*, when you are so much more to him."

The resident pain along the length of Isabel's esophagus flared, as if the organ were being wrung. She plucked up her gloves and the string bag in which she'd brought food to her mother from the big house. "I'm glad that you think so."

"Why don't you stay here and rest? You look so tired." Mrs. Lyon did not add that Isabel had a better chance of securing Mr. Clemens if she appeared well rested and youthful.

"I'm fine." Isabel did not mention that yesterday her doctor had told her to get in bed and stay there until her nerves settled or risk permanent damage to her system.

On the walk back to Stormfield from her house, Isabel tried to settle herself by savoring the view of the deforested hills, paralyzed under a shroud of snow. Razed of all but a few trees lining the road—The King would have a view—his lands, blinding in the midmorning sunshine, spread out as far as one could see. Closer at hand, the shadows of the naked surviving trees striped the white road like the bars of a prison. Frozen drops clung to the rusty bramble leaves poking here and there from their glittering cover. A brook thrashed mutely against its clear lid of ice. Save for the groan of the trees in the wind, the shuffle of her rubbers on the sleigh tracks, and an occasional protest from a small bird, silence reigned.

Here at Stormfield The King would finish his autobiography, the culmination of his career, a project that he had started nearly forty years earlier and, though running thousands of pages, wasn't done yet. He seemed afraid to put it to rest, as if ending the work would be the end of the man. Isabel still could not believe that she had her own little house on the Stormfield grounds, a saltbox that dated back to the Revolution—the Lobster Pot, The King called it, his Christmas present to her. She had not expected to get this house or, indeed, any reward when she had directed the construction and decoration of Stormfield. All she had wanted was to support The King's work and to make him happy, and she believed that every little detail—the Italian-style loggia with its view of the hills; the Orchestelle player piano set up in the library; the wooden cherubs crouching over the fireplace—did so. Surely she'd outdone his wife.

Inside the mansion, Isabel kicked off her galoshes by the front door, shed her coat and hat in the cloakroom off the foyer, and went to the kitchen, which smelled of The King's breakfast of bacon and hotcakes drenched with maple syrup—the only meal of the day he might do more than pick at, unless you counted his nightly dish of radishes.

In the pantry she came upon the new butler, Horace, a raw and gangling eighteen-year-old youth from a local farm. His knobby wrists stuck out four inches beyond his shirt cuffs as he gingerly arranged the tea set upon its silver tray. Isabel would have to tell the new maid to stop boiling his shirts so long. And where was his suit coat? Horace was serving the most famous man in the world, not sexing chickens.

He glanced up, the silver creamer cradled in his callused hands, then looked back down quickly. A blush flooded the hollows of his cheeks. He had been unable to meet her eyes since discovering that her bedroom in the big house adjoined The King's.

"Were you able to polish all the silver yesterday?" she asked.

"Yes, ma'am."

She hated how he wouldn't look at her, as if she were some sort of fallen woman. "Are you enjoying your work here? Not everyone has a chance to serve so many interesting guests."

"Yes, ma'am."

Perhaps teasing him would soften him. "You can't say that you didn't like when that pretty actress Billie Burke visited us the other day."

Horace opened the lid of the sugar bowl and began to fill it from a paper sack, his face glowing like a horseshoe heating over a blacksmith's fire. An awkward moment passed. "Miss Clara sent word that she is coming, ma'am."

The pressure in Isabel's sternum flared at the mention of The King's daughter. "Did she say when she would arrive?"

"No, ma'am."

"Have Teresa make up Miss Clemens's room, please." She worked on lightening her tone. "Our Clara does insist on fresh linen."

"Yes, ma'am." Horace still wouldn't look at her. Isabel told herself it was because she was his superior and a good two decades older than he was. He probably had difficulty with other adults. Surely that was it. He definitely lacked training in manners. In truth, he made a terrible butler, but since the night of the burglary in September, after which all the servants but the maid Katy had fled, experience was not the most important qualification one needed to join the Stormfield staff. The local farmers said that the staff had bolted because of the burglars, but that wasn't really the reason why. Clara had fired them because of what they had seen, then threatened to ruin them if they talked. They were afraid of her. Rightly so.

Isabel gave him a comrade's smile. "I had better go see if The King is ready to descend."

"Yes, ma'am," he mumbled, her smile wasted.

The smell of bacon accompanied Isabel up the stairs. She was halfway up, the thick strand of coral beads that she always wore thumping against her breast, when the doorbell chimed. She flinched, then chided herself, *Don't be silly. It isn't Clara yet.* At any rate, Clara did not ring; Clara barged in like she owned the place, which she would, as soon as she could shove her father off this mortal coil.

Isabel checked the watch pinned to her shirtwaist. It couldn't be Miss Keller already. Her train wasn't due in to Redding until 3:45, and Giuseppe still had to greet them at the station and bring them back in the sleigh. Another thought froze her footsteps: *Reporters.* They had been showing up lately without Isabel inviting them, hoping for some scandal, and not just because of the burglary. Bully the help all Clara wanted, she couldn't control every wagging tongue in the nation.

Isabel waited while Horace clomped in from the dining room to answer. A man's elegant voice, accented with a whiff of the British Isles, wafted up from the foyer. Relief flooded Isabel's chest: dear

Ralph. As The King's business adviser, Mr. Ashcroft was the head of the Mark Twain Corporation, the company formed to exploit the Twain name, and the only person in the world who began to understand the difficulties Isabel faced in managing The King. Just hearing Ralph's voice soothed her. She turned around to greet him.

A faint metallic clank drifted through the house: tap-tap-tap-TAP. Beethoven's Fifth. The King was knocking on a radiator, his signal for her to come. Ralph would have to wait.

Upstairs, she rapped on The King's door.

"Come in."

She entered, releasing a cloud of cigar smoke. The world's most revered folk philosopher was sitting unselfconsciously on the bed, the hair around his ears damp from his bath. He wore white silk shorts and nothing else.

"You forgot me."

She laughed in spite of herself. Her King could always make her laugh. "No chance of that. I just popped down to the Lobster Pot to see Mother. How is your story coming along?" He liked to work in bed, mornings.

The King's drawl was as unhurried as an African potentate. "Terrible. The well is dried up."

How many times had Isabel heard that in her six and a half years with The King? "Dictating your autobiography usually unsticks you. I'll see if I can get Miss Hobby to return."

"No."

The abruptness of his tone startled Isabel.

More serenely, he said, "I want you to write it down for me." He took a draw on his cigar. "Like we did in the old days."

She glanced at him, then kept going toward the wardrobe. She knew the rules to this game. She kept emotion out of her voice, the hope, the love for him that burned inside her all the way down to her toes. "All right."

Aware that no one else alive had the privilege of such an intimate view of the great man, Isabel took her prerogative of studying him, albeit from her peripheral vision, as she opened the wardrobe. His head, crowned with a drift of silver and robed with a pelt of mustache that retained some of the orange and black of his youth, seemed overlarge for his body, as if it contained a brain larger than most men's. Beneath that beautiful head, his wiry body had a defiant virility, a scrappy knowingness that thrilled her. The slightly sagging chest flesh beneath its thicket of white curls spoke to her not of age but of his years of worldly experience. At seventy-four, he held himself with the amused confidence that a younger man could only pretend to, a confidence that invited you to let down your guard even though you knew he would not be doing likewise.

She kept her voice neutral. "I heard Mr. Ashcroft downstairs."

The King's response was to teeter his cigar languidly between his fingers.

She took a shirt from the wardrobe and shook it out. From long habit, she inspected the garment, specially made for The King with the button in back of the collar. In one of his autobiographical dictations, The King had recounted the apparently hilarious incident of when he'd discovered the collar buttons missing from three such shirts and, bellowing curses, pitched them out the window of his Hartford home. Isabel had cringed. Too easily, she could imagine his roar and the offending items flapping to the lawn like swans that had been shot, his wrath far out of proportion to such a minor irritant. His shirts, indeed all of the objects scattered around Stormfield, held within them the potential of provoking a similar eruption, mines waiting to be set off by his terrible temper. She didn't know what would cause a man to be so volatile.

She looked up from her inspection. "Should I tell Mr. Ashcroft that you're busy today?"

"Tell Ashie—" He stopped. "Wait a minute, what's your pet name for that English bastard?"

She kept her expression cool as she brought over the shirt. The King himself had dubbed Ralph "Benares," after the holiest city in India, where dying pilgrims went. If Ralph could bring new life to

The King's already robust bank accounts, The King would think him holy, indeed.

"Tell *Brazierres*," The King drawled scornfully, "to go home." He sucked deeply at his cigar, as if to draw sustenance from it. "Remind me to stop and think next time about hiring an Englishman to promote America's Sweetheart, will you? He creeps around like an English fog."

"Oh, you're America's Sweetheart now?"

He smiled around his cigar. "The Belle of New York, America's Sweetheart—same difference."

"I'll make sure it's on your next playbill."

"My next playbill"—he blew out smoke—"will be for my funeral."

"Please. You are outliving us all."

"Not if Halley's Comet has anything to say about it."

Isabel wished he had never read that article in the *Times* about the return of the comet next year. Even before the article came out, he made too much of being born under it, as if it held some kind of magical power over him. It disturbed her that he kept claiming it would take him with it when it soared through the skies in April 1910. He claimed that he and the comet were two "unaccountable freaks"—they came in together, and together they must go out.

"Put on your shirt," she said.

Cigar in teeth, he shrugged on the shirt and turned his back for her to button his collar. She used her wrist to push his hair from his nape—she knew his mane's surprising weight, being the one to wash and rub it dry for him every day—and then fastened his collar. He smelled good, like a scented cake of shaving soap. By day's end, the smell of smoke would sheath him like armor.

"Clara is coming today," she said.

Only the tightening of his jaw indicated that he had heard her. He took his cigar from his mouth and slowly tapped it against the ashtray on the bedside table. "Did you place the telephone call?"

"Yes."

He took a languid puff. "You know, someone could have Wark killed, and who'd ever know who'd done it? Everyone would think that his wife was behind it."

Isabel kept quiet. It was best in these situations to let The King get control of himself on his own. He did not really mean that he would kill his daughter's lover—the man couldn't bear to move a sleeping kitten from the pocket of his billiards table. The reality was that The King himself was the one in danger. He was increasingly suffering from pains in his chest, searing constrictions that would drop him into a chair and blanch his face to the color of an onion paring.

He smoked in silence as she moved on to the rest of his shirt buttons. She was getting his cuff links from the chiffonier when he said, "Miss Keller here yet?"

She returned to him and waited for him to raise his wrist. "We have plenty of time until her train arrives, or I wouldn't have risked going to see Mother."

He watched her poke the stem of a link through a cuff hole. "How is the old dame?"

"Mother? The same."

"I shouldn't call her that. I've got twelve years on her."

"You don't look it."

He kissed her cheek, brushing her with his mustache. "I knew I liked you."

Isabel fastened the link. "Liked?"

Their eyes met. Let him look away first; she wasn't afraid. Let him see her lips, remembering their kisses.

He looked at her mouth, then back up into her eyes. His expression softened into affection.

Before she could respond, he switched hands with his cigar, then raised his other wrist for her to work on. "How long did Miss Keller say she was staying?"

"Three days. She leaves Monday."

"I agreed to that?"

"You asked her to stay ten. Don't worry, I made nice for you."

"Ha. Good. Well, Helen's a sweet girl. Think I should invite her to be one of my Angelfish?"

"Isn't she a little old for that?" Isabel busied herself with his cuff. "Anyhow, I suppose she's occupied with her new book just out."

"I'm going to ask her anyway."

This wasn't about his little club for girls. Who cared about them? They were like daughters to him—better than daughters, he said, because they did not cause him grief. They were not her competition.

"Don't be jealous, Lioness."

"I'm not jealous." She pulled back from him, finished with his sleeves.

"You are. I see it in your mouth."

"I am not jealous."

"Clara says you are."

"Clara is a troublemaker."

"You're damn right about that." He pecked her again on the cheek. "Get my pants."

2.

January 8, 1909
Stormfield, Redding, Connecticut

THE SNOW GLAZING THE King's front lawn was blue in the gathering twilight. Shivering in a wind that held the stony smell of winter, Isabel aimed her attention not at the horse-drawn sleigh jingling its way up the drive, but at a large chip in the paint on one of the thick wooden spindles of the balustrade behind which she stood. The balustrade was supposed to have been made of solid stone, but in the last phase of building the house, Clara had suddenly demanded a large private suite, so sacrifices had to be made. The fountain on the rear terrace had been denied its statue of Cupid; the house faced with a thinner skin of plaster; the balustrade cheapened. Now this chip, the size of a silver dollar and roughly the shape of The King's home state of Missouri, served as Clara's smug agent, there to remind Isabel who really was in power.

Making a mental note to ask the caretaker to paint the spot immediately, Isabel changed her focus to the sleigh coming to a halt on the other side of the offending baluster. It was a new sleigh, two-seated, leather-cushioned, black-painted, and gold-trimmed, all to the lordly tune of $463. Isabel knew this because she had bought it. The King had said not to spare any expense. He always said not to spare any expense.

Although already sufficiently wealthy—he was the best-paid

writer in the world, the lord of the literary lions—The King had the habit of believing himself on the verge of striking it even richer. Not even his devastating bankruptcy in the previous decade, which had forced him on a worldwide tour to pay off his debts, had cured him of this belief. His very well-being seemed to hang upon his expectation of a forthcoming financial bonanza. He could never get enough.

The horse settled in with a last jangle of bells against its muscular haunches. The King's coachman, Giuseppe, hopped down and folded back the hood of the sleigh to reveal three passengers huddled under a shaggy buffalo robe. He helped out the first of them, a willowy young woman who was pretty in a fleshy-cheeked Germanic way, with chestnut locks curling from under the vast drooping brim of her hat. She waited on the shoveled flagstones, stiffly alert, her eyes as pale blue and empty as medicine-bottle glass. A squat woman in a tight coat stepped down next, followed by an athletic gentleman wearing round wire glasses. When he took his place next to the younger woman, she brightened.

The King drawled over his shoulder to Isabel, "Look, Helen smells me. She knows everyone by their scent."

Miss Keller broke from the others and, with quick careful steps, ran to The King and threw her arms around his neck. Her voice was curiously hollow when she spoke.

"Mark."

Isabel suppressed a sigh as The King kissed her on both cheeks. She wished people would not call him Mark, not even Helen Keller. Mark Twain was not a real person. The person they were addressing was Samuel Clemens. But The King never corrected anyone on this. Instead, something inside him seemed to shift when he heard it, as if the mortal Sam Clemens were stepping aside for his slow-moving doppelgänger, Twain.

Miss Keller let go of The King, then felt his hair. "You still have it."

"My mane? Thank the Lord. I'd be like Samson without it—weak as a hatchling."

"No, I mean your halo."

He held Miss Keller at arm's length to inspect her beaming face, then reeled her back in slowly. "And they say this girl is blind." He kissed her on the temple, then reached out to the other woman. "Miss Sullivan—excuse me, Mrs. Macy. If Helen is the Eighth Wonder of the World, then her genius of a teacher is the Ninth. Glad to see you again, dear."

Mrs. Macy trundled forward with a flap of coat hem, her round face growing florid. Short-necked, stout, and tense, Anne Sullivan Macy was the very opposite of the ever popular languid and lithe Gibson Girl. She almost quivered with barely suppressed anxiety, which seemed to center in her finely cut pursed lips. Yet at The King's greeting, her face unclenched, giving her the doe-eyed smile of a dreamy child. Isabel thought how beautiful she must have been when she was young.

Her companion leaned in front of her, thrusting forward his large chin as he offered his hand to The King. "John Macy, at your service." When The King switched gears to accept the handshake, Mrs. Macy's smile dissolved, returning her to her frumpy state.

"Good to finally meet you, Macy. You've got a nice little harem here."

An uncomfortable snort served as Mr. Macy's laugh. "It's a pleasure to meet you, sir. I'm your great admirer."

"Tell me that at the end of your visit."

Another snort. "This is quite a spectacular place," Mr. Macy said, looking around. He had a nice mouth, Isabel noticed, with firm expressive lips, white teeth, and that Ivy League jaw. One sleek brow insisted upon arching over his wire spectacles and into his sheaf of hair, making him appear both skeptical and bemused. Isabel had met Miss Keller and Mrs. Macy last year when they'd come to dinner at The King's house in New York, but not Mr. Macy. He was not what she expected of Mrs. Macy's spouse. She'd imagined a kindly, thickening gentleman with a gold dental bridge that flashed when he smiled.

She found herself wondering if Miss Keller knew how attractive her teacher's husband was.

"You like it?" The King reached into his wool suit coat, the same white as his nimbus of hair, and pulled out a cigar. "It's my Tuscan villa, here on American soil. I expect to go pick grapes at any minute, or find Michelangelo's cradle in the attic."

Mr. Macy's beautiful jaw hardly moved when he spoke. Perhaps it was limited by its weight. "I can see how authentic a villa it is. Although the snow does hamper the effect."

A shadow of displeasure passed over The King's brow.

"The Tuscans only *wish* they had snow to make their villas look this beautiful," Mr. Macy added quickly.

The King considered him a moment, then nodded, the diplomatic crisis averted. "The only detail missing from this setup is a foul-tempered donkey to chase down my guests." He spread out his arm and then waggled his fingers, beckoning Isabel, now exhaling, from behind him.

"This young lady," he said as she stepped forward, "oversaw the building of this pile—she and my daughter Clara. Forgive her for not including the donkey. One tried to kill her when she accompanied my wife to Italy as a social secretary. She has no love for asses anymore."

"I never did," Isabel said. In spite of The King's smile at her joke—he rarely laughed, the world's leading humorist rarely laughed—the burn flamed up behind her breastbone. When could they stop pretending that Clara would ever lift a finger to please her father and that Isabel was just his secretary? He didn't have to marry Isabel. She'd seen too many marriages that were nothing more than legal contracts, having little to do with love and respect. She didn't need that. She just wanted his acknowledgment of their mutual devotion. She just wanted him to claim her.

She introduced herself, reminding Mrs. Macy and Miss Keller that they had met, to which Mrs. Macy responded that of course they remembered her, she had spoken so enthusiastically about her recent trip to Bermuda with Mr. Clemens, to which Miss Keller added in her cavernous voice, "Yes, you stayed at the Princess Hotel with Mark." She smiled as if proud of having remembered this detail.

Mrs. Macy's plump hand lay still in Miss Keller's palm during the brief, embarrassed silence. The King twitched his unlit cigar. Her smile unchanged, as if she were unaware of the others' discomfort, Miss Keller then offered her own hand for Isabel to shake, putting it uncannily close to where a sighted person would have known to place it. As Isabel took it, she wondered if Miss Keller could smell her as she had smelled The King. With a start, she wondered what her own scent was.

"I grew up on a farm," Miss Keller said. "We didn't have donkeys, but we did have a goat named Sal that insisted on butting me. I braced myself as soon as I smelled her coming."

"Mere butting would have been child's play for Miss Lyon's Italian donkey," The King said in his unhurried way. "He had murder on his mind. I'm just glad he didn't get his hooves on her. Death by Ass would be a shameful way to go."

As Mrs. Macy spelled Mr. Clemens's quip into her student's hand, Isabel glanced at her King. It was when she had lain in bed, bruised and shaken from the attack by the frenzied animal that The King had first spoken of his feelings for her. He had touched her hair and told her haltingly how much he'd come to depend on her—how much he and his daughters had come to depend on her—now that his wife's illness kept her locked away from him. When he spoke of the donkey now, did he not recall this scene?

"I think Helen is in danger of succumbing to Death by Ass," said Mr. Macy, "when people snap their fingers in front of her face or clap next to her ear to see if she notices."

Miss Keller laughed after Mrs. Macy signed his words into her hand. "Or when they ask me if I can see colors."

Mr. Macy laughed affectionately. "As if red felt differently than blue."

"Often someone will quiz me, asking what color his or her coat is. If I guess wrong—"

"She tells him," said Mr. Macy, finishing her thought, " 'If you knew, why did you ask me?' "

The two laughed as Mrs. Macy spelled their conversation. Isabel noticed Mrs. Macy watching her husband, her eyes intense under the slivers of her brows, even as her fingers flew. Mrs. Macy, Isabel suspected, knew exactly how handsome her husband was.

"You'd better stay on your toes, Helen," said The King. "There are a lot of goddamn asses running loose in this world."

Mr. Macy spoke louder, as if to cover for The King's profanity. "Actually, I myself nearly succumbed to Death by Horse once. Helen had taken it in her mind to get a stallion for our farm in Wrentham. She thought she'd make a pet of him, feeding him apples and dubbing him Whitefoot for his one white sock. Well, the first time I put our dear Whitefoot in harness, he threw me from the wagon and proceeded to bash the vehicle to bits against the stone wall surrounding our property."

Miss Keller, who'd been following the conversation from Mrs. Macy's fingertips, exclaimed, "I loved that horse! I hated to sell him. We didn't give him enough time to adjust."

The King was patting Helen's arm in amused sympathy when Mrs. Macy said flatly, "The horse was shot for killing a cabman. It was not the kind creature Helen likes to think it was."

Her husband stared at her, his errant brow edging higher above his glasses.

Isabel said briskly, "It's much too cold to be out here. Won't you please come in?"

• • •

Soon Miss Keller and Mrs. Macy were cradled in a roll-arm sofa before the fire, the former swanlike in her shirtwaist with its high lace collar, the latter, doughlike, her head cleft like a Parker House roll by the severe part in her hair. Mr. Macy perched near them on a plump velvet chair, flicking his nails with nervousness. Across from him, Isabel readied to preside at the tea table while The King, as usual, puffed on his cigar and prowled.

Horace brought in the tea things.

Miss Keller sniffed. "Orange pekoe, isn't it?"

Horace looked up from where he was setting down the tray. Red lakes spread across his cheeks until his understanding of her unusual speech sank in. "Yes, ma'am, it is."

She nodded happily when Mrs. Macy spelled his answer to her. "And that's strawberry jam with the toast."

"You're just showing off," said The King, "making the rest of us look weak with our poor noses. You ought to hire yourself out for crime cases, Helen—the police would love you, although their bloodhounds would be jealous. Miss Lyon, will you dole out the tea?"

Isabel gripped the silver teapot. The King's words had triggered the sound of baying bloodhounds in her mind, sailing her back to the night of the burglary. Alerted by thumps downstairs, and then by the sound of a door closing, Isabel had stumbled from his bed and gone to the window, only to see the burglars on the back lawn, bashing open the doors of the locked sideboard that they had dragged outside. She'd seen the glint of the silver teapot as one of the thugs held it up to the moonlight: the very teapot now in her hand.

His cigar smoldering between his fingers, The King pulled a straight-back chair close to the sofa and Miss Keller, then took the hand in which Mrs. Macy was not busy spelling words.

Miss Keller turned toward him. "Hello, Mark," she said in her mechanical voice.

Isabel sighed. *His name is Sam.*

He put Miss Keller's hand on his face. "Read me so Mrs. Macy can take her tea. I tend to do all the talking in a room, anyway."

"Mrs. Macy," Isabel said, "would you like to sit next to me? The fire is especially warm here."

Mrs. Macy reluctantly moved away from her charge, her chained magnifying lens bouncing on the shelf of her bosom. Soon Isabel had distributed the refreshments and The King was dominating the room in Mark Twain fashion, his shadow terrifying the others on the wall. He once told Isabel, after giving a dinner for eighteen worthies from New York in his former Fifth Avenue home, that he felt a good host should monopolize the conversation so his guests could be free to enjoy their meal. Mark Twain should entertain so they could relax. She had wondered then how the real Sam Clemens bore up to the burden that Mr. Twain so frequently imposed upon him, and had turned to him to ask. But he had shut his eyes as if to nap, his beautiful head sinking into his pillow, the subject closed.

"I want to congratulate you again on your recent book," The King was now telling Miss Keller. "I had Miss Lyon read *The World I Live In* to me from cover to cover. I only fell asleep in the middle of it twice."

Miss Keller smiled as she took his meaning from his lips through her fingers. "Considering that it was one hundred ninety-five pages—"

"One hundred ninety-five pages with only four pictures," The King interjected. "Miss Lyon flashed them at me to keep me awake. I dozed through Kipling's *Just So Stories*, and he had over a dozen pictures. Now I know why he called his stories 'Just So.' But I think he forgot the second 'so.' "

Isabel shook her head, knowing how much The King admired Mr. Kipling. The two kept up a lively correspondence, for which she penned The King's letters. She could hear the affection in her King's voice when she took his dictation for them, even as he made the evilest cracks. It often seemed that the more Mark Twain loved people, the harder he was on them, as if any real affection must be made into a joke.

"I wanted to call my book *Sense and Sensibility*," said Miss Keller, "but that title was already taken. It didn't seem like a smart way to go after fighting that charge of plagiarism."

"Now, there's a group I'd like to introduce to Miss Lyon's donkey! Shame on those jealous old bullies, tormenting a twelve-year-old girl who obviously had not copied a single word. To a man, I'd say they were no better than a barnyard jackass, but that wrongs the jackass."

Miss Keller laughed as Mrs. Macy continued to stare at her husband, who was straining at the edge of his chair as if that might get him closer to Miss Keller and The King. "I'll always appreciate how you came to my rescue, Mark," Miss Keller said. "How I laughed in spite of my tears when you called the plagiarism committee a 'bunch of dull pirates.' "

Dull and hoary pirates, thought Isabel as The King turned away his face to suck on his cigar. Who were *disciplining and purifying a kitten.* She had taken that letter from dictation, too. Although it had been six years ago, she remembered The King delivering those lines to her. He had smiled impishly at her, like a boy trying to amuse, even though Clara had sat across the room glowering at them, waiting for her father's attention. Isabel had felt self-conscious then, during the first year of her employment, when Mr. Clemens had put her before his family. In time she had come to expect his attention whenever he was near, and to suffer greatly when he gave it to someone else.

The King blew out a lavish cloud, then put Miss Keller's hand back on his mouth. "Not even those old turnips could accuse you of being unoriginal in *The World I Live In*, Helen. Pegging a person's character through the feel of the hands—I thought it was brilliant. Of course, I might be especially partial to your mode of reckoning, seeing how you wrote that my own flippers were 'whimsical' and 'droll.' "

"I believe the rest of my description read, 'The drollery changes to sympathy and championship.' " Miss Keller peered earnestly into space, though her voice remained flat. "I can feel that, Mark. I can feel your kindness and your lovingness. I am so very grateful for them."

"You caught me out." The King kissed her hand.

Miss Keller's winsome face glowed.

Mr. Macy put his cup on his saucer with a clink of bone china. "I fear Helen was talking about me when she referred to the friend whose hands gave away his aggression. She said his hands' 'impatient jerk' alerted her to a forthcoming argument." Mr. Macy's tone was meant to be playful. "Do I argue that much, Helen?"

"Get over here, Macy," said The King. "She's going to have to read that off your lips, not mine."

Mr. Macy needed no further invitation to spring from his chair and onto the sofa, to the place where his wife had been. He put Miss Keller's other hand on his lips, repeated his accusation, and, with glasses glinting, watched for her reaction.

Miss Keller gleamed. "John, you know I can never reveal that person's identity. But if you recall, I also said in that passage that I could feel this friend start when a new idea shot through his head. It is a thrill to feel this person's probing intelligence."

"A thrill? You also said that you could feel his soul wrap itself in darkness. That you could feel his grief." Mr. Macy's laugh held no mirth. "He sounds like less of a thrill and more of a burden."

Isabel glanced off as if she had intruded into a personal scene. Miss Keller couldn't see how she gave herself away. But how was she to know how much we must keep to ourselves?

The King pushed from the sofa. "Who wants to go look for Michelangelo's cradle with me?"

"Not everyone is done with their refreshments," Isabel protested.

"They'll wait." The King drew up Miss Keller and, with his hand at the small of her back, guided her toward the loggia. Mr. Macy started to follow and then stopped to collect his wife. Isabel fell in behind them, pretending not to see Horace's embarrassed glance as she passed him at the door. At least someone acknowledged that she was more to The King than just a secretary.

3.

January 8, 1909
Stormfield, Redding, Connecticut

ISABEL FOLLOWED THE KING and Miss Keller's party down the hall, savoring the soft cushion and autumnal palette of the Persian carpet under her strapped pumps. The authentic Bokhara, woven in her favorite dull greens and rusty reds, had been purchased after much haggling with a dealer on Broadway in New York. The King had no idea of its quality or the trouble to which she had gone to get it, nor would he ever care. He might have been feted around the world by royalty and men of mark, awarded an honorary degree from Oxford University in England, and made a boon companion of the rich and powerful in New York, but at heart he was a Mississippi steamboat pilot whose idea of luxurious decor was that found in a New Orleans brothel.

Isabel wished she had known him in his piloting days, before Time and his wife had tried to tame the animal out of him. How lucky Livy Clemens had been to possess such a magnificent beast, with his flowing auburn mane and powerful lusts, a man who could dance the Schottische until dawn on the deck of the ship that he captained and then steer the four hundred tons of cargo, wood, and pressurized iron through the sucking black depths of a snag and sail it home. Women couldn't resist him. Long before he was famous, if there was only one woman in a crowd, he'd be the man to bed her. Isabel knew this because he bragged about it to her often, which both interested and repulsed her.

She remembered The King telling her such a story several years back. He'd been dictating his autobiography to his stenographer then, Miss Hobby. He was in bed, of course. After Mrs. Clemens died, he always wrote or dictated in bed—he did whatever he pleased in all things. He had on a velvet wrapper, vermilion, his favorite color. Isabel had given it to him for his seventieth birthday.

"Have I talked about the all-male dance I attended while I was a prospector in Nevada?" He had been addressing Miss Hobby but kept his gaze on Isabel, who'd been standing by with a sheaf of letters for him to sign.

Miss Hobby, a young woman whose moist olive skin and blunt features put Isabel in mind of a salamander, had looked up with colorless eyes from her typewriter. "No."

"Good. Take this down."

While Isabel waited, The King told of a night in a ramshackle barn in which 160 female-starved miners decided to hold a dance in spite of the dearth of women.

"It was a pitiful sight," he said, watching Isabel, "grown men shuffling through the sawdust in each other's arms, serious as schoolboys at a funeral. Half of them wore kerchiefs to play the part of girls. The other half wore their own greasy hats. Hot smelly wax rained down from the wagon-wheel 'chandeliers' slung overhead, peppering the whole sorry, untrimmed bunch."

The King ignored Isabel's gesture for him to sign the letters. Instead he pulled a cigar from his robe pocket. "So there we were, half-singed and fully drunk, tottering along to the fiddle music, our six-shooters thumping on our legs. We had resigned ourselves to waiting for a fight to break out for the evening's entertainment, when into the barn flounced a girl. Wearing a red dress. That stopped just short of her knees."

He reached for his matchbox, struck a match, then after lighting his cigar, waved it out. "Her name was Etta. Etta Booth. She was fifteen years old, and her dull stump of a mama was called Maude."

Isabel affected boredom.

"The fiddle screeched to a halt," said The King. "Those candles hadn't time to drip another cruel drop before one hundred and sixty tin cups of punch appeared before that girl. One hundred and sixty hairy arms were proffered up to dance. One hundred and sixty dungarees peaked with hope. And who do you suppose, among all those cups, arms, and dungarees, sweet-talked the girl into going out back to see the moon rise over the slag pile?"

Isabel shoved the letters in his hand. "I can't guess."

He laid them on his wrapper front and took a tug at his cigar. "Miss Hobby?"

Miss Hobby raised her salamander's face, her fingers splayed on the typewriter keys.

He blew out smoke. "Scratch that story. I've got to tell it in a different way." He nodded at Isabel. "It seems that my editor here does not approve."

Isabel dared not look up at him. He'd called her his editor. No one was good enough to be his editor. The only other woman he had allowed to edit his work was his wife.

He hesitated as if shy when Isabel met his eyes, then let a corner of his mouth inch up. They had confronted each other, no grinning allowed, while Miss Hobby ripped the paper out of the typewriter and rolled in a new piece.

• • •

Now The King had stopped in the hallway and was placing Miss Keller's fingers below the ledge of his mustache for her to read his lips. "We have come, my dear, to the beating heart of the universe: my billiards room."

Toying with her coral necklace, Isabel entered behind Mr. and Mrs. Macy. The space, thickly paneled in mahogany, papered with scarlet brocade, and bursting at the seams with potted palms, tufted leather chairs, books, pictures, and a tassel-hung billiards table, was not to her taste, but she had known her King when she'd furnished it. "How about a game of billiards, Helen?" he asked.

She laughed as she read his mouth. "I have no sight. I can't."

"The kind of billiards that gets played around here, you could. Plenty of people who come to this table have less skill than you have sight, though they claim to be to the cue stick what Edison is to light."

"Speaking of Edison," said Mr. Macy, edging closer, "you heard what he said about you—something to the effect that an average American loves his family; if he has any love left over, he generally selects Mark Twain."

"Now we know why they call him a genius." The King spoke as languidly as a maharaja riding an elephant through Delhi. "But as smart as he is, it would have been my friend Tesla, not Edison, mentioned in one breath with electricity if Tesla hadn't given up. He got discouraged when he lost all his papers in a fire, and he let Edison grab the glory. The moral of the story is," he said, glancing at Isabel as Miss Keller felt his lips, "don't ever give up."

Miss Keller laughed. "I won't!"

Behind them, Mrs. Macy toyed with the fringe of a lampshade as if at a loss for what to do with her hands when she wasn't spelling into her student's palm. Isabel remembered her to be much more talkative the last time they had met. She and Helen had bantered at the dinner table as if they were twins conjoined at the hands, finishing each other's sentences and arguing between themselves. Mr. Macy hadn't been there.

"I play billiards," said Mr. Macy.

Mrs. Macy pulled back her chin and looked at her husband. "You do?"

Even though Mr. Macy pushed up his glasses, the one brow remained stubbornly arched over them. "Not very well, but yes."

"Good," said The King. "We'll lay bets. How's tonight, after supper?"

"Be prepared for a long night of it," Isabel told Mr. Macy. "The King demands his pound of flesh."

"I am up for the challenge. Evenings at the Harvard Club have prepared me."

"You play billiards there?" said Mrs. Macy.

Mr. Macy made one of his exhalations of amusement. "Of course I do."

Mrs. Macy stared at him. "I thought you were working."

"You're on, Macy." The King gestured to the row of photographs of pretty adolescent girls and pictures of fish wreathing the room. "Like my Angelfish? I call this room 'The Aquarium' in their honor. It's our meeting place when they come. Helen, would you like to be one? All you've got to be to join is young at heart."

And to be female, Isabel thought. Boys were never invited. And to be a dewy-skinned beauty. And to flirt with the old man as if he were fourteen.

"Or, if you'd rather," The King added, "you could scuttle down to the Lobster Pot—Miss Lyon's house—and knit with her and her old mother. Your choice."

Isabel stared at him as Miss Keller exclaimed, "Me?"

"You do love to swim, Helen," said Mr. Macy. "You'd make an excellent fish. She goes out with our dog when we go to the Cape. I'm trying to teach her how to do more than just a fair dog-paddle."

Our *dog?* Isabel glanced between husband and wife. Was everything shared between student, teacher, and the teacher's husband in that household?

"Helen doesn't have to swim," said The King. "She just has to wear at all times the Angelfish pin that I give her and to write letters to me." He pointed to a handwritten list tacked on the wall, then produced a match from another pocket.

Mr. Macy thrust his heavy chin forward and examined them. " 'Angelfish Club Rules.' It's all here."

"Miss Lyon can give you one of the little pins I award my minnows. I had Tiffany make them in New York. Run and get one for Helen, will you, Miss Lyon?"

"That would be lovely," said Miss Keller, "but I don't want to trouble you, Miss Lyon."

When Isabel paused, The King shooed her with his cigar. "Helen's waiting. Hurry up."

Isabel stalked up the stairs and switched on the light in The King's bedroom, so angry that she was short of breath. She was not imagining it. After all they had been through, he was treating her shabbily, punishing her in front of their guests. She had been working hard to repair their relationship since the night of the burglary, looking the other way when he was unkind to her, putting up with his little girls, throwing him frequent parties to fill his bottomless need for love. She could not make it clearer that she was sorry for what she'd done. When would he ever forgive her?

She gritted back tears. She didn't have to take it. She could just leave him and never come back. He had no idea how much he needed her. He had no clue how to manage his career, cajole his creditors, schedule appearances, arrange travel, write letters, plan his day, hire household help. It was she who had to buy presents for his daughters, Clara and Jean, to set the amount of their allowance and dole it out monthly, to prop up Clara's singing career. It was she who'd had the heartbreaking job of arranging for Jean's care in the sanitarium after she'd seen what a danger Jean had become to herself when she was left unattended. It was she who communicated with the doctor and who wrote often to Jean to keep her spirits up. For all his ordering her around and showing off to guests, The King was helpless as a baby. She kicked his slippers under the bed. He couldn't even button his own shirt collar.

When she opened the wardrobe door, his crimson Oxford gown billowed out. How proud he was of that gown, wearing it over his white suit whenever he got a chance, to dinners in the city or playing billiards with guests. What was wrong with him that he always had to make such a spectacle of himself? Why did he have such a burning need to dominate a room, whether it contained three guests or three thousand, and to suck all the love from everyone in it? He needed to take every ounce of love, yet never gave back a drop.

One by one, she pulled off the lids of the robin's-egg-blue boxes lined up in a wardrobe drawer. When she glanced up, she was met with her reflection in the mirror mounted inside the door. She stopped to inspect. A lavender half-moon formed a delicate depression under each eye. Dear Lord, her eyes were beginning to sink into her head. The rest of her facial flesh, while not plump with the juices of youth, was by and large firm for that of a forty-five-year-old woman, although her mother's out-pouchings were sprouting along her jaw. Overall, her features were even and pleasant. It was a handsome spinster's face. A handsome spinster. Was this really her life?

There was a tap on the frame of the bedroom door. "Knock, knock."

Isabel flinched, then turned around. Ralph Ashcroft leaned into the room. "May I come in?"

"Ralph." She patted her coral beads, composing herself. "The King is in the billiards room."

"You mean the Aquarium?" His wry grin, with his neat red lips, only added to his attractiveness, and his English accent didn't hurt. Isabel told herself that it was just his pointed Vandyke beard she was responding to. Any man with one looked rakishly handsome, especially if he had such dark eyes and lashes. Age was on his side, too. He was thirty-three, twelve years younger than she. She never forgot that.

She resumed looking for a pin.

"Anyhow, it's you who I wanted to see." Ralph came over. "Who's the new Angelfish? Let me guess—Helen Keller, although she's on the mature side for a Fish. It certainly wouldn't be Mrs. Macy." He noted Isabel's frown. "I saw them getting out of the sleigh."

"Don't be uncharitable, Ralph."

"Uncharitable? I am thinking of your King. After all, it is my job to protect his image. You would think that he would be aware of the headlines, of the whole 'Girl in the Red Velvet Swing' scandal."

"Oh, I think he is." He had certainly studied Evelyn Nesbit's sulky pictures in the paper long enough, after making Isabel read the parts in the articles about how his friend Stanford White, the wealthy architect, installed a swing in his New York apartment for the girl to perform on.

"I do believe that Stanford White caused a greater uproar by having kept a girl since she was sixteen than by being murdered by her jealous husband five years later. Americans are terribly shocked by sexual urges."

"And the English aren't?"

"If Mark wants to remain the most beloved man in America, he needs to stay away from the girls."

She glanced at him, then resumed rifling through the Tiffany boxes. "His name is Samuel. And he does nothing wrong with them."

"How would you know?"

"He just wants their attention."

"He wants everyone's attention."

"Don't we all?"

"Not really. Some of us are more selective of whose attention we want." He leaned in as if to kiss her neck. She caught the light scent of his shaving lotion before she dodged away.

"Ralph."

His smile faded. "Someday, not only am I going to kiss you, but you are going to kiss me back."

"I wouldn't wait if I were you."

"You know that I care about you. And I can feel that you care about me, too. Why don't you listen to your heart and let me in?"

She held up an azure-enameled pin. "What do you think of this one?"

He studied her. "I don't know why you deny yourself a chance at happiness, Isabel. But I think that someday you will allow me to treat you the way you deserve. Let me know when you do."

She examined the pin as if its selection mattered to her. "Are you coming to meet Miss Keller?"

"And watch Sam flirt with her? No."

"She's blind!"

"He isn't."

"You are terrible." She walked on even as her traitor body longed to stay.

• • •

"I'm ashamed to admit that we had inferior burglars." The King picked up a cue stick, placed it on the table, and bent over as if to shoot.

Isabel stopped at the billiards room door, the Angelfish pin in her hand. She should listen to her doctor. She should go home, plan a new life, take up with Ralph.

The King lined up his imaginary shot. "They left a trail that even an amateur could follow. In fact, an amateur did find them—my daughter's accompanist caught them red-handed on the train out of Redding. Who knew that an ivories-tickler could have such gumption? You may have heard of him in the papers—Charles Wark?" The Macys shook their heads as Mrs. Macy spelled the question to Miss Keller. "Our family owes him a large debt of gratitude. I am sorry that he is accompanying another singer these days." The King faked his shot.

Isabel stepped forward. "Would Miss Keller like her pin?"

The King leaned on his cue stick. "I take part of the blame for those bumblers wanting to burgle me. I gave them the wrong idea by calling this place 'Innocents at Home' in an interview with the *Times.* I named it for my Angelfish, but I suppose I made us sound like easy pickings, like taking a cookie from a baby. When I was casting about for a new name, I had wanted to call it 'Twain's End,' but that seemed to spook Miss Lyon. She knows my fellow freak, Halley's Comet, is coming around to claim me next year." He tried to engage Isabel's gaze.

She wouldn't look at him. "I know no such thing. I thought it should be 'Autobiography House.' 'Stormfield' was Miss Clemens's idea."

"Are you writing your autobiography?" Mr. Macy asked The King. Isabel allowed Miss Keller to remove the piece of jewelry from its box. She took it from her and fastened it on the younger woman's high collar then stood back, thinking to excuse herself.

"I started it forty-four years ago," said The King. "I can't seem to finish it."

"How does one write one's life story?" said Mr. Macy. "Did you begin with your birth?"

"I tried that," said The King, "then realized where that was going."

"To the present?" said Mr. Macy.

"No. To Twain's end." He glanced at Isabel. He thought it was so easy to win her over.

Mr. Macy produced one of his silent laughs. "You put me in mind of some kind of horror story, where the fates keep spinning out your thread as long as you write about your life. Keep telling your life's story, and you live forever. You stop and—" He drew his hand across his throat.

Helen received his words from Mrs. Macy. "Don't you ever stop, Mark! Everything that comes from your heart is pure gold. The everyday man lives vicariously through you, the small-town Missouri boy who grew up to be the friend of kings and emperors. Everyone wants to be Mark Twain."

He pulled on his cigar. "Even me."

She dropped Mrs. Macy's hand and happily took his arm. "I remember when we met. I asked you how you chose your pen name. You said that you liked how 'mark twain' was the riverboat pilot's term for safe waters, that it suited you because sometimes you were light and on the surface and sometimes you were—

Mr. Macy stepped in and put Helen's hand on his lips. "Deep."

Mrs. Macy got out of the way. "Isn't dark the opposite of light?" she said querulously.

"How clever that 'twain' means 'twin,' " Helen said in her hollow voice. "Mark Twain is Samuel Clemens's twin."

"We're like the Siamese twins Eng and Chang," drawled The King. "We may share a body, but we don't necessarily get along, isn't that right, Miss Lyon?"

Isabel looked away.

"Like Jekyll and Hyde," said Mr. Macy.

Helen laughed. "Mark, can you tell that we have been reading *Dr. Jekyll and Mr. Hyde*?"

"When?" Mrs. Macy sat down hard. "I haven't read it."

Mr. Macy lowered Helen's hand to speak to his wife. "I've been reading it to Helen after you go to bed. She's had insomnia, and I wanted to practice my signing skills."

The King stole away Helen and pulled her toward the billiards table, where a black kitten slept in one of the gold mesh pockets. He put her hand on the sleeping animal.

"A cat! Oh, Mark, you know how I love them."

"I believe cats are the smartest creatures on earth. Unlike dogs, who will stay and let an idiot mistreat them, cats won't stand for it. They don't like how they're being treated, they leave." The King rolled his gaze to Isabel.

She stared back. She didn't want this. She didn't want to go. She couldn't believe that he wanted it, either.

"Cats are very intelligent," said Miss Keller.

Mrs. Macy heaved herself upright, snatched Helen's hand, and put it on her face. "I thought you preferred dogs."

"I love all animals," Miss Keller said, her face radiant.

"You can't," said Mrs. Macy. "What about snakes? Or spiders? Or rats?"

Her husband frowned. "Annie." He spelled something into Miss Keller's hand.

The front door slammed. A female voice rose from the foyer. Clara.

"You stupid bumpkin! What are those reporters doing outside?

I said to get rid of them." Above Horace's abashed murmur, her voice grew louder as it trailed through the house. "Where's Isabel? If she's so damn good, why are those leeches still out there?'

Her footsteps stormed in their direction.

"I can't speak for all species." The King hit another ball, setting it rolling until it tagged another with a soft click. "But I believe that man is the only animal that blushes. Or needs to."

The party watched the door, save Miss Keller, who was smiling at Mr. Macy with the adoration of a lover.

PART TWO

The Critic, June 1904

MARK TWAIN FROM AN ITALIAN POINT OF VIEW

Mark Twain's life is regulated by a system. All day long he is at work; during the good part of the night he strolls alone about the immense grounds of the villa, meditating and shaping in his mind the sketches which are destined to make future generations laugh—and to enrich his publishers. If you met him, you might think he was one of the ordinary people who are weary of life, and that he was turning over in his mind a plan for ending it once and for all. The man is occupied by a rapid procession of memories of all the things which he has observed on the varied stages of human life. Out of this confused mass of visions and recollections, Mark Twain picks out the most delicious comic figures.

When the amount of his work becomes oppressive, he has a secretary, an intelligent American girl, to whom he dictates letters and articles.

4.

Mid-September 1889
Hartford, Connecticut

IT WAS ONE OF those damp September evenings in Hartford when the air thrummed with the urgent cries of insects and the sense of impending change. Isabel, twenty-five years old and, as their governess, as beloved by the younger members of the Whitmore family as their pet Newfoundland dog, had just been summoned from her book and her bed under the low slanted ceiling of her third-floor room. Down in the parlor, as the homey muffled clatter of dishes being washed drifted in from the distant kitchen, her employer, Mr. Whitmore, balding, brown-eyed, and slope-shouldered, plucked at his cuffs as he explained the situation. A gentleman couldn't make it to their regular Friday-night card game at the home of Samuel Clemens—perhaps she knew Mr. Clemens as the author Mark Twain? An emergency substitution was needed to fill out the table. He cleared his throat, then looked up at her sternly, his bristly graying mustache stacked like a beaver dam across his face. Would she come along with him?

Isabel agreed, secretly pleased that Mr. Whitmore recognized her ability to converse with gentlemen. Her own father had been one, distinguishing himself as a professor of classical languages at Columbia and as a successful businessman who owned one hundred acres of prime property overlooking the Hudson River, a mansion in Tarrytown, and an estate on the Hudson called "Spring Side." He had raised Isabel to do more than just marry well, although that was, of course, the ultimate goal. From the moment three-year-old Isabel stunned her father by picking out words from *The New York Tribune* while she sat on his lap at the breakfast table, he had been determined to educate her, her sex be damned, in the subjects that he so loved. He taught her Aristides, Solon, and Themistocles. He drilled her on Ancient Roman history. He transferred his love of Greek mythology to her so completely that she named her dolls after goddesses. His teaching culminated in his bringing her with him on the train to New York City. There he would stop at his club, where he would position young Isabel, wearing a bow that dwarfed her head, within a circle of leather armchairs and proceed to have his friends parry with her on which was the greater civilization, Ancient Greece or Ancient Rome. Then, after a brief visit at a Bleecker Street tenement, where she would eat cookies with a girl her age while he disappeared in a back room with the lady who lived there, he would take her to the university to watch him lecture.

When she grew older, she dreamed of traveling to Greece and Italy with a husband who would be every bit as tall, handsome, and wise as her father. But he died when Isabel was nineteen, and with him, her comfortable life. The acres overlooking the Hudson were seized by the bank that held their note; the mortgage was called on Spring Side; the house in Tarrytown, Isabel's mother's ropes of pearls, her father's two-thousand-thirty-six-volume library—all were sold. When the lady from Bleecker Street paid a visit to Mrs. Lyon, prompting Isabel's mother to shoo her three mostly grown children from the room to protect them, there was nothing to offer her, threaten all she wanted.

Isabel's younger sister was soon situated in a hasty marriage, and her brother, Charlie, drifted to New York, but who was to care for Mrs. Lyon? At a time when Isabel's friends were busying themselves with debuts and subsequent impressive marriages, Isabel remained with her mother in a rented mansion that they could not afford, taking in sewing or constructing pincushions for sale. It had been after an evening of stuffing wood shavings into pink heart-shaped velvet covers that she'd reread *Jane Eyre* and conceived of a steadier, possibly less depressing source of income: becoming a governess.

Her mother objected—no Van Kleek, no Lyon, had ever stooped to such a thing—but neither, Isabel reminded her, had they hawked pincushions among their wealthy friends. Only after Mrs. Lyon had been reminded of Jane Eyre's eventual marriage to her rich employer, Mr. Rochester, had the former Belle of Tarrytown come around.

• • •

Mr. Whitmore twitched his mustache at Isabel in a nervous smile, then tapped on the door with his walking stick. Isabel had never spent a moment alone with her employer, and now here they were, on Mark Twain's covered porch, with a host of cheeping crickets as their only chaperones.

Mr. Whitmore cleared his throat. "Mark's got quite a place here."

"Yes."

A horse whinnied in Mr. Clemens's stable. Out on the street, a carriage whirred by, its lit lantern jittering.

"I hope you are enjoying your employment in my home. The children aren't being too difficult, I presume?"

"Not at all. They are a credit to their parents." Isabel was too absorbed in trying to make sense of the design of the Clemens house to fully grasp his discomfort. Tall, redbrick, and rambling, the mansion was a circus of gables and porches and chimneys, as though its owner had thought if one of a certain feature were good, a half-dozen might be better. Isabel was studying the patterned orange brickwork that belted the house like Indian beads when a fierce face appeared in the sidelight.

The door swung open. A maid, perhaps in her early thirties—

Irish, by the look of her ruddy skin and wiry black hair, and handsome in a gritty sort of way—allowed them in, her chin tilted up just enough to show her contempt.

Isabel had been at the house once before, delivering a book for Mrs. Whitmore to Mrs. Clemens, but had not gone inside. She was not prepared for the wallop to the eye delivered by stepping into the entrance hall. The walls seemed to fly at her in a jumble of angles—silver and brown triangles shimmered like fish scales from each crimson panel. Across the multilevel ceiling tumbled geometric stars vibrating with black and crimson dashes until they were sucked up into a dazzling three-story vortex of stairs. Mirrors and chandeliers glittered. Doors and interior windows opened to rooms throbbing with objets d'art. Penetrating this ambitious display was the prosaic smell of roast chicken, along with the smoke of cheap tobacco.

"Upstairs," said the maid.

"Thank you, Katy." Mr. Whitmore touched Isabel's back so briefly she might have imagined it. Away from his home, he seemed uncertain how to act around the family governess, this not-quite-servant, yet clearly not-gentry creature with a thicket of dark hair twisted up in a heavy knot.

Isabel trudged her way up the flowered carpet of the stairs, aware of Mr. Whitmore's gaze upon her back. They reached the third floor.

"Here we are," he said. She stopped and waited for him to open the door. He looked into her eyes, longer than he'd ever done in his own home. Drawing in a breath, he turned the knob. She walked into a blue cloud of smoke.

The green baize expanse of the billiards table dominated the cramped red-papered space. The nearby folding card table and the two men sitting at it seemed an afterthought. Etchings of drinking vessels and smoking pipes winked from the frosted glass of the far windows. A rack of cues idled on one wall. Only a small desk littered with papers, a wall of pigeonholes jammed with manuscripts, and a set of bookshelves hinted that more was knocked around this room than celluloid balls. In this flamboyant, spacious mansion, all the endeavors of the man of the house seemed crammed into this one small space, as if he'd been forced to take refuge beneath the rafters. *Refuge from what?* Isabel wondered.

Touching her back again, Mr. Whitmore introduced her to the first gentleman, although she already knew him from the Sunday post-church promenade, he strolling with his wife, and she following the younger Whitmore children, prompting them to walk straight and be silent, which they did because they worshipped her. Like others of his class, the gentleman had eyed her and said nothing; she doubted he knew her name. But she had known his: Reverend Twitchel, but called Joe by the others.

He smiled mildly. "You don't mind if we smoke, do you?"

Isabel hated smoke. "Not at all."

Mr. Clemens—Mr. Whitmore introduced him by his pen name, Mark Twain—squinted at her as if sizing her up. Or maybe he was just squinting from the smoke snaking up from the cigar wedged between his fingers. At fifty-three, he was handsome in an almost violent way, his gray eyes too piercing, his cheekbones too raw, his arched nose somehow sexual. Although he was only sitting there and smoking, his energy seized the cramped room. His avalanche of silver-shot auburn hair, even his mustache—a coarse, impenetrable, orange and black buffer between the world and the man—was aggressive. Its twin haystacks lifted from his face when he frowned, as if creatures were readying to crawl out from under them. Isabel wanted to touch it, much as one was tempted to touch a cactus.

His speech was as slow as a lion licking its claws. "We don't usually have ladies up here. You're going to see things ladies don't like to see. Smell things ladies don't like to smell."

"With you, Mark," said Mr. Whitmore, offering her a chair, "she's more likely to hear things ladies don't like to hear."

"Damned if you aren't right. Unless she's not a lady." Mr. Clemens rolled the tip of his cigar against an ashtray. "Then she won't mind as much."

Mr. Whitmore flashed Isabel a sympathetic look. "You'd better be careful, Mark. Her father owned the land that they're building the Bear Mountain Bridge on. Miss Lyon, you'll be my partner, all right?"

Isabel nodded.

Reverend Joe sat back in his chair, bumping into the billiards table. "Is that fiasco done yet? They've been working on that bridge for decades."

"So you're a rich girl," said Mark Twain.

Was. Was a rich girl.

He tapped away more ash. "My wife, Livy, is a rich girl. She bought this place. Do you like it?"

Reverend Joe coughed.

"Excuse his rough manners, Isabel," said Mr. Whitmore. "He's from the West. His wife has tried to tame him, but she's not done yet."

Mr. Clemens continued to smoke and stare as Isabel settled in her chair. She wouldn't let this comedian, this former "Wild Humorist of the Pacific Slope," unnerve her. She might be just a governess, but she was no one's joke, especially not a nouveau-riche Westerner's. She removed her gloves as the first hand was dealt. Mr. Whitmore played his card.

"What's the news on your typesetting machine, Mark?" Reverend Joe put down his ten of spades. "Don't worry, Miss Lyon, our man Twain is going to be richer than his wife once his new investment takes off. He'll leave Carnegie in the shade."

"I say Mark should stick with his writing," said Mr. Whitmore. "There's something about that machine that makes me uneasy. Too many moving parts that could fail. It doesn't look good that Mr. Paige has had to ask for so many infusions of cash to prop up his creation."

Mr. Clemens reordered the cards in his hand. "When Paige and I are counting our money from it, don't say I didn't invite you in on the action, Whitmore. It takes an old typesetter like me to know that automatic typesetting is the wave of the future. I intend to ride it all the way in like a Sandwich Island surf-bather on his board—only not naked, like they were. At least, not most of the time."

Mr. Whitmore glanced to see if Isabel was scandalized. She wasn't, except by Mr. Clemens's cocksureness. He gazed around the table, his eyes cooling with triumph within their ginger fringe while he laid down his card: an ace of spades.

Isabel had no spades to follow suit, but she did have trump. Playing it would take away the lead from Mr. Clemens. She placed it carefully on top of his card.

Mr. Clemens's face hardened. The very air in the room seemed to contract. Around the table, eyebrows danced and smirks flickered, but not a word was said until the hand was played out and Isabel picked up all of the remaining tricks.

The men broke out in a roar—except Mr. Clemens.

He touched his cigar to the ashtray as he studied her. "Now, who'd you say you were?"

Mr. Whitmore took up the cards to shuffle them. "Come on, Mark. She's just the governess. Take it easy on her."

"She was only doing what anyone else would do with trump," said Reverend Joe. "You yourself say to never nibble when it comes to cards."

"I say to never nibble when it comes to everything," growled Mr. Clemens. "But that only applies to me."

Isabel glanced away, but his gaze drew her back to him.

"How'd you get to be a governess," he said slowly, "if you're so rich?"

"Mark," protested Mr. Whitmore.

"Bad luck," Isabel said.

From behind the arrogant tilt of his nose, behind the hillocks of his mustache, behind the belligerent tendrils of his smoke, he studied her.

"Luck. Huh." He drew on his cigar, then slowly let it out. "It is lucky to begin life poor; it is lucky to begin life rich. Both are wholesome. But to begin it prospectively rich! Now that is foul luck."

He flicked ash from his cigar. "My father had land in Tennessee, hundreds of acres. He expected money to come pouring in from it at any moment, to lift my family out of poverty and restore us to our rightful place among kings. When the riches had not yet come by the time I was grown, I thought I might goose my true destiny by prospecting in Nevada. Along with a couple other aspiring tycoons, I took myself into the hills, where we found a creek just spoiling for despoilment. We followed it up to a fork, and then, consulting Fate, took the branch to our left. There we dug and we dug until we had made the most enthusiastic, *emptiest* hole in the territory. Desperate now for cash, I saw that I might write a little piece for the local paper. I liked writing it, and people liked me writing it. I traded in my pan for the pen and never looked back, something I never would have done if I had found the mother lode."

"Is this another of your tall tales?" asked Mr. Whitmore.

"It's our good fortune that you failed," said Reverend Joe. "*Tom Sawyer* is part of the American canon now, as is *Huckleberry Finn* and your Mississippi book."

"And *The Prince and the Pauper*," said Mr. Whitmore, "and *Roughing It*. And *Innocents Abroad*. What other pieces of your genius did I forget?"

"*A Tramp Abroad* and *The Gilded Age*, but who's counting?" Mr. Clemens took a pull on his cigar. Smoke tumbled out with his words. "Funny thing is, if we had turned right where that creek forked, instead of left, we would have stumbled across a vein that was one of the richest in Nevada. The mine is still putting out today. I would have been richer than Carnegie, Gould, all those robbers. So am I lucky or not?" He stubbed out his cigar. "None but the Deity can tell what is good luck and what is bad before the returns are all in."

"Amen," said Reverend Joe.

Mr. Whitmore kept his anxious watch on Isabel. "Amen."

Mr. Clemens leaned back, folded his arms, and then pinned his gaze on Isabel. "Play."

• • •

Mrs. Whitmore was a small woman, like Isabel, and pleasant-looking in her middle age in spite of the turned-down grooves at the corners of her mouth which put one shamefully in mind of a ventriloquist's dummy. The unfortunate grooves were deepening as she watched Isabel slip black rubbers over her shoes that rainy November night. "Another card game?"

"Apparently so." Isabel flattened any trace of delight in her voice. Only a fool would be honored that Mr. Clemens refused to play his Friday-night cards without "the little governess," as he called her, after that evening a number of weeks back. Even the term lessened her—the professor's accomplished daughter had become a diminutive nanny. There was nothing to celebrate, although she'd come to relish Friday nights more than the Fourth of July.

Mrs. Whitmore fingered the filigree edge of the brooch at her throat. "How does Mrs. Clemens like having her house invaded every Friday night?"

"I don't know." Isabel snapped on the other boot. "I haven't spoken with Mrs. Clemens."

Mrs. Whitmore cocked her head. "In all these weeks?"

"No." Isabel straightened. "I've met their daughter Susy briefly—"

"Now, she's an odd duck! So peculiar, did you notice? As high-strung as a Thoroughbred."

"—and I have heard Clara's voice when she was speaking downstairs—"

"Of course you have. She's quite the outspoken girl, in a very outspoken family."

"—but I've only caught a glimpse of Mrs. Clemens while passing her room on the way to the card game. At least I believe it was her. She stepped out of sight before I could see."

The tinkling sound of a music box wafted into Isabel's memory.

She felt once more the sadness radiating from that room, as if a creature were struggling to be freed with the silent anguish of a butterfly beating within an overturned glass. She shook off the disturbing feeling.

"She must be interesting. It must be amusing to be married to Mr. Clemens."

"You think so?" Mrs. Whitmore's gaze went to Isabel's hair. Isabel had taken extra pains to brush and re-pin it into a twist and, in a burst of energy, had crowned it with her garnet and pearl comb, a relic from her past.

Mrs. Whitmore kept her gaze on Isabel's comb. "I know that Livy was supposed to have fallen down skating when she was sixteen and that walking has been difficult for her since then, but she spends so much time in her room—more than you'd think a fall twenty years ago would warrant."

Isabel plunked on her hat, covering her hair none too soon. "I didn't know of her injury. I'm sorry."

"Sometimes I think her old skating wound is the least of it." Mrs. Whitmore brought her gaze down to Isabel's eyes. "I suspect that Mr. Clemens—"

"Mr. Clemens what?" Mr. Whitmore came down the stairs.

Mrs. Whitmore raised the pitch of her voice. "Mr. Clemens curses entirely too much."

Mr. Whitmore nodded coolly at Isabel before smiling at his wife. "That he does. I don't think Livy will ever take the country boy completely out of him. He's as rough as a cob, in spite of that hulk of a house."

Mrs. Whitmore shook her head. "That house! What a spectacle! That is what comes of having more money than sense. I don't care that it's bigger than ours—poor Livy!"

"Poor neighbors," said Mr. Whitmore, buttoning his coat.

"Poor neighbors?" said Mrs. Whitmore. "The rest of them are every bit as colorful over there in Nook Farm as he is, what with Harriet Beecher Stowe wandering like a ghost in house slippers in and out of everyone's house, now that she's lost her mind, and her sister Isabella Hooker harboring all those suffragettes who keep landing themselves in jail. I shouldn't be surprised if Mr. Clemens finds himself in jail someday, wild as he is." She handed her husband his hat from the rack. "It wouldn't be the first time, from what I understand. Livy said that when he was wooing her, her father tried to turn him away after details of his unruly past came to light, but Mr. Clemens just had to have her and she just had to have him. I wonder if she's so glad now."

"Of course she is." Mr. Whitmore clapped on his hat. "They are happily married."

Seventeen-year-old Frederick trampled down the stairs, his dark hair flapping into his eyes. His cheeks, already pink with youth, reddened when he saw Isabel.

"Where are you going in such a hurry?" asked his mother.

"To a play with some fellows." He grinned at Isabel. "Miss Lyon, they asked if you could go."

Mr. Whitmore touched Isabel's back. "She may certainly not." Mrs. Whitmore's gaze went to her husband's hand. Isabel moved within her own skin, willing his touch away. Mr. Whitmore unknowingly dropped his hand. "Which fellows are you going with?"

"Russell and Theodore. They would really like Miss Lyon to go." Frederick threw his striped scarf over his shoulder. "You ought to, Miss Lyon. We'd be more fun than Father's crowd."

"Watch it," said Mr. Whitmore.

"We aren't a bunch of old men who come home smelling like they've been rolled in ashes."

"Off with you!" said his mother, whisking him out the door. She turned to her husband when Frederick had gone, tucking her arms under her bosom. "Shouldn't you and Isabel be going, too?"

Mr. Whitmore pecked her on the cheek. "We'll be back." He opened the door for Isabel. His carriage was waiting for them under the porte cochere. "We can't walk tonight," he said when she paused. "Too wet."

She got into the carriage. He sat heavily next to her. The vehicle shuddered forward with a clatter of hooves on wet paving blocks. Over the stony smell of the rain, she inhaled the spicy scent of his flesh doused with shaving lotion.

Silence mushroomed between them as they rocked within the musty leather walls of the carriage, the rain drumming on the roof. She ached to adjust the space between them. The heat of his leg next to hers made her want to squirm.

She kept her voice light. "I wonder what ridiculous story Mr. Clemens will tell us tonight."

Mr. Whitmore cleared his throat, then inched his leg closer. After a moment he said, "I'm worried about Mark. You know that I handle some of his business . . . ?" There was more than a hint of pride in his tone.

"Yes. I'm sure he must be grateful."

"Mark pays three thousand dollars a month to Mr. Paige for development of that infernal typesetter he so loves, resulting in an investment that is nearing three hundred thousand. Not even Mark Twain can afford to throw that kind of money down a pit. I'm afraid that he's going to lose everything."

"Surely he knows what he's doing."

"Just because a man is intelligent doesn't mean that he has sense."

Just then the carriage jerked to a stop, throwing them forward. Mr. Whitmore flung out his arm to catch her, brushing her breast. He snatched away his arm as if singeing it on an iron.

"Jimmy!" he bellowed out the window. "What in God's name are you doing?"

The driver shouted back. "A dog, sir! It ran out."

Mr. Whitmore blew out his breath and threw himself back, rubbing his offending arm. He edged away, to Isabel's relief.

"I'm just saying that Mark isn't the hero that you think he is," he said testily. "He has absolutely no mind for business, although why anyone would expect that from a humorist, I wouldn't know."

"Does anyone expect that from him?"

"I should think that his wife might find that to be an admirable quality."

They spoke no more until they reached the Clemens house shortly thereafter.

• • •

Mr. Clemens threw down his jack of spades in disgust. "Even Christ couldn't take tricks with these cards."

Isabel coolly put her ace on it, then scooped up the deal.

Mr. Clemens sat back and smoked his cigar. "Your girl is ruthless, Whitmore," he drawled. "Do you really trust her with your children?"

"Do you expect her to let you win," Mr. Whitmore said almost peevishly, "like one does with a little child?"

"It wouldn't go unappreciated. But she won't. She's as cold as a San Francisco summer." Mr. Clemens caught Isabel's gaze. He let his sights travel to her garnet and pearl comb before languidly picking up his drink.

Aware of his admiration, she posed for him as she sorted through her cards. "Better to be cold than unlucky."

"Better to be unlucky than dead." Mr. Clemens took a gulp of whiskey. "Wait a minute—I'm not so sure of that."

They exchanged a smile that was limited to the eyes, the art of which Isabel had not fully valued before making Mr. Clemens's acquaintance. Who knew that forcing a grin away from your mouth drove it directly into your heart? She craved the game within the game that they had invented over the weeks, in which he protested her cruelty and she rewarded him with mock aloofness. No boys she had met when she was marriageable had been half as much fun. Suddenly, she was very glad she had worn the garnet and pearl comb.

"When does your next book come out, Mark?" Reverend Joe played his card. "What's the name of it again?"

"*A Connecticut Yankee in King Arthur's Court.* Comes out next month by subscription."

The men held up their glasses. "Congratulations."

Mr. Clemens raised his cup, then tipped his chair back on two legs. "Thanks, but this is my literary swan song, boys. I am done with this unsatisfactory business."

"Unsatisfactory?" said Reverend Joe. "You're the most widely read author in America."

"And the most uncomfortable. Even with Howell editing instead of Livy—that goddamn eye infection has been plaguing her all year—I had to take out the most important bits. Now these truths burn in me, and they can't ever be said. Do you know what a damned prickly feeling that is?"

When he saw his friends' discomfort, he rocked forward. "Gentlemen, I got a telephone call today—Paige expects to start production Monday. Say hello to the new Prince of Printing."

They clinked glasses, Mr. Whitmore rather reluctantly.

Isabel sipped her water. "What truths, Mr. Clemens?"

Mr. Clemens put down his drink. For once he looked at her neither fiercely nor flippantly but with a growing seriousness. A knock came on the billiards room door.

"Who is it?" Mr. Clemens shouted.

The haughty Irish maid opened the door.

"Yes, Katy?"

She blinked as if taken aback by her employer's unmasked expression. They looked at each other longer than a servant and master should.

"Mrs. Clemens is asking for you."

He rose without questioning her.

When he returned to the room perhaps a quarter of an hour later, he was his old self again, making salty remarks and dry observations. The party broke up before midnight, with the gentlemen half tipsy and Isabel steeped in smoke. As she was spiraling down the flamboyant staircase with Mr. Whitmore, she thought she heard a woman crying. Gripping the newel post on the second-floor landing, she paused to listen.

"Wouldn't you say that was right, Miss Lyon?" Mr. Whitmore said, continuing his conversation. He saw that she was listening to something elsewhere. "What is it?"

The crying stopped. The very air seemed to be holding its breath.

Uneasy, Isabel started forward again. "Nothing."

• • •

Months passed. The card games were suspended due to one or another of the gentlemen being called out of town, and then the summer season intervened and everyone escaped to the countryside. To Isabel's disappointment, the Friday-night games did not reconvene in the fall. Mr. Whitmore claimed that as busy as he was at work, he wanted to spend his evenings at home, and encouraged her to join the family circle.

One November afternoon, the weather outside as dreary as her life, she was giving the younger Whitmores a history lesson when Frederick, now eighteen and only a visitor to the nursery, spoke up. "I like this place, Pompeii." He swung the leg he had hooked over the arm of the leather chair. "It's gruesome."

The youngest boy, thirteen-year-old Harold, gaped up from the rug before the fireplace. "Miss Lyon, were the people really caught in the act of whatever they were doing?"

"Well," said Isabel, "yes. The volcanic ash rained down on them and covered them completely, then hardened, forming perfect casts. They were caught bent over tables, sitting against walls, crawling, even—"

"In bed?" Frederick thumped his leg against the chair.

Eleven-year-old Ruth jumped up when her mother entered the room. "Mamma! Miss Lyon is telling us about the most terrible place."

"Pompeii," Isabel informed her employer. "We are studying the Roman empire."

Mrs. Whitmore nodded distractedly. "Isabel, may I speak to you a moment, please?" Once she had drawn Isabel into the hall, she said,

"I'm asking a favor of you. I have a dear friend in Philadelphia who is in great need. Emilie Dana has just returned from abroad, where she lost her seven-year-old son to meningitis."

"I'm so sorry," Isabel murmured.

"It is a sad story. To lose one's child! There is nothing worse." She sighed deeply, the corners of her mouth furrowing. "Well, now there's the daughter to care for, ten-year-old Millicent, and I fear Mrs. Dana is not up to mothering her. She asked if I knew of a governess—and well, they need you more than I do now. It would be just until they get settled in."

Isabel let what her employer was asking sink in. "You want me to go to Philadelphia?"

"Yes. Just for a while."

"But your children—"

"Oh, they'll survive. This is only temporary. You'll like the Danas. Mr. Dana is a gentleman professor, like your father—he teaches art. He's not a boring old banker like Mr. Whitmore." She smiled pointedly.

Isabel blinked at her. Was she being let go?

"I told Emilie that you would be there tomorrow. You don't mind, do you?"

Isabel thought of her mother, now living with her sister in Farmington, only an eight-mile ride away. Philadelphia was hundreds of miles beyond that—there would be no more Sunday visits. She thought of the Whitmore children in her charge. They would grow up without her. After a little while, they would not even notice she was gone, or when they did think of her, they would experience only a twinge of melancholy, like one did when remembering a favored childhood dog. This was not her home. They were not her family. She was only perched here, allowed to stay on as long as it suited them. Even if she'd done nothing to encourage Mr. Whitmore's advances, even though she kept him at arm's length, there was nothing to keep her here should Mrs. Whitmore grow too uncomfortable.

Isabel's own good behavior couldn't save her. Her mistake had been in not understanding that.

"When do I go?"

"There's a train at eleven-twenty-three in the morning."

Isabel thought briefly: *No more card games with Mr. Clemens.* And then put such dreams out of her mind.

"All right." She kept her sigh to herself, for pride's sake. Pride was all she really had.

5.

November 1902
Riverdale-on-Hudson, New York

IT WAS A VENERABLE old gentleman of a house, bearded with ivy, wrapped with a porch, and capped with a slate mansard roof. Commanding a view of the Hudson River at its most impressive, and situated just a few miles outside of New York City near the quiet rail-stop of Riverdale, the fieldstone mansion looked as if it could have been the cradle of a great man, and it was. The sitting president, Theodore Roosevelt, had spent two years of his boyhood here.

Now Isabel stood on the same broad boards of the porch on which Teddy, in short pants, would have once thrown marbles. She peered again at the letter of instructions from Mrs. Olivia Clemens that she held in her black-gloved hand, as if a study of the hurried handwriting might explain how she'd come to be there. Her—the underpaid and overeducated companion to Philadelphia socialite Millicent Dana—a private secretary! She had no idea what a private secretary did. Heaven forbid that she should be asked to operate a typewriter. She knew no more of stenography than did a chimpanzee. But when the position with Mrs. Clemens was mentioned by Mrs. Whitmore (who had remained friendly with Isabel over the past thirteen years, once she had isolated Isabel from her husband), Isabel jumped. She needed the extra fifteen dollars a month that

Mrs. Clemens promised; she had her mother to support. And although life with Millicent had offered voyages to Europe, trips to New York, and photography lessons and other excursions into the art world of Philadelphia in which Mr. Dana was a distinguished player, she'd grown tired of shirking the embraces of married gentlemen or bachelors before they were wedded to fortunes. Without an inheritance, she would never be considered as a potential partner for the men in the circles in which she ran. She liked this new idea of being a secretary for Mrs. Clemens, of doing a man's work for a woman. In two weeks, Isabel would be thirty-nine—not too late for a fresh start.

The door swung open, exposing Isabel to a face she had not seen in over a dozen years. "Hello, Katy."

The maid, with her high cheekbones and ruddy coarse skin, was still roughly handsome in her fierce Irish way, although time had thickened her body within its starched and ruffled pinafore and had spun gray wires into her black pouf. By the tough set of her mouth, it did not appear to have sweetened her much.

"Do you remember me?"

"The little governess." There was a mocking edge to her voice. "To the rear. And be quiet. Mrs. Clemens needs her rest."

The floorboards creaked as Isabel took a step backward. "Should I come another time?" With a sinking heart, she pictured the train ride back into the city and to the boardinghouse that smelled of canned peas.

"I said to the rear." The door thudded shut.

Isabel would not be dispirited. She needed this job. Holding her hat against the wind and her letter crushed against her chest, she navigated the side lawn.

Uncut withered grass, rippling sideways, released its herbal scent as it crunched beneath her boots. Brown leaves tumbled before her. In the near distance, across a sloping expanse that could be traversed quickly with a pony cart, stood a step-down shelf of bare trees lit oddly from below, as if they stood on the edge of the world. Beyond them, in a rocky canyon over a mile wide, the Hudson River, its deep blue skin scaled with whitecaps, lumbered toward the sea with saurian unconcern.

Isabel stopped to look out over it, the wind banging her skirt against her boots. She'd grown up with a similar grand view. In her mind, she saw herself as a four-year-old. Her mother was lounging on a rug with her toddling sister on the lime-green lawn of Spring Side; her baby brother slept in a pram. Her father made her sit next to her mother, and then he put the infant, heavy as a small sack of sand, into her arms. When Baby Charlie had scowled up at Isabel with his double chin and furrowed brow, a petulant worm being pulled into the light, love had surged through her bony chest. Gritting her teeth against the overwhelming pain of it, she squeezed his arm. He cried out.

"Charles!" her mother exclaimed. "Take him away from her."

Isabel's heart had broken as her brother had been wrenched from her. Even now, as she looked out over the majestic river, she could taste the bitterness of being misunderstood.

The sound of a woman singing penetrated her thoughts. Isabel listened: it was Schubert's "Ave Maria," sung with more volume than control. The warbling came from a massive chestnut tree located a whack of a croquet ball across the lawn. Stairs led up the side of a tree to a wooden shelter tucked among the spreading boughs.

A gravelly drawl punctured the singing: "Could you at least wait until I get down?"

Isabel felt a jolt. She hadn't expected to be affected by him after all this time. It had been at least a dozen years. She reined herself in. He was an old man in his sixties now. He wouldn't remember her. His wife had been the one to hire her.

Boots with soles much scarred by match strikes appeared on the board steps descending from the treehouse, followed by gray trouser legs riffling in the wind, a flapping coat, and a mane of silvered hair. Their owner saw Isabel as soon as he hit the ground. He stopped. The trauma that she'd heard had befallen him in the intervening years—losing his daughter Susy to meningitis, suffering from bankruptcy, embarking on a worldwide speaking tour to pay off the debts on the Hartford house, in which he could no longer afford to live—seemed not to have defeated him. He stared at her from beneath those frightening eyebrows, as bold as ever.

The singing ceased. Velvet pumps, slim ankles in black hosiery, and then a fluttering lavender skirt hem piped in black came down the steps. "I'm getting very good, Papa. Everyone says so. Would it grieve you so much to compliment me every once in a while?"

He wouldn't stop staring.

"I won't let you discourage me, Papa." The singer hopped the last step to the ground. With a bushy mass of auburn hair that resisted the restraints of a pompadour and the endearingly stooped figure of a shy child, the young woman, of perhaps thirty years in age, instantly charmed. Her features were rounded and girlish yet accurate copies of her father's—she was what he would have looked like as a pretty girl. Although her black straw boater was pinned to her pouf in a jaunty tilt, she ducked her head further when she stood next to him, her submissive air contradicting her hat.

"Clara." Mr. Clemens kept his gaze on Isabel. "I believe your mother's new secretary is here. This is Miss Lyon."

The long ribbons of her hat jerking in the wind, Clara briskly crossed the lawn, hand extended, to Isabel. "Welcome to our home. If you ever call me Miss Twain, you will be instantly dismissed."

Isabel laughed until she saw that Miss Clemens was serious.

Mr. Clemens ambled his way over. "So you're a secretary these days. Well, if you are as good at secretarying as you are at sharping cards, my wife is in good hands."

Clara looked between them.

"We met at your father's Friday-night card game when I was working for the Whitmore family," Isabel explained. "I didn't think you'd remember," she said to Mr. Clemens.

"It's funny what Papa remembers," Clara said, "and what he doesn't."

Her father tipped back his head to inspect Isabel at his leisure.

"I must be time-traveling," he announced when he was done. "You look exactly the same. Clara, did you thunk me on the head with a crowbar?"

"He's talking about the main character in the *Connecticut Yankee*," Clara said impatiently. "He got hit in the head and went back in time. Not everyone has read your books, Papa."

"You mean Hank Morgan?" said Isabel.

Mr. Clemens performed his old trick of smiling with his eyes. "I think you are going to work out just fine."

"She has yet to talk with Mamma."

He patted his breast pocket for a cigar, ignoring his daughter. "You must be a whiz at shorthand."

"I'm afraid I'm not," said Isabel.

"Then," said Mr. Clemens, drawing out a cigar, "you must know your way around a typewriting machine."

Panic electrified the skin of her forearms. "I'm sorry. I should have been clearer with Mrs. Clemens as to my experience, but Mrs. Whitmore did urge me to apply. Perhaps I'm not right for the situation."

Mr. Clemens clenched an unlit cigar in his teeth and held out his hand for the letter that Isabel had been clutching. She gave it up.

He looked it over. "So my wife doesn't want you staying with us."

"You don't have to be rude, Papa. Please excuse him, Miss—"

"Lyon," said Isabel.

"—Miss Lyon. My father thinks Mark Twain is above the rules of civility. Perhaps you've already noticed that."

Her father ignored her. "You ought to stay with us. This old pile is a regular rabbit's warren of rooms. I'm sure we could scare one up for you. Don't let the fact that Teddy Roosevelt once lived here spoil it for you. I try not to."

Mrs. Clemens had been clear in her letter that Isabel was not to stay with them. Had there been an incident with a previous live-in servant?

She took back the paper. "I've made inquiries. I know of a comfortable room nearby if Mrs. Clemens finds me right for the position."

"If you insist," said Mr. Clemens. "But I'm throwing you out if you insist on banging away on one of those goddamn typewriters. I won't have one in the house."

Did this mean that she had the job?

"What are you talking about, Papa?" Clara cried. "You do have one in the house. He wrote *A Connecticut Yankee* on it. He was the first author ever to have used the machine for a book."

"I didn't want to show off."

"Liar. You always want to show off." Clara seized Isabel's arm, then lowered her head in challenge. "Miss Lyon is Mamma's, so don't try to claim her."

Isabel let Clara lead her to the house. When she turned around, Mr. Clemens was lighting his cigar. He glanced up, and then grinned at her with his eyes.

6.

March 1903
Riverdale-on-Hudson, New York

ISABEL WAS DRAFTING A check when Clara came to the office door of the Riverdale estate, a dress draped over each arm. She held them up with a swish. "Help me decide."

Isabel put down her pen, glad for company. Five months on the job, and she still had not met Mrs. Clemens. Oh, she had heard the chiming of Mrs. Clemens's music box wafting through the silent halls, had heard the quiet click of Mrs. Clemens's bedroom door being closed by the doctor after his frequent visits, had felt Mrs. Clemens's spirit penetrating the house, or at least she thought she did—she suspected that was what gave the place such a lonely, desperate atmosphere, in spite of Mr. Clemens's playfulness when he entertained reporters or his few friends. Perhaps what Isabel felt was their loss of Susy. Even eight years after the death of the eldest Clemens girl, no one would speak her name. Grief seemed to permeate the air. Clara, Jean, and their father drifted around in the gloom like fish in an aquarium, rarely making contact with each other or Isabel, who was mostly left alone save for when Clara dropped bills on the office desk, a practice she'd unceremoniously begun two weeks after Isabel's arrival. No one seemed to be in charge of the day-to-day affairs of the estate, not even Mr. Clemens, who was locked up in his billiards room—writing, he said, although the constant muffled syncopated click of the balls said otherwise.

"Of course."

"I can't ask Katy," said Clara. "Her taste is hopelessly garish. She used to dress up when she first started working for us—if a gown wasn't low-cut and scarlet, she wouldn't have it. Papa refused to let her go out in them."

Mr. Clemens bothered himself with his employees' attire when off duty? But Isabel held her tongue, not wanting to alienate her rare visitor.

Clara raised the garments. "Which should I wear to the party tomorrow night?" To Isabel's look of surprise, she added, "Mother is feeling better. Dr. Quintard said it would be safe for me to take the evening off."

In the five months that Isabel had worked for Mrs. Clemens, the doctor had ordered her employer to keep to her bed, no visitors allowed. Mr. Clemens himself was only granted one two-to-five-minute visit a day—if Mrs. Clemens were up to it, which was not often. Weeks went by without his seeing her. Clara, on the other hand, disappeared into her mother's room for the greater part of each day. Jean, if she decided to come in from the stable or the woods, was usually allowed in, too. For everyone else Mrs. Clemens remained out of sight, as strangely elusive as Mr. Rochester's first wife in *Jane Eyre*.

It seemed odd that Mr. Clemens should be so restricted when their daughters weren't, and that Clara should be required to spend all of her time in the sickroom though a very capable professional nurse was in residence. Isabel's own mother would have been frantic for her to be out in the social swirl, meeting marriage prospects, instead of wasting her prime marketability years at bedside. If nothing else, surely Mrs. Clemens would have liked for her daughter to get some fresh air.

"The pink or the green?" Clara lifted each arm in turn, displaying a pink brocade featuring voluminous mutton sleeves on one and a heavy green satin with a high neckline of sheer netting on the other. Isabel herself owned three dresses: a secretarial shirtwaist costume, a navy day dress, and an evening gown that had been lovely when she debuted in it twenty-one years earlier but now made her look like a Civil War widow. Her salary of fifty dollars a month paid room and board for her mother and her, but it did not cover bolts of satin. It didn't even allow her to feel secure. She and her mother were still assembling pincushions for sale upon an evening, stockpiling them against adversity.

"How formal is the party?" she asked. "What is the occasion?"

"See? Katy wouldn't have known to ask that. I'm so glad that you work here now, although Katy would not agree. What did you do to set her so against you?"

Isabel thought of Katy's refusal to serve her coffee, to bring her the mail, or do any other little service for her. She was especially chilly if Isabel was speaking with Mr. Clemens. "I was born, evidently."

"I shouldn't laugh. It's no joking matter. As hot-tempered as Katy is, I wouldn't want her against me."

"Believe me, I don't relish it."

Clara didn't really hear, her attention returned to her clothes. "It's just a dinner at my friend Marie's house, but there will be several musical gentlemen there, and I want to look"—she plucked a piece of lint from the pink dress, then shrugged—"desirable."

"I like you in the green."

"I look good in green," Clara agreed. She pressed the gown against herself as if to model it.

Isabel smiled at Clara's unapologetic vanity. It seemed a forgivable flaw in someone who devoted all her time to her ill mother.

"Don't tell Papa about the gentlemen," Clara said abruptly.

"I won't."

Clara saw her frown. "You don't know how Papa is about men. He cannot bear for them to be near me." She went to the door and carefully closed it. "When I was sixteen and we were staying in Marienbad, he locked me in my room for three weeks after a young German army officer paid me a call at our lodgings. I had met him in a café with Papa. I'd never even spoken to the man." Clara glanced over her shoulder before continuing. "Papa banished him as if he were a criminal, and locked me in my room. He only let Katy in to bring me trays of food. For three weeks, he made me a prisoner. I didn't get out until Mother came home. And you know what she did?"

Isabel shook her head.

"She laughed."

Isabel pushed away her disbelief. "They were trying to protect you."

"No, they weren't, especially not him. You don't know—sometimes he is frightening. It comes out of nowhere."

Clara hitched the dresses over arm and reached for an envelope on the desk. "How many does he get? Fifty invitations a day? Everyone loves good old clever Mark Twain." She put down the envelope. "I see him talking to you, Isabel. He likes you. He's the one who suggested that we hire you. Katy says he's in love with you."

"Katy!" Isabel scoffed.

"I know. She can be absurd. We keep her around because she's as loyal as she is coarse. You're my friend, aren't you?"

"Of course I am."

"Don't let him turn you against me. He will. I swear to you, he will. He's not happy unless everyone loves him and only him. He won't even let anyone love his own daughter. That's why I so rarely have friends. He steals them."

Isabel straightened the blotter on her desk. He'd hired her?

"I shouldn't have told you this."

"No, I understand."

Clara took Isabel's hand. "Thank you." She pressed Isabel's fingers. "Friend."

When Clara left, Isabel picked up her pen. Before she could go back to settling accounts, her sights strayed to an old family photo on the wall. Grouped with Clara and little Jean on the porch of their Hartford home, Mrs. Clemens seemed to be willing herself from view by smiling at her lap and clamping her frail arms to her sides, reducing her figure to a sliver. She appeared hardly bigger than her robust toddler, Jean. Yet her handsome tousle-haired husband, paired with a disgruntled-looking Susy, nearly throbbed with virility and well-being as he sucked on a thick cigar. It was as if he were tapping Mrs. Clemens of her very lifeblood, growing stronger as she grew weak.

Isabel had pushed aside the checkbook and was writing her private thoughts in her daily reminder when the closed door was cautiously opened. Thinking that it was Clara with more dresses, Isabel stashed her journal in her desk and rose. "Wait—I'll help you."

Mr. Clemens inched his head around the jamb. "You will?" he said in a falsetto voice.

She dropped back into her chair.

When Mr. Clemens stepped inside the room, Isabel was astonished to see that he was still in his nightshirt, over which he'd wrapped a blanket gown. His bare legs were slender and muscular for a man of sixty-seven—unusually youthful, like the rest of him—and as sleekly furred as a mink. He had black felt slippers on his feet.

He shut the door behind him. "I have a secret mission for you."

She folded her arms tightly, suppressing a smile. "You do?" She could not help but enjoy the absurd fact that one of the most famous persons in the entire world had just shut himself in with her, wearing only nightclothes and slippers. This would have to go in her journal.

"I want to get Mrs. Clemens a necklace. To cheer her up. I need you to go into town to Tiffany's to pick one out."

"Thank you for asking me, but I'm afraid that I don't know her taste."

"Her taste?" Mr. Clemens scratched the back of his neck. "Why, Livy's taste is your taste. She was brought up rich, like you."

Isabel could not understand why he so often mentioned her former wealth in their conversations, when her plain clothes, humble salary, and rented cottage near the tracks marked her as someone long out of the swim with the wealthy.

"Wouldn't you rather have the pleasure of choosing for her?"

He pulled the belt of his robe tighter. "My pleasure is in the giving. I've always had my secretaries buy for me. My nephew Charley bought her a fine enough diamond, and he was the worst secretary I ever had. The crooked little swindler destroyed me financially, but I'm not holding that against him, may he burn in hell."

Technically, Isabel was Mrs. Clemens's secretary, but of course, he knew that.

"I've been seeing ropes of red beads on the girls around town."

"You must mean coral. Coral is stylish now."

"I knew you'd know. Get her a whopping big strand at Tiffany's, would you? I like to see a woman in red." He swept his gaze over her. "You'd look good in it, too. How come there aren't any fellows around here, trying to take you from your work?" He stepped to the desk and, leaning so close to Isabel that she could smell his flesh, peered over the envelopes. "You hiding one behind there?"

"Not hardly." She laughed uncomfortably. "Unless one has risen from these scraps of paper like Adam springing from the dust."

He gazed down on her, considering. "It wouldn't be the first time. One has loosed itself from my pages, and now the beast is in control. You've heard of him—Mark Twain? 'Known by Everyone, Liked by All'? I hate the rascal."

She looked to confirm that he was joking, but he had caught sight of something outside the window. He paused, propped over the desk and Isabel. "I never noticed those were out there."

Before Isabel could ask him what he meant, the door flew open.

Mr. Clemens drew back slowly as Clara stopped, the dresses swishing in her arms.

Isabel stared at Clara in declaration of her innocence.

Shutters banged closed behind Clara's eyes. She turned to her father. "What are you doing?"

"Planning a surprise for your mother."

"I'll say," she said bitterly. "I thought you were never doing this again."

"Clara."

She spat out her words. "You are indecent in that nightgown, Papa. Go upstairs right now!"

"I'm comfortable. Miss Lyon doesn't mind, do you?"

Isabel straightened a stack of envelopes.

"Upstairs, Papa! Now! You are embarrassing Miss Lyon."

He raised his brows at Isabel. "Am I, Miss Lyon?"

"You are embarrassing me," said Clara.

"Well," said Mr. Clemens, "heaven forbid I should ever do that."

He strolled out, slippers scuffing against the floor.

Clara waited until he was out of reach. Her voice was tight. "I told you he was trying to win you."

"There is no winning. I'm just a secretary."

Mr. Clemens's stage whisper floated down from the top of the stairs. "Psst. Miss Lyon."

"You sure you want to deny it?" Clara asked Isabel.

"Miss Lyon," Mr. Clemens called. "Is my whelp gone yet?"

Against all her better instincts, against every effort to master herself, Isabel chuckled.

Clara sniffed as if struck. "You laughed."

"I'm sorry. He's just so . . . unexpected."

"Oh, Miss Ly-on!" he sang.

Isabel pressed her lips together, but the more she fought off the laughter brewing in her chest, the closer she came to erupting.

Tears thickened Clara's voice. "He won't even leave me you." She stormed from the room.

Isabel protested to the empty air, then remembering, looked out the window to see what he had commented upon. Through the railings of the covered porch she saw a bare hydrangea bush, its remaining withered flowers bobbing silently in the wind.

7.

April 1903
Riverdale-on-Hudson, New York

THE FOLLOWING MONTH, THE wind, sweet with the greenness of April, lifted Isabel's hat as Jean Clemens handed her the inlaid-pearl opera glasses. "Look. Up near the house, on that shrub."

Isabel twitched her skirt from where it had caught on the grass, then took the glasses from the youngest Clemens daughter. She and Jean were near the edge of the lawn, where the property commanded the Hudson. Mr. Clemens had encouraged Isabel to indulge his daughter in her outdoor romps, and Isabel didn't mind. She welcomed a break from the paperwork that was descending upon her desk with the persistence of Sisyphus's rock, and she genuinely liked Jean, though there was something about her that made Isabel sad. Outwardly, Jean seemed to have everything—a world-famous father, money, intelligence, and, with her strong chin and Greek-goddess nose, healthy good looks. At nearly twenty-three, she was still a tomboy, not only in her appearance—she refused to wear a corset under her plain white shirtwaist and brown corduroy skirt, or to fashion her hair in anything but a single dark braid—but in her ungraceful movement as well. She spoke in the same way she moved: bluntly, plainly, no mincing allowed. Yet as sturdy as she looked, there was something vulnerable about her, something broken, like the stray dogs and cats she was continually nursing back to health, like the dray horses in the city for which she bought freedom whenever she could.

"It's a bluebird," said Jean.

Isabel squinted through the opera glasses.

"Calling for its mate. Hear it?"

Isabel squirmed under the nagging pain of her attire as she listened to the bird's plaintive murmur. The steel-ribbed busks of her corset painfully forced her small breasts up and her narrow hips back, as was the fashion. Her belt added fresh agony, driving the steel stays into her flesh. Why had she cinched her belt so tightly? In addition, she had left off her jacket to display her figure, and now she was cold. What folly to think that Mr. Clemens would notice her small waistline. Why should he? Why would she want him to? This was what happened when you were neither fish nor fowl, too low in status to attract high men, too high in status to attract low men—you ridiculously yearned for your married, much older employer.

"They mate for life, you know," said Jean. "Well, unless another bird forces them apart."

Isabel glanced at her guiltily.

"Or one dies." Jean sighed. "The survivor won't abandon its mate. I saw that happen to a pair of Canada geese in the city. A trolley had killed the female and the male wouldn't leave. He frantically circled the body, dodging wagons and carriages until a cabbie ran over him."

Isabel chased away the unpleasant image, concentrating instead on the bluebird, his head and wings a vivid azure against the orange of his throat. Maybe it would not be wise to tell Jean that last week on a trip to the city for Mr. Clemens, she had seen a stuffed bluebird just like this on a woman's hat, complete with mate, nest, and eggs. The woman was her friend Win Cattelle, whom Isabel had run into at a stationer's on Fifth Avenue. Isabel remembered the bluebirds on the hat distinctly, for she had stared at them steadily while Win told of their friend Olive's strange infatuation with a man many years her senior.

"So disgusting," Win had said, tugging at her gloves. "Everyone will think Olive is a shameless fortune hunter."

Isabel had agreed that it was a most unsuitable affair.

Jean nudged her with her elbow. "Look, there she is—his wife. Isn't she a darling? Everyone looks at the boy bird with his bright blue, but I think the girl's quiet colors are nicer. Not everyone needs to be such a show-off."

Isabel shot her a sidelong glance. Jean's father was the biggest "show-off" Isabel had ever met. People adored him for it, including her. She knew exactly from whom he'd drawn his scheming adventurer Tom Sawyer: his own irrepressible self.

She gave back the glasses to Jean. "How is your mother?"

"You'll have to ask Clara. I haven't seen Mother in weeks."

"You haven't?" Although Isabel still had not met her employer, receiving her orders via Clara or with a sneer from Katy, she had assumed that Jean made regular visits to her mother's bedside.

Jean lowered the opera glasses. "I guess you don't know. I've been banned from Mother."

Isabel grasped for a response. "Why?"

"I make her sad."

"Jean! You would never make anyone sad."

"I scare her."

Isabel sighed. "Jean. You couldn't scare a"—she looked across the lawn—"bluebird."

"I do," said Jean. "I scare Mother, and one more scare might kill her. We all have to do everything we can to preserve her. We can't survive without her—none of us."

Isabel thought of the photograph, and of the wisp of a woman being whittled away by her husband in it. "I'm sure she'll get well."

Jean's prominent chin crumpled. "The only person I scare more is Father."

"That can't be," Isabel murmured, even as she pictured Mr. Clemens leaving the room whenever Jean entered. She had thought it was just a coincidence—he was a busy man and, in spite of the languid mode in which he moved, a restless one. He never stayed in one place long. He could not even remain seated at dinner. From behind the servants' screen in the dining room, Isabel had watched him prowl around the Belgian-lace-clothed table, smoking one of his pungent cigars, as his friends, perhaps William Dean Howells, or Henry Huttleston Rogers of Standard Oil, ate their meal. Of course, Mrs. Clemens never joined them.

Jean's cheeks had gone red. "It's not just that he doesn't find any interest or entertainment in me, which he doesn't. There's something wrong with me."

"Oh, Jean—" Isabel broke off when she saw that the girl was serious.

"I have fits. They started when I was fifteen. We thought it was an isolated incident, but then I kept having them. No one is to marry me—an epileptic can't have children—but the awful fact is, even if I were well, Papa would never let me marry."

"Jean."

"It's true. He won't let any of us. He hates the thought of us with men. No wonder Susy turned to someone he thought he would not object to. But that turned out to be the biggest mistake of all."

This was the first anyone had spoken of Susy. "I'm so very sorry."

"I shouldn't be telling you this."

"You don't have to if you don't want to."

A mourning dove burst whistling from the grassy verge. "Poor Susy. She was his favorite—he made it quite plain to us. He seems not to have the insight to see how that might hurt Clara and me." Jean watched the bird. "It turned out that getting the lion's share of his attention was unlucky for Susy, though I'd be lying if I said I wasn't jealous." Jean's gaze went toward the house. She seemed to shrink into the high collar of her shirtwaist.

Isabel turned to see Mr. Clemens ambling from the terrace with its empty stone urns, a cigar between his slender fingers. "Well, look who's out here," he called. "I thought I was going to have to smoke this thing alone."

Jean galloped off, as ungainly as one of her abused horses. The wind groaned in the trees as Isabel waited for him. He stopped next to her. "What's wrong with her?"

He gazed out over the river and drew on his cigar. Under the bluff, a train approached on the tracks by the water, its rumble growing.

Isabel felt disloyal to Jean for remaining with him. Yet she did not want to go. She tried to strike a cheerful note. "Did you know that bluebirds mate for life?"

He drew in a long breath. "Just another example of how low a form of life mankind is. When it comes to decency, even birds beat us."

"Humans mate for life," Isabel said. It came out as a warning.

Her tone drew his glance. "Do they?" He tugged on his cigar. "Show me a couple that has been faithful in spirit, if not in action, for their entire marriage, and I'll show you the day that river down there changes directions. Humans just can't do it."

An onrush of blood stung Isabel's face. She could feel the train roaring under her feet as it neared.

He blew out smoke. "Livy and myself excluded, of course."

"Of course."

They stood looking at the water as the train shrieked below them. Isabel wondered what the loss of a child—two children, if you counted the baby son who'd died several decades earlier—had done to the Clemenses' marriage, and what toll Mrs. Clemens's infirmity might have taken on it as well.

He raised his voice. "You can't beat this view of the Hudson."

"It's magnificent." With a dig of steel stays, she turned away to wait out the passing train, her bones trembling with its vibrations.

At last the train lumbered away, leaving a ringing quiet. Birdsong swelled into the void.

"Damn trains," said Mr. Clemens. "They're as inelegant as an elephant at a tea party. A steamboat's the thing. How I yearn for the days when I piloted them. What a life! I mean to set it down in my autobiography—as unflinchingly truthfully as a lying human can do."

"You're writing an autobiography?"

"If you call the cowardly stabs I've made at it 'writing.' It's a daunting proposition, Miss Lyon, telling the whole truth about yourself. Ever try it?"

"No. I'm not sure I'd want to."

He was quiet a moment. "I keep trying, but my pen gets in the way."

"People would want to hear everything about you."

"Would they? I think they might want to hear about Mark Twain; about Samuel Clemens, maybe not as much. They wouldn't care for some of the things I've done. I don't know if even my beloved twin Twain could take the heat if I told the unvarnished truth about myself."

She remembered Jean's accusations, then shook them off. "Then varnish it."

He smiled. "I like you, Miss Lyon. Wish I knew you back in my steamboat days."

She could not look at him, glowing as she was.

"Those were the days," he said with a sigh. "There is no man who rules so absolutely, so independently of the opinion of others, so aware of and greedy for his awful responsibilities, as a riverboat pilot. I thought I was king."

"You would make a good king," she said stoutly.

"Would I?"

She could not resist the pull of his gaze. She turned around to look at him. "I think so. You move like one."

"I do? If only you knew what I came up from, you wouldn't say that. We were poor enough when my father was alive, but after he died, we were so frantic that I had to leave school and go to work at the age of twelve. But I'd like to be king." He tossed his graying auburn mane and held out his cigar like a scepter. "How's that?"

She bowed to him. "Your Highness."

"What am I king of?"

She thought of his fondness for cards. "Hearts."

He nodded. "Right." He put out his other hand. "You may kiss the royal mitt."

She gazed at his wedding band shining from within a sparse thicket of hair. When she looked up, he lifted his hand.

She returned his bold look, then leaned forward and kissed his knuckle. The salty taste of his skin stayed on her lips after she pulled back; she smelled the tarry smoke of his cigar.

The laughter in his eyes settled into seriousness. They took a breath and, as one, turned toward the river. Below, a ship, trailing smoke from its single black stack, navigated the broad and sparkling seam in the earth.

The drawl left his voice. "Way up here, I feel like Christ looking out over the world, with Satan at His side, offering Him power over all the dominions."

"Does that make me Satan?"

He laughed, the first time she'd heard him do so. "By God, Miss Lyon, you are a lioness."

Breathing hurt her chest. She ached all over from happiness.

"What would you wish for, if you could have that power?" she asked.

"A submerged reputation." He looked down on her, eyes shining. "The man who gets that market, his fortune is made, his livelihood is safe. People will never go back on him. An author may have a reputation that is confined to the surface, and lose it. He becomes pitied, then despised, then forgotten, then entirely forgotten: the frequent steps in a surface reputation. A surface reputation, however great, is always mortal, and always killable if you go at it right—with pins and needles, and quiet slow poison, not with the club and tomahawk."

His gaze grew intent. "But the submerged reputation, down in the safe water, down mark twain deep, is different. Once a favorite there, always a favorite. Once beloved, always beloved. Once respected, always respected, honored, and believed in. What the reviewer says never finds its way down into those placid deeps; nor the newspaper sneers, nor any breath of the winds of slander blowing above. Down there they never hear of these things. Their idol may be painted clay, up at the surface, and fade and crumble and blow away, but down below, he is as indestructible as gold."

The birds calling, the groan of the trees, the train steaming into the distance, fell away. They smiled at each other, not just with their eyes but with their whole selves—there was no need to hold back.

"What would you have, Lioness? With your power over the dominions."

She caught her breath. She had never been asked. She had never asked herself.

The fierceness was gone from his face. He beheld her deeply, his gray eyes gentle with sadness. "You have to ask, Lioness. In this life, you don't get what you want unless you ask."

He raised his gaze and then stiffened.

Isabel turned around to see a frail hand extending from an upper-story bow window of the mansion. It waved a lace handkerchief until the wind snatched the bit of cloth away. The handkerchief, white as the sunlight dappling the Hudson, pitched and sailed languorously toward the terrace. The hand withdrew.

"Livy. She's calling me." Mr. Clemens threw down his cigar and stalked to the house, sending the pair of bluebirds up and away.

Isabel crushed the smoldering nub under her boot, then, after checking the window, picked it up and touched the damp end where his mouth had been.

8.

June 1903
Riverdale-on-Hudson, New York

OH DEAR, IT WAS humid, and it was only June! Mrs. Lyon patted her face with her handkerchief as she surveyed Isabel's hair, assessing the work to be done. How was she to fix the mess her daughter had made of it in time for her gentleman caller and still make them a lovely tea? The Wild Men from Borneo had tidier coiffures. Shaking her head, she tucked her hankie into her belt and then plunged into battle with the teasing brush.

"How many years has Mr. Bangs taught at Columbia?" She furiously back-combed. "You did tell him that your father taught there for eighteen years?"

Isabel scraped the chair armrests with her fingernails, as if warring against the urge to spring from her seat. Mrs. Lyon renewed her grip on Isabel's hair to keep her from moving. Not only was John Kendricks Bangs a Columbia man, but charming, sweet, and pleasantly even-featured in a bald, Humpty Dumpty–ish but nice way. He was a famous humorist (although not as famous as Mr. Clemens), and still Isabel said that she found him as boring as unsalted bread. Did Isabel consider that he was still in mourning? His wife had died only two months earlier—of course he was not at his best. Isabel should not be so judgmental.

"Be still!" Mrs. Lyon seized another hank of her daughter's hair as if apprehending a criminal. "I see a gray." She isolated the offender with the point of the teasing brush, grasped it by the root, and yanked. She produced her culprit. "There."

Isabel glanced at it, then rolled her gaze away with a sigh.

Mrs. Lyon cleaned the excess strands from the brush and then stuffed them into the ceramic hair receptor on the vanity. From a quick stirring of the pot with her little finger, she gauged that she had just about enough hair to roll together a new rat—a fresh rat was the secret to the fluffiest pompadour, didn't you know. She could see why her daughter would be disturbed by the gray. It was 1903, which—goodness!—made Isabel almost forty. Almost forty and unmarried. To be graying before achieving wedlock must be a terrible shock. Mrs. Lyon had not been gray at this age, although she was already married with two children. Her hair had been thick as a fox's pelt, and had glowed with hints of russet. She had not had grays until Charles died twenty years ago, although then they had come in droves. In truth, it was a miracle that at Isabel's age, she hadn't had a shock of hair as white as thistledown. It had not been easy being married to a man as handsome and as vain and as unfaithful as Charles had been. How often had she needed to look away and pretend he was not having relations with another woman?

"Don't worry, dear. That's the only gray I saw."

Isabel stared into the mirror.

Mrs. Lyon resumed back-combing her daughter's hair. Gracious, Isabel needn't take one silly gray so hard. How about having to deal with your husband's illegitimate child—alone? There wasn't a person in the world with whom she could talk about it. Isabel knew nothing of it—none of the children did. Mrs. Lyon had protected them from the knowledge and borne the shame of its existence by herself. Not that she expected their thanks for shielding them. It was just what a mother did.

"Now, tell me about Mr. Clemens." She picked up the next section of hair framing her daughter's face. "Where did he take you in New York? Wherever you went, you simply ruined your hair. It's so damp, it will hardly take a back-combing. You might as well have toured the Niagara Falls on the deck of the *Maid of the Mist.*" She presented the lank hank as evidence.

"What?" Isabel appeared to swim out of a daydream. "It rained."

"I know it rained. It rained so hard here that I couldn't see across the street from our window. Why didn't you stay inside until it stopped?" Mrs. Lyon dropped the hank, then reached for a towel and began to blot Isabel's hair.

• • •

Isabel glanced away from the mirror. Her mother's dabbing had jiggled free a disquieting recollection from that morning. Isabel had arrived at the Clemenses' home earlier than usual, to catch the 8:50 train to the city with Mr. Clemens. The air was cool as she had crossed the side lawn, a cardinal warbling *birdie-birdie-birdie* and the dew glistening on the grass. She had just taken her gaze from the river—she had grown even fonder of the view since sharing it with Mr. Clemens—when she saw him on the terrace, tipped back in a wrought-iron chair. Katy stood over him, rubbing his hair with a towel.

For a moment, Isabel had not recognized her. A smile had transformed the maid's sour face into that of a fresh-faced pretty girl. She was singing some sort of hymn, to which Mr. Clemens listened with closed eyes, seemingly unabashed by his bare chest and his bare feet, with which he rocked his tipped chair. Isabel had hiked quickly back toward the front of the house, discomfited by the intimate scene.

Now Mrs. Lyon repeated, "What were you doing in New York that you couldn't stay indoors?"

Isabel's gaze trailed over to the pot with a hydrangea plant sitting next to the bed. A kitten was batting one of the heavy blue heads. The cat had come from a litter of one of Mr. Clemens's cats; Clara had given it to her. "We were busy."

"Too busy to get out of the rain? What will Mr. Bangs say about this hair?"

Isabel refrained from saying that she did not care what Mr. Bangs would say about her hair. She did not care what Mr. Bangs would say about anything. As her mother vigorously reapplied the brush, systematically teasing one section until it stood up on end before moving to the next, Isabel slipped into her thoughts. Soon the rhythmic tugs to her scalp gave way in her mind to the sound of clopping horse hooves.

She saw herself with Mr. Clemens, two hours after the disquieting scene earlier that morning. His derby crowned his tempest of clean hair as he jostled along companionably next to her within the horse-drawn cab. They were making their way down Broadway, an automobile puttering ahead of them, its pneumatic tires pummeling the Belgian blocks of the street. Trolleys rumbled past with a scowling driver in front and riders clinging to the grab-rails in the back. Schools of men in straw boaters and women in white dresses and huge hats fluttering with ribbons flowed purposefully down the sidewalks, the tide of humanity in flapping summer-weight cloth dwarfed by the elegant entrances of stores adorned with gigantic lanterns, columns, and extravagant awnings.

The broad brim of her hat brushed her shoulders as she shifted toward the cab window to look up. Where Fifth Avenue and Broadway crossed at Twenty-Third Street, the just-completed Fuller Building, the tallest and strangest of the new "skyscrapers," loomed on its triangular lot like a twenty-some story slice of wedding cake.

"Magnificent." Mr. Clemens leaned over her to view it. He smelled like smoke, wool, and man. She tried to make nothing of the fact that his arm was resting against her breast.

"Want to stop and see it?" he asked.

She reminded herself that it wouldn't be right for Mrs. Clemens's secretary to appear alone in public with Mr. Clemens. "No, but thank you."

"Really?" He sat back. Isabel's breast tingled where he had made contact. "You looked pretty interested."

Even in the shade of the cab's interior, she could feel the intensity of his eyes. Although she would not look into them, she knew exactly their color: gray, with a tendency to soft green when he was happy. She yearned to see if they were soft green now. "No. But thank you."

"Just as well." He pulled a cigar from his coat, then fished a match from his pocket. "You could lose your virtue out there."

Isabel acted as if she had not heard.

He struck his match against the sole of his shoe and watched her as he lit a cigar. "The wind whips around that devil's flatiron like a Missouri cyclone"—he puffed as he waved out the match—"wreaking the most awful havoc on the ladies' skirts. It has gotten so that a squadron of policemen has to patrol the sidewalks around it. Any casual 'scientist' who makes too close a study of the effect of wind on skirts is told, 'Twenty-three skidoo,' and gets familiarized with the street out front of that number."

Isabel glanced through the netting hanging over the edge of her hat. "I don't believe you. You're making that up."

"Now, Lioness, I thought I had trained you better than that. What do I say about stories that sound like whoppers?"

" 'The more it sounds like a whopper, the truer it is.' "

"Good girl. You'll make a fine secretary yet."

She laughed. She was thirty-nine, and he made her feel like a girl. "I am trying."

"Try harder. Rogers thinks he's got the best secretary in the world. I want to make him jealous."

"I'll do my best, but I am just your wife's social secretary."

"The hell you are. I have purloined you from Livy, and now you've got to make me look good. Why do you think I hired you?"

"I thought I was Mrs. Clemens's employee."

"Have you ever talked with her?"

"No."

"Then how could she have hired you? I'm the one who wanted you. Those card games we had were the last I had a good time, the last I felt *in charge*, before"—he scowled—"before everything went to hell." He knit his warlike brows. "I'm counting on you to take me back to those happier days. I want you to sail me back there. You think you can do that for me, Lioness?"

"I'll try." She meant it. She'd do anything for him.

He squeezed her hand. "That's my girl."

They joggled south down Broadway, a private bubble of camaraderie surrounding them as their cab navigated the sea of machines, horses, and people. At last, past City Hall, past St. Paul's Chapel, past Trinity Church, they arrived at an elegant skyscraper several blocks short of the base of the island. In spite of its prominence above its neighbors, the Standard Oil Building, with its eleven white stone stories, was marked solely with a black 26 between the massive columns of its entrance. A trip across the marble tomb of a lobby and then skyward in a brass elevator cage took them to the stronghold of the person against whom Mr. Clemens had pitted her: Katherine Harrison, secretary to Henry H. Rogers, the ranking director of the Standard Oil Company.

Wearing an expression that she hoped struck the right note between serenity and seriousness, Isabel gaped inwardly as Miss Harrison led the way to Mr. Rogers's quarters. At over six feet in height, Miss Harrison towered over Mr. Clemens. The top of Isabel's voluminous hat didn't reach the bottom of her shoulder blades. Miss Harrison had outfitted her Amazonian figure in a man's shirt and coat over a tailored skirt and had pulled back her dark blond hair in a severe bun. She was said to be the best secretary in the world and was certainly the best paid. At ten thousand dollars a year, she made more than twenty schoolteachers combined.

When she turned around at Mr. Rogers's office door, her face held all the emotion of an anvil. "You two chat," Mr. Clemens told her and Isabel. He entered the office. "Henry, you old pirate!"

Miss Harrison stepped over and sealed the door closed, then looked down upon Isabel without speaking. Chatting, it seemed, was a waste of her expensive time.

An electric fan—the latest in conveniences—droned in a corner.

Isabel's dress rippled in the hot air blown from its black metal paddles as she faced her competition. "I'm very glad to meet you, Miss Harrison. Someday I should very much like to be as respected in our field as you are."

Miss Harrison glanced at the elaborate hat for which Isabel had paid a quarter of a month's wages. "Really."

Isabel shored up her confidence, fast eroding like a sandcastle at high tide. She was not a child. "What advice can you give me on how to be a first-rate secretary?"

Miss Harrison paused. "Never get personal."

"Yes. Yes, of course. Thank you. I mean, what skill do you recommend that I work on?"

"Never getting personal."

Mr. Clemens and Mr. Rogers strolled out of the inner office. Erect as a rifle stock, Henry H. Rogers stood about a hand taller than his secretary. With his white hair parted down the middle to form two opposing bulwarks, and a mustache bristling like a timber breastwork, he seemed of a different, bellicose race. He looked like he might be one of the richest men in America, and he was.

He nodded slightly. "Good afternoon, Miss Lyon."

Isabel nodded back, surprised that he knew her name. They'd never spoken. On the occasions when he'd come to dinner with Mr. Clemens, she'd remained properly out of sight.

He clapped Mr. Clemens on the shoulder as he spoke to Isabel. "Nice that Mrs. Clemens let you slip away to keep this old buccaneer out of trouble."

"Miss Lyon is not Mrs. Clemens's property anymore." Mr. Clemens raided his own suit coat for a cigar. "I've commandeered her. That's what we pirates do."

Mr. Rogers let go of him, still smiling. "What does Livy say about that?"

"She doesn't mind. I'll get her a new one." Cigar between his fingers, Mr. Clemens put his arm around Isabel's shoulders. "This model suits me fine. I'm not trading you her for Miss Harrison, so don't even ask. She's just the right size for throwing, should a bomber give me a scare—pint-sized, just the way I like them."

Mr. Rogers's mustache lowered. "You've lost me, Mark. To what are you referring?"

Mr. Clemens snapped his fingers as if to remember. "Who was that tycoon who threw his clerk at the villain who threatened him with a bomb?"

"Russell Sage," Miss Harrison said coolly.

"That's right. Russell Sage. Didn't do much for the clerk, but it sure saved Sage's hide."

Isabel felt the weight of Mr. Clemens's arm on her shoulder as he bantered with Mr. Rogers. A fog of shame had begun to infiltrate her mind, preventing her from following their speech.

"What do you say about a ride in Rogers's motorcar?" Mr. Clemens asked her.

She nodded numbly.

"Have you ever been in one?"

She shook her head. The corners of her mouth were leaden.

He looked at her a moment longer, then removed his arm to sign some papers that Miss Harrison produced. Soon they were ushered into one of Mr. Rogers's motorcars, where Isabel spent the first automobile ride of her life turned away from Mr. Clemens. Miserable in the open backseat behind Mr. Rogers's goggled chauffeur in a duster, she was jostled north up Broadway. Gunmetal clouds roiled overhead, darkening the crowds and skyscrapers. The temperature was dropping. A storm was soon to come.

"These things give a body a shaking," Mr. Clemens shouted over the roar of the engine, "right where they need to be shaken. A man could get a massage just going to the haberdasher."

She said nothing.

A wind whipped up Broadway as they passed the gushing fountain in City Hall Park, tipping Isabel's hat forward at a precarious angle. A second gust lifted it from behind, ripping it from its pins and tumbling it toward the driver.

Mr. Clemens snatched it in midair. He turned around and held it out to her. "You need to pin it better."

"You're getting too familiar," she said suddenly.

They confronted each other, the car bumping along.

His tone was bitter when he spoke. "You society girls. Always trying to civilize me."

"I'm not a society girl."

"You were."

"Not for a decade. Not for two decades. Why do you insist on humiliating me with that?"

A red spot the size of a thumbprint appeared on each of his cheeks. "You don't know humiliation. Humiliation is living above the store that your father lost. Humiliation is having your mother make a deal with the devil so you can eat supper that night. Humiliation is growing up to be goddamn bankrupt, just like your goddamn bankrupt father."

"I'm sorry." She turned away, not caring that the wind was tearing at her hair. Trolleys passed in both directions, clanging on their tracks under the boiling black sky.

"Damn it," he demanded, "talk to me."

The motorcar sputtered by the crowd of men clustered around a pushcart selling oysters, its awning flapping madly. Boys on the sidewalk hawked newspapers to the men rushing past with their collars turned up to their hat brims.

"There are rules, Mr. Clemens."

"I know," he said viciously. He scraped off his hat, then ran his hand through his hair. He gave her a fierce look. "Livy's getting better."

She breathed out. "Then she won't need me anymore."

"That's not true. We are going to need you more than ever. We'll be out and about—we'll need you to schedule things. Keep us on target. I'm going to take up my autobiography again. I'll need you to type it up."

She looked up at him.

"Please," he said harshly.

She turned away, letting herself sink into the vibrations of the car. At the lower edge of Union Square, great mounds of dirt, the tailings of the excavation for the subway system tunneling up the eastern edge of the park, surrounded the forlorn equestrian statue of George Washington. The statesman's steed bowed its bronze head under the oppressive skies as a cable car roared past, unable to regulate its speed on Deadman's Curve at Broadway and Fourteenth. Their motorcar had turned down Fourteenth and was jittering its way north along the western side of the park when Mr. Clemens, raking his hair, glanced to his right.

"Wait! Driver—stop!"

The car swerved to the curb. Before Isabel could make sense of what was happening, Mr. Clemens clapped on his hat, threw open the door, jumped out, then pulled her along.

"What are you doing?" She glanced back at her hat on the blue leather car seat. She was bareheaded and disheveled in the city with the husband of her supposed employer.

"Just come." He tugged her toward rows of flowering plants in pots on display at the weekly flower market at the northern rim of the square.

"I can't."

"Yes, you can."

"It's going to rain."

"I don't give a damn."

He pulled her over to a clay pot from which fat blue flower heads drooped from their spindly parent. "How much?" he asked the boy tending the pots.

The boy was scratching his short-pants cuff with the side of his shoe, counting the coins Mr. Clemens had given him, when Mr. Clemens thrust the pot at Isabel. "Here. Hydrangeas. My favorite."

"For your wife," she said firmly.

"For you," he said equally firmly.

"I can't accept this."

"They're just hydrangeas. A man can give his secretary hydrangeas. What is wrong with that?"

She wanted to cry.

"Take it. Although you've taken all the fun out of it." At that moment, the sky opened. Rain drummed against the sidewalk and pelted their heads and backs. They ran under the awning of a nearby milliner's shop, Isabel hugging her pot.

At the curb, rain bounced from the chauffeur's cap as he struggled to raise the cover over the car. When done, he splashed over with an umbrella, then shepherded them to the vehicle. Isabel slid inside, soaked to the skin. Locks of her hair were peeling from her bouffant like the skin from a banana.

Mr. Clemens took off his hat. He looked equally drowned, with tips of his hair plastered to his face. Only the top of his head was dry. "Take her home, Pat."

"What about you, sir?"

"I'll take the train. Stop now."

"We're not near the train, sir."

"Damn it all, I said stop."

As soon as the driver had braked, Mr. Clemens was out and waving away the car. He ducked under an iron marquee.

Isabel pivoted with a crunch of leather seat to look out the window as the car pulled away. Well-wishers were approaching Mr. Clemens in the driving rain. He looked up at her from the gathering crowd, then turning his back to her, launched into entertaining them.

• • •

Now, at the vanity in her bedroom, the tugging on Isabel's scalp had stopped. In the mirror, Isabel saw her mother balling a wad of hair. Once the rat was suitably shaped, Mrs. Lyon positioned it behind the wall of robustly back-combed tresses that she'd so tirelessly created.

"I'm going to quit my job," Isabel said.

"What? Why? He's famous. You might meet a successful gentleman through him if Mr. Bangs doesn't work out."

"I want to use my skills in the city."

"Good heavens. Why would you want to do that?"

Isabel lost control of her emotions. "Mrs. Clemens has gotten better." She stuffed her pain back into a box, but not quickly enough. Mrs. Lyon was watching her in the mirror.

Her mother's voice rose. "Have you talked with her?"

"No. Not yet."

Mrs. Lyon vigorously smoothed her daughter's hair over the rat. "Then Mr. Bangs's attention is coming just at the right time. But I suppose the Clemenses will make a big play for you to stay. Mrs. Clemens will need you more than ever if she's becoming more active."

"No, she won't. She's got Clara. And Mr. Clemens."

"Mr. Clemens!" Mrs. Lyon scoffed. "The man cannot be bothered to lift a finger. Are you still doing all of his accounts? What's wrong with him that he cannot manage a single business affair? No wonder he went bankrupt. He's so proud of paying back his creditors—touring around the world to do so—when he shouldn't have lost it all in the first place."

A knocking sounded at the cottage door.

Mrs. Lyon gasped. "Mr. Bangs! He's early. Oh dear, I haven't filled the sponge cake! How does one do these things without staff?"

The knocking came again.

"I'm coming!" called Mrs. Lyon. No devil pitchforking her hands could have made her more quickly spread the rest of Isabel's hair over the rat, twist it, and then rapidly fire pins into the base of the knot she'd created.

They could hear the door opening.

Mrs. Lyon looked with horror at Isabel in the mirror. "Mr. Bangs is coming in!"

A voice came for the parlor. "Miss Lyon?"

Mrs. Lyon gasped. "It's Mr. Clemens!"

Both women listened with held breath to the approaching footsteps. Mr. Clemens appeared in the bedroom doorway. "Yes, it is."

Mrs. Lyon cleared her throat. "Mr. Clemens, of course you realize this isn't proper. Isabel will be out—"

Mr. Clemens clenched his hands at his sides, then walked quickly over to where Isabel sat. He stood over her until she looked up at him. "My wife wants to go to Italy. She'll get better there. I agreed to take her as soon as we can get passage."

Isabel nodded. Tears stung her eyes.

"You're coming with us. She needs you. You've got to come."

"I can't," Isabel whispered.

Mr. Clemens turned to Mrs. Lyon, watching the pair with her fingers to her mouth. "You, too," he said brutally. He turned back to Isabel. The flesh under his eyes twitched as if electrified. "Say you'll come. Tell me that you'll come. She needs you." He knotted and unknotted his fists. "I need you."

A salty lump prevented Isabel from speaking. She nodded.

9.

June 1903
Riverdale-on-Hudson, New York

UNFOLDING ARMS CROSSED OVER the rigid ruffles of the pinafore that encased her trunk like a candy wrapper, Katy rapped on the telephone closet in which Isabel was placing a call.

"Hold the line, please," Isabel told the "hello girl" at the switchboard office. She cupped the receiver to her chest, then wiped the perspiration from her brow with the back of her hand. The humidity had intensified since her trip into the city with Mr. Clemens earlier that week. Even with every window in the house open, the nook under the stairs was close; it smelled of mold and furniture wax. "Yes?"

"She wants you."

Seven months' association had done little to smooth Katy's permanently raised hackles toward Isabel. If anything, their relationship had deteriorated, try as Isabel might to be kind. The best policy was to keep out of Katy's way, a feat not easily managed, as they served the same master in the same strained household.

"I'm placing a call for Mr. Clemens," Isabel told her as politely as possible. "Please tell Miss Clara—"

"Not Miss Clara," Katy snapped. "Mrs. Clemens."

So this was it. She would finally meet Mrs. Clemens. Even after Clara's joyous reports that her mother was out of bed and walking around her room, and after Mr. Clemens's announcement that

Mrs. Clemens wished to go to Italy, Mrs. Clemens had not summoned Isabel, nor had Isabel expected to be called. Isabel had gotten used to the arrangement, to the point of almost believing that there was no real Mrs. Clemens. She had come to prefer it this way.

"I will place this call later, thank you," Isabel said into the receiver. She hung it on its hook, feeling slightly nauseated.

Sweat blossomed under the arms of her shirtwaist as she followed Katy up the stairs. She had done nothing to cause offense to Mrs. Clemens, she reminded herself. She had said nothing to encourage Mr. Clemens's attentions, had done nothing that could be criticized. Even if she had certain feelings, she would never act upon them. To do so might part her from him forever.

Katy stopped at Mrs. Clemens's bedroom door. "If you break her heart, I'll kill you."

A bubble of guilt burst beneath her breastbone. "Don't be absurd."

"I'm warning you." She opened the door.

The room, hot and darkened by heavy curtains, smelled of camphor, talcum, and roses. The shadowy walls, papered in a large, vaguely flowered print, seemed to respirate the too-sweet scent. It engulfed the great carved bed in the center of the room, which, as Isabel's eyes adjusted to the gloom, revealed itself to be a carnival of wooden cherubs frisking along the headboard and squatting upon the mahogany posts. A chill streaked up Isabel's spine when she realized that her employer was reposing below them. Mrs. Clemens's slight body barely raised the coverlet from the mattress. Was she asleep?

"Miss Lyon."

Isabel flinched.

Mrs. Clemens's weak voice carried a patrician Northern accent, elite, like that of Isabel's own people. "Please shut the door and come in."

Isabel did so as, with a scrape of linens, Mrs. Clemens struggled to sit. Her thin gray tresses trembled against her nightgown as she fought against her pillows. Isabel rushed to her.

"I am fine." Her employer coughed wrenchingly into a handkerchief and then continued in an imperious wheeze. "I must do things for myself. Youth—my husband—coddles me too much. How am I to walk among the olive trees in Italy if I don't build up my strength?"

Isabel stood back as Mr. Clemens's wife, breathing heavily, wound the glossy rosewood music box next to her bed. The tottering opening chimes of "Für Elise" tinkled into the hot, quiet room.

"How may I help you, ma'am?" In her life of service, Isabel had never called her female employers "ma'am." Using their proper names had allowed her to keep at least a shred of pride.

Mrs. Clemens pointed with a thin finger. "Could you hand me my robe, please."

Isabel fetched the black silk wrapper lying over the back of an oval chair. Mrs. Clemens allowed Isabel to hang it upon her bony shoulders, and then dragging her legs off the bed, tied it around herself. She drifted to the window to the tinny pinging of the music box.

"I understand that you are feeling better," Isabel offered. "I am glad."

Mrs. Clemens parted the drapes. Sunlight flooded in through the wavy glass windowpanes, bleaching her profile. The sockets of her eyes were large and her nose scant; her forehead was as high, rounded, and white as the bone beneath it. Yet from across the room, Isabel could see that something fierce shone within Mrs. Clemens's dissolving earthly shroud, as if the diminishing of her flesh were exposing the spirit beneath it.

The teetering notes pealed as Mrs. Clemens gazed out the window. Grasping the drapes for support, she did not bother to turn to address Isabel. "When we are in Italy, you must find your own lodgings. Make it close enough that you can attend to my husband each morning and far enough that there will be no going back and forth between your house and mine at night." The music slowed as she revolved to face Isabel. "Youth is from the South, you see. His family had slaves. Tradition was that the master of the house had free access to the female servants. Youth has told me this fact himself. I think he has never completely freed himself from that mind-set, although he denies it." Mrs. Clemens smiled. "Have you ever been to Italy?'

Isabel tamped back her shock. "Yes. With the Danas."

"I love the flowers there," said Mrs. Clemens. "There are no hydrangeas, though. At least I don't remember seeing them, and Youth makes such a fuss over them. Doesn't he?"

The tinkling crept to a single metallic twang.

A heavier, painful gas seemed to have replaced the air in Isabel's lungs. She couldn't breathe.

"Wind the box up, dear. I didn't do a good job of it."

Isabel stepped to the table. She cranked the brass handle on the polished box, guilt wedging against the back of her throat.

"It's all right, dear. He told me that he gave you the hydrangeas. He tells me everything." She nodded in time when the music began. "That is why I have had to restrict his visits with me. He tells me so much more than I want to know. He always has, foolish boy. His complete candor is terrible for my health, although I suppose it's good for his. I seem to serve the function of sucking the poison from his wounds—I've never been good at spitting it out."

She eased toward a velvet couch, coughing. Isabel put down the box, vibrating with its efforts, as Mrs. Clemens slowly lowered herself into her seat.

"Is there anything I can do for you, ma'am?"

"I can see why Youth chose you," said Mrs. Clemens. "You stand up to him even as you worship him. He can't resist either in a woman, especially when done simultaneously. I did the same once."

The music tinkled along in its dainty pirouette.

Isabel found her tongue. "Mrs. Clemens, with all due respect, you and I have never spoken. How can you say these things about me?"

Mrs. Clemens closed her eyes. "Youth got me this music box years ago. He told me that he got it in a San Francisco whorehouse. I didn't know whether to believe him. Our Samuel—if he seems to be lying, he's telling the truth. Perhaps you've discovered that by now." She laughed. "He has revised his story, saying he bought it for six-hundred-fifty dollars in Geneva. He told me another time that he bought it for Katy in New York, then took it back from her. Which do you think is the fiction?"

She opened her eyes. "Clara likes you, Miss Lyon, and so does Jean, and for that I am eternally grateful. They haven't many friends, I'm afraid. Mark Twain has extracted a terrible price from them. But you make them happy, and for that you will always have a place, if not actually in my home, then near it."

Isabel's value to Mrs. Clemens was not as a secretary, it was now clear, but as a companion for her grown daughters. For them she had allowed her husband to hire Isabel. And now Mrs. Clemens understood that their companion had fallen in love with the master. How Mrs. Clemens must loathe her.

"I've upset you," said Mrs. Clemens. "I'm sorry. That was not my intention. I shock myself with what comes out of my mouth these days. I seem to have lost my ability to temper my words. I've been stripped of my protective covering—the unadulterated truth just comes spilling out. It's not an attractive quality, I fear. No one wants to hear the actual truth. Not even me." She reached for Isabel. Her hand was as delicate as a wren's foot when she grasped Isabel's fingers. "Please go with us to Italy. You'll make the girls so happy, and it's a beautiful place. I'm not so bad. I promise."

"Your offer is generous, and I thank you, but I have my mother to consider."

"Oh. I thought she was coming. Youth told me that he invited her."

Isabel thought of her mother, already bragging to the butcher yesterday about their upcoming trip to Italy, as Isabel had paid for their chop.

The music jingled more slowly, winding down once again. "She'll adore it," said Mrs. Clemens. "I think we shall all be happy in the warm Italian sunshine. I was happy there once, when Susy was alive. We were all happier when Susy was alive."

The door swung open. Clara's glare of surprise was so like her father's. "Miss Lyon, I didn't know you were here. Mamma, you said you needed a nap!"

"Don't chase her off; I sent for her. I'm feeling quite peppy at the moment."

"The doctor says five-minute visits."

Mrs. Clemens leaned her head back against the chair. "A prisoner of my own rules."

The music stopped. The vibration of the final note gently strummed the air.

"We were just finishing." Mrs. Clemens coughed feebly. "Thank you for coming, dear. Let me know if you need trunks for the voyage. We have plenty. Clara, be a dear and crank up the box."

• • •

That night, Isabel stopped typing to massage her sore fingers. She leaned forward to advance the page trapped against the roller of the typewriting machine, then, by the flickering yellow light of the oil lamp, examined the nine lines of type that she had achieved in a half hour's time. She sat back, too warm in her high-necked linen shirtwaist. The walls of the parlor in the rented cottage seemed to close in around the table at which she sat. Everything irritated her since leaving Mrs. Clemens's room earlier that day—the sound of her mother's chewing at dinner, the hesitant drip of the leaky kitchen tap, the feel of her own hair growing oily.

Her mother looked up from her mending. "Does Mr. Clemens really think that clackety instrument is an improvement over the work of a good old-fashioned scribe? My father's clerk could put out a beautifully penned letter in half the time it takes you to peck on those keys, and he didn't give one a headache while he was doing it. Surely Mr. Clemens could afford a good clerk."

"Modern businessmen have lady stenographers to take their dictation and typewrite their words. Or they employ lady typewriters, if dictation isn't required. Mr. Rogers uses one."

"What a terrible trend."

"I rather like typewriting. I'll get better at it." She had no choice but to improve. She would need the skill once she left Mr. Clemens.

"And you will have fingers as fat as that German butcher's once you do. The brute strength it takes to press those keys! You won't be able to fit a ring on your finger when you are done, mark my words. What will Mr. Bangs have to say?"

"Nothing, I fear."

"That's not true. He likes you, I can tell." In a singsong voice, Mrs. Lyon added, "Better keep your ring finger ready!"

Isabel sighed. What was wrong with her that she did not want to wear Mr. Bangs's ring? She did not want to bring his slippers, she did not want to bear his children, she certainly did not want to share his bed. But he was half Mr. Clemens's age and had lovely dark eyes. He was not married. He did not have a sick wife who was her employer, an intelligent, fierce wife who hid in an invalid's body.

A knock sounded upon the door.

Mrs. Lyon looked at her daughter. "Mr. Bangs would never come this late! He's a gentleman."

Her blood throbbing, Isabel thought of one who was not a gentleman. In spite of his mansion, his friends at Standard Oil, his trips around the world, his endorsement by dukes and kings, he was not a gentleman, not at all. She opened the door.

Mr. Clemens glared at her. He clasped his hands behind his back, the way he held them when he dictated letters or when he was thinking about his writing. "She talked to you."

Fury blazed up inside her. She stepped outside on the slab of stone that served as a porch, then closed the door against her mother's curious gaze. "Your wife? Yes, she did."

"What'd she say about me?"

She shook her head.

His expression sharpened to the point of cruelty. "If I'm going to know you and you're going to know me, you have to tell me."

"I'm your wife's secretary. You don't have to know me."

"You know you're more than that."

The urge flared up to strike him. She didn't want to be more than that. To be more was shameful and degrading. She would be hated for disrupting the beloved family of the most loved man in America.

A growing rumble marked the approach of a train to the nearby station.

He brought his hand from behind his back. He thrust a framed picture at her. She took it and held it up to the light of the window. It was his photograph. "For when I can't be with you."

She looked at him, incredulous. This was her reward for risking everything? She should smash it on the doorstep.

The train whistle moaned in the night.

"She said that you used to have slaves."

He pulled back.

"That masters had access to their female servants."

He drew in a breath, then burst into one of his rare laughs.

"It's not funny," she said when he did not cease.

He leaned forward and kissed her on top of her head. "Good night, Lioness."

He melted into the night as the train thundered into town, its brakes screeching, metal upon metal.

10.

November 1903
Florence, Italy

MRS. LYON REPOSITIONED HER hatpin, repeatedly stabbing her chignon until she found traction. How was she to keep her hat on her head when she was being tossed like a lettuce salad with Isabel, Jean Clemens, and that rude maid Katy down the filthy streets of Florence? In the States, they would have called this "cab" in which their teeth were being loosened a wagonette. It amounted to no more than a covered cart. The passengers were given the same rough ride as their precious luggage, trunks containing pieces of heirloom Van Kleek china. All around them, people were on foot. Where were the decent carriages in this city?

They rattled past an applecart attended by a pretty woman wearing a shawl on her head and an apron wrapped around her slim waist. Her Charles would have stared. Men liked that kind of thing, shawls and aprons and such. Why? Did it remind them of their nannies? For a man of Charles's stature to fall for an apron and the poor Italian girl wearing it—their own maid!—when his own children were babies: it was a terrible pill to swallow. And then for Charles to set her up on Bleecker Street, unbeknownst to Mrs. Lyon, after Mrs. Lyon had dismissed her! What a shock it had been when the little fortune hunter had come begging after he'd died, demanding money for his alleged bastard child. The only thing that had crushed Mrs. Lyon more was when her own beloved son had passed away—of a heart attack, her poor angel!—when he was a youth of twenty-seven and in the pink of health. Why did such bad things happen to good people?

Mrs. Lyon shuddered, although for a day in late November, it was not as cold as the Tarrytown of her youth. In fact, it was pleasantly warm—unseasonably warm, Jean Clemens had said when she met them at the hotel, having arrived in Italy with the rest of the Clemens family several weeks before them. Mrs. Lyon reminded herself that she would do well to keep an open mind about this place, to try to enjoy it. Isabel had presented the move as an opportunity to experience European culture firsthand, with the cream of royal society, no less, and it was true that Mr. Clemens had procured an estate from an Italian countess. The most famous man in the world could do that. Let Mrs. Lyon's friends in Tarrytown say that *they* had lodged in aristocratic accommodations in Europe, no matter how well their husbands had invested.

But as the shoddy vehicle shuddered across the bridge by their hotel (dirty, small, no hot water, hard cookies for breakfast), only to come upon naked Italian urchins diving off the bank into the muddy brown Arno, Mrs. Lyon was having her doubts. Why, here they were, approaching one of the most important palaces in town—at least according to Jean, and one did wonder about anything she said—and there was yet another statue of a man with his parts on full view. Had they never heard of loincloths in this town? Even the Catholics back home knew to artfully drape them over their Jesuses. And now Jean was putting her lorgnette to her eyes to look, although *that* needed no further magnification. It was the size of a prize crookneck squash.

"I don't know how you can stand looking at it," Mrs. Lyon cried.

The maid Katy, who'd been glaring at the sky as if it might levitate her from the wagon, threw her a disrespectful look. Mrs. Lyon would have given her notice then and there if she were hers.

"Looking at the dog?" said Jean. "The one at Hercules's feet could be the twin of my little Rosie. I found her in London. She snapped so much that Mamma didn't want me to keep her, but I knew she was sweet. You can't judge a creature's temperament when it's in distress."

"Oh." Mrs. Lyon lowered her gaze from the crookneck squash and squinted at the recumbent stone animal. It was a wolf, wasn't it? "Have we much farther to go?"

"Mother," said Isabel, "all around us are the treasures of the Medicis. Can't you just enjoy them?"

Jean trained her glasses up where Mrs. Lyon was sure that she shouldn't. No wonder Mr. Clemens insisted upon a constant chaperone for her, although she was a grown girl of twenty-three. Isabel claimed that the two Clemens daughters were too sheltered for their own good, but Isabel was not a mother and did not understand.

"Our villa was built by a Medici," said Jean. "Cosimo the First used it as a summer retreat."

"Retreat!" Mrs. Lyon bleated. "That sounds far."

"It's not bad. Only up into the hills. We look down over the city—you can even see the Duomo. There are lots of birds up there. You'll love it."

Birds! thought Mrs. Lyon grimly. She wondered once more what was wrong with Mr. Clemens's youngest daughter. Isabel had hinted that something wasn't right about the girl, but Mrs. Lyon couldn't get it out of her. Isabel was so loyal to that family that it was unhealthy. As much as Isabel wanted to think that she was one of them, she wasn't. Mrs. Lyon feared that it was all going to come to tears.

"There's the Duomo," Jean announced.

Mrs. Lyon gazed at the building rising from the stones of the street. Gaudy, if you asked her. The builders had crosshatched the white facade with so much orange and green marble that it was as plaid as a Scotchman's kilt.

Jean tipped her lorgnette toward the matching chunk of marble across the way. "And that is the Baptistry. They say it's the oldest building in town."

The squatty octangular structure looked like a giant's sugar bowl. Mr. Astor wouldn't stable his horses in it. But Mrs. Lyon kept her comment to herself, recognizing that she was peevish after a night on that small Italian bed. She had expected to be disturbed by carts and wagons trundling past the windows—these people put their dwellings cheek to jowl with the streets—but she had not banked on the constant clanging of church bells and the relentless crowing of roosters. She felt certain she heard pigs rooting nearby. How she wished for a glass of baking soda and water to settle her digestion and a quiet session viewing *The Gardens of the World* on the beloved stereoscope that she'd left at home. She glanced at Isabel. The child was absolutely glowing. She went in for this foreign nonsense. Well, Mrs. Lyon wasn't going to spoil it for her. If her only unwed child, now that her dear son was gone, wanted to see Europe as a secretary to a humorist's family, then Mrs. Lyon was going to go along and make sure Isabel didn't get hurt. And perhaps find an Italian count to marry her.

They wound their way through streets lined with stone buildings the color of dust. Mrs. Lyon kept her thoughts in check as the buildings thinned out and the road became dirt, winding its way upward between stands of pointed cypresses, a few pines that looked oddly like bottlebrushes, and green-gray groves of olives. The houses, always stucco, always yellow, got scarcer as their horse plodded uphill. Soon they had left civilization completely and were up where they could look down on the orange tile roofs of Florence, up where donkeys and goats grazed in the long grass under the olive trees, up to where there was nothing but stone walls on both sides of the road, walls so high in places that only the tallest oaks appeared over them. The road had become a chute of rock so narrow that two wagons passing would scrape their sides on it. Mrs. Lyon felt like a rat in a colossal maze.

"Are we almost there?" Her voice had grown tremulous.

"Not quite. Hear the blackbirds?" Jean closed her eyes and sighed over the rattling of the cart. "There's no sadder sound in the world."

Mrs. Lyon dabbed her perspiring upper lip with her handkerchief. Blackbirds! Who could listen to blackbirds at a time like this, when they were in the middle of nowhere among people who spoke in gibberish and thought nothing of statues with their members dangling about, and she and Isabel did not even have lodgings! Mrs. Clemens had been very clear, Isabel said, about their not staying in the countess's palace. She had insisted that Mrs. Lyon and Isabel find lodgings elsewhere. Mrs. Clemens let this coarse Katy stay in the home, but not Isabel and her. It was rude, plain and simple, when they had a palace all to themselves. One might wonder if something had happened between Mr. Clemens and a servant now that Mrs. Clemens couldn't bear one in the house. Mrs. Lyon sniffed into her handkerchief. Maybe she should have done the same with her maid Poppy from the start, to have kept her from the hands of her goat of a husband. If she had, maybe there would not be a young woman who'd grown up in New York without a papa.

"We're here!" said Jean.

The wagon driver halted his horse at the blunt round-topped stone towers of the entrance. Mrs. Lyon thought wildly of tumescent male parts, then blinked away the thought as the driver hopped down, applied his shoulder to the iron gate, and pushed until it gave way with a rusty squawk. Pounding down a rutted road lined with a palisade of pointed cypresses, Mrs. Lyon patted her lips and throat, until, finally, they arrived before a dusty stone edifice. She stared, her handkerchief to her mouth. The place was bigger than Christ Episcopalian in Tarrytown.

It was large, but plain. There was no tower, no turret, no portico, no grand porch, just rows of windows with shutters as tall as a painter's ladder. A porter helped Mrs. Lyon, stiff in the hips, down onto the gravel courtyard. She had not quite unkinked herself when Jean took her by the elbow.

"You must see the garden."

While the driver unloaded their belongings, Mrs. Lyon let herself be frog-marched to the back of the house. At least the view there was more satisfactory. Three covered stone arches graced the door, their shade extended on either side by the arbor that ran the length of the house. Beyond the gravel walkway, an enormous garden stretched out before them. The countess must have put her money here, for it was a lovely garden, with a tall boxwood maze and a fountain around which rosebushes were still blooming in November.

Isabel caught up with her and Jean, with Katy trailing, unwelcome, behind. "What do you think, Mother?"

The excitement in Isabel's voice made Mrs. Lyon uneasy. "I'll reserve my judgment until we find lodgings."

Jean rubbed the ears of the dog that had come bounding out. "Papa said that there's a *villino* on the grounds that is nice. A clockmaker in Florence rents it."

"Is he a noble, too?" asked Mrs. Lyon. She was looking at the garden, wondering if she might take cuttings home to show off to the ladies of the Tarrytown Garden Club, when Mr. Clemens himself stepped out smartly from under the arches, the pebbles ringing under his feet. His face lit up when he saw Isabel: *Too bright!* thought Mrs. Lyon, nearly gasping. *Too bright! He gives himself away.*

He pulled in his smile but kept his eyes on Isabel. To Mrs. Lyon's dismay, Isabel was gazing back at him as if no one else could see her.

Mrs. Lyon glanced guiltily at Jean. "Isn't this place lovely?" But the odd girl had raised her glasses to look at a bird and was paying no attention.

Mr. Clemens growled, "What took you so long?" He wasn't talking to his daughter. Nor was he talking to Mrs. Lyon. Nor Katy, who was marching away with a furious crunch of gravel. No, he wasn't talking to them at all.

11.

December 1903
Florence, Italy

ISABEL LINKED HER ARM through Clara's as they strolled across the piazza, pigeons bobbing like comical windup toys before their buttoned shoes. She breathed in deeply, filling her nose with the smell of wet marble and bronze splashing from a fountain as they passed. Above them loomed the fearsome Palazzo Vecchio, wearing its crenellations like a stony crown. A crowd had gathered in its shadow before a Christmastime puppet show. Walking past the spectators vying for a view, Isabel thought that their earthy odor of dirty wool and flesh mingled almost pleasantly with the street smell of rot and horse dung on stone paving block. She smiled at her irrational exuberance. The world stank, and she loved it! Why not revel in the commonplace? Why not embrace the smelly, the comical, and the homely? How good it was to be alive! The babble of Italian, the endless barking of dogs, the clop of hooves ringing on rock—they were a symphony to her ears, especially when blended with the throaty drawl of Mr. Clemens, lecturing Jean, just ahead.

Clara leaned in to Isabel. "What do you think of Florence so far?"

They walked from shadow into winter sunshine. Isabel withheld her answer as Clara let go of her arm to raise her parasol. Its shade did not quite reach Isabel, but she didn't mind. It would obstruct her view of Mr. Clemens.

"I love it here." Isabel realized she should curb her enthusiasm. Mrs. Clemens had not yet regained her strength; the move overseas had not yet produced the miracle cure that the family had hoped for. She saw no one save Clara and Katy and, on occasion, Mr. Clemens, but then only for a minute or two. But surely Mrs. Clemens might still improve.

• • •

From the deep shade of her considerable hat brim, Clara studied her mother's employee. Miss Lyon had been unreasonably enthusiastic since arriving at the villa several weeks earlier. She got rather too big a thrill from living in Italy. Certainly, Americans went giddy over the place, but Clara wouldn't have guessed that Miss Lyon, with her polish and her privileged upbringing, would be among them. She usually kept herself pulled together with the extra care of a rich person without money.

Clara, on the other hand, was genuinely unimpressed with things Italian. Of the many European cities Clara had lived in, Florence rated only a lukewarm nod. It was a town built ages ago by men showing off for one another, each one trying to top the others with palaces or statues or gardens. A pissing contest, Papa would call it, like little boys seeing who could pee the farthest. *Vienna* was the city that held Clara's heart, Vienna with its music, its sophistication, and its attentive, gentlemanly men. It was in Vienna that the great pianist Theodor Leschetizky had said his male students suffered from "Delirium Clemens" whenever Clara came to his studio. Dear, dear man. Dear, dear students. As soon as Mamma was well, Clara was taking the first train back.

"I guess Florence is interesting enough," she told Isabel, "if you like dead people."

Two paces ahead of them, Papa stopped. He leaned on his walking stick as Jean marched off, her small box Brownie camera clutched before her like a shield. Clara saw Jean's quarry: a skeletal white horse tied to one of the crumbling stone buildings on the edge of the plaza.

"Only Jean kodaks ugly horses in one the most beautiful cities of the world," Papa said when Clara and Isabel caught up with him. "I'm proud of her."

"I wonder where the owner is," said Clara. "She'll be giving him a card from the Humane Society, placing him under citizen's arrest."

"Heaven forbid, Clärchen. Then I'll have to cool him down in my schoolboy Italian. And you know how well that works."

Clara laughed. "You wouldn't believe how many horses Papa bought for Jean the last time we lived in Florence," she told Isabel, "just to make peace. And not one of them was fit to ride."

"At least we'd have a place to put them here." Papa threw down his cigar. He had not yet acknowledged Isabel's presence, Clara noticed. "There's plenty of space under your mother's bedroom."

Clara felt herself expand with pride. Her father didn't often give her his full attention. He was usually too busy telling stories to visitors, or entertaining reporters, or looking at things to see how he could fit them in his work. "I cannot believe that wretched countess makes us stable our horses under Mamma's bedroom while she keeps the stable building and the connected apartment for herself and that big Roman steward of hers. The countess was supposed to have left the grounds when we moved in. You'd think she'd be ashamed, living with that steward under our very noses."

Walking stick tucked under his arm, Papa ground out the smoking stub on the paving stone. "If they weren't disturbing your mother's peace, I wouldn't so much mind the horses down in the cellar, polkaing with the flies. All that clomping around takes me back to a gentlemen-only miners' ball I attended in Nevada."

"You should put these things in your autobiography, Mr. Clemens," said Miss Lyon—too brightly, Clara thought.

He moved his gaze to her. "I suppose you're right."

Clara took her father's arm possessively. She was surprised that he had not taken the bone she'd thrown him and gone on a tirade about the countess. If there was anything that enraged her father the quickest, it was loose women. "I can't believe you aren't throwing a fit about the horses under the house, Papa. Poor Mamma can't escape them, bedbound as she is. Why aren't you raising Cain for her? I've seen you throw a bigger tantrum over snapping a pencil lead."

"You don't give your father credit," Miss Lyon said. "The creator of the *Personal Recollections of Joan of Arc* must be the most tender-hearted of men. How is your wife? I haven't seen her."

"She's got the bedbug habit. But she's holding her own."

Clara peered at her mother's secretary. The woman was glowing like Joan herself, in the throes of a beatific vision. Clara looked up at her father. He was lit up, too.

"*Joan of Arc* is my favorite book," he told Miss Lyon. "How did you know that?"

Miss Lyon shook her head.

"He's only said so enough times in the newspapers," Clara muttered.

"Never has there been a human animal who was so noble and so brave." Papa's eyes had gone quicksilver, like they did when he was excited. "Joan was completely free of self-interest and personal ambition. She didn't *want* to have to lead France to fight the English, but she did because God asked her. I've been in love with the Maid of Orleans since I was twelve and found a page from a book about her blowing down the street."

Clara withdrew her arm from his. "Didn't *Joan of Arc* sell the worst of all your books, Papa?"

He didn't seem to hear her. "If one more person comes up and tells me how much they admire *Tom Sawyer*," he told Miss Lyon, "I might possibly brain them. He's just a prankster who's out for himself. There's not an important idea in that book, yet that's the one that I'm known for. What does that say about people?"

"You told Susy and me that Tom Sawyer was you as a boy," said Clara.

"No more talk of Tom!" Papa scowled as if being playful, but

Clara could see the telltale red spots of anger appearing on his cheekbones.

His anger did what it always did—fueled hers. If he wanted to fight, she'd fight! "Gladly. I'd be happy to be rid of Mark Twain altogether. He's been nothing to our family but a nuisance."

"Nothing to us," said Papa, "but the person who butters our bread."

He looked down his squashed nose at Miss Lyon. You could almost see his ruffled feathers smoothing. "If I ever wanted to be shut of Mark Twain, this would be the appropriate place to do it. We are standing on the spot where the Mad Monk of Florence, Savonarola, put his match to that famous pile of books and art. He said that anyone who tossed treasure on his Bonfire of the Vanities would be guaranteed a country home in the afterlife."

Miss Lyon raised her skirt from her ankles to see the street. "Do you mean—the fire was right here?"

Papa's gaze went to her ankles. "Close enough."

Clara stared between them. Papa had chased their childhood nurse, Rosa; he had chased their governess, Miss Wright; he had chased Mamma's nurse, Miss Sherry, when she'd gone with them on their lecture trip around the world. He'd sworn after Susy died that he'd stop—he claimed his sins brought the curse on his house, and Clara believed that. But then he'd chased Mamma's new nurse until she got sent off—her boat was leaving Italy as Miss Lyon's arrived—and now Clara was stuck with Mamma's care by herself. The man had not the decency to keep his britches buttoned, yet he could not bear if a fellow so much as looked at his daughter.

"You know they burned the monk a year later," Clara said bitterly. "Same spot. He asked everyone to give up their pleasures, and it seems that people don't like that."

Papa looked up from Miss Lyon's ankles. He reached in his jacket for a fresh cigar. "You seem surprised, Clärchen."

Clara turned to Isabel. "Savonarola thought he would rule forever, but he didn't. He was just in power for one short year. Never take anything for granted, Miss Lyon. Nothing ever lasts."

Jean trotted back to the group. "The villain says he will increase the horse's rations, but I don't believe him. Papa, will you buy that horse, please?"

"Why not?"

"You will?" Jean threw her arms around him. He patted her, shooting a cool glance at Miss Lyon before puffing his cigar at Clara. "I'll get you that cameo you were looking at earlier, too, Clara."

"I don't want it. I want to go home now." Clara turned on her heel and, with a kick of skirt hem, marched across the plaza. She didn't know whom she hated more, Mark Twain or Samuel Clemens.

• • •

Isabel navigated the tumult of the piazza, inwardly scolding herself for not having been aware sooner of Clara's feelings. Of course Clara felt threatened. Isabel sympathized with her. She knew too well the wrenching queasiness that came with detecting a whiff of one's father's desire. She remembered with sickening clarity the overlong gaze of the lady on Bleecker Street when they had gone again to visit, and how carefully Father had avoided looking at her. It had been his avoidance that had tipped off eight-year-old Isabel. Yet Mr. Clemens and she had not acted on their feelings; Isabel would never allow it. But Clara would have no way of knowing this and would hate her as much for mere suspicion than if Isabel had actually succumbed.

A row of pinafored girls led by a nun marched between Isabel and Mr. Clemens and his daughters, separating Isabel farther from them and giving her room to shake off her discomfort. What had she done other than adore a man whom millions of others adored?

She resumed her walk, passing a trio of English women, their hats bent together as they consulted their tour book, their gentleman escort eyeing the newfangled automobile parked across the plaza.

She allowed herself to luxuriate in remembrances of the day. She pictured her walk downhill behind Mr. Clemens and his daughters this morning, running her gloved fingertips along the rough stone wall beyond the villa gates, on their way to pick up the electric tram into town. She then saw herself strolling through the vaulted rooms of the Uffizi, reading her copy of the newest Baedeker's travel guide to Clara as they examined the Botticellis, the da Vincis, the Titians, and the Raffaellos. She saw herself in the plaza between the Duomo and Giotto's Bell Tower, watching the bony little brown boys flock around Mr. Clemens as he distributed a pocketful of change, his walking stick pressed under his arm. Her memory came to rest upon the Ponte Vecchio, where she was ambling along with Mr. Clemens, absentmindedly gazing at the jewelry shops that had lined the bridge for centuries, while he told her about the aborigines of Australia. Was there a place that Mr. Clemens hadn't been?

They had left behind Clara, who'd stopped to admire a cameo pin, and Jean, kodaking a basket of Italian greyhound pups just inside a jeweler's doorway. Acutely aware of Mr. Clemens's presence by her side, Isabel had paused before a shopwindow, where a heart-shaped ruby had caught her eye.

"You like that?" He stopped next to her, closer than he should.

She did not adjust her distance. "I saw one just like it in New York before we left, in a shop on Maiden Lane, near Broadway. I don't usually care much about jewelry, but I was with Mother, and she wondered what had drawn such a crowd." Three boys in jackets and short pants ran by, kicking a ball and shouting in Italian. "A number of us were looking at the ring—it was quite big, maybe the size of a walnut shell—when an older man came in with his younger mistress and, as if we weren't there, bought it for her. We were all in shock."

Mr. Clemens peered down his fierce nose at her. "What was the shocking part—the contours of the ruby, that someone bought it, or that the old man liked a young woman?"

Heat washed over her. "I must sound so provincial."

A man and woman, respectable in fine clothes, nodded as they passed. "*Buongiorno, Professore.*"

Mr. Clemens tore his gaze from her. "*Buongiorno, buongiorno.*"

Clara came flouncing back. "That thief wanted two hundred and fifty lira for that cameo, can you believe that?"

Then Jean drifted up, and the four of them made their way over the crowded street toward the Pitti Palace and its art treasures, their party frequently addressed with nods and *Buongiorno, Professore*s. Although Mr. Clemens walked with Jean, Isabel could feel him reaching out to her. Keenly Isabel willed her inner self to let him know that she was reaching back.

At the palace, they broke into pairs, the Clemens girls not willing to wait on their father when he was accosted by a couple from Indianapolis just inside the first salon of the Palatine Gallery. It pleased Isabel to wait for him. She stood back with her Baedeker's and watched him perform. How he radiated charm without effort, grace without caring what kind of impression he made! *Take me as I am*, he seemed to say, *you can't hurt me*. He was irresistible.

Once freed of his Midwestern admirers, he walked with Isabel through the rest of the gilded salon and into the next, she reading aloud from her copy of Baedeker's, he strolling along with his walking stick under his arm and his hands behind his back. " 'Raffaello, Number Sixty-one, Agnolo Doni, and Number Fifty-nine, Raffaello, his wife, Maddalena Strossi Doni, from his Florentine period, circa 1505.' "

She stopped to examine the portraits of the wiry, cruel-mouthed young man peering suspiciously from under his black hat, and his heavy-faced wife, whose mismatched eyes registered hurt, hatred, and determination from beneath her black rickrack headband. Isabel shuddered to think what kind of treatment Signora Strossi Doni bore at the hands of such a husband.

"Do you aspire to money like this?" asked Mr. Clemens of her.

Isabel looked away from the pictures.

"This place. This was someone's house." He raised his walking stick to indicate the sumptuous room of the palace, with its frescoed ceilings, rococo moldings, and scarlet silk brocade walls covered with milestones in the history of art. "Don't you wish it was yours?"

She laughed. "No."

"That's because you grew up with money. This place looks pretty good to a boy born in a two-room shack."

She lowered her book, sensing that something important was being said.

His eyes went stern. "I had a house nearly this fine in Hartford. Me. Little Sammy Clemens. You remember it from our card games? At least in my mind, it was this fine. It was the loveliest house that ever was. I lost it due to my own stupidity. It was payment for my crimes." He looked in Isabel's eyes. "I've committed a lot of crimes, Miss Lyon."

"I'm sure that you haven't."

"Are you? You shouldn't be. I'm a dangerous man, Miss Lyon."

Carefully, she said, "You're beloved by so many, sir."

"You know you break my heart when you call me 'sir.' "

"I'm sorry." She looked blindly at a white marble statue, then back at him. "What should I call you?"

"Sam. Just call me Sam."

In that moment, he looked strangely vulnerable, a sensitive boy trapped in the flesh of an aging, worldly man. She said it tenderly: "Sam."

The peaks of his craggy brows softened. "That sounds good."

She turned to the wall, then raised her guidebook. " 'Number One-seventy-one. Tommaso Fedra Inghirami. Humanist and Papal Secretary.' " She failed to hide the emotion in her voice.

"Imagine that: another secretary. But not nearly as good-looking as you. And likely not as much of an inspiration to his boss."

She lifted her gaze to his.

"I'm glad you didn't laugh," he said. "I wasn't joking."

He had a wife. An ill wife, one so infirm that she could not leave her bed.

"You inspire me, Miss Lyon. I appreciate how you take me seriously. Most people laugh no matter what I say. That's what makes me so dangerous. The things people let me get away with because I make them laugh."

She wanted to embrace him. "It's not as if you murdered someone."

He lifted his cane and, as if probing a wound, gingerly pressed a spot on the scarlet brocade. "Oh, I've done in a few. Even my brother, Henry."

It took her a moment. "Your brother died in a steamboat accident. He was a hero. I read about it."

"I gave him too much opium, Miss Lyon."

"If you did, you didn't mean to."

"I didn't?"

Why was he telling her these things? She raised her book. A tremor entered her voice. " 'Number One-sixty-five, Madonna del Baldacchino.' "

"I killed Susy. If I'd stayed home instead of tramping all over the world, piling up money to show that I was not bankrupt, seeing how much I could make people worship me, she never would have died. I destroy everyone I love, Miss Lyon. Stick with me, and I'll destroy you."

He said love. His wife is back at the villa, too ill to move.

He followed her into the next salon, empty of people save the portraits of those long dead. He touched her arm. "Isabel."

She looked up at a portrait of a beautiful veiled woman who gazed down with a mysterious smile. Isabel scanned the picture frame for a number, then ran a trembling finger down the page of her Baedeker's. " 'Number Two-forty-five. Raffaello, *La Velata.* The artist's mistress.' " She stopped.

"I've got the Twain Touch, Miss Lyon. Everyone I love best suffers. Susy, my wife . . . others."

Her voice cracked. "Why do you tell me this?"

"Because you're in deep."

At that moment they became aware of the sounds of swishing cloth and shoes upon the marble floor. They moved apart as Jean marched in.

"Papa, where have you been? We are already done with the museum."

The party had then quickly finished their tour, Isabel consulting the Baedeker's and reading passages, her mind not catching a word of it, and Mr. Clemens following along with a tap of his stick.

• • •

Now, across the piazza, Mr. Clemens and his daughters had been stopped by an Italian gentleman—near Isabel's age, she judged—exquisitely dressed in a black fedora and a soft gray morning suit crossed by a gold chain. Isabel closed most of the distance between herself and her employers, but she did not get too near. She was not part of the family.

Mr. Clemens leaned on his walking stick as he smoked his cigar. He raised his voice. "Get your pen and take that down, Miss Lyon."

She came forward, self-conscious in his presence.

"She wasn't listening, Papa," said Clara. "Her head has been in the clouds."

"Ah, Firenze will do that to a person." The gentleman smiled at Isabel. "I have lived here much of my life, and it still has that effect on me."

"The beauty of the place, every little thing—the very air—overwhelms," said Isabel, more warmly than she intended.

"Nothing is more attractive than enthusiasm." The gentleman fixed her with an earnest dark-eyed gaze. "Luca Aleghiri, Count de Calry, at your service."

"This is Isabel Lyon," Mr. Clemens said.

"My mother's secretary," said Clara.

Mr. Clemens picked at a paving stone with his stick. "The count just revealed why everyone has been calling me *Professore*. It seems that I bear an uncanny resemblance to a professor at the university in town. Here I thought everyone felt that I should have an advanced degree based on my looks alone. This will be a good item for my autobiography."

"Papa has been writing it for years," Jean said fondly. "Nothing ever comes of it."

"Did you need a pen and some paper, Miss— Pardon me, I did not catch your name."

"Lyon."

"As in the beast," said Clara.

"Lyon—a noble name." The count bowed to her. "I live quite close by. My home is just across the river, between the Ponte Vecchio and the Ponte Santa Trinita." He turned to Mr. Clemens. "I shall be pleased for you, for your entire party, to join me there."

"We need to get home," growled Mr. Clemens.

"Perhaps after Christmas?" asked the count.

"We don't celebrate Christmas," said Jean. "Not since my sister died."

After the count absorbed this strange information, addresses were exchanged. Mr. Clemens then led the way to the electric tram stop, his daughters reluctantly following. A tram approached, its trolley pole sparking on the overhead power line.

"Why didn't you let us go to the count's home?" Jean asked once they'd entered a tramcar.

"I didn't like the way he looked at you," said Mr. Clemens.

"Me?" Jean settled on a wooden bench. "He didn't even look at me. Not like he looked at Isabel. But I found him very interesting. Those dark eyes."

From the tram ride to the north of town, to the hike back up the steep walled road to the villa, the party was quiet save for Jean, planning the purchase of the emaciated white horse. They passed through the iron gates of their rented estate—still open at that hour—and walked down the long private road to the mansion. There Isabel left the group with a quick goodbye and began the hike home.

She strode down the graveled paths, through the overgrown maze, and across the grassy wooded parkland, then pushed on another half mile through untended forest. At a tile-roofed *villino* in a clearing, her mother attended to the rose vines trellised over the porch.

"Aren't they just marvelous, Isabel—roses!" Mrs. Lyon cupped a bloom as if it were the face of a baby. "In December! I just can't get over it. Don't you think I should bring some inside?"

"What?"

"Clip some sprays."

"Yes."

Mrs. Lyon tilted her head to inspect her daughter. "Isabel, what is it?"

"Nothing." She lowered herself onto the porch steps.

"You're acting peculiar," Mrs. Lyon declared. But she left her daughter to go get scissors.

There was a crunching of dried grass and snapping of twigs. Mr. Clemens waded through the overgrown brush of the woods, avoiding limbs on the ground and vines that hung from the trees. Isabel stood slowly.

"Where's your damn pen?" he said when he saw her. He ducked under a gnarled branch and kept coming.

Isabel could barely speak. "Inside."

He stopped in front of her, too close. Close enough to caress him.

He looked down upon her, the skin twitching under his eyes. "I'm writing my goddamn autobiography. You're my secretary—you're going to take it all down. I'm not paying you to look gorgeous. You have to work if you're going to be around me."

"I'll work," she whispered.

"I'm going to work you to the bone. You're going to write and write and write until you're sick of hearing me."

"I won't get sick."

"I'm going to tell my whole life's story if it kills me, and you're going to write it down. You're going to keep me from using my pen. You're not going to allow me the writer's obsession of revising my words, you're not going to allow me to alter the truth, you're not going to let me do anything but talk until everything comes out. Get your pen, damn it, before I change my mind."

Isabel rushed into the house.

Mrs. Lyon was rooting through her sewing basket. "Isabel, have you seen the scissors?"

Isabel grabbed a pen, a sheaf of paper. "Don't come out. Stay here."

"What?" Mrs. Lyon ran after her.

Drawing a breath, Isabel let herself outside.

When he saw her, his face crumpled in relief before he could blacken his expression. He bit off the words harshly. "All right. Let's begin."

12.

January 1904
Villa di Quarto, Florence, Italy

MR. CLEMENS WAS PROWLING his private reception room when Isabel entered. The floor-to-ceiling French windows had been thrown open though the weather had gone cold just after Christmas. Even as painted wooden Christ Childs had lain in their mangers all over Florence, her mother's beloved roses had turned a deathly coral. Now brisk air swept in past the statues of angels guarding Mr. Clemens's room, stirring his blaze of white-streaked hair, trembling the ends of his undone bow tie.

"Where have you been?" His tone was such that to a stranger, it might seem like he disliked her.

It had been ten days since that first dictation. When he had finished that evening, he'd ordered her to burn everything she had just written, *now,* and then had stalked back through the woods, leaving her standing in the falling light with the inky pages in her hands. Later that night, when she reread what she'd been too overwhelmed by his presence to comprehend, she saw between smudges—she had written in such haste that she'd smeared the ink with the side of her curled hand—that what he'd spun was not autobiographical but was a story about an unnamed boy in a river town, like *Tom Sawyer* and *Huck Finn.* He had not mentioned himself. Because it had come from him, she could not bear to destroy it, so had tucked it away in the lid of a suitcase.

But a week passed after his visit, and still he did not return to her little *villino*. When Isabel reported to the villa each day to pay bills, prepare checks for deposit, and to manage the family's correspondence—her instructions were to turn down all invitations with the exception of the King of England, should he write—she strained her antennae to detect if he might be thinking of her. She felt nothing.

She saw him only once, on the third day, when he passed her in the entrance hall on his way to breakfast. He nodded and shambled on, his footsteps echoing from the ceiling frescoed with angels. The following day, when she approached the villa from the gardens, she saw Mrs. Clemens, swathed within a tartan blanket, being wheeled in a wicker invalid's chair onto the balcony, her butler carrying an iron tank of oxygen behind her. When Isabel waved, a white-gloved hand arose from the nest of red plaid.

Was a new development in Mrs. Clemens's illness causing her husband's withdrawal from Isabel? Over and over she replayed the evening when he had come to her. She could not see what she had done wrong. She had given up on the prospect of working with him on his autobiography, and was beginning to think she should go back to the States if she so offended him, when he sent for her via Katy, whose contempt did nothing to put her at ease.

And now he was asking Isabel where she had been? Where had *he* been?

"I've been up to the villa," she said, "but after I did the work there was for me to do, and you didn't call for me, I took time off for Christmas with Mother."

"Your work was to take my dictation for the autobiography."

"I didn't know we were still doing that." Why was he being so gruff? "I feared something had happened to your wife."

"Livy's fine."

She did not look fine. Isabel waited for him to continue.

Like every window in the palace, the French window before which he'd stopped was protected on the inside by a fitted wooden door, this one laid back against the ocher plaster wall. He snatched the handle of the lock mechanism on the protective door and began to shoot the heavy bolt up and down, up and down. "I had pegged you for someone with a little more initiative."

"You gave me no indication of what you wanted."

Click, clack. Click, clack. "You're disappointing me, Miss Lyon. Please do not disappoint me."

"I will do whatever you need. But I cannot read your mind."

"I hoped you could."

She could see he actually meant that.

Click, clack. Click, clack. "This isn't doing much for my flow of thought. Sit down."

Reluctantly, she slipped into the chair at the desk. He let go of the latch, rubbed his mustache as he regarded her, and began: " 'This villa—' "

Just like that, he was going to resume his dictation? "Wait!" She scribbled with her pen. Dry. She tried another.

" '—is situated three or four miles from Florence.' "

She caught up. Soon she heard nothing but the steel nib of her pen scratching and his words, his everyday perfect words. Over an hour later, he stopped. For the first time since he had begun, he darted a glance at her, oddly shy. She beheld him, a little shyly in return, and in truth, felt flattered, mindful of her role as witness to a great and baffling man's work.

• • •

And so it was that they were in his reception room several days later, the wintry countryside smell of cold earth and dead grass wafting in through the French windows that Mr. Clemens kept open regardless of the weather. A bell tolled in the distance; there came a far-off bleating of a goat; blackbirds whistled their melancholy tune. Unwelcome distractions, all of them. Nothing must disturb Mr. Clemens, his dagger brows aimed at his nose as he paced, hands behind his back, smoke escaping from the cigar between his fingers. Within the room, only the buzzing of a lone fly—hatched in the wrong season and doomed to spend the single day of its life battering at the glass transom above the closed door to the hall—and the crush of the wool rug under Mr. Clemens's boots broke the silence. Isabel noiselessly laid down her pen, rubbed her cramping fingers, then picked it up, waiting for the truth of his life to emerge.

So far during their sessions, he had talked only of the Villa di Quarto and of the woman who rented it, Countess Massiglia, for whom his contempt grew daily. The subject had not yet become personal, but this was his way, both he and Isabel assumed, of his working into the meat of things. Truth would come.

Mr. Clemens took a pull on his cigar. "Where were we? I've lost track. Read where I left off yesterday. I can't seem to think today."

Isabel scanned yesterday's pages as the fly buzzed at the transom glass. " 'There are four rugs scattered about like islands, violent rugs whose colors swear at each other and—' "

"Right. Right." He puffed his cigar, then opened his mouth to start. Just then, from what seemed to be directly below one of the windows, came the alternating honk and squeal of a braying donkey. Each cry increased in volume and abrasiveness, as if the animal's outrage were feeding upon itself. Isabel jumped up to close the windows.

"No, leave them."

Clinging to the casement latches, Isabel glanced across the terrace. She could see the long low stucco stable building at a right angle from the villa, with its crooked row of cypresses jabbing up behind and the two-story stucco carriage house attached to the far end. In this carriage house, the countess, the former Mrs. Paxton from Philadelphia, carried on her affair with her steward while her titled second husband served on a diplomatic assignment overseas. The donkey was tied to a ring in the wall toward the middle of the stable building.

The door to the carriage house flew open. A woman with hair a red that didn't occur in nature fled down the steps and toward the hedges surrounding the garden. Isabel watched as, bottle-red hair and her paisley shawl flying, the countess, still lithe and beautiful in her middle age, strode for a break in the shrubby border, oblivious to the donkey bucking at his tether at the sight of her.

A young man, naked to the waist, even in this chill, slammed out of the house. Isabel held her breath as he pursued the countess. He caught her on one of the graveled paths of the unruly garden, where, his shoulders rippling like the haunches of a beast, he tipped her back and kissed her.

"I wonder if that's the one who bit off the thumb of one of the countess's men."

Isabel jumped. She had not heard Mr. Clemens come up behind her. Out in the garden, the steward slid his hand up the countess's dress.

"Supposedly," said Mr. Clemens laconically, "he's vicious."

She thrust herself away from the window. "Who?"

"That damned donkey. Who else?"

Mr. Clemens left the window. He stopped before her, close enough that she could feel the disruption he made in the air. He stood staring down at her as, across the room, the fly stabbed and stabbed at the glass.

"Did you—did you want to dictate?"

He turned to grind out his cigar in an ashtray on her desk. "Oh, yes, Miss Lyon. I want to dictate."

She fumbled for a pen.

He caught her wrist.

He was waiting for her when she looked up. "Not that way," he said.

She clung to the pen as he ran his fingers up her arm, blazing a tingling path across the flesh under her sleeve, then across her chest, perilously close to her breasts. He found the bare skin of her neck, where he lingered, stroking her throat. She felt her mouth part.

The door was thrust open. They jerked away from each other.

Katy hove into the room, her broad face bunched with hostility. She looked from one to the other. "Mrs. Clemens wants you."

Mr. Clemens patted his pockets for a cigar. "She does?"

"Not you, sir." Katy thrust her gaze at Isabel. "Her."

"Me?"

"You'd better go," said Mr. Clemens.

Isabel followed Katy's rigid form down the hall. What had Katy seen? Isabel vowed never to put herself in such a position again.

Several yards from Mrs. Clemens's bedroom door, Katy turned and blocked the way. "You think you're smart, but you're playing a fool's game."

"I'm not playing any game, Katy." Isabel sounded guilty, even to herself.

"Other people have been his favorites. It never lasts."

"I really don't know what you're talking about."

"You think you're better than me, with your pretty face and fancy accent. You just watch yourself. I know what you're up to. So does everybody else."

Isabel squeezed by her, catching her yeasty scent.

"Two minutes," Katy said as Isabel reached the door.

She stepped into the bedroom. Sunlight flooded in from the floor-length windows. Isabel raised an arm to shade her eyes.

"Youth tells me that you have begun working on his story."

Isabel squinted in the light. Across the room, beneath a brass headboard wrought into a heart the size of an extravagant box of chocolates, Mrs. Clemens lay propped against a pile of pillows. The whimsical design of the headboard, full of flourishes around the heart, seemed a cruel joke for a sickbed. Its occupant was far more ill than Isabel had been told. Her disease had progressed in the nearly seven months since Isabel had spoken with her. Now the bones of Mrs. Clemens's skull strained against her skin in such a way that every contour could be clearly traced, from the rounded bulge of her brow to the delicate hinge of her mandible. The flesh on her hands had melted away to the point that it was barely discernible; hers were a graceful skeleton's hands. Yet the wasting away of her physical body somehow made her look younger, even girlish, as if her suffering were erasing the years. Isabel could not help but stare, trying to comprehend how this could be.

Mrs. Clemens stared back calmly, grunting slightly with each breath.

Isabel found her words. "We've begun his autobiography—I mean he has. He's dictating it to me." *Don't be flustered. You have done nothing wrong.*

"I have heard," Mrs. Clemens said with a wheeze. "He thinks he's hit on the way to tell the truth about himself."

Isabel covered her alarm at Mrs. Clemens's worsened shortness of breath. "Yes, he's very excited. I'm honored to be able to help him. I don't think anyone has ever written a completely truthful autobiography."

"The truth." Mrs. Clemens's laughter turned into a cough. "Have you ever met a person with such a burning need to tell the truth—"

"It's very honorable."

"—yet who is so incapable of telling it?"

Isabel swallowed. "He has lived a long and rich life. I think he just wants to share it."

"Does he? By describing the carpets in this place?"

Mrs. Clemens took gasping sips from a glass of water at her bedside. Outside, the countess's donkey brayed as if its heart were breaking, its cries faint through the closed windows.

"He told me what he talked about yesterday. Rugs. That seems like thin material for an autobiography." She watched Isabel. "I see you agree."

"Actually, he was quite amusing."

"Don't tell him that if you want to keep his eye. He loses respect for anyone whom he amuses. As successful as he has been with his humor, that is just about everyone."

Isabel glanced at the oxygen tank that had been set up by the bed. Near it sat Mrs. Clemens's music box, silent.

"Do not misunderstand me. I'm glad that he is working on his autobiography, Miss Lyon. His publisher wants it, and Youth thinks that he'll make money on it, and nothing makes Youth happier than the prospect of making money."

Isabel grasped for safe ground. "Everyone will want to read it."

Grunting softly with each breath, Mrs. Clemens waited until Isabel stopped smiling. "If you care about him, let him talk about the rugs in this place, Miss Lyon. Let him talk about the wall color. Let him talk about the shutters. Just don't encourage him to tell the truth about himself." She paused, panting slightly. "No one wants to hear about the deepest part of another person's heart. It's too unbearable."

"He—"

Mrs. Clemens raised a wren's claw to stop her. "Not even Youth would still be loved by his readers if he bared his soul, Miss Lyon. In his heart, he knows this. That's why he flirts with spilling it. He loathes himself, Miss Lyon, and everyone's adulation only makes him loath himself more."

It took Isabel a moment to wrench out the word. "Why?"

Mrs. Clemens wheezed for a moment. "Why does he hate himself?"

"No, why do you tell me this?"

"Because I love him, Miss Lyon. I always have. No matter what he's done to me."

"He loves you, that is clear."

"I know. He does. Or at least he loves the idea of me. But having Sam Clemens's love is hard on a person. You're going to need every scrap of your strength for it."

"Mrs. Clemens—"

"I don't have time to pretend, Miss Lyon." She paused to swallow, then regained her breath. "My heart is not strong. I can spare no energy on pretense. But that doesn't mean I want things thrown in my face. Spare me that, please."

The door opened behind Isabel. Katy thrust in her face. "Time, ma'am."

"We were through." Mrs. Clemens melted back onto her pillows. "Katy, help me with my air."

Katy strode over and began to unfurl the rubber tubing from the iron tank of oxygen.

"Oh," said Mrs. Clemens.

Isabel turned around.

"And take this." Mrs. Clemens gestured at the music box. Katy's hands stilled upon the tubing. "Go on. Take it. See if you can get Youth to tell you the truth about it. I'm done with it."

Isabel scooped up the silent box next to Katy and reeled from the room. She stashed the hateful thing behind an urn in the entrance hall, then had the presence of mind to find Jean, to whom Mr. Clemens had assigned the job of turning Isabel's pages of handwriting into typescript. Once she had pressed the day's dictation into Jean's hands, she collected the music box and turned homeward. Tomorrow she would make the five-mile walk into town and book a passage home for her mother and herself. She would leave now, while her reputation and conscience were intact. Oh, she loved him, she loved every part of him, but that didn't mean she could have him. She could never have him. He was his wife's, his daughters', his readers' around the world. Who would be a friend to the mistress of Mark Twain? No one, not even her mother.

She entered the overgrown boxwood maze surrounding the fountain—ironically, the fastest way home. Clutching the music box, her feet crunching on the gravel of the path between towering hedges that smelled of cat piss, her mind wandered to the countess and her steward, and the violent lovemaking that she had witnessed in this garden. She batted at the jutting branches, their stiff leaves as small as mouse ears, as she realized, perversely, that she hoped she would come across the lovers. She hoped to see their bodies twisting together, lusted to hear the wet smack of their flesh, their animal cries. The skin of her throat throbbed from the memory of Mr. Clemens's touch as, in her mind, their limbs, their groans, became hers and his.

She glanced over her shoulder. Someone was at Mrs. Clemens's window.

Correcting herself with a sharp sniff, she quickened her pace on the spongy gravel. She looked again. Whoever it might have been was gone.

Fear washed over her. He was married, *married*, and she'd let him come too close.

She heard a rustling in the hedges. She changed her tack, taking an offshoot that bore to the east, away from the stables and the countess and her steward—out of her way home. She could bear to see no one now.

The rattling came again. Closer. The hair tingled on her arms as the animal in her sensed danger. She quickened her pace and listened, hyper-aware, over the noise of her steps on the gravel. A blackbird tootled, out of sight. From the direction of the olive grove beyond her house, goat bells tinkled, soothing and sweet.

The shrubbery rent with a crack. Something crashed through the greenery. A glimpse through the hedges revealed the donkey, pounding toward her, no longer a docile barnyard creature but something murderous, with eyes white, ears flattened, teeth bared.

She raced down the overgrown tunnels, her corset digging her ribs. She hit a dead end, retraced, ran faster. Branches snapped behind her. The thudding, the furious breathing, closened. A glance showed her pursuer gaining ground. She heaved the music box. It bounced from its haunch and smashed on the path with a ringing chime. Still the animal kept on.

She stumbled out of the maze and into the tangled woods, where the grade turned sharply upward. She scrambled uphill through the waist-high undergrowth, tripping on roots, on rocks, ripping her dress on brambles. Over her shoulder she caught a glimpse of the beast weaving uphill through the trees. Through more brush, she stopped dead: a tumbledown stone wall blocked the way.

Erected centuries ago to protect the olive grove on the other side, the crumbling rocks served as a home for lizards and snakes and now as a barrier for escape. She ran along it, faint from the heat, from the relentless clench of her corset, gasping for breath—choking like Mrs. Clemens. Justice! Justice!

Ahead, a wooden stile jutted into the leaves piled at the base of the wall. She dashed for it, moaning with relief, then scrambled upon its rough plank, grabbed the fence posts, and swung over a leg. Her skirt caught. She yanked at it as the beast stormed up and bit at her, long yellow teeth clacking. She tugged until the cloth ripped, sending her tumbling to the other side. She was sprawled on the ground, spent, dizzy, when her gaze trailed down the wall. Twenty yards away, the stones gave way to a gap through which the animal could easily pass.

She skittered on hands and knees to the closest olive tree, a twisted gray specimen as ancient as the wall, then cowered behind the clump of long grass at the base of the trunk, waiting to be found.

Shouts rose in the woods. "Signorina?"

She forced wind into her lungs. She squeezed out a reedy "Here!"

Over the buzzing in her ears, she heard the men's cries. There was a sturdy thrashing through the undergrowth, shouts, and then a single heartbroken animal scream.

Isabel's sights swam up through the lowering blue fog as the steward bent over her. *Handsome,* decided her inner self, ascending calmly into the branches of the olive tree above her reclining body. *His teeth are so white.* Her ears registered his thickly accented "Okay?" and, puzzlingly, the sound of distant weeping and the ring of a broken chime.

The deep blue twilight became a crushing black.

13.

February 1904
Villa di Quarto, Florence, Italy

CLARA PULLED THE BEDCLOTHES over her mother's shoulders, flattening the perky lace of her nightgown. The covers always slid down when Mamma slept propped up like this, and then Mamma would wake and say her hands were cold. Clara would have to rub some warmth into them, which was ridiculous when this faded Italian bordello boudoir was so hot that you could boil a pot of pasta in it.

Tucking the ironed sheets around her mother's wasted neck, Clara peered into her sleeping face. She *was* looking healthier, and astonishingly younger. Clara was not just imagining it. While Mamma's cheeks were not yet pink, her skin was taut and unwrinkled, perfect as marble. She looked like a child.

Coincidentally, her convalescence had begun on the day Miss Lyon was attacked by that absurd donkey. That same day, Mamma rose up in her bed, stood, and staggered to the window. Katy had seen it. Just two weeks later, Mamma was getting herself to the window and standing there for whole minutes at a time. Soon she would be strolling into the dining room, then outside to the garden, then into town to marvel at the art like everyone else. Anyone could be her companion then, it wouldn't be limited to Clara—Papa, Jean, Miss Lyon, any of them could do it. Especially Miss Lyon, who was certainly getting paid enough. Fifty dollars a month! And then Clara, good, faithful, *deserving* Clara, could catch the train to delicious Vienna, back to the conservatory, to where men got to their feet when she entered a room. They jumped up for *her;* Clara Clemens, the star contralto, and not for Papa.

She could see herself in Herr Leschetizky's studio, waiting patiently as two handsome students fought to accompany her on the piano. She would choose between them, brightening one's day by promising that he could play for her, then telling the other—the blond, she had a weakness for blonds, with their gleaming gold whiskers—that he could take her to dine, causing the poor yellow-haired dear, looking so downcast, to beam like the sun in this hothouse. The two of them would step out in the evening, down the beautiful Ringstrasse glittering with cafés and men with top hats and canes and women in delectable furs. Other gentlemen would nod at her, but *her* blond young man would tighten his hold, his arm sinking into the fur of her wrap as he murmured to her in his rich Austrian accent.

"Miss Clara."

Still smiling up at her swain in her mind's eye, Clara turned around. Katy, as rigid and squat as one of the bronze cupids in the Donner Fountain in Vienna, waited in the doorway.

Clara went to her, irritable at being taken from a good daydream. "What do you want?"

"Miss Lyon is asking for you."

Clara rolled her eyes. Now? But she had better go. She didn't want to alienate Miss Lyon. What a shock it had been when she was attacked. Whose secretary gets mauled by a donkey? She might as well have been boxed by a sheep. And for her to have been laid so low! Miss Lyon had been bedridden for more than a week, lying in her bed as limp as a hot water bottle, while the Clemenses' bills went unpaid and their letters unanswered, the checks from Papa's publishers undeposited. Clara had visited her every day, hoping to cheer her up, to get her up and moving. She couldn't give out, not when Clara needed her most. How would Clara ever get back to the conservatory in Vienna if Miss Lyon were unwell? Clara had begged Papa to go see her—Miss Lyon was sweet on him, that much was apparent, and he might make her rally—but Papa would only make one perfunctory visit to her cottage. He was gone for under an hour: Clara timed him. So while Clara took no small satisfaction from knowing that their affair had shriveled on the vine, as all of Papa's peccadilloes eventually did, the timing was terrible. Couldn't he have waited to break Miss Lyon's heart until after Clara had gone?

But then, suddenly, surprisingly, Miss Lyon was out of bed and so was Mamma, and both of them hale and happy enough. If Clara could just coax everyone along, her soul-numbing days of being buried alive would be over. Clara had earned her escape; no one was ruining it for her now.

Miss Lyon was waiting in the entrance hall. She was a tiny little thing, dark as an Italian herself, and almost pretty with good health, especially for someone who had just nearly died. In fact, Miss Lyon was positively glowing. Maybe it was all those visits from Don Raffaello, the parish priest, who'd kindly looked in on her when she was ill. Let's face it: some women are greedy for the attention of any man, even a celibate.

"I'm sorry to have taken you away from your mother," she said when Clara got closer, "but a puzzling situation has come up. A certain dressmaker in town claims that he made you a traveling ensemble." Miss Lyon pointed her pert little nose at the bill in her hand. "A certain Signor Muratore. He has a shop on the Duomo plaza—does that sound familiar? When I went into town this morning, I looked him up and told him that he must be mistaken, no one in this family plans to travel, but he insisted he was correct."

No good falsehood would spring to mind. Clara glanced at Katy, who was dusting a piece of statuary with her apron. Clara was fishing for a lie from her by telepathy when, down the hall that ran the length of the entire first floor, a door opened. Papa leaned out. "Oh, there you are, Clärchen. Just who I was looking for. Come here."

Did he ever consider that she wasn't free to drop everything at his command? "I was speaking to Miss Lyon."

"I want you to see something." He ignored Miss Lyon; she might as well have not been standing there.

"What is it?" Clara asked, feeling a little better for Miss Lyon's snub.

"A surprise."

Clara frowned at the bill in Miss Lyon's hand. She never would have guessed that Italians would charge their customers so fast. They were so slow about everything else. "Coming."

"You can come, too, Miss Lyon," Papa said—as an afterthought, Clara noted with satisfaction.

They trooped down the hall with its kaleidoscope of threadbare rugs, Katy following. They came to his bedroom, the largest in the house, fitted out with a fireplace in which a boar might be roasted, and erupting with cascades of lemon satin over the windows and bed.

Miss Lyon hung back by the door, Katy behind her, while Clara stepped forward, a daughter's privilege. "What did you want, Papa?"

"Look at my little prisoner."

Clara followed his gaze to a water goblet that had been placed upside down on the Persian carpet. Underneath it was a lizard, shaggy with peeling skin. He was the same rust red of the pattern on which he crouched.

"I almost stepped on him."

Papa's writing must not be going well if he was excited about a lizard. She had seen him struggle with writer's block a thousand times before. He claimed that it didn't bother him, but it did. She recognized the moodiness, the tendency to focus on trivial matters, the quickness to anger. But writers' children knew how to deal with these things.

"Isn't he smart?" she exclaimed in the voice one would use to cheer up a small boy. "He knew to go on the bit of the carpet that was just the color of himself. He's hiding in plain sight—isn't that clever!"

"Not so clever," Papa said in that slow way of his, "if it almost got him stepped on."

"Are you going to keep him for a pet, Papa?" she said brightly.

"Should I?"

"Mamma might like him. She's getting so much better." She noticed Miss Lyon, lingering in the doorway. Katy had gone. "Miss Lyon, help me catch him."

Miss Lyon hesitated. As harsh as Katy was, Clara thought, *she* never hesitated. She was as loyal as she was belligerent. Clara was taking Katy with her when she went to Vienna, to protect her from any unpleasant men. Let Miss Lyon hesitate all she wanted at Mamma's bedside.

Finally, Miss Lyon came over—wasn't that grand of her?—and, one knee at a time, Clara got down next to the upside-down goblet containing the ragged little fellow. When Clara laid her head on the dusty carpet to examine him, she could see his heart beating through his thin skin.

"He's so fragile! How am I going to move him without hurting him?" She sat up. "Give me that," she ordered Miss Lyon, indicating a piece of stationery on Papa's bedside table.

Miss Lyon stepped forward and picked up the paper, then, glancing at it, stopped.

Clara snapped her fingers. "Give it."

Miss Lyon did as told.

Still on her knees, Clara looked at the paper. Papa's handwriting. Her gaze went to the top of the page. *Dearest Lioness.*

Papa dug in his coat pocket for matches. "Aren't you going to slide it under his feet?"

Clara snapped, "Yes," but couldn't move. It was as if poison were leaking from the ink on the paper into her hands, sickening her, paralyzing her.

Papa ambled over, took the paper from her hands, and turned it over. Supporting himself with a chair, he got down next to her, his unlit cigar still between his fingers. He lifted a side of the glass rim and slowly slid in the paper. "We Clemenses," he drawled, "are true bleeding hearts. I got it from my mother. She shamed me for throwing a stone at a bird when all it was doing was singing its song." He gently knocked the edge of the paper against the creature's immobile feet. "Have you ever seen a family that got so worked up about the welfare of a lizard?"

Clara scrambled upright. "Oh, we're kind folks, we Clemenses, saviors of reptiles, champions of birds. The only creature we'd mistreat is our own slave."

Miss Lyon took a step back.

Clara smiled grimly. "Tell her, Papa. Tell Miss Lyon about your slave. Tell her what your father did."

Papa patiently coaxed the lizard to step first with one foot and then the other onto the paper. "My father," he said, concentrating on his task, "was a quiet man, a good man. He was a lawyer by trade. He never struck me but twice—for lying, it turns out, a fine example of his restraint when he could have used those same grounds to beat me every day of my life." He sat back on his heels. "But he did whip our slave. Whenever he felt the need. It was a master's right."

"I wish you'd never told me that when I was a little girl," Clara said bitterly. "I don't know why you couldn't have kept it to yourself." She turned to Miss Lyon. "So you see, we are not who you think we are."

"No one is ever who you think they are, Clärchen. You're not telling Miss Lyon anything new."

A cow lowed in the distance; chiffchaffs wheedled outside the open window as the three stared at the reptile, motionless under the glass. Clara glanced up just as Papa caught Miss Lyon's gaze. She saw the understanding flowing between them.

"Why isn't he moving?" Clara exclaimed. "You've hurt him!"

Miss Lyon dropped next to Papa, lifted the glass, then blew on the creature, stirring its shreds of skin. She looked up at Clara. "I think he feels too safe. He doesn't realize he should run."

"Then he's a fool." Clara reached down, snatched the lizard by the tail, strode to the window, and flung him out.

Papa pushed himself up, using the chair. "Congratulations, Clärchen. You just killed him."

Clara was looking outside, stricken, when the maid Teresa rapped on the doorjamb. "Excuse me, ma'am, but your mother is calling for you. She is not feeling well."

Clara felt the fury rising in her. "Tell her no! Tell her I'm not coming!"

"But Signorina—"

The shock in the servant's eyes only goaded her. "Tell her I hate her!"

"Clara!" snapped her father.

She turned on him, so cool, so hard, so perfect and impenetrable. Something burst within her. "Why doesn't she just die? How I wish she were dead!" She swept the papers from her father's desk. "How I wish all of you were dead!"

Miss Lyon flung herself forward to save Papa's papers. The sight of her grasping at them set Clara on fire. Screams tearing her throat, she heaved chairs, threw books, smashed lamps. The clunk of metal, the splintering, the shattering spurred her, as did the servants appearing in the doorway, blinking stupidly. She rushed at them, howling, enjoying their terror, and then hurled herself at the mantelpiece. One swipe of her arm nearly cleared it. She stopped. At the end of the mantel, alone on its tripod, stood a picture of Papa and Susy dressed for their parts in a play that Susy had written. With a shriek, Clara grabbed it with both hands and raised it over her head.

The butler, Ugo, tackled her. She fought against him, scratching at his homely face, at his garlicky breath, relishing the pain of his rough hands upon her.

"Let her be!" Papa roared.

Reluctantly, Ugo loosened his grip.

She shoved away Ugo, then clutched the picture to her chest.

Her voice was in shreds. "Susy hated you." She flung the words at her father. "She hated you, you know."

He lit his cigar. "I know."

"Everyone hates you."

He waved out his match. "No, Clärchen. Just the ones who truly know me."

Katy bustled in and took in the scene with a woeful look. "Oh, Miss Clemens!"

"They're killing me," Clara sobbed hoarsely.

Katy cradled Clara to the bolster of her breast. "Oh, Miss Clemens, what have you done?" She escorted her mistress, clinging to the portrait, past the rest of the gaping staff.

14.

March 1904
Florence, Italy

HIS DERBY CLAMPED DOWN against the March drizzle, Mr. Clemens held the umbrella over Isabel. "Warm enough?"

She flexed her cold fingers within her gloves. "Yes."

They exchanged a smile before Isabel turned to face the iron-strapped door of Count de Calry's riverside palace. It was a miracle that they were there. Mr. Clemens rarely called upon anyone; he turned away visitors to his house. The humorist who was loved around the world, Isabel was finding, did not generally like people. Yet when Mr. Clemens was considering the invitation to call on Count de Calry and Isabel had remarked, while filling her pen with ink to decline it, that she wondered what the inside of a real Florentine palace looked like, he had agreed to go—*if* his secretary could come. Mr. Clemens had been especially kind to her since he had come to the *villino* after the countess's beast had attacked her, when, lightly touching her hair, he'd admitted how much he'd come to depend on her—how much he and his daughters had come to depend on her. Theirs had become a special friendship. Couldn't a secretary and her employer have a special friendship?

The door creaked open upon ancient hinges. A heavy-lidded manservant showed them into a marble hall that smelled of the muddy Arno, which the palace overlooked. They waited, raising eyebrows at each other, until footsteps echoing from the high ceilings announced the arrival of the count. He entered, all smiles and sleek in a finely cut suit.

"Signore Clemens!" He shook Mr. Clemens's hand, then took Isabel's hand, kissed it, and stood back to behold her with eyes as brown and noble as a stag's. "The esteemed secretary." He offered her his arm. "Shall we?

The smell of musty cloth intensified as Isabel strolled with the count up a grand marble staircase and through a hall hung with tapestries, Mr. Clemens trudging behind them. They came to a room littered with bronze statues, glass-fronted cabinets full of curios, pots of ferns, armor, paintings, an elephant's foot. "My private lair," explained the count.

Once they were comfortably seated, the manservant who had answered the door carried in a tray and, after placing it on a marble-topped table, cranked up the phonograph and set the needle on the wax cylinder. Isabel swelled with well-being as the phonograph began scratching its way through an orchestral piece. She was in an exquisite palace in Florence because the man she adored had wanted to make her happy. God does not put many such days into a woman's life.

The cheery splash of wine against crystal echoed from the coffered timber ceiling as the servant filled their glasses. The count waited until his manservant finished before asking Mr. Clemens, "And how is your wife?"

A white halo had sprung up around Mr. Clemens's ears, the impression made by his derby. He leaned forward to get his glass. "Improving."

Isabel nodded politely at the servant's offer of an olive crostino; a cloud blotted her sunshine. Yes, it could be said that Mrs. Clemens was improving. After her heart attack brought on by Clara's rampage three weeks earlier, anything was an improvement. Isabel could still see the physician testing his steel syringe as Mrs. Clemens, held up by Katy, clawed for air. The subcutaneous injection of brandy had done its work immediately, causing Mrs. Clemens to melt back into her pillows with a groan. Mr. Clemens had sunk into a chair, head in hands, as Isabel turned on her heel to go find Clara and report to the despairing young woman that she had not killed her mother, as she feared. Clara had not left her mother's bedside since that day, sleeping on a cot next to her at night.

"Please do tell me that you have had a similar shouting attack," Clara had said to Isabel later. "Surely you or someone you know has had such a fit before?"

"Of course," Isabel had lied. In truth, she had never seen such madness. The violence of Clara's outburst still astonished her. What kind of pressure must the woman be under to crack so completely?

Now the count said, "I look forward to the honor of meeting Mrs. Clemens soon."

"Livy's a fine woman," said Mr. Clemens. "A rich one, too, until I impoverished her."

The count, reaching to retrieve his wine, paused.

"This one was rich, too," said Mr. Clemens, nodding at Isabel, "but she lost her fortune before I could get to it."

The count laughed. "You are as humorous as they say." He raised his glass. "*Cin cin.*"

Mr. Clemens saluted in return.

"And your daughters?" asked the count. "How are they?"

Mr. Clemens sampled the wine, then smacked his lips. "That's good." He put down his glass. "Jean is busy saving horses. If any of yours go missing, come out to our stables, she might be ministering to them there. Or just keep them fat and healthy—then she won't look twice at them."

"A lover of animals," said the count. "Very admirable. And the other?"

Mr. Clemens drew in a breath as if still absorbing the fact that he had only two daughters now, since Susy's death. "Clara? She's with her mother. The two are as thick as thieves. As huddled together as they are night and day, I suspect that they're forming an in-house chapter of the Woman's Christian Temperance Union against me.

Miss Lyon and I are forming our own club in response: the Goats Among Sheep."

Isabel sipped, feeling the count's curious gaze upon her. Mr. Clemens had used that expression privately when explaining to her why he was no longer letting Jean type his dictations. His off-color thoughts were fit only for goats among sheep, he said, of which he and Isabel were two. While Isabel knew he was joking, she also knew the count may not understand that. Mr. Clemens was increasingly reckless in his speech these days, as if he took a perverse satisfaction in pushing the limits of others' tolerance. Or perhaps he had always been this way, and as a member of his inner sanctum for more than a year and a half now, she was becoming more exposed to it, or perhaps Mrs. Clemens, when well, had simply curbed it.

But while Mr. Clemens's reputation might withstand whatever outrageous statements Mark Twain threw at it, could hers? The count would get the wrong impression of her. Yes, Mr. Clemens and she were spending more time together each day, working on his autobiography, or ranging over the wooded grounds of the estate as he talked and she listened, or playing cards in the evening at his house. Yes, they went to concerts in Florence and investigated the excavations of the Roman ruins in Fiesole: every day was an adventure. But they did nothing improper, nothing that two good friends wouldn't do together. They would not let themselves cross the line that they'd nearly slid across before being interrupted by Katy.

The count cradled the base of his goblet like a breast. "Are you writing anything new?"

"My autobiography," said Mr. Clemens. "I've finally found a way to trick myself into telling the truth. I dictate my thoughts to Miss Lyon here, then she writes them down before I can change my mind. I've no chance to pretty up the truth, there's no time to shave off any warts—she's too quick for me."

Isabel laughed with affection. "It's a very natural approach."

The count trained his stag's eyes upon her. "I see."

"This way," said Mr. Clemens, glancing between them, "the author cat doesn't have much chance to rake the dust over the nuggets in his work. The truth is right there on the surface, its smell undisguised from the clever reader." His hand went unconsciously to his coat pocket. "Mind if I smoke?'

The count looked both intrigued and repulsed. "Be my guest." As Mr. Clemens pulled out a cigar, the count asked, "Why would you wish to reveal so much? In your autobiography, I mean." He slightly lifted his index finger. His man rushed forward and lit Mr. Clemens's cigar. "It sounds . . . dangerous."

"Thank you," Mr. Clemens said to the manservant. He blew out smoke. "You're right. Being ruthlessly truthful may not make me friends. That's why I won't let the bulk of my autobiography be published until a hundred years after I die."

The count raised well-groomed brows. "That is a long time. Your readers will be disappointed."

Not as disappointed, Isabel thought, taking a sip of wine, as she would be. She would be long gone before the world knew of her part in his telling his story.

"Perhaps you will write a story based on Firenze sometime," the count suggested.

Mr. Clemens glanced at Isabel. He had written such, decades ago. Neither the Florentines nor Americans had come out well. He had made his name on *Innocents Abroad*, but if he wasn't reminding the count about the book, she would not, either. She felt the thrill of being his co-conspirator.

"If I don't write a book set in Florence," drawled Mr. Clemens, "it won't be for lack of scenery."

The count inclined his elegant head. "We do have our share. And the world's greatest art—Michelangelo, Botticelli, Raffaello—"

"I adore Raffaello," Isabel said.

"You have excellent taste, Signorina Lyon. He is well represented here."

"He had done a portrait in the Palazzo Pitti that greatly moves me," she said. "*La Velata*. The woman comes to life—you can feel her playful spirit just by looking at her."

"Ah, yes. The painting meant a great deal to Raffaello. It was of his mistress, you see."

Isabel nodded.

"Perhaps you did not know that Raffaello died as a result of a night of passion with her. This woman, the daughter of a baker, must have been a formidable lover." The count took a sip, watching Isabel over his glass. "Or so the story goes."

"For my artistic money," Mr. Clemens interjected roughly, "give me Leonardo."

The count paused to switch gears. "Leonardo was Tuscan by birth, as you know, but he spent too much time in Milan, in employ of the duke, and died in France. Still, you can find much of his life here, and his works." He put down his glass. "Have you been to the Uffizi?"

"On occasion." Mr. Clemens exchanged looks with Isabel. They had been there together many times, as well as the Accademia, the Bargello, and the Pitti Palace, which held a special sentimental value that Isabel felt keenly. "Educate me," Mr. Clemens would say as they strolled the galleries, his deep-set eyes intense upon her. "Refine me." A thrill would warm her to the tips of her toes.

The count watched them with a growing smile. "You may be interested to know that Leonardo conducted an experiment with his flying machine outside of Firenze, on the rocky cliffs near Fiesole."

"Where?" Isabel said. "We've been in that area."

The count grinned as if he'd caught them out. "Monte Ceceri—do you know it? It can be reached along the road from Firenze. The cliffs are quite high there. Leonardo's assistant jumped from the rocks to demonstrate the machine."

"Did it work?" asked Mr. Clemens.

"No."

"What happened to the assistant?" Isabel asked.

"He died. Or broke his legs. I do not know which."

"I suppose the assistant had an interest in which," growled Mr. Clemens.

The count rubbed his brow with this thumb, contemplating Mr. Clemens. He turned to Isabel. "So you like Florence, Miss Lyon?"

"I admire it very much."

The phonograph stopped. The count lifted his finger. The manservant stepped forward to rewind the machine.

"Should you ever leave, if you wish to guarantee your return, you must rub the snout of the bronze boar in the fountain by the Mercato Nuovo before you go. It will assure that you come back."

"And you believe that?" asked Mr. Clemens.

The count dipped his head. "It is a charming local legend."

"Heaven forbid one should stint on charm," Mr. Clemens muttered. Isabel could feel her employer's mood turning, although the count had been nothing but gracious. However, when the scratchy music started again, Mr. Clemens nodded admiringly at the servant. "He's a jack-of-all-trades."

The servant's hooded blue eyes did not blink.

"Paolo knows no English and cannot understand you," explained the count. He took a sip. "This house has twenty-eight rooms—"

"The house I just sold in Hartford had twenty-five," Mr. Clemens interjected.

A blink registered the count's annoyance. "—and yet I have only six servants. Paolo is one of the reasons I am able to have so few. That, and I do not encourage marriage between my servants when they fall in love. And, my friend, they always fall in love. That is human nature, yes? We are always falling in love."

Mr. Clemens stared at him.

The count smiled. "I am just immoral enough to let them carry on under my roof. It makes for a very happy house—I get their work, they get their pleasure. It is a fair bargain, yes?"

Mr. Clemens stood. "Thanks for the wine."

The count's smooth veneer ruffled as he rose to his feet. "But you only just arrived."

"Miss Lyon, are you coming?"

Soon Mr. Clemens had collected his hat and they were out on the street along the Arno, among groups of women in rain capes and men carrying umbrellas, although the sun had begun to shine. Isabel did not try to catch up as he walked ahead of her, letting him put distance between them until, in the middle of the Ponte Santa Trinita, she stopped.

Mr. Clemens made it to the statue of the naked Roman god at the end of the bridge. He turned around slowly. "What?" he called.

Isabel gazed into the Arno, its brown water churning around the stone pilings of the bridge. The March wind, full of the reptilian smell of the river, tugged at her hat.

He came back to her. "What?" he demanded again.

"You may not care about your reputation, Mr. Clemens, but did you think of mine?"

"I was thinking about yours. That's why I left."

"To leave so rudely will ruin his opinion of us."

"Do you think I was going to sit there another second? That man has no more morals than a cat."

"Why? Because he acknowledged that his servants fell in love? Or must employees simply be beasts of burden, incapable of emotion?"

"You're not talking sense. I was protecting you."

She held her hat against the wind as she looked up at him. "Would *you* make your servants marry?"

"Yes. I would. As a matter of fact, I have done so before. I made one of my footmen marry a maid whom he had spoiled."

"Spoiled?"

"She was a virgin when she started out," he said angrily. "She wasn't by the time he was done with her. I call that spoiled."

"Even if they loved each other? Who gave you the right to control them?"

"I was doing her a favor! What has got into you? You should be admiring me and thanking me, not giving me grief."

"Must you always play God? You don't own them. Last I heard, slavery was illegal."

His face darkened. The drawl had left his speech. "Don't even say that word. You don't know anything about it."

She had gone too far to stop; she found that she wanted to hurt him. "Slavery? It's true, I don't know anything about it. And I'm proud I don't."

"How easy for you to gloat over a decision that was made for you by birth. You never had to decide. I bet you never even saw a colored person before you were ten. How do you know what you would do if you were brought up like I was, being told that our peculiar institution was wholesome and good? How do you know you wouldn't strike a slave or worse?"

A boy dressed in velvet short pants skipped by with his upright father. Isabel waited until a flock of women passed, chatting in Italian. The bridge was deserted save for the two of them.

"I don't really want to fight with you, Mr. Clemens."

"Then why are you provoking me?"

"I don't know!" She blew out a breath. "What *am* I to you, Mr. Clemens?"

He jerked back his head. "You know I can't answer that."

"The count seemed to know."

"Damn him!"

"I feel—I feel like you are leading me on."

"Lioness, you tell me: what choice do I have, when I want you but can't have you?"

She clung to his words even as the impossibility of the situation became clear. She walked away before the pity she felt for him, hunched and alone, made her turn back.

She wandered down narrow streets. She deserved more than this, more than being a friend who wasn't really a friend, a secretary who wasn't really a secretary. At the end of the day, she was nothing.

Turning her thoughts in her mind, she was surprised when she looked up in the Piazza della Repubblica and saw the Clemenses' maid. "Katy?"

Katy thrust out her chest in defiance but would not meet Isabel's eyes. "What are you doing here?"

"I might ask you the same." Isabel peered into the windows of the Café Gilli at the crowded tables inside. "Is that—Clara?"

"Go away!" Katy demanded.

Through the glass, Isabel watched Clara chat with the gentlemen surrounding her. When a young man leaned in to speak in her ear, she drew up her shoulders with delight.

Mr. Clemens shambled up. "Katy?"

Her guilty expression sent his gaze over her shoulder. The blotches on his cheekbones flamed as he registered the scene within the café. He loped into the restaurant, followed by Isabel.

"Papa!" Clara jumped to her feet.

"Who is home with your mother?"

"Teresa. Mamma was better today! She said I could go."

"Who are these men?" He gestured at the group of young Italians at her table.

"They are from the music school!"

"Up," he told her. He threw down some lira on the table. "Keep your filthy hands off my daughter."

"They know English!"

"Good. Then they know what I mean when I tell them to keep their goddamn peckers in their pants."

Clara rushed from the restaurant. She ran through the narrow streets, dodging tourists and shoppers, and then ducked into the loggia of the Mercato Nuevo, where she wove between the market stalls, glancing over her shoulder for her father. He caught her by one of the pillars.

Holding her arm, he handed her his handkerchief. "Clean up your mouth."

"Papa! You're making a scene."

"Wipe it!"

She wiped off the tint on her lips.

"Button up your coat. I won't have my daughter looking like a whore."

Tears rolled down her face as she fastened her jacket. "Why do you do this to me? I've done nothing wrong."

"Give me your hat."

Clara was unpinning it when Isabel caught up with them. "Sam! Don't!"

He grabbed the hat from Clara's hands, ripped a glass cherry from its brim, and hurled it to the street. "Is this what you want men to do to you?" He ground the ornament into the stone of the street as he plucked off another. "Use you and then crush you?"

"I wasn't doing anything!"

He pulverized another cherry under his heel, then another.

"Don't punish her," said Isabel, "when you are truly angry at—"

He stopped. Isabel saw that she did not have to finish the sentence for him to understand.

"Angry at whom?" Clara wiped at her eyes.

He shoved the denuded hat into Clara's hands. "Miss Lyon, take her home. Her mother needs her." He turned on Katy. "You're supposed to take care of her. You disappoint me."

Clara swept away. With a venomous glance at Isabel, Katy followed.

15.

April 1904
Villa di Quarto, Florence, Italy

MAESTRO LUGARNO'S TUFT OF mustache, the size and texture of a baby vole, teetered on his lip as he crumpled his face in pain. A moan seeped from his vocal cords. Fastidious in his expectations of his students, although not so much in his dress—his dull black suit bore gravy stains from the tripe sandwiches that he favored—he had reached his breaking point at twenty-five minutes into Miss Clara Clemens's lesson that morning. The Monday, Wednesday, and Friday lessons in preparation for a public concert later that month were not enough. Her father the American *celebrità* had said that his daughter had already received some instruction in Vienna, that she needed only a little brushing up and she'd be ready to go. But after two weeks of instruction, the maestro had lamented to his wife about the devil's deal he had made. There was no pay enough. A cow had more talent.

"No! No! NO!" His tight coat lifted above his belly when he waved his arms. " Again!"

The pianist's wife, a stringy woman as concave as her husband was convex, struck the keyboard. Clara tried once more to match the note.

"No, Signorina! Don't you hear it? Again!"

The keyboard clanged. Clara sang.

"No! Signorina! No! You will be my death! Again!"

Clara's face went the red of a *pomodoro*.

The maestro mopped the sole black curl in the center of his pate. "Signorina Clemens, how are you to sing like a bird with your head hang down like a donkey?"

Isabel, on the sofa with a portable desk on her lap, whittling her way through the Clemenses' mail, discreetly gazed away. Clara looked ready to plow the maestro with her brow.

"What is that you do with your neck? Are you a vulture? Up! Up!"

Clara raised her chin higher, her eyes round with murder. She had been ready to kill the man since the day he'd first come to the villa, five days after her father had ruined her hat. Of all of the instructors at the observatory, her expression said, this was whom Papa picked? If he meant to make up to her for destroying her hat and her reputation in town, he had sorely missed the mark.

"*Buono!* Now—again!"

The maestro's wife banged the keyboard. Clara attempted to match the note.

"Now hold it! Hold it! Hold it!"

Clara was trembling with sustained effort when Mr. Clemens strolled in. Instantly, the room felt too full to Isabel, as if his energy crowded everything in it. The piano playing stopped.

"Keep on," said Mr. Clemens. He dropped heavily next to Isabel. "How is she doing?"

Isabel nodded false enthusiasm, shifting her legs under the lap desk. She'd kept her distance from him since the disruption in town.

"For your august papa," said the maestro, "we start at the beginning of the piece." His wife flipped through the sheet music then, at her husband's signal, attacked the piano. Clara began to wrestle with Schubert's "Gretchen at the Spinning Wheel."

Mr. Clemens sat back and tapped his boot in time. He lifted his thicket of brows at Isabel.

Isabel smiled as if they were on good footing. They were not. There were no more adventures, no excursions. Their interaction was limited to one strained hour each morning of dictation for his autobiography, conducted with the door of his room wide open and Katy and the rest of the staff coming and going. After that, Isabel retreated to her office at the other end of the floor, where she performed her secretarial duties for the entire family. In the afternoon, she was free to pursue her own interests. She had taken up watching birds, cataloging the flora and fauna on the estate, and learning Italian, activities that she found so much more satisfying when done with her neighbor, the parish priest, Don Raffaello Stiattisi, a young man who seemed as lonely in his little rectory built into the wall of the estate as she was in her *villino*. Her mother discouraged their friendship—he was not marriageable and therefore was a waste of time—but Isabel welcomed it. He had kept her heart from eating itself.

The maestro's wife played through several sheets of music, her mouth pursed like a drawstring bag, while Clara sang. Mr. Clemens leaned toward Isabel and whispered, "I always thought that Schubert's music is better than it sounds."

Clara stopped. "Papa. I can hear you."

Mr. Clemens got up. "Don't let me stand in the way of artistic genius," he said loudly. "Keep going, Clara. You sound beautiful." He nodded toward the French windows for Isabel to follow him.

As Clara continued her warbling, they stepped outside onto the terrace, under a trellis from which bunches of just-blooming wisteria dangled. When he stood next to her at the balustrade, she did not adjust her distance. Rightly or wrongly, she savored the feel of his energy.

"Smells sweet," he said. "Sweeter than hydrangea."

"Don Raffaello calls the wisteria *glicine*." She let the word roll from her tongue as her friend had taught her: *gly-she-nay*. "They are blooming early this year. Did you know that these flowers"—she gestured to indicate the trellis running the entire length of the terrace—"are probably all from one trunk?" She pointed toward the stables, where a purple clump draped over the door. "That might be part of the same plant, too. An old plant can spread over fifty feet."

"Never underestimate an old plant." He laid a finger on the back of her hand.

She moved her hand. "But though beautiful, the plants get destructive with age. Don Raffaello says that the vines eventually crush their supports, or if they grow up trees, they strangle them."

"You must be spending a lot of time with the young father to learn all these fascinating facts."

"He's wise. And I fear that he's very lonely."

"I'd be lonely, too, if I were lodged in that little tower of his like a fairy-tale princess."

Isabel pictured her friend showing her the parts of a wisteria cluster in his strong, tanned hands. "He's hardly a princess."

Mr. Clemens watched her, his gray eyes sharp under erect brows. "Shouldn't he be out saving souls instead of talking to pretty unmarried ladies?"

"I think he'd be happier if he had more souls to save. Besides the estate, he has only the families along the Via Santa Maria to attend to."

"How about the countess and her lover? They should keep him busy."

She glanced at him. "Are you afraid that they won't get to heaven?"

"Heaven! I wouldn't wish it even on those two. What a queer idea the human creature has for his heaven! He naturally places sexual union far and away above all other joys, yet has left it out of his paradise."

"Above all other joys?"

"I'd say so. The very thought of sex excites him. The chance of it sets him wild. In this state he will risk life, reputation, heaven itself." He looked down his nose to Isabel. "Anything to make good that opportunity and ride it to the overwhelming climax."

This man had forced his footman to marry his maid after he'd "spoiled" her. He had shamed his daughter just because men admired her, had insulted Count de Calry for letting his servants have love affairs, had despised the countess for indulging in relations with her steward, and yet he spoke cavalierly to Isabel about sex. He truly must think of her as a goat among sheep. She was not complimented.

"You cannot shock me, Mr. Clemens, try as you may."

He burst into a laugh. "By God, Lioness, I've missed you."

She gazed off in the distance at the splashing fountain, furious with herself for imagining him taking her in his arms.

He curled his fingers around hers. "What are we going to do about it?"

"You cannot think I'm influenced so easily." This time, she did not move her hand.

A French window rattled just down the terrace. They stepped apart as Mrs. Clemens crept onto the terrace, her thin gray braid catching against her white robe.

"Livy!"

"I came out to smell the flowers." The weakness of her voice made Isabel wince.

"Livy, I'm glad to see you up." Mr. Clemens strode to her side, Isabel following at a respectable distance.

"The flowers are nice here, but there aren't as many as in the Sandwich Islands. Hawaii, the natives call it." Slowly, she reached up and touched a budding cluster. "I was fascinated by the variety of flowers in the Sandwich Islands, although my husband seemed more fascinated by the women. But it was rather a heaven on earth." She paused to cough. "What luck for him that in Hawaii," she continued, more wheezy now, "women saw no shame in taking a man they wanted, no matter if he were married, though maybe that dulled the pleasure of the conquest for the man." She turned to Mr. Clemens. "Did it?"

"Livy. You're not well." He put his hand to her shoulder to guide her inside.

She shrugged him off, surprisingly strong for someone so ill. "Do you like wisteria, Miss Lyon? *Glicine*, I think they call them."

A chill slithered up Isabel's spine. "Yes."

Mrs. Clemens slowly raised her eyes to a dangling mass. "It's likely that this is all the same plant. Did you know that the runners can spread for fifty feet or more?" She smiled when she saw she had Isabel's attention. "The vines will eventually crush their supports or, if they grow up trees, strangle them." She turned to her husband. "Youth, why look glum? It's a beautiful day."

Clara came out. "Mamma!"

"I heard your singing. Lovely. Schubert, yes?"

"I know how much you like Schubert. I asked the maestro to include a number in my program." She slid out her lower lip, a nearly-thirty-year-old child. "I was going to surprise you with it."

"It's not your fault, dear. Sound travels. You can hear everything in this terrible old house."

The flesh twitched under Mr. Clemens's eyes. "Livy, you must go to bed."

"Not yet, Youth, not yet. But it won't be long now."

He gritted his jaw. "Go," he ordered Isabel.

Isabel walked away, sick with dirtiness. His wife was protecting what was hers. Isabel could not blame her.

Yet Isabel could not release him. Nor could she save herself.

16.

June 1904
Villa di Quarto, Florence, Italy

OLIVIA CLEMENS SAT IN her chair, listening to crickets. It was her least favorite part of the day, when the light dissolved into darkness. The gloaming. Eventide. Twilight. Dusk. For this hour to have so many names, it must have troubled the ancients. As a girl in Elmira, before her health had become delicate, she'd liked this time best, especially in summer, when there were fireflies to capture and a white moon to watch rise, after which she would drag herself indoors, sticky and tired from playing, to sit in the warm soapy water of a tin hat tub. Now the folding of day into night held none of these delights. Twilight felt purely ominous: the ending of a chance; the dwindling of time that would never repeat itself; a loss. The earth itself seemed to hold its breath during these fading minutes, as if afraid of what was to come. The lingering made the surrender so poignant, until the light finally . . . went.

She was on the villa terrace during this gloaming in June—the fifth of the month, nearing the longest day of the year. She'd had Ugo, with his brute's face and lamb's heart, move her chair outside from the bedroom. Youth and the girls were downstairs playing cards, just like in the old days in Hartford. She could hear him tease them—he was in one of his rare jolly moods. For the moment, the girls were not tiptoeing around him and his temper; Jean was not out sacrificing herself for her animals; Clara, thank God, was not singing.

Poor Clara. Her singing was bound to let her down someday. Olivia had not been able to go to the three recitals in town, but she could imagine them: Clara yodeling as if to save her life before a crowd there to see Mark Twain's daughter or, better yet, Mark Twain himself. At the end of Clara's performance, Youth would give them what they wanted and stand up to applause that was heartier than it had been for the anxious young contralto onstage. Clara hadn't a chance. No one did, really, against Mark Twain. Not even poor Youth himself.

Olivia's sigh blended with the rasping of the crickets. It was wrong, what she was doing to Clara, not responsible of her as a mother at all. She should not make her daughter spend so much time with her when Clara should be out discovering her own life. When she was Clara's age, she had borne three children and lost one of them; another baby would come two years later, conceived in England, during those halcyon times when Youth's talent was being discovered and she was his beloved wife. She—quiet, serious Olivia Langdon, an invalid who'd spent six years of her youth confined to her four-poster—was married to a man so vibrant and virile that he electrified any room he entered, be it a parlor, a ship's dining room, or a concert hall. Such an exciting life! He had been a terror in bed; oh my, Olivia had lived for that. She had ignored her doctor's warnings that she could not withstand childbirth, that the marital bed would kill her, that her body was too delicate to take the violence of a man's sex. Well, the doctor was right about all of those things, but not in the ways he had meant.

She fingered the padded silk of the armrests. Clara. Poor, greedy, headstrong, tempestuous Clara. Just like her father, but without her father's mitigating wit and intelligence. She was all appetite and no wisdom, with plenty of vanity thrown in—like her father, she had an excess of that. The pair of them needed praise like the rest of us needed oxygen. How could Olivia let Clara, made so vulnerable by her narcissism, loose in the world without a mother to guide her? Olivia had to get well—she *willed* herself to do so. She had made the mistake of acquiescing to Youth's insistence of keeping the girls at home when they were small and not allowing them to go to school, or much of anywhere else without their parents. She'd not been thinking. How were the girls to deal with the world when they'd had no exposure to it? Why was Youth so against letting them out? No wonder Susy had run wild during the semester she went to college. It was like sitting a girl raised by wolves to dinner at the Waldorf with the expectation that she'd fit in beautifully.

And then there was the problem of Jean. Olivia closed her eyes. Cruel, cruel time of day—it always brought out her regrets.

A terrible braying cut through her repose. Her lids jolted open. That unfortunate beast, wounded now with a gash to his head, was more dangerous than ever. His condition could be remedied by simply turning him out to a field, but the countess kept him tied up, too busy with her lover to care. Olivia peered toward the stables. A light shone in the window of the carriage house. She saw the countess and her lover draw together, their silhouettes framed within the rectangle of yellow light. The big Roman steward cupped the countess's elbow, then drew her to him by the waist. He grasped her hair at the nape of the neck and pulled back her head to kiss her.

Olivia shifted in her chair and let out a long breath. Sam used to kiss her like that. She'd been frightened of him at first. Just looking at him had terrified her. He'd shown up at her parents' house wearing a sealskin coat and hat—fur side out, like a beast—with boots to match. He looked like a trapper or prospector or criminal or worse. Mamma refused to let him in. Only her brother, Charles, overhearing him at the door and coming to identify him, had saved him from being run off.

"This is the chap I was telling you about," Charles had said, introducing him in the parlor to the family. "From my voyage. Sam Clemens the newspaperman—you know, Mark Twain? Funniest man I ever met."

With his storm of wavy red hair, his chiseled face, and those frightening gray eyes, Sam Clemens seemed anything but funny. Before Olivia knew it, he had grabbed her hand and was shaking it. He hung on too long. When she got her hand back to herself, she had cradled it, now a precious thing, for the rest of the night. No man outside of the family had ever touched her. She was twenty-two.

Sam Clemens had then vanished from her life for weeks, only to pop up in New York City, where she and Charles had gone to see the great writer Dickens. Mr. Clemens intercepted them at their hotel, flashing the better tickets he'd gotten, then sat with them in the center of Steinway Hall. How aware she had been of his energy throbbing next to her, even when Mr. Dickens strode out onto the stage, looking neither left nor right but bearing down upon the podium with his luxurious goatee and the side wings of his hair brushed stiffly forward, as if he were being blown in by a gale.

"Someone should advise him about his hair," Olivia had whispered to her brother. "He looks like a Scotch terrier." She could feel Mr. Clemens turn and stare so long at her that she was sure she had offended him. Perhaps Mr. Dickens was his idol. She hazarded a glance.

"You, dear lady, are brilliant."

Two weeks later, she received a note in the mail containing a clipping from a San Francisco newspaper, in which Mark Twain had described Mr. Dickens's hair as giving him the appearance of a Scotch terrier. Mark Twain also announced in the article that "there was a beautiful young lady with me—a highly respectable young white woman." He did not mention to his readers that later that evening he had told the beautiful young lady that he planned to be bigger than Dickens. Richer, too. And she had not laughed.

Now Olivia smiled, half conscious of the lovers in the carriage house across the garden. How Sam Clemens had wooed her! She'd believed that he would indeed outstrip Dickens if he applied himself as vigorously as he did to winning her. She turned him down repeatedly, the animal in her wary.

But how often do we listen to the animal in us? In spite of his rough Western ways and alarming restlessness, in spite of her father worrying that young Mr. Clemens was just after her fortune, he being penniless and she a coal heiress, she couldn't resist him, broken down by his winsome letters full of flattery and appeals to cure him of his drinking, cussing, and tobacco chewing. He begged her to "sivilize" him, and she jumped at the role, calling him "Youth" although he was ten years her senior. He told her in his letters that the only kind of women he ever got, he didn't want; he wanted a respectable woman, like her. If he could just marry a woman as beautiful, smart, and cultured as she, why, he'd become the kind of man he knew he should be. Couldn't she help him, please?

Olivia would hold his letters to her breast, trembling. She yearned for him to take her in his arms and ravish her. Oh, and when he finally did, after a thrilling two years of courtship and breakups and tearful reunions—

Olivia closed her eyes again, remembering the first months of her marriage. He had tried to be tender, calling her his little girl, his sweet, delicate, fragile little girl, stroking her, petting her, until his kisses became so passionate she thought he would eat her. He made her scream out in ecstasy, her body tearing with pleasure.

She smiled now and opened her eyes. The lovers across the way were gone. Loneliness swooped in, devouring her like the night swallows the day. What had happened to her and Youth? She still loved him, and he still loved her in his self-centered way. At least she thought he did. Maybe you couldn't call what he had felt for her "love." It was need, it was desire, it was dominance, but love? In their thirty years of marriage, had he ever known her? Had he ever asked what she had on her mind or how she felt about the girls, what made her the happiest, what she was fearful of, what she wanted for dinner?

It wasn't all his fault. Instead of facing him, she had retreated to her room, a trick she'd learned as an adolescent. When she tired of his trampling over her and the girls, of his restlessness, his blustering, his preening, his ambition, his relentlessness, she had run away. She had confined herself to her bed, pretending she was sick until, after years of constant feigning, she had become truly ill.

Well, if she had willed herself into this wasted state, she could will herself out of it. There was still time. She was only fifty-eight. She needed to work on her walking, to get up her strength, to go into town, to see Clara perform, to see the art. This was Italy! Romantic, life-affirming Italy! And it was June—she glanced across the way—the time for lovers. Sam and she could be lovers again. Her heart hurt with a pang of desire.

She heard whistling. Youth? She sat up, then felt her face as if unsure she was still there.

"Livy, what are you doing outside?" His voice was bright. His good mood encouraged her.

She clutched at the velvet armrests. "Sam, I want another chance."

"Chance? Chance at what? Winning the church raffle?"

She coughed. Traitor body. "Sam, I'm serious."

"You're always serious. The most serious little girl I ever met. I don't hold it against you."

She could feel her energy flag. "Sam, please. Listen."

He noticed her face. "All right." He got closer to peer at her in the lamplight cast through the open door. "You ought to get back in bed. My little girl needs her rest."

"No, Sam. I want to be up. I want to live. I want—I want to go to the Pitti Palace."

"The Pitti Palace?" He laughed. "What has gotten into you?"

"Sam, I've been thinking. I've been throwing away the years, hiding from our problems, when I should have been facing them straight on."

The crickets pulsed into the silence. She could feel his frown.

"We've had big problems, Sam. Your moods, my moods, Susy—"

"You need to go to bed," he said sharply.

"I want to talk, Sam. All these years, I haven't talked. I want to get well."

She could hear his swallow. "I came to say good night, Livy. They're trying a new kind of communication tonight, out in the hills. The army is flashing lights in Morse code to communicate over distances. They're stationed between Fiesole and town. Miss Lyon's seen them—she said they look like fireflies up in the trees."

Her heart jolted. "Miss Lyon."

"She knows just where to stand to see them best. That funny little priest showed her. You get better, and you can join us."

"Miss Lyon." Olivia's energy drained from her.

"She's waiting down in the entrance hall. It starts as soon as it's dark." Olivia could sense his impatience. "Let me take you inside." He took her elbow.

"I don't want to go in." She planted her feet.

He drew her upright. A wave of yearning—for life, for love, for what had been—buckled her knees. He caught her as she was falling.

"Kiss me!" she whispered.

"Ugo!" he shouted. "Ugo! Help me!"

"Sam!" Her lungs seemed to be closing. "Sam!"

"Ugo, hurry."

The butler hastened out the door. "Signora Olivia!"

"Help me with her!"

Ugo gathered her up into his arms. She felt as insignificant as a bag of sticks.

Inside, she looked up at her husband when she was propped against her pillows.

"Are you all right?"

She couldn't answer.

"You gave me a scare!"

She looked up at him, tears flooding her throat, robbing her of air.

"You rest up."

She listened as he walked away. Down the hall, his voice rose up again, and then a plinking on the piano. She recognized the song, his favorite, reserved for celebrations. He had played it for her on the first morning in their first house. The day before, the whole wedding party had taken a private train from her hometown in Elmira up to Buffalo, then, in sleighs, had merrily set out for a housewarming in their brand-new house. Sam had rented it at Papa's urging, sight unseen.

When they had arrived at the elegant three-story house, Sam had been fit to be tied. They would never be able to keep up the rent! Her father was trying to make him look bad! He'd been about to have a tantrum in front of the entire wedding party when Livy said, "Don't you see? Papa bought this for us. It's ours—we own this house now, free and clear."

After the guests had gone, Sam and she had explored the house. He had touched the sky-blue velvet chairs and the scarlet sofa, the wallpaper and the crystal lamps. She had followed after him, smiling, with the pleasure of watching a small boy receive a train set.

"Livy, it's perfect."

"Papa remembered: a piano. He knows I couldn't live without one. I don't even know—do you play, too?"

Sam had sprung over to the instrument and dropped down on the stool. He sang as he struck the keys: " 'Go chain the lion down . . .' "

"So you do play."

He raised his hands from the keyboard. When he looked at her, the fire in his eyes took her breath away. "You don't know the half of my talents."

She'd never felt so wicked or so alive. "Show me."

With a whoop, he had jumped up, scooped her in his arms, and carried her upstairs.

Now another jolt rocked her chest. She clutched her breast against the crushing pain. Her lungs, her airways, were as unyielding as stone. She opened her mouth to scream, but there wasn't enough air.

She clawed at her sheets as the piano rang out downstairs. Her husband's husky voice joined it.

"Go chain the lion down,
Go chain the lion down,
Go chain the lion down,
Before the heav'n doors close."

He came to her, young now. So young, so beautiful, with that red hair. She had always loved his wild red hair. And his eyes—oh, when he looked at her like that, with those quicksilver eyes. There was never a more beautiful beast.

He touched his lips to hers. Her mouth melted against his warmth, melting, melting, dissolving, receding, as the darkness grew ever bright.

PART THREE

The New York Times, August 18, 1904

"MARK TWAIN" LEASES HOUSE.

Gets Lower Fifth Avenue Residence for a Term of Years

Samuel L. Clemens, "Mark Twain," has taken a lease of the four-story brick and stone dwelling 21 Fifth Avenue, at the southeast corner of Ninth Street. Mr. Clemens evidently intends to make his residence in this city for some time, as he has secured the house for a term of years. He will occupy it early in the Fall.

The New York Times, November 26, 1905

MARK TWAIN: A HUMORIST'S CONFESSION

On the Eve of His 70th Birth Anniversary He Admits He Never Did a Day's Work in His Life.

Mark Twain will be 70 years old on Thanksgiving Day, and he has never done a day's work in his life. He told me so himself, sitting in onc of the cheerful, spacious rooms of the old-fashioned stately New York house which he will probably call his city home as long as he lives.
I probably started upon hearing this unlooked-for statement from the lips of the good, gray humorist, for he repeated emphatically:

"No, Sir, not a day's work in all my life. What I have done I have done, because it has been play. If it had been work I shouldn't have done it.

"The fellows who groan and sweat under the weary load of toil that they bear never can hope to do anything great. How can they when their souls are in a ferment of revolt against the employment of their hands and brains? The product of slavery, intellectual or physical, can never be great."

17.

January 1905
21 Fifth Avenue, New York

WINTER DAYLIGHT, WHITENED BY the falling snow, streamed through windows as tall and arched as those in a church, illuminating the books in Mr. Clemens's library as if they were holy. The Greenwich Village mansion did have the feel of a house of worship, Isabel thought, with its vaulted ceilings, Gothic windows, and sheer size—no accident, as it had been designed by James Renwick, Jr., the architect behind Grace Church and St. Patrick's Cathedral there in town. Any sort of ecclesiastical hush was broken, however, by the constant clicking of billiard balls and the blasts of creative cursing that radiated up from the basement. Since October, when Mr. Clemens had rented the house—four months after Mrs. Clemens's passing—only his recent bout of bronchitis had subdued the tapping and swearing, replacing it with a hacking that echoed through the vaulted halls. Isabel heard her employer coughing now, vaguely worrying her, as she beheld the library bookshelves shining in the sun.

From floor to ceiling on three walls, the spines of the books had been arranged in a perfectly gradated rainbow. Shades of vermilion blended into rust; mellow sienna melded into tobacco brown; chocolate became inky black. Someone had put countless hours into this project—Jean? She had little time, what with giving out Humane Society citations to the cabbies just down the street in Washington

Square and rescuing cats from alleys. Isabel hadn't noticed the work going on, having been busy tending to Mr. Clemens, ill in bed and sullen for the past two weeks, and with moving her mother into a boardinghouse just around the corner. Isabel's own room was above Mr. Clemens's. The rule that all female servants other than domestics had to reside off-premise had ceased with Mrs. Clemens.

Isabel took one last appreciative gaze at the colors fanning out on the walls around her, then stepped forward, grasped two books by the spine, and dropped them to the Persian rug. She slid out two more, let them fall, *thud*, *thud*, then repeated, until a landslide of books was slithering around her buttoned pumps.

She was just about to release two more when a gilt word caught her eye: *Pitti*. She dropped the other book as she opened *The Treasures of the Pitti Palace*. She turned the pages of the collection of colored photos until she found what she was looking for: Raffaello's painting of his mistress. How the man must have loved this woman. And for them to have had such a night of passion together that it killed him!

"What are you doing?"

Isabel shut the book. In the doorway, Katy shook with such fury that the ruffles of her pinafore trembled. The recent return to New York, Mrs. Clemens's death, or just the effects of time had taken their toll on her. Her face had a squashed look, as if her skin had softened and gravity were having a field day with it. Only her fierceness had remained evergreen.

"What are you doing?" she demanded again.

Isabel realized now who had created this beautiful, useless library arrangement. "I'm sorry, Katy, but books have to be arranged by subject, not color. Who can find anything this way?"

"Miss Jean liked it."

"I like it, too, but it just isn't practical. But I completely agree, the books do look prettier this way."

"Don't you look down your nose at me!"

Isabel sighed, then tried again. "This must have taken hours of your time. I apologize for ruining it."

"I hear your disrespect."

Wearily, Isabel removed more books. "I wish we could get along, Katy, since neither of us is going anywhere."

"Aren't we? I wouldn't be so sure of that."

Isabel would not respond to her bait.

Katy spoke over the books thumping on the rug. "Just wait till Miss Clara gets back."

"Miss Clara understands that I am here to serve her family. I only do what her father wants." She doubted the words as they came out. Clara did not know or care what her father wanted. If she knew what he wanted, she would want the opposite. She so vehemently blamed him for her mother's death that it had broken her own health. She had not spoken to him or Isabel since the funeral, after which she immediately put herself into a sanitarium on Fifty-Ninth Street, where she would not receive his or Isabel's letters.

"He'd want the books arranged in a manner that would make sense to him," Isabel continued truthfully. "Please try not to take it as a personal affront."

Katy's voice rose. "What makes you the expert on what he wants? You don't know him, not like I do."

"You're right—you've known him much longer than I have."

"There's more to it than that."

"I suppose that his wife's maid would know him very well."

Katy's ruddy face went crimson; her eyes glimmered with loathing. "He and I understand each other. We come from the same place."

"Ireland?" Isabel pulled down more books as if Katy's stare weren't boring into her.

At last Katy said, "You'd better watch yourself. Miss Clara hates you, and don't you forget it."

They turned when they heard coughing in the hallway.

Mr. Clemens trudged in, dressed in his robe and slippers, an unlit cigar between his fingers. "Who hates who?"

"Nobody, sir." Katy swiped at her fallen pompadour.

He leaned against a leather wingback to fish in his pocket for a match. "What is it about a hen fight that so satisfies a man? Let me draw up a chair to watch. Just make sure no one flies off the handle and kills a body like our neighbor Dan Sickles."

Isabel felt a stab of offense. She was not a hen, nor did she like the idea of him thinking she had invited Katy's hostility. But she submerged her hurt feelings beneath relief that Mr. Clemens was moving around and joking. He'd spent both Christmas and New Year's in his room, glum and uncommunicative, not cheering up even when the steel magnate Andrew Carnegie dropped by with a case of rare whiskey. Usually, the homage of the rich and powerful was a tonic to her employer, but he had only sipped from his tumbler, morose, as the bewhiskered Carnegie, with a boyish grin that undermined his pretense to modesty, remarked casually about the English king's drop-in visit to his "little castle" in Scotland. When Mr. Clemens did not try to top Carnegie's story, missing his chance to tell of having walked a mile with the king while taking the waters in Homburg, Isabel had been worried indeed.

She blinked the memory away and mustered her good humor. "Old General Sickles?" She pictured the one-legged former Civil War officer being helped down the steps of his Fifth Avenue mansion across the street, then being ladled into his open carriage.

"Old General Sickles shot his wife's lover, I'm sorry to report. The lover was a bigwig, too—Philip Keyes, a U.S. attorney and the son of the man who wrote 'The Star-Spangled Banner.' When young Dan fired that gun, he shot himself into a world of trouble." He lit his cigar, sucking on it to get it going. "But he claimed that seeing the pair together made him temporarily insane, and damned if the court didn't let him go. Temporary insanity was a new defense at the time, and it worked like magic. Don't know why we don't all use it whenever we run off the rails." He broke off, coughing.

"Please don't smoke, sir," Katy said. "You haven't been well."

He waved her off along with his cigar fumes. "Oh, a little tobacco heart never killed anyone. I'm as hardy as a stump. It was Livy who was fragile." He took a long draw on his cigar. "The doctor only gave me two minutes with her a day for all those years because I could kill her with my words. I laughed at him. Who kills people with words? Me, evidently." He looked at Isabel. "Why didn't you stop me?"

She was as wounded as he meant her to be. He had bottled up his anguish for these past six months, and now he was releasing it in front of Katy.

Katy gently took his arm. "You didn't kill her, sir. No one did. It was her time." As one does with a small, hurt boy, she carefully turned him around and, with her stubby hand on his back, walked him to his bedroom, leaving Isabel standing among the fallen books.

• • •

A deck of cards in her hand, Isabel confronted Mr. Clemens's bedroom door that evening, trying not to take its firmly closed state or his absence from dinner as a personal message. She hated playing cards, and the daily silent rounds that she'd endured with Mr. Clemens since his wife had died had not improved her love for them. But if a deck were to be her Trojan horse, if it could bring her and Mr. Clemens to a truce, so be it. She knocked on the door.

"What?" It was Katy's voice.

Isabel sagged. "I'll come back," she called.

There was a brief silence.

"No," called Mr. Clemens from inside the room, "come in."

She let herself in. Mr. Clemens sat on his bed, naked to the waist. Katy stood next to him, holding a small green jar. Isabel's gaze went directly to the exposed flesh of his chest. "I didn't mean to interrupt."

He lay back against the piles of white pillows. No sultan in a harem looked more comfortable. "What did you want, Miss Lyon?"

She thought of the time she had come upon Katy drying his hair back in Riverdale. She held up the deck. "Hearts," she said awkwardly.

He patted the other side of the bed. "Come here. Sit."

Regretting her need to be with him, she obeyed. Katy uncapped the green jar. The release of camphor and menthol overwhelmed the room.

"Deal," Mr. Clemens said after Isabel reluctantly sat.

She shuffled the cards, pretending not to be disconcerted by the sight of Katy rubbing the ointment on his chest. She could not keep her gaze from the glistening salt-and-pepper hair springing under Katy's fingers.

"Are you just going to shuffle all day?" said Mr. Clemens.

Isabel dealt the cards upon the bedspread as Katy finished massaging in the Mentholatum and then laid a thick one-foot square of white flannel on his chest. Isabel picked up her cards and arranged them in her hand as he shrugged into his shirt while Katy held it. When Isabel glanced up, Katy was looking down upon her master with naked tenderness.

Mr. Clemens scooped up his cards as Katy buttoned his shirt. "What's wrong, Lioness?"

She shook her head. How had she not realized that she was not the only employee in love with her master? She should have seen it in Riverdale when she'd caught them alone, or any time they were in the same room, now that she thought of it. How blind we are to things we can't imagine.

"Thank you, Katy." He shifted to adjust the plaster under his shirt as he positioned his cards. Katy went over and stoked the fire, necessary on this cold night even though the house had a modern furnace. Reluctantly, the maid left the room.

They played several hands. The blood rose in Isabel's face as she pictured herself carrying on a flirtation with him at the Pitti Palace, at her *villino*, back in Riverdale, everywhere. What made her think she had any more chance with him than Katy ever did? She hoped that he got some enjoyment out of them. Pull up a chair, enjoy the hen fight between servants!

Mr. Clemens stopped the game to unbutton his shirt, wipe his chest with the flannel, and pitch it across the room. "Thing stank."

Isabel wanted to leave.

"You aren't trying to talk my leg off for once," he said, buttoning up.

"Sorry."

They resumed playing. He took another trick. "Are you letting me win?"

"No."

"You sick?"

"No."

They threw down more rounds; Mr. Clemens scooped them up, winning each hand. "You've got terrible cards. Just look at them! Products of the devil and his ancestors. You must be as cool as a saint on ice not to boil at the sight of them."

She didn't feel like laughing.

A rattling came at the windows. Both looked up. "Sleet," he said. She could feel him watching her. "Pour me some of Carnegie's whiskey, why don't you?"

She put down her cards and retrieved the bottle on the nightstand. The whiskey splashed into a crystal tumbler.

"Queen Victoria's distiller made that stuff," he said as she poured. "Her son Edward only lets it out to a chosen few. Carnegie got a supply, and now there are only three people in the United States currently sipping that stuff—Carnegie, the president, and me. Hell, make it four. Pour yourself a glass."

She grimaced.

"Go on." He waggled his fingers for her to pour. "Don't make an old man drink alone." He raised his glass when she was done pouring. "To the New Year."

The liquid burned its way down her throat. Across the room, the sleet hissed against the windows.

He watched her drink. "Do you like it?"

"No!" But she kept drinking.

Several hands later, he said, "I shouldn't have said that to you earlier."

There were many things he should not have said to her in their years together.

"About Livy," he said.

She finished her glass and put it down. The top of her head seemed to be floating toward the vaulted ceiling.

He slapped down a card. "It's not your fault that I killed her."

She tightened her jaw to stabilize herself. "You didn't kill Mrs. Clemens." It was vanity, really, that he thought he controlled his wife's very breath—vanity or madness.

"I should have been more careful with her. How did I not see she was in such a bad state?"

She could not bear his anguish, as wrongheaded as it was. "She had been feeling better that day. Clara had told me. Everyone was so encouraged."

"She really was better?" His eyes begged her to confirm it.

His vulnerability deflated her anger. "Yes, Clara said. She was up walking more than she'd been in months."

"I shouldn't have let her walk so much! She hadn't walked more than twenty steps at a time in the last five years. Since she was a girl, she couldn't walk over a hundred feet. Why'd she think she could start now?" His tears shone in the firelight. "I loved her, you know. People said that I married her for her money, but that wasn't true. Oh, I loved her money, don't get me wrong, and I loved how she made me respectable, or at least tried to, but that's not why I had to have her." He took a drink, then set down his glass. "She was just a *little* girl, you see, frail as a child. It was as if I could hold her in one hand. I was so honored that she trusted me not to crush her." He sighed. "But I did. I crushed her every day."

A crash came from the street outside, the screaming of horses, shouts. Isabel went to the window.

Below, the streetlight cast a sleety glow upon an overturned carriage. One of the pair of horses had fallen on the ice. While two men struggled to extract a woman from the side of the vehicle, the downed animal stabbed at the glistening street for purchase. The mare became tangled in her lines, dragging the other down upon her. She rolled back with a shriek.

Mr. Clemens came up behind Isabel as a bystander ran to help the screaming horse. Isabel turned away, face in hands.

He cradled her head against his chest. "It'll be all right."

She heard his beating heart. Slowly, she looked up, sleet hissing against the window. He kissed her, then pressed her to him again. His voice rumbled against her ear. "Lioness, what are we going to do?"

A shot rang out. She could feel herself shaking.

He gathered her closer. "Poor horse. Nothing to be done when they're broken like that."

18.

March 1905
21 Fifth Avenue, New York

MRS. LYON COULD UNDERSTAND why Isabel had insisted upon dragging her to the moving picture show the other week. The studio, so common with its rough wooden benches and pressed tin ceiling, had smelled distressingly of foreign food and unwashed hair, but the action in *Rescued by Rover* made up for it. Mrs. Lyon had gaped at the jerking images, as keen on them, she supposed, as an immigrant beholding the distant skyscrapers of Manhattan when descending the gangplank to Ellis Island. The picture show was an interesting improvement over her beloved stereoscope after all, and she admitted as much to Isabel. Mrs. Lyon could admit when she was wrong. It took a big person to do so.

What Mrs. Lyon could not understand, however, was the thrill Mr. Clemens got in riding this underground death trap. Her ears ached from the racket of their subway car banging along its tracks like a coffee tin full of pennies. The passengers were all jumbled together like mulligan stew, Italian street repairmen in filthy overalls next to Russian shirtwaist-factory girls next to Negro men in celluloid collars next to bowlered clerks reading the *Sun*.

When she had entered the domed cast-iron kiosk to the Astor Place station, Mrs. Lyon had asked Mr. Clemens if they would be riding in a first-class car. Yes, he had said in that maddeningly slow way of his as they went down the steps to the tracks. They were all first-class. She was questioning how that could possibly be as she gazed dumbfounded at the tiled walls decorated with plaques of beavers—beavers, of all things, so crude to someone accustomed to the classical nude statues of Florence—when a train rumbled up, shrieking like Grendel being hewn by Beowulf. Higgledy-piggledy, the rich, the poor, and the middling had piled into what amounted to covered coal cars fitted out with benches. Mrs. Lyon entered with all the dignity one could muster when an Italian organ-grinder with a monkey on his shoulder was nudging one's back with his instrument.

Once seated behind Isabel and Mr. Clemens, Mrs. Lyon tried to catch the eye of the woman dressed in furs in the seat across from her, traveling with her maid, to commiserate about this sorry state of affairs. But the woman had been too busy smiling at Mr. Clemens to see.

Now they screeched along their subterranean circle of Hell. Mrs. Lyon adjusted her neckpiece, a single mink clasping its own tail between its needle teeth, an adornment she had owned since her debut. Its glass eyes were a little dull, a situation she had not improved with some shoe black, and it had a thumbprint-sized patch on its left haunch where the skin was rather too visible, but it and she looked respectable enough, especially when she held her chin high. You could always tell a person of quality by how she held herself. Her straight back was one of the perilously few things that elevated her above the coatless young clerk across the aisle, still wearing his arm garters and slumped like a sack of navy beans upon his bench. Once Isabel married Mr. Clemens, there would be no question of Mrs. Lyon's respectability. Mrs. Lyon could slump like a cooked noodle out in public if she cared to, and there would be no mistaking her rank. Her daughter's elderly humorist was a very famous man.

Isabel *would* marry him someday. It was done, you know. Why, Isabel's former suitor, Mr. Bangs, had married his secretary just the previous year. Mrs. Lyon had seen Mr. Bangs and his secretary-wife with her own eyes this past November, riding through the Washington Square arch in a shiny new carriage. Mrs. Lyon had kept her head down as they passed, ill with her daughter's bad fortune. It should have been Isabel sitting in that brougham! But now it seemed that Isabel was the luckier for not having married him, leaving her free to wed a much bigger fish. If Mrs. Lyon could read the signs right, wedding bells should be ringing any day now. Funny how often bad luck was good luck in disguise.

And to think that just a few months ago, Mrs. Lyon never would have given a thought to them as a couple. Whatever closeness they had enjoyed before Mrs. Clemens passed away—purely professional, mind you—had been dashed by Mrs. Clemens's death. Mr. Clemens had taken her demise hard, although not as hard as his daughter Clara, who immediately took to swathing herself head to toe in black veils *if* Isabel could get her to rise from her bed, which believe you me was not often. As soon as they were back in the States and her mother was buried, the girl locked herself in a sanitarium near Central Park. She was languishing there to this day. She would not even entertain a letter from her papa!

Now the train screamed to a stop. Mrs. Lyon held her handbag tightly during the exchange of people getting off or on. It was just the sort of place where riffraff preyed on their superiors, looting them when they were helpless. She stared at the well-dressed woman with the maid, trying to catch her eye to let her know that she had a compatriot in the fight against rabble, but the woman seemed more interested in the buttons on her glove. Gripping her bag until the tin can was back in motion, Mrs. Lyon finally gave up on the woman and let her mind wander to more pleasant places.

It was two months ago, in January, that Mrs. Lyon had noticed the encouraging change in Isabel and Mr. Clemens. Oh, they had been playing cards all evening for a number of months after Mrs. Clemens's passing, sometimes with that poor, wild Jean. He did things like give Isabel his letters to mail and had her send his telegraphs and place telephone calls and so on. Then, what seemed like overnight, just after the evening when that horse had to be put down right in front of Mr. Clemens's house, Isabel and he became inseparable. He gave her his stories to read. He taught her to play on his Orchestrelle organ. He had her trotting with him all over town and filling in at home as his hostess.

Oh, the people they had to their table! Businessmen like Henry Rogers and Andrew Carnegie, writers like William Dean Howells and Thomas Bailey Aldrich, scientists, musicians, even professors. Sometimes Isabel had Mrs. Lyon join them for dinner, as they did when they had in Mr. Clemens's doctor friend from Vienna, Herr Heinrich Something-or-another, just last week.

Mrs. Lyon sighed as she bumped along, thinking about that evening. It was just like old times when her Charles was alive, when every night it was another intellectual come to dinner. As she and Isabel were putting on their gloves before going down to table, Isabel had warned her to keep her silence. Mr. Clemens liked to be the one to entertain. Mrs. Lyon had nearly laughed. Isabel was telling *her* how to comport herself? Why, she and Charles had hundreds of these dinners! When an awkward pause arose at the Clemens party as they were waiting for that rude maid Katy to bring in the turtle soup, it was Mrs. Lyon who had known just how to bridge the gap.

"What will you do whilst you are in New York, Herr Doctor?" she had asked the young physician.

"I am here to lecture at Columbia University—"

"Columbia!" Mrs. Lyon clapped together gloved hands in delight. "My husband was on the faculty of Columbia! His textbook on Latin is still being used there. Perhaps you've heard of him—Charles Lyon?"

Young Herr Heinrich inclined his sleek head, the ribbon of his pince-nez dipping onto his stiff white shirtfront. He was dark, like Charles had been, and almost as handsome, and he spoke in a sophisticated Germanic accent. His shirt studs looked to be made of good jet. All in all, he could be a decent catch for Isabel. "I have not," he said. "I apologize."

"Isabel," she said, "was brought up in learned circles. Do you know that she once sat on Horace Greeley's knee and called him Uncle?"

"He must have had an awfully knobby knee," said Mr. Clemens.

Isabel had gazed into his eyes perhaps a pinch too fondly, especially if she didn't wish to discourage Herr Heinrich.

"Why do you say so?" asked Mrs. Lyon.

"Well," drawled Mr. Clemens, "it made her cry 'uncle.' "

Isabel grinned at him—overly amused, Mrs. Lyon thought. Was she the only one who noticed Herr Heinrich's confusion? "Mr. Clemens is teasing us," she explained to him. "The mark of a humorist," she added.

Katy came in with her tray, along with that sweet girl Teresa whom Mr. Clemens had brought back from Italy.

"What are they getting up to at Columbia these days?" asked Mr. Clemens as Katy placed the soup dishes before him. He smiled up at her absentmindedly. Katy looked straight back at him, too long, too hard—much too forward for a maid. Mrs. Lyon resolved to have a word with Isabel about it.

Herr Heinrich watched Teresa set a dish before him. When she was through, he said, "My colleagues in cell biology have recently discovered what they call an XY chromosomal system in humans. Every individual creature's sex is determined by the presence—or not—of the Y chromosome. The default sex is female, who have two X chromosomes but no Y."

Mr. Clemens took a sip of soup. "You mean we are all girls until we get this Y?"

"Yes." Herr Heinrich laughed. "And no. It does not work quite like that. My colleague Edmund Beecher Wilson could explain it better."

Mr. Clemens cocked his head, spoon in fist. "Edmund Beecher Wilson? Edmund *Beecher* Wilson? It would be a Beecher who discovered the biology of sex."

Mrs. Lyon looked with alarm at Isabel. It was the hostess's job to steer a conversation from the rocks of poor taste. But Isabel just smiled at Mr. Clemens in encouragement.

"Have you heard of him, Heinrich? He was one of the most famous preachers in America. One of the busiest in bed, too."

"Oh my," gasped Mrs. Lyon, even as Herr Heinrich sat up.

Mr. Clemens continued. "I don't know if you heard, Herr Heinrich—it was pretty big news here—but he was tried for adultery with the wife of a friend."

"Do you think it might snow tonight?" said Mrs. Lyon.

"Where Herr Beecher erred," said Mr. Clemens, "was that he should have publicly denied the affair the day it appeared in the papers. He should have countered the husband's accusations and lied with all his might. There is no more holy a time to lie than for the honor of a woman."

"The only time holier," said Isabel, "is when one must lie to save one's own skin."

Mr. Clemens regarded her, his mustache cocked in amusement. "Lioness, I did not know you were such a cynic."

"A heavy snow will nip the crocuses!" Mrs. Lyon bleated.

"What happened to this Beecher?" asked Herr Heinrich.

"Beecher?" said Mr. Clemens. "Nothing. He has gone down in history as one of America's great preachers."

"And the lady?"

"Mrs. Tilton? As one of America's great whores." He stared openly at Isabel. To Mrs. Lyon's horror, Isabel stared right back. What was she doing? She would secure neither gentleman, condoning such talk.

Mrs. Lyon was going to turn this conversation around. "Herr Heinrich, tell us about the exciting work you are doing here at Columbia."

He pulled his fascinated gaze from Mr. Clemens and Isabel. "My work? I am studying the nervous system. For this, I am dissecting a body that has been preserved on ice for one and a half years. It has become so soft, I can separate the muscles and nerves and pick them up without cutting—very useful."

From adultery to corpses! Mrs. Lyon closed her eyes in pain.

" 'It.' " Mr. Clemens lowered his spoon. "Don't you mean 'he'?"

Herr Heinrich's pince-nez rode his frown. "Pardon me?"

"Who is your cadaver?"

"I saw the most curious automobile today!" cried Mrs. Lyon. "A green contraption called a 'Ford.' "

When Herr Heinrich just stared, Mr. Clemens said, "What's his name?"

"Oh. I see. My cadaver." Herr Heinrich smiled slyly. "I have given him a name. 'Fritz.' "

"No, what's his real name?" The edge in Mr. Clemens's voice made Mrs. Lyon blink.

The doctor laughed uneasily. "I don't know."

"Have you ever stopped to think," said Mr. Clemens, "that your 'Fritz' has a family? A wife? A son?"

The doctor's eyes cooled. "Cadavers are most commonly criminals."

Mr. Clemens stared down his beak of a nose, his gray eyes sharp. "Well, cut nice, Herr Doctor. Fritz could be some boy's pa."

The rest of the dinner had gone badly. After that, Herr Heinrich could say nothing that Mr. Clemens would not take exception to. Once he'd gone—with no invitation extended to stay and play billiards, a break from the usual custom—Mr. Clemens had turned to Isabel when they retired to the drawing room. Mrs. Lyon had been helping herself to a chocolate from a box on a marble-topped table, wondering how she might have saved the night.

"I don't like him," Mr. Clemens said.

Mrs. Lyon had looked up with a mouthful of nougat. She saw Isabel reach out and squeeze his hand.

Mr. Clemens bit off the words. "My father had an autopsy. I saw them cut him up through the keyhole of his bedroom. I was eleven." When he fearfully met Isabel's gaze, she pressed his hand again. She said nothing, she asked no questions, just looked at him.

Mrs. Lyon's hand dropped back to the box of candy. Unthinking, she returned the remainder of the piece of chocolate back to its crinkled brown wrapper. It wasn't Mr. Clemens's awful statement that had rattled her. She never understood half of the crude strangeness that came from his mouth. But she had seen that look before, decades earlier, when she and Charles were in the entrance hall of Spring Side, returning from some morning calls. The butler had just given Charles the telegram with the news that his mother had died. Mrs. Lyon had been crying into her handkerchief when Poppy, tidying the hall table, put down her feather duster, went to Charles, and, bowing her head, squeezed his hand. Charles had shuddered, but he didn't look at her. He didn't need to. The sympathy that flowed between them was as intimate as that of two lovers after an act of passion . . . the sort of sympathy that only those who had shared their bodies could experience. Realization had scooped out Mrs. Lyon's core, hollowing her out so quickly that she had nearly dropped to her knees.

Choking down that mouthful of nougat in Mr. Clemens's parlor, Mrs. Lyon had drawn a life-giving breath. She must not fret over the disastrous dinner with Herr Heinrich, nor linger over the heartbreak of that terrible, searing memory. She should rejoice: *Isabel and Mr. Clemens have that sympathy.* Isabel could win the prize.

Now, trundling underground in this deafening keg of nails, Mrs. Lyon glanced at Mr. Clemens and Isabel, sighed, then went back to counting the number of pelts in her neighbor's coat. Twenty-six, that she could see. When the woman looked up, Mrs. Lyon would give her a knowing smile. They were peers, you know, and like liked to be with like as the world went topsy-turvy beneath them.

19.

August 1905
Dublin, New Hampshire

"MISS LYON! YOO-HOO!"

The heels of her white boots ringing on the boards of the covered porch, Miss Norma K. Bright, twenty-two, as blond as butter and crammed full of deviled ham sandwiches and lemonade from lunch at Mr. Clemens's summer home in New Hampshire, strode toward Isabel with all the confidence of the young, the beautiful, and the coddled. Miss Bright was one of the many stripes of wealthy artists who summered in the inspirational shadow of Mount Monadnock, all of them hoping to escape the heat of the city while turning out creative work, Mr. Clemens among them. Having recently published a collection of poetry for children, Miss Bright clearly felt on top of the world—or maybe she had always felt that way.

"You disappeared!" she cried. "I had hoped I'd find you out here."

Isabel turned regretfully from the hemlock-fringed view of the mountain, and from a happy memory with Mr. Clemens that she had been savoring. "Just getting a breath of air. I hope you enjoyed your lunch."

Miss Bright patted her stomach, sunken beneath her white lawn dress. "Stuffed!"

"Good."

Miss Bright seized Isabel's arm. "I wanted to talk to you before everyone else came out—your boss is in there showing off his copy of Helen Keller's new book."

"He's very fond of her."

Miss Bright gave her a conspiratorial smile. "He's very fond of *you*, I'd say. I saw the way he looked at you at lunch."

Isabel studied her, wondering if Miss Bright was always this brazen or if the success of her poetry had emboldened her. "We've been working together for a number of years now."

"How many?"

"Three."

Miss Bright twisted her head in a teasing look. "A suitable period for an engagement."

Was it because Isabel was older, poorer, or less successful that made the girl think she could be so forward with her? "He lost his wife just last summer."

"A shame. Do you get along with his daughters?"

"Miss Bright, please."

The girl tented her nose and mouth with her pretty hands. "I'm sorry. I must sound rude." She put down her hands. "But it's really quite adorable how he dotes on you. One can't help wondering if there might be wedding bells."

Isabel glanced inside the house, flattered in spite of her annoyance. Did he actually seem to dote on her? Well, she had nothing to hide. And surely it would seem like more of a case of her doting on him. She picked out his clothes, arranged his activities, accompanied him on trips, conferred with his daughters' doctors, read his works in progress, even washed his hair, taking the chore from Katy—all of which she did with pleasure. The result was that his writing was flowing out of him this summer like it hadn't in years. Bold, angry, thrilling stories and articles like "The Mysterious Stranger," "King Leopold's Soliloquy," "3,000 Years Among the Microbes," "The War Prayer," and her favorite by far, the preciously personal "Eve's Diary," poured from him. His exuberance on the page spilled into their relationship, forging a closeness that no one would understand—certainly his daughters couldn't. Not even she and Mr. Clemens did. They did not speak of it. To acknowledge it, to look too close, might make it disappear, like the shoemaker's elves once the shoemaker discovered them. Oh, but she could feel it. Being with Mr. Clemens filled her with so much happiness that it frightened her.

"I'm just his secretary, nothing more."

"Well, people are interested in you."

Isabel plucked at the coral necklace that he had given her, thinking of all the times she had been patted, kissed, or had her hand grasped by both men and women so they might touch someone close to the great man. One woman, after kissing her on the forehead, had asked how she ever managed to come to work for such a saintly man, as if Isabel somehow maneuvered her way into his confidence. Isabel had "managed" nothing. The most wonderful things in life came of their own accord; you just had to be open to them.

Even one of their guests this afternoon, the author Thomas Wentworth Higginson, presently indoors admiring Helen Keller's book with Mr. Clemens, had captured Isabel's hand earlier that day and clung to it, saying he wanted to hold the hand that guided Mark Twain. Once she got over the shock of it, such behavior only brought out Isabel's protectiveness toward Mr. Clemens. How like a hunted animal he must feel, with everyone wanting a piece of his hide.

"Have you ever thought of writing an article on Mark Twain?" asked Miss Bright.

"Mr. Clemens, you mean."

"No, I mean Mark Twain." Miss Bright lowered her voice. "No one cares about Samuel Clemens, do they? He's just a salty old man from Missouri. But Mark Twain—"

"Excuse me?"

Miss Bright put her hand to her mouth. "Oh, dear. That must have sounded terribly harsh. I'm sorry, it's just that, well, that's all he would be if he hadn't created his Mark Twain character, do you see what I mean? But of course, he did create Mark Twain, and he is a genius! Mr. Clemens made himself into a character that the whole world loves. Bravo!"

Colonel Higginson lumbered outside, the floorboards groaning under his feet. His thick skin, crosshatched with weathering, as well as his drooping eye bags, jowls, and mustache, lent him the air of a tired walrus, although there was a spark in his saddlebagged eyes, as if a nimble boy were encased within his heavy carapace of flesh. "What are we applauding out here?"

"Mark Twain," said Miss Bright. "Colonel Higginson, please help me convince Miss Lyon that she should write an article about Mark Twain. Wouldn't it be the candy to hear from Mark Twain's secretary's point of view?"

He rotated his bulk toward Isabel. "Why, that's an excellent idea. Miss Lyon, would you consider it? I think my friends at *The Atlantic Monthly* would snap it right up."

"I really couldn't."

"Why ever not? I am warming to this idea. Who knows Mark Twain better than his secretary?"

"Unless it was his daughters," said Miss Bright.

Isabel drew in a breath. Currently, Clara and Jean were in their beds, Clara still in the sanitarium in New York, and Jean upstairs recovering from another epileptic episode, neither available to rhapsodize about their father. Even before her self-imposed confinement, Clara had nothing to do with her father after her mother died. And Mr. Clemens would have little to do with poor Jean, especially now that her seizures were coming more often than ever. He could not bear to see Jean in her agonies. At the moment Isabel was trying to figure out how to tell him about Katy's report from this morning—that, while in her fit, Jean had attacked Katy with the intention to kill. Isabel didn't know how Mr. Clemens would react if he thought Jean might be dangerous to others. Already she was such a danger to herself.

"Mr. Clemens is a very private man. I don't think—"

"Mark?" The colonel laughed. "I have never met such a glutton for the spotlight. Bet he'd be the first to admit it if you asked him. That's what we all love about him—he's so honest about himself, flaws and all."

Isabel agreed, hoping the subject was dropped.

"I do confess," said the colonel, "that I am completely intrigued by the secretary angle."

She suppressed a sigh. "Well, thank you, but it wouldn't be right. It would be a betrayal."

"It would only be a betrayal if you said something scandalous about him." Miss Bright lit up. "*Is* there something scandalous?"

"No!" Isabel tried to laugh.

The colonial looked down upon her with shrewd amusement. "Do you realize how important you are, the influence that you have over him? This brings to mind a story I once read, about a mighty king whose life was governed by the words of his valet, no one suspecting it, least of all the king. The king thought he was ruling, yet by a single word, the servant could turn the better judgment of his master."

Katy came out with a tray of lemonade, offering it to everyone but Isabel. The colonel took a glass before continuing. "In this case, the valet used his power to cause the king to condemn as worthless, as utterly self-seeking, the service and homage of the real one who gladly gave himself to the king. The king cast out the loyal servant, never seeing that it was only jealousy in the other."

"Sounds like *King Lear*, only with servants instead of daughters," said Miss Bright.

"I don't have that kind of influence over Mr. Clemens, I assure you." Isabel lifted a glass from the tray as Katy passed.

Mr. Clemens swaggered onto the porch, escorting the colonel's grown daughter Margaret, who was pink-cheeked with excitement. Isabel was struck, as always, at how his face was as ruggedly handsome as that of a forty-year-old, his figure as hard and upright, as if he were too fierce to age.

"Just the person we were talking about," said the colonel. "Mark, what do you think of Miss Lyon here writing an article about you for *The Atlantic*?"

Mr. Clemens stopped across from Isabel and cast his coolly aggressive gaze upon her. "Whatever the secretary wants, she gets."

"Oh-ho!" the colonel cried.

Isabel was too drawn in by Mr. Clemens to care about their meddling guests. She could feel his spirit bridging the space between them, filling her with its warmth. Happiness burned down her throat like whiskey.

"Oh, do tell us his secrets," said Miss Bright.

"Yes, Miss Lyon," said Mr. Clemens. "Do tell them some of my secrets." He shook his head at Katy, who was offering him a drink.

The wind picked up, tugging at the ladies' skirts. It hissed through the ranks of fir trees that marched into the distant mountains as, in her mind's eye, Isabel saw him reading "Eve's Diary" to her last month. She had listened, his customary after-dinner plate of radishes sitting untouched on the table set up on this very porch while the daylight reddened and then drained into a smoky gray. She'd lit a lamp, then sat back in its throbbing glow as fireflies rose into the treetops.

A lump had scalded her throat when he'd finished and taken off his reading glasses. "Well, what do think?" he asked.

"Eve tells all the reasons why she could love Adam, but those aren't really why." Fireflies signaled as she'd swallowed her tears. "She loves him because he's hers."

Just then a rocket, a leftover from Independence Day, had soared over Mount Monadnock. It struggled toward a heaven it couldn't reach and then, in a piteous burst, fell to earth in despair. They had looked at each other with shining eyes. The very world seemed to have been created just for them.

Now she told Miss Bright, "He eats radishes every day."

"Radishes!" Miss Bright exclaimed.

Mr. Clemens glanced away in amusement.

"They're good for the digestion. Some nights they're all he will eat." Isabel would never give him away.

The wind sent a sheet of newspaper tumbling across the lawn. Katy appeared inside at a porch window and, watching Mr. Clemens, closed it with a bang. He flinched unconsciously at the noise.

"Should we go in?" Isabel asked the group.

Mr. Clemens turned his gaze toward the mountain. "Not yet. I like it out here."

"Then tell us something else," the colonel said to Isabel, "about the great and powerful Twain."

Down the way, Katy banged another window shut.

Another memory poured before Isabel's eyes. She saw herself writing in her daily reminder at her desk just last week, during an afternoon rainstorm. In the midst of an entry, as lightning lit the room, she heard a rapping on her ceiling: *tap-tap-tap-TAP.* She had paused but, hearing nothing further, resumed writing in her journal.

Tap-tap-tap-TAP.

She put down her pen and went up to Mr. Clemens's room. He was at his window, in his dressing gown, clasping his hands behind him, one turned out in that dear way of his. A scratchy symphony was playing on his phonograph. On his bed, a cat was giving itself a bath, the sound of its licking audible over the music.

"Did you want something?" she asked. Thunder boomed, closer now, sending vibrations through the floor.

"Hmm?"

"You knocked."

Just then, the phonograph crackled with the familiar strain of Beethoven's Fifth Symphony. He tapped his foot along with it. *Tap-tap-tap-TAP.*

"Oh."

He quirked his mustache. "If I had known that's all it took to get you up here, I would have done it a long time ago."

"If you don't need me, then—"

A flash of lighting illuminated his shock of hair. "Come over here. I want you to see this."

At the window, he had slid his arms around her from behind. Conscious that they were in his bedroom, that his forearms were crossed over her ribs, that his sensitive hands with their tapered fingers, an ink-stained callus on the side of his index finger, were near her breasts, she lifted her gaze to the storm sweeping toward the mountains. White fissures sliced the curtains of rain slanting from the black heavens. Thunder jarred the house. At the edge of the lawn, the fir trees reached up as for mercy, their supplications lit up by the relentless lightning.

Mr. Clemens tightened his hold until she could feel his every contour pressing into her back. She dared not move.

By and by, the terrible ecstasy beyond their window died away, until the only sounds were the hissing of the phonograph needle at the end of the cylinder, their breathing, and the purr of the now sleeping cat.

Mr. Clemens's mustache had brushed against her cheek when he spoke. "Is that you, Lioness, or the cat?"

"Me," she had said.

Now Isabel told Miss Bright, "He loves cats."

Miss Bright shook her head. "Give us something juicy!"

"I'm afraid that's as juicy as it gets. Let's leave the writing to Mr. Clemens, shall we?"

Farther down the porch, another window was slammed shut.

Miss Bright put her hands on her hips. "Well, if you won't write the article, then we will just have to get the maid."

"Ha!" said Colonel Higginson. "Perhaps *she'll* air Mark Twain's laundry." He smiled at Mr. Clemens.

Thunder rumbled in the distance. Mr. Clemens stared off toward the mountains, past the fir trees standing guard.

"Maybe we should go inside," Isabel said, just as the first fat drops began to fall.

• • •

Later, after the visitors left, Mr. Clemens picked at his dinner, a fricasseed meat so delicious that Isabel sent Katy to the kitchen to fetch the cook, Marjorie.

A slight girl with the flinty face so common in the region, Marjorie came in wiping her hands on her gravy-stained apron as Katy stood behind her, her brow thick with disapproval.

Isabel lowered her fork. "This meat is divine, Marjorie. What is it?"

The girl fought back a delighted smile. "Frizzled beef, ma'am."

"Frizzled?"

"You frizzle shaved smoked beef in butter until it curls, then cook it with hot cream and a beaten egg."

"Well, it's delicious."

Rubbing the callus on his index finger, Mr. Clemens glanced up absentmindedly. Perhaps mistaking his remoteness for displeasure, Marjorie bobbed in a curtsy. "Thank you, ma'am." She fled the dining room, brushing past Katy.

Katy remained at the dining room door, watching. Isabel would not let her presence bother her. "Jean seems to be feeling better tonight," she told Mr. Clemens.

He grunted.

"She was up and around when I took some dinner to her room, thank goodness." Isabel took a small bite. "I do fear that she's getting worn out."

He stared blankly.

"I'm placing a call to Dr. Peterson in the morning." She stabbed another bit of meat. "I wonder if we should increase Jean's medicine. Her attacks seem to be on the increase—it makes me very uneasy. She had three on Monday and then one today." She took a breath. "There's something I should tell you about."

Mr. Clemens snorted. "Colonel Higginson thinks *The Atlantic* won't publish 'What Is Man.' "

Isabel put down her fork. "About Jean."

"*The Atlantic* is too cowardly to publish anything with an original idea."

Isabel knew the article well and thought it brilliant, although she did not agree with it. She could see why a mainstream publication like *The Atlantic* might shy away from a story that concluded Man was no better than a machine when it came to making moral choices. According to the tale, Man would always do what he was premade to do; he was no more in control over himself than a hammer. Man would do whatever benefited himself, first and foremost. There was no real thinking about it, no such thing as free will.

"Maybe a more forward-thinking magazine would be a better fit. As for Jean—"

"That's how it has been my whole life: whenever I'm not playing around and delivering a straightforward truth, the target hasn't the strength of mind to receive it."

Isabel glanced over her shoulder. Katy was still there.

"Higginson told me about an Englishwoman." Mr. Clemens wiped his mouth with his napkin. "A Miss Allonby, who wrote a book she ambitiously called *The Fulfillment.* He said she couldn't publish it while she was alive because people couldn't stand the bare-bones Truth of it. So the poor dear recently committed suicide, in order that her book and all its Truth might be given to the world." He threw down his napkin and got up from the table. "She thought that only from the grave could one have freedom of speech, but poor deluded woman, she won't even have it there. Miss Allonby's relatives edited everything out of the book."

"That's terrible."

"That's why I want you to be the editor of my letters."

"Me?"

He paced on the other side of the table. "You're the only one I can trust. Even Livy was hell-bent on tidying me up. She cleansed me until I was fit for mass consumption, but sometimes she took the 'me' right out of me—usually, if she could help it. Clara would be worse. I am as embarrassing to her as breaking wind in church. And Jean . . ." He sighed. "She's got her own battles."

"She does." Before Isabel could say more, he came over and stood behind her.

"So will you do it?"

She twisted around to look at him. "Edit your letters?"

He nodded.

"I'd be honored."

He rested his hands on her shoulders. "Don't let Clara get her hands on them. Don't let her tamper with my autobiography or, God help us, write my biography when I'm gone. She'll have me singing in the choir every Sunday and helping Civil War widows across the street."

"I'll do whatever you want."

He patted her head.

• • •

Late that night, Isabel awakened with a rush. A disturbance in the air hovered over her as she struggled to orient. She was alone in her third-floor bedroom in the New Hampshire house. Mr. Clemens's room was below hers. They had spent the evening talking, sipping his "Carnegie" whiskey; she'd played the piano for him—Beethoven's "Moonlight Sonata." As the music rippled under her fingers, he'd lain back on the sofa, his pipe between his lips. He'd watched her, boring into her soul, as his chest rose and fell to the rhythm of her left hand stroking the bass. She pounded the strident notes of the treble, her heart crying out to him, until she broke off and, trembling, strode upstairs. If he came to her, she would let him in. It was time, now, for them to act. She waited, naked in bed, woozy with drink, listening to the insistent crickets. She shut the window against them and then, in the spinning blackness, fell asleep.

She awakened. The air near her cheek swooshed softly as if pushed with exquisite wings. Samuel? She opened her mouth to call for him—

What if it were Jean come to her for help? Or a staff member—she was in charge of the house. What would they think if she cried out in her bed for Mr. Clemens?

She felt it again: a quiet fluttering. A displacement of air so slight, so delicate, she seemed to imagine it. She held her breath to listen.

Silence.

Slowly, she reached out for her nightstand and carefully felt its smooth surface for her box of matches. Fingertips grazed cardboard; stealthily, she gathered the box to her and struck a match. A flame flared up. Movement in a dark corner caught her eye. Her gasp put out the flame.

"Hello?" she whispered.

No answer.

She struck a second match. Shaking, she held it out like a sword. "Hello!" she said louder.

In the weak glow, a soft brown creature fluttered toward the ceiling in the shadowy corner.

She hiccupped a laugh. A moth! It was just a moth, a *Cecropia* as large as her open hand, evidently trapped inside when she'd shut the window.

Her scalp tingled with relief. "Poor fellow. I'll let you out."

Shaking out the match, she got out of bed. She was crossing the room in the dark when she heard the click of a latch.

The door gently closed.

20.

December 1905
21 Fifth Avenue, New York

CHRISTMAS PURCHASES WERE TO be made, their selection critical enough that the elite shoppers of Simpson Crawford were able to ignore the monster in their midst. Clara Clemens was among the anointed, judiciously examining hats in the perfumed, humming beehive of the most exclusive department store in New York.

Isabel, being without funds, was free to contemplate the beast: a mammoth Santa Claus that swelled up toward the glass dome of the six-story atrium like a genie freshly let from its bottle. Its noggin alone was taller than two grown men stacked head to toe. The behemoth clutched an armful of baby dolls so defiantly to his chest that he appeared to be taking them hostage. It was by far the most enormous Santa that Isabel had ever seen, outstripping all the decorative Right Jolly Old Elves she'd admired as a girl when her mother had taken her shopping at tony stores like this.

"How do I look?" Clara modeled a flat-topped amber velvet picture hat with a glossy brown bow on its brim.

Isabel pulled her gaze from the yuletide ogre. She shifted her hold on Clara's coat, folded over her arm, and then juggled Clara's fur wrap, hat, and muff. "Wonderful."

It was true. Clara shone. She had emerged that fall from a year in the sanitarium like a butterfly from a cocoon, her slightly pudgy girlish softness hardened into a womanly beauty. She had a gravity to her, an attractive confidence that she hadn't had before her hospitalization. Yet as much as Isabel rejoiced in her recovery, the metamorphosed Clara unnerved her. This Butterfly Clara had all the Caterpillar Clara's endearing bad habits, like lowering her head as if to bowl over anyone in her way, or smiling too broadly when complimented, but in her newfound hardness, she was a foreign creature: Clara, yet not, as if goblins had replaced the real Clara with one of their own in the night.

Isabel shimmied back Clara's coat on her arm to pick up a moss-green hat awash with veils. She casually turned it over. Clara watched her, then looked in a mirror and rearranged a lock of auburn hair curling from under her hat. "If you're looking for a price tag, Simpson Crawford doesn't use them. The theory is that if you need to know the price, you can't afford it. I suppose you wouldn't know that unless you shopped here." She raised her dark brows as if in pleasant surprise. "Maybe you do shop here. Now that you're not paying rent, you must have all the money in the world."

Isabel caught her breath. Who was this goblin child? The truth was, Isabel could hardly bear her. She'd noticed Clara's new cruel edge immediately after returning to New York from the summer season in New Hampshire, the first they had seen each other in a year. Even as Isabel was pulling back from a one-sided embrace, Clara announced that Isabel needed to find lodgings elsewhere; her mother's old rule was being enforced.

The bottom had dropped out of Isabel's heart. Didn't Clara know that Isabel had arranged for Clara's medical treatment during her hospitalization, that she had written to Clara nearly every day because her father hadn't the time, that she had found a manager when Clara announced that she wanted to sing professionally? Isabel knew when she wasn't welcome. She promptly gave her notice, but Mr. Clemens convinced her to stay and ruled that she would keep her third-floor room in the house. Give Clara time to adjust, he had said. It would all work out.

A sophisticated clerk floated up on strapped pumps, assessed Isabel's plain clothes, then turned to Clara. "Amber suits you," she said in the rounded voice of an aristocrat. "Do you like a toque? This one is very French." She held out a hat in amber and apricot.

Clara took on a frostily superior tone. "They were wearing toques in Paris when I was there a few years ago. Surely they're not wearing them *still.*"

Isabel contained her eye roll. The clerk had probably just gotten off the boat from Ellis Island. Aristocrats did not work in department stores any more than they worked as secretaries. And as much as Isabel worshipped Mr. Clemens, she knew his backwater pedigree. Neither woman was the royalty they pretended to be.

Her gaze drifted back to the troubling Santa. Now that she thought about it, the titan's wild white hair and mustache were much like Mr. Clemens's, which made her like it better. She smiled to herself, picturing Mr. Clemens bending over the game table in his billiards room last night, his glorious shipwreck of hair shining in the ruby glow of the Tiffany lamp suspended overhead. He had invited her down to the lower-floor room via the famous notes of Beethoven's Fifth Symphony rapped on the radiator, now their code for her to come to him. She could still see him straightening when she entered.

"Listen." He had leaned on his cue stick and cocked his ear toward the basement window, through which the sidewalk could be seen on the other side of their iron fence.

She'd gone over, rubbing her arms against both her anxiety of having just been accused by Clara of moving the furniture in the parlor, and the cold air sliding through the window. She peered outside. The light of a streetlamp revealed the clean gaiters and pressed pant cuffs of a man standing just beyond the fence. He was singing "Danny Boy" in a voice so rich, so full of longing, that it made her heart hurt.

Mr. Clemens strolled over. " 'The pipes, the pipes are ca-all-ling.' " He stopped next to her. "He's been yowling like that for some time."

Isabel sighed. "He sounds like all the misery in the world." She curled her hands, icy from the cold, under her chin. "It's beautiful."

"The man is probably dead drunk, but that doesn't lessen your heartache." He took her hands, then rubbed them. "What's wrong, Lioness? You've been dragging along with your tail between your legs."

Your daughter. She shook her head.

"As soon as I finish my autobiography, I am taking us someplace warm. Like Bermuda. You ever been to Bermuda, or did your old boss take you there, too?"

"I haven't been."

"Then you and me, we're going. Just us."

As conscious as Mr. Clemens was of his image, he'd never risk ruining it by traveling alone with an unmarried woman. Mark Twain the beloved family man would never stoop to such scandal. She searched his eyes. Was this his strange way of proposing marriage?

He broke their gaze to peer out the window. Suddenly, he swept up his arms, making her flinch, then whistled as he stretched his hands high. He dropped his arms only to whoosh them up and whistle again.

"What are you doing?"

"I'm giving the fellow the Chinese applause."

"The what?"

"In San Francisco, the Chinese show their appreciation by imitating a sky rocket. Clapping pales in comparison once you've gotten a good Chinese send-off."

He went closer to the window, then whistled and waved, whistled and waved, until the singer bent down, peered between the iron railings, and, spotting Mr. Clemens, bowed.

Katy burst into the room. "What was that sound?"

"My Chinese applause? Katy the Librarian, you have eagle ears."

She looked between Isabel and him, breathing hard. "I thought you were in trouble," she said petulantly.

After Katy left, nothing more had been said about Bermuda. Isabel had stored it in her heart, waiting for clarification.

• • •

Now Clara said, "Miss Lyon, wait while the clerk boxes them up, will you? Be a dear and give her my account, please."

Isabel found the noble salesclerk and Clara watching her. "Yes, of course."

"I can have the boxes held until you're done shopping," said the clerk, "or perhaps you'd like them sent to your home."

"No, Miss Lyon will wait for them. She loves to help."

Isabel met Clara's cool green gaze. "Go on, do more shopping, I'll catch up. Which department will you be in?"

"Dresses." Clara laughed for the clerk's benefit. "Isn't it obvious?" She swished her dress, a rose-colored silk that made Isabel's black wool look dowdy. "All I have are rags."

Twenty minutes later—according to the clock across from the Christmas leviathan—balancing two hatboxes and the rest of Clara's wraps, Isabel rode the clacking wooden steps of the escalator up to meet Clara. She stood by as Clara tried on gown after gown, keeping the clerk, an older Frenchwoman with a red pincushion on her wrist, busy with buttoning, fastening hooks and eyes, and strategically draping material. How many decades had gone by since Isabel had shopped like this with her mother? She remembered a certain blue velvet gown that showed off her girlish waist. The clerks had gathered to exclaim how beautiful she looked.

"Here, Miss Lyon." Clara plucked a dress from the final selection the clerk had brought out on hangers. She laid it across Isabel's arms. "This is for when I go to church on Christmas Eve. And this is for New Year's Day breakfast. And this is for New Year's Day lunch."

The clerk looked doubtfully at the heap upon Isabel. "Let me have them sent to you, madam."

"No, no. Miss Lyon will carry them. She's indispensable, don't you know?"

Isabel felt sick.

The dresses, once boxed, proved too much for any mortal to carry in combination with the other packages, but Clara was able to make her point by insisting that Isabel at least bring home the hats. Isabel was able to make *her* point by carrying them. Soon they were out on Sixth Avenue, where the roar of the elevated train, the murmur of the teeming crowd, and the shouts of men hawking fir trees and mistletoe intensified Isabel's headache.

She was gritting her teeth against the clanging of a Salvation Army worker at her kettle and the shouts of children running to Christmas display windows when Clara, marching ahead, suddenly stopped. Isabel ran into a nurse pushing a baby carriage.

"Watch it!" the woman exclaimed.

Isabel apologized.

"You are hopeless." Clara laughed. She fished a coin from her coat pocket and dropped it in the red pot.

The caped woman dipped her bonnet in gratitude. "Merry Christmas."

Her charity dispensed, Clara led the way over to Fifth Avenue, much quieter and brighter out of the shadow of the cast-iron El tracks. "I've been thinking about Christmas," she said over her shoulder. "You should take it off, go home to your people."

They stopped at a cross street to let pass a double-decker electric omnibus chock-full of gaping tourists. Isabel's people consisted of her mother, who lived in a room around the corner, and her sister and brother-in-law, who were busy raising their family in Farmington.

"Thank you very much," said Isabel from behind her wall of boxcs. "But I hate to leave Jean. Her seizures are getting so frequent. Is there someone who can keep an eye on her?"

"She's my sister. I don't need you to tell me what to do with her."

The omnibus chugged by as Isabel grasped for words. First hospitalized for a year and now wrapped up in making an American singing debut, Clara had not had to deal with her sister's care. She was unaware of the signs of an oncoming seizure and had no idea what to do even if she could recognize them. She—and everyone else—relied on Isabel to take care of Jean, and as much as Isabel loved Jean, even she was terrified of the seizures. Her fear was not that Jean would hurt her, as Katy claimed she had done, but that Jean would hurt herself. Only Katy had witnessed Jean's seizure-induced violence, painting a horrifying scene in which she'd feared for her life. Jean never attacked anyone else.

"Isabel, is that you?"

Isabel juggled her load to find the speaker. Next to her at the curb, beneath a wide-brimmed mink hat, beamed Betsy Trompert, whose father had been in business with hers.

"It is you!" Betsy tried to hug her but, thwarted by the boxes, could only laugh. She brought forward two young girls buttoned up in rabbit fur and ribbons. "These are my granddaughters, Ellis and Elisabeth. Girls, I'd like you to meet one of my oldest friends, Isabel Lyon—or is that your name still?" She slid forth the sly look she'd perfected as a girl playing with Isabel on the bluffs of Spring Side. "I hear that you are to marry Mark Twain."

Before she could speak, Clara leaned in and produced a hand from her muff. "I'm Clara Clemens, Isabel's employer. Don't make me kill you by calling me Mark Twain's daughter." She laughed as if she were clever.

Betsy drew back. In the awkward pause, she saw the boxes in Isabel's arms. "Simpson Crawford," she said. "Lucky you! They have the nicest things." She took in Isabel's drab clothes. Confusion bridged into pity in a single blink.

The omnibus cleared. Betsy grabbed her granddaughters' hands. "Must be off—I'm taking the girls to see the windows at Siegel-Cooper. Good to see you, Isabel." They hurried across the street and down the sidewalk.

Clara sighed, then shook her pretty head. "Too bad Siegel-Cooper is the other way." Her expression cooled as she and Isabel set off. "You really must stop this hideous talk about Papa and you."

Kindness was not working, nor was diplomacy. "What if we were to marry, Clara? Why would that be so hideous?"

Clara flashed her a look. "Don't make me laugh."

• • •

That evening after dinner, Isabel sat before the towering carved mahogany wall of the Orchestrelle, pumping out Schubert on the player organ as her stomach knotted. How perfectly the tormented strains of the andantino suited the absurdity of the scene. Just across the room, Clara was arguing with her father about Isabel, every word of her protests perfectly audible, as if Isabel were a stray whose owners were arguing over whether to keep it.

"They're saying that you're going to marry her, Papa. That snide smirk on people's faces when I deny it, as if they are sure that I am lying—I cannot bear it."

"I never took you," he said, "as such a tender little shoot."

"I don't know what's worse—you actually marrying your *secretary*, or you keeping her under our roof and *not* marrying her. It's scandalous, Papa. Mamma would never allow it."

"Probably not, but there's a new sheriff in town."

Isabel kept pumping.

"It's not working out to keep her, Papa. She thinks she's the boss! When I fired Marjorie last week, Miss Lyon had the nerve to fight with me to keep her, as if she is in charge of employing our cook!"

"She was in charge of just about everything while you were gone, Clärchen. I needed her to be. She did a good job."

"Well, it can't go on. Having her here humiliates me. I'm the one who is running this house now, and you need to tell her so."

There was a silence. Isabel could feel them looking at her.

Mr. Clemens drew a breath. "I think you just did."

Isabel slid her foot off the pedal. With all the dignity she could muster, she rose and marched stiffly out of the room. She was packing her trunk when a knock came on the door. Mr. Clemens opened it before she gave her permission.

"Can I come in?"

"Clara wouldn't like it."

"I'm not worried about Clara." He ambled over to the bed. "What are all these?"

Folding a shirtwaist, she glanced over at the spread, where the fruits of hours of her labor had been lined up so that she could count them. "Pincushions."

"You collect them?"

"I make them, and my mother sells them to her friends."

"You need the money?"

Her skin prickled: he truly was not aware of her poverty. The man had no idea she couldn't afford a new dress, or hat, or shoes. He could not lift his head from the loving bosom of the world long enough to notice that everyone in his own household was struggling in one way or another.

He picked up a pincushion shaped like a swan. "I was reading up on my hero, Gibbon, while you were gadding around with Clara today. You know how I love his histories."

Gadding around. She laid the shirtwaist in the trunk.

"It seems that as a youth, our Edward Gibbon fell in love with a girl from Geneva. He was set on marrying the girl, but his father said no, the girl was of no consequence. Gibbon, it is said, never got over it. But I guess the girl did pretty good. She married the French comptroller-general, Necker, and produced Madame de Staël, the most revered female writer in France."

She plucked a shirtwaist from the wardrobe. "I'm not sure what you are saying with this story."

He put back the pincushion. "Isabel, please stay. I need you more than you need me."

She faced him straight on. "She made me stand with the servants at your birthday dinner last month. When I got to Delmonico's, they barred my way. Do you know how foolish I felt, all dressed up in my ancient debut gown, being turned away by the maître d' when I tried to enter the dining room?"

"You didn't miss anything. Colonel Harvey padded the place with all his Harper and Brothers friends. It was hardly a party for me—more like a benefit for his books. But you're right, you should have gotten in."

"She purposefully humiliated me out in public today. I won't go into the details, but let's just say that she's given my old friend plenty to gossip about."

He picked up another pincushion, a black silk cat. "Clara's not a happy soul. I don't know why she finds so much pleasure in hurting others. She seems to think that fate is out to destroy her, and it's true that she's accident-prone. Most of her childhood, she nearly died almost every day. When she was a three-year-old, the nurse caught her teetering out on the edge of the balcony of our fifth-story hotel room—that's our Clara. But she takes bad luck stalking her too personally. Bad luck is on everyone's tail; it hasn't singled her out for special treatment."

She roughly folded the shirtwaist. "Clara is only part of the issue."

He put the pincushion on top of the folded waist. She looked up.

"Lioness, don't go."

"Give me a reason why I should not."

She saw the fear in his eyes. He looked away. "Damn it, you know me better than any living person."

"Sometimes I think I don't know you at all."

"Yes, you do. You know me, and yet you still like me."

" 'Like!' "

"That might be more important than loving me."

"Oh, Sam."

He gathered her to him. His neck was warm against her face. "God, I need you."

"If I stay, I need help with Jean. She's getting worse—we have to face the situation. I'm frightened for her."

"Shut up, Lioness," he said into her hair. "Just say you'll stay. For Jean. For me." He kissed her hair. "Especially for me."

She closed her eyes. "Will you take me to Bermuda?"

He pulled back from her. "Is that what you want?"

She wanted his commitment to her. She had given him everything. But she was not going to beg.

She nodded. "Yes."

He kissed her hair. "Book the trip."

PART FOUR

The New York Evening Mail, April 1906

EDITORIAL

Things have reached the point where, if Mark Twain is not at a public meeting or banquet, he is expected to console it with one of his inimitable letters of advice and encouragement. If he deigns to make a public appearance there is a throng at the doors which overtaxes the energy and ability of the police. We must be glad that we have a public commentator like Mark Twain always at hand and his wit and wisdom continually on tap. His sound, breezy Mississippi Valley Americanism is a corrective to all sorts of snobbery.

21.

September 1906
Norfolk Gymnasium, Norfolk, Connecticut

CLARA HAD SAILED THROUGH her concert program. Now here she was, in the finale, singing the Bach/Gounod "Ave Maria," with a grin threatening to shanghai her face. People would say it was nerves, it being her American debut, but it wasn't; it was joy. Pure unmitigated joy. Finally, *finally*, she was up onstage, doing what she was born to do. Hadn't Papa said that she had crawled out of the womb ready to give a show? Even as she quaked now from her vibrato, she almost laughed. She could picture her infant self lighting up slick uterine walls with a candlestick as she squirmed her way out into the world.

Mr. Luckstone frowned over his shoulder as he massaged the piano keys. Oh dear, he could see she was cracking. Focus!

She closed her eyes, concentrating on the force of the music surging through her body and out of her mouth. When she opened them, she saw the tarpaulin-covered shapes of the gymnastic apparatus hulking like tan dinosaurs against the sides of the wood-paneled walls. Someday she would laugh about debuting in a gym. How quaint her beginnings would seem when she was playing Carnegie Hall, the Wigmore, and the Wiener Musikverein in Vienna. From the smallest mustard seed comes a mighty tree! But even here tonight, among the dumbbells and pommel horses, her audience was stellar: reporters from *The New York Times*, influential people from

New York: the Gilders, the Harveys, the Rogers . . . Charles Edwin "Will" Wark.

She touched her throat for drama, just as she had rehearsed at this point in the piece, and cast her gaze upon Will Wark, down in the front row.

Just look at him with his crinkly blue eyes, straight sandy hair, and thick muscular body of a *man.* His chest nearly popped out of his shirt, yet when he smiled, he was a just boy—a Tom Sawyer!—and he was smiling at her now. He'd come all this way to Norfolk, when his concert schedule was full accompanying other singers. She hadn't spent much time with him in New York, always within musical circles, never alone, but there was a spark between them; it wasn't her imagination. Yet she had to get over it. Will Wark was married.

She filled her tremolo with despair. Few knew of Will's marriage—he seemed to keep it secret, for some reason—but Clara had made inquiries. Why were the good ones always taken?

A flash of white caught her eye. Two rows back, Papa's head nodded forward in a nap. She felt her vocal cords constrict.

She paused as the strains from Mr. Luckstone's piano expanded throughout the gym. She had begged Papa not to come. He had said he wouldn't address the crowd, that he'd be quiet, but Papa could no sooner be quiet than could a monkey not hoot. He'd get up and steal the spotlight, and Clara would be forgotten. Her importance in the room would shrink to the level of a footstool.

She jumped back into the music.

Oh, Papa looked innocent, with his chin propped upon his snowy shirtfront. But as sure as she was singing now, he would spring to life the minute the music stopped and, refreshed by the goodwill that she had created, would commandeer the crowd.

Maybe tonight would be different. Maybe Papa actually realized how much this night meant to her. So far he had obeyed her, by not bringing Miss Lyon, and by not sitting in front or wearing his freakish white suit. Why had he taken to wearing that, just when everyone was turning to seasonal black? *Mein Gott*, the man was desperate.

Clara attacked the long crescendo to the finish, with all its pleas to the Virgin Mary.

Santa Maria!

"It's September," Clara had told him last week when she'd met him on their staircase and he was in that damn white suit. "You can't wear that."

Santa Maria!

"I'm calling it my 'dontcareadam suit.' I'll be polite. I'll ask before I come to dinner, 'Madame, do you mind if I wear my dontcareadam?'"

Maria!

"You look like a Southerner."

He laid his hand upon the banister. "You think I look like a Southerner, Clärchen? That might be because I am a Southerner."

"You are not. You live in New York."

Maria!

"Oh, but I am one, Clärchen. My family had the slaves to prove it."

"Yes, but Grandmother let them go."

Pray for us!

"My mother told you that?"

"Yes."

"She shouldn't have."

For we are sinners.

"Why?"

He had started down the stairs. "Because it was a lie."

Clara's crescendo grew until her whole body shook. If only people knew about him. Yet there he slept, looking as guileless as a baby, the most beloved man in the world. God, she hated him.

The music broke off.

When the piano resumed, the tempo was calmer. Clara shut her eyes and let the music comfort her. This was her moment. Hers. Not her father's. Hers.

She caressed the final notes like a mother soothing a child. *Amen. Amen.*

The piano music floated to its finish, and with it, her most tender voice, reduced to a single grain of sweetness.

And then it was done.

She stood there, her every fiber ringing from the music that had passed through her.

Her people jumped to their feet.

• • •

The bouquets of roses rustled in Clara's arms as she took her third bow, the applause reverberating in her ears. Her manager, Louden Charlton, hustled out next to her, the coat of his checked suit flapping. "And who would like to hear a word from Mark Twain?"

The applause intensified as if that were what her audience had been waiting for. Papa waved them off.

She smiled over the rose blooms. She would murder Mr. Charlton in the morning.

"These people have come all this way to see you," he said. "What do you have to say about your daughter's performance?"

Her glare would have killed a lesser man. But Papa got slowly to his feet, then shambled to the stage. "Now that took some bravery. Let me tell you about my first time before an audience. I wrote the book on stage fright—well, that and a few other tomes."

The crowd—Clara's crowd—caressed him with fond chuckles.

Some twenty minutes later, laughter was shaking the very dumbbells on their rack. When people calmed down, Papa rubbed his shirtfront. "I got up here to thank you for helping my daughter, by your kindness, live through her American debut. And I want to thank you for your appreciation of her fine singing"—he lifted his chin in mock pride—"which, by the way, is hereditary."

Clara pushed past her manager, past the shrouded parallel bars, past the rapt pair of women clutching copies of *Huckleberry Finn* near the door. Laughter chased her as she spilled onto the lawn surrounding the cedar-shingled building. The cool night air, the crickets hunkered in the cold grass, even the horses stamping at waiting carriages, seemed to vibrate with love for her father.

No one came for her.

At last she heard the closing of a screen door. "Clara?"

She turned around as Will Wark strode across the grass.

"Clara, what are you doing out here? They're looking for you."

He stopped before her. In the porch light, she could see that his boy's face was crumpled with concern. She could feel the warmth of his solid body.

"He's ruined it for me," she said.

"Who?"

"My father."

When he stepped closer, he seemed so troubled, so innocent and sweet, that her anger dropped away. He looked like a boy who had lost his pet turtle.

"It doesn't matter," she said. "I don't care." And finding that she really didn't, not at this moment, she laughed.

"Well, I do. I care. Are you all right?"

"I am now."

"You were great in there. You're something special." He pushed a lock from her cheek. How did he play the piano with such thick fingers? "Clara Clemens, how'd you get to be so wonderful?"

She kept her face upturned to his. "You are terribly kind."

"I'm not kind, I'm honest. You're wonderful. And beautiful. A fellow doesn't stand a chance against falling in love with you. You must have a hundred beaus."

"Not so many." She felt the solidness of his body in the space between them. She searched his eyes, the evening air cool against her hot face. The laughter coming from the gymnasium melted away as his gaze reached down inside her, grasped her heart, and tugged it back to him. She gasped from the actual physical pain of it.

"What are we doing?" he whispered.

She could feel her light flooding out of her and into him, and his sweet light pouring back. So this was love, this was the ecstasy that she'd missed all those years she'd been locked away with her mother, those years of nearly total isolation that had started as a child. It wasn't getting away from her now.

She seized his face as if to devour it.

22.

January 1907
The Princess Hotel, Bermuda

MR. CLEMENS'S LINEN-CLAD KNEE jiggled against Isabel's thigh as their cart, drawn by a sleepy mouse-colored donkey named Blanche, crunched down the white pulverized limestone road. The muted pounding of the sea below the cliffs could be more felt than heard on this windblown stretch of Warwickshire Parish, where white houses cloaked with scarlet hibiscus bushes studded the rolling green hills. The bend in the road revealed the sea stretching out before them, startlingly turquoise and clear.

Isabel closed her eyes and felt the salt breeze wafting through her veil. There were no dinners at Sherry's to attend, no young actresses to entertain, no curious well-wishers to turn away from the house. Clara, as her father put it, was warbling across Europe. Jean was off getting treatment for her sickness. At last Isabel and Mr. Clemens had gotten away to Bermuda, six months after agreeing to it. But they had not come alone.

As they bounced along in the cart, the sun smiling upon her hat and shoulders, Isabel pushed down the nerves that had been churning her stomach since Mr. Clemens had announced last week, after several cancellations, that he was ready to sail. Would she please rebook a passage for them, he'd asked as her heart rose—and get one for Reverend Joe Twichell. Her heart had plummeted. They were going to Bermuda with Reverend Joe? How could Mr. Clemens have allowed him to horn into their plans? Couldn't Mr. Clemens have said no?

She had endured Clara's abuse, indeed, she had turned her into a friend. She'd sought and secured Jean's place at the best facility for epilectics in the world, hopeful for a cure. Upon his insistence that she be at his side, she'd played his hostess to perfection, performed her secretarial duties to exhaustion, and would have done the same with her wifely duties, too, had he let her. Oh, they had cuddled and fondled, had kissed and tantalizingly stroked, but they had not yet consummated their love, although not by Isabel's choice. She was sure that she made it clear she was willing. Her commitment to him could not be greater had they been married. That he gently sent her out after heating her up made her feel like the worst kind of tramp. Yet he encouraged her affection and put his hands on her whenever he could—when just out of sight of others, and there were always others in the house, Jean, Clara, Katy, his multitude of fans. Isabel did not know how it felt to be with him without knowing that someone could walk in on them at any moment. And now, having finally shed the clinging Reverend, here they were, just the two of them, with Blanche the donkey and the sighing turquoise ocean as their only witnesses.

Mr. Clemens spoke up, the first since Blanche had clopped from the shade of the Princess Hotel portico perhaps a half hour earlier. He had been quiet, too. "I was thinking how much this place reminds me of home."

She sifted through his tone to gauge his mood. They had not discussed where they were going when they set out. He had appeared at her room and told her to get her hat, they were going for a ride. Just you and me. She had tried not to read too much into it, even as her heart raced.

"It reminds you of New York?"

He shook his head. "Missouri," he said, pronouncing it as he always did: *Miz-ur-ruh*. Of all the places he had lived in the world—

San Francisco, Nevada, Connecticut, all over Europe, New York—he still called Hannibal home.

"Hannibal," she said, clarifying. "Because of the water?"

"Not Hannibal. I meant Florida, Missouri, the town where I was born. No water there. It was prairie land, nothing but long grass and loneliness, stretching all the way to the horizon. The sky crushed you with its vastness. A sky like this one."

She gazed up, holding her hat, as he continued.

"I can still remember Jennie raising me up to look at it. I was just a little shaver, three years old, maybe, or four—couldn't be older than that because we moved before I was five. I remember a hawk overhead, one lone brown wheeling hawk, the blue of the sky showing through his fringe of end-feathers. Jennie wanted me to see him, so she held me up, but it made me mad."

"So you've always had a temper," Isabel said with affection.

He smiled. "It didn't sneak up on me as an adult? No. I was angry because that hawk wouldn't come down for me to touch him. If I couldn't touch him, why, I didn't care about him. When I told Jennie that, she said, 'You're going to grow up mad if you think that just because you want something, you're going to get it.' "

"Who is Jennie?"

He glanced at her, then shifted the reins to one hand to feel his pocket for a cigar. "You didn't ask me why Bermuda reminds me of home."

"Because of the sky?"

He shook his head. "You notice that half the faces here are dark? Well, that gives me comfort. I have always felt most at peace when in the company of Negroes." He gave up on his cigar hunt. "Back in Florida, I used to go out to the slave cabins to play with the boys my age. I didn't even know we were different. When I found out, it hurt me to think how they must have felt when they found out they were slaves. What must that have done to their minds?"

"Was Jennie a slave?"

"Ah, Jennie." He sighed, then chirruped on Blanche, who raised her head but not her speed. After a while he said, "I was seven when my mother whipped her. My mother, the same person who would scold me for doing anything as violent as waking up a cat. To see her threaten anyone with a horse whip, especially my Jennie, tore the rug right from under me. And to hear her shout! I'd never heard such terrible words. They singed my soul like a branding iron: *You black whore.*"

He was silent a moment, as if gathering courage.

"Mother snapped the whip," he said quietly, "but Jennie grabbed it. So Mother sent for Father, and Pa came roaring home. My brothers, my sister Pamela, and I watched as he dragged Jennie outside, bound her hands with leather reins, and whipped her with a cowhide. I wanted to kill him. I wanted him dead. And I knew I would do whatever it took to accomplish that goal."

The donkey's hooves crunched on limestone. Isabel found that she was holding her breath.

"When it was over, and Father had stormed away, and Mother was weeping in the house, I crept out back to be next to Jennie. She was lying in the dust, all in a heap. I whispered that I was sorry, real sorry, but that did no good. She did not move. So I lay down next to her and, shyly, crept my hand upon her arm. And as I lay there begging God to help her get up so we could run away together, I saw that the skin of her forearm was paler than the freckles on my hand. How could Mother call Jennie black if she was whiter than me in places?"

He stopped the cart. From the distance came the moan of the turquoise sea, collapsing on the beach. "I've never told anyone that. Not even Livy. Her family was as abolitionist as mine was slaveholding. It would have made her hate my mother. But it wasn't Mother's fault that Jennie got whipped. She didn't cause everything that happened to Jennie." Gripping the reins, he turned and glared at Isabel in defiance. "I did."

She wanted to touch him but was afraid. "How could it be your fault? You were just a little boy."

"I wrote *Huck Finn* and *Pudd'nhead Wilson* and 'A True Story, Repeated Word for Word' and my Congo piece and what-all to make up for it. I'll take the heat for showing man's ugliness and absurdity, for his capacity for casual, bloodcurdling cruelty to all living creatures. I'll sin against half my countrymen, as one hot critic has charged, by turning against the South. But nothing, nothing, eases the guilt of what I did to Jennie."

She searched his anguished face. Whatever it was that he imagined that a seven-year-old boy could have done, Isabel saw that there was no convincing him otherwise.

She took off his hat and, smoothing his hair, looked into his eyes. "I'm so sorry, Samuel." She stroked his cheek. "I'm so very sorry."

He slid his arms around her. "I loved her. I loved her more than anything. I thought I was going to marry her."

They held each other, the surf groaning in their tropical Eden. What had become of his Jennie?

Before she could gather the courage to ask, she heard the crunch of hooves on the coral road.

He sat up, putting back on his straw boater. A cart with a lone Negro jostled by. Mr. Clemens tipped his hat.

"We'd better get back," he told Isabel.

They spoke little on the way back to town, and only then anodyne remarks like how the sand in the southern coves was pink, and how whitewash on the pyramidal roofs of the houses was blinding in the sun, yet each impersonal comment kept a foot in the door cracked open by his admission.

In time they came to the docks of Hamilton. She was gazing up at the white balconies of the wooden buildings along Front Street, bracing herself for their return to the hotel, when Mr. Clemens guided Blanche up Reid Street.

She looked at him questioningly.

"We've got to get you in some better clothes."

She smoothed the skirt of her white linen ensemble, suddenly aware that her blouse was thinning at the elbows from a decade of ironing. It was the best of her two warm-weather dresses.

He stopped before the most expensive clothing store in town. "Do you think an emporium that only deals with the carriage trade will accept customers who came in on a donkey?"

"It didn't work well for Jesus."

He shook his head in admiration. "Lioness, you are a tiger."

Soon he was sitting in a flowered chintz chair with his hat on his knee as Isabel swished before him in a yellow silk dress. "Like it?"

He tapped two fingers on the arm of the chair: *tap-tap-tap-TAP.* Then he sat back and crossed his legs, a sheik admiring his harem. "Back home in Mizurrah, Jennie would have called you the 'Queen o' de Magazines.' "

She knew how privileged she was that he could speak Jennie's name to her.

He sat forward. "From now on, I want to see you in rich, soft, clinging silks. I want to see you in splendid colors. I want people to recognize when your comet goes by, flashing with beauty, and to clap their hands in appreciation."

Her chest filled with elation. "I hardly think this dress will do that."

"Then put on another." He sat back. "I'll wait."

• • •

Isabel was wearing the yellow dress when they entered the Princess Hotel an hour later. The lobby smelled sweetly of lilies. Vases of them covered every marble-topped table within the elegant, cool hall, and yet their strong scent only partially penetrated Isabel's consciousness. Her awareness was centered on the hand Mr. Clemens had placed upon the small of her back as he guided her toward the brass doors of the elevator.

They gazed at each other, mindless of the white-jacketed boy polishing the mirrors that hung from every wall. A red spot glowed high up on each of Mr. Clemens's cheeks; his eyes shone like quicksilver. He pushed on the button again, breathing hard. His excitement made Isabel's heart beat even faster. This was it.

He was going to let her in. They were going to pledge their bodies to their union.

The brass doors parted. Out walked Reverend Joe Twichell in a boater and white flannels, still tall and handsome in his old age, a grin lighting a face that seemed all the more kindly with his downward-slanting mustache and eyes. "There you are. I've been looking for you. I've hired a carriage to take us out to Devil's Hole."

"We've been out," growled Mr. Clemens.

Reverend Joe looked between them, his smile dimming as he noticed their tension. "The carriage is waiting."

"Well, I need a nap."

"Miss Lyon, too?"

Mr. Clemens glared at him from beneath belligerent brows. "I don't know what she wants."

But he did know what she wanted. She wanted him, with every scrap of her being. She would throw propriety out the window, along with her reputation, because he meant that much to her.

Reverend Twichell covered his awkwardness with a laugh. "We've come all the way to heaven, and you're considering a nap? Don't tell me that this is the same Mark who walked with me the hundred miles between Hartford and Boston."

"You seem to forget," Mr. Clemens growled, "that we only made twenty-eight miles of it. And that about killed us."

"Who noticed? The papers surely didn't care. Mark Twain was taking a walk. You could spill your tea and the papers would be full of it. The world can't get enough of their beloved Mark Twain." He gave his friend a pointed look. "They are watching your every step."

A footman in the livery of the hotel approached them. "Your carriage is waiting, sir."

It crushed Isabel that Mr. Clemens seemed almost relieved as they strolled out to the portico, where a drooping horse patiently awaited.

• • •

Less than an hour later, she found herself peering into a clear emerald pool flashing with colorful fish, Reverend Joe at her elbow. Every carriage on the island seemed to be parked on the bright white road behind her. Beyond the jam of carriages, in the shade of a large cedar tree by an inn, a flock of ladies in picture hats and gentlemen in boaters crowded around Mr. Clemens. *Let him entertain them*, thought Isabel, turning away. She would not protect him. He could have insisted on claiming her as his woman, and he didn't.

"See anything?" asked Reverend Twichell.

At the bottom of the clear depths of the pool, perhaps twenty feet down, skulked a gray fish the size of an ice wagon. Wafting side fins comically small for its bulk, it sat with its lower lip thrust up, all too human in its petulance.

"It's a grouper," he said when she didn't answer.

She felt as peevish as the gray monster looked.

The aw-shucks slant of his eyes enforced Reverend Joe's disarming smile. "I think what you're doing for Mark is a great thing."

She kept her gaze upon the fish. "And what is that?"

"Taking care of him. God knows our Mark can't take care of himself."

She did not want to have this conversation. "There seem to be little blue fish nipping the gills of that big fish."

He peered down into the pool. "They're cleaning him." He drew in a breath. "Miss Lyon, as Mark's best friend, I must speak up: I'm afraid that you're making him lazy."

"Lazy!"

"Livy tried to reform him, and for her, he worked at being a gentleman. But lately, I see him falling back into his wild ways. He's drinking more, he's swearing more, he's as confrontational and rude in his writing and in his manners as when I first met him. He's become a complete boor."

Isabel watched the fish. At a speech in New York several weeks back, Mr. Clemens had stopped mid-lecture to berate a woman in the audience whose only offense was that she was knitting. He scolded her until, glowing with shame, she had stuffed her needles and wool into her bag. Isabel had radiated with her own shame for him, then chalked it up to his exhaustion, as she attributed most of his uncivil acts. It was tiring being the most famous man in the world.

"I knew him before his marriage," said Reverend Joe. "In fact, I married Mark and Livy. The Mark Twain of the 1870s was not fit for polite company. Livy had her work cut out for her."

"His name is Samuel."

He smiled gently. "You're right. Samuel. Don't get me wrong, Mark—Samuel—even when wild, is a genius. But left to his own devices, he's his own worst enemy. He's rude and bad-tempered, the most mercurial man I've ever met. His friends know to take the good with the bad, but his public doesn't."

"Mr. Clemens is over seventy. He has earned the freedom to behave however he likes."

Reverend Joe half gasped, half laughed. "Are you joking? He'll be hated. People will turn against him in droves. And more than anyone I've ever met, Mark—Sam—whatever you want to call him—needs to be loved. Miss Lyon, you have to save him from himself."

"I don't understand," she said, understanding completely.

"Mark needed Livy. She edited everything he wrote." He paused as the knowledge bounced between them that Isabel currently served in that role. "She kept him from indulging in his appetites—as you know, he's pretty wild in his extremes." Again he paused, underscoring the understanding that if anyone knew of Samuel Clemens's mania, it was Isabel. "His girls are terrified of him, even his dear Susy was, but Livy wasn't. You wouldn't think that such a little mite of a woman, so sickly, could stand up to him, but she did, and he adored her for it. Livy was his great guiding star."

"Livy is dead," she said with a vehemence that shocked even her. She backpedaled quickly. "I will not go against his wishes. It's my great pleasure to make him as comfortable as possible so that he may write. Look at all he has produced this past year and a half—an output unmatched since he was young. Do you think he could have done this unprotected? No. He must not be harassed, must not have unnecessary matters brought to him that he might fret over. He must be saved from all anxiety." She thought of their earlier conversation. "He's had enough of it in his life."

He looked at her long and hard. "Marriage to a man like Sam must seem appealing, Miss Lyon. He is worshipped around the world. You'd be worshipped, too. Livy was."

"That's not why I'm here, Reverend Twichell. I don't want attention. It's insulting that you might think so."

"Mark will eat you alive."

"Please don't call him Mark. If you only knew how it tired him."

"No, Miss Lyon, in this case, I do mean Mark. Mark is the one who's going to hurt you. Mark will do anything to further himself—Mark would step on his own mother if he thought it would benefit him. Mark will never let Sam marry you. Mark's got a certain image to uphold, an image he painstakingly crafted over the years, the image of a devil-may-care rascal who was tamed only by the love of his life, his brilliant wife, Livy, and his adoring daughters. Marrying you would ruin that story, Miss Lyon, the story everyone loves, and Mark won't let you."

"I can't believe that you are speaking so hatefully about your friend."

Reverend Joe looked over to where Mr. Clemens was entertaining the crowd. "Come to think of it, Mark isn't really my friend. He's no one's friend. There has never been a more self-serving creature. The man I'm trying to protect is Sam."

Isabel took her gaze from the small blue fish nipping at the sedate gray monster. "And I am as well. He won't tell you this—he won't tell anyone this—but he gets vertigo when he's feeling stressed. He almost fell last week when he got up to light the gas. I only know because I came in and found him sitting in a chair, looking gray. The pressure is killing him. Who's going to take care of him if I don't?"

"His daughters."

"Ha! Clara won't and Jean can't; Jean has life-threatening struggles of her own. He has no one, unless you want to count his maid Katy."

He took off his hat, wiped his high forehead with his handkerchief, then put his hat back on. "The fact is, Miss Lyon, you can't keep living under his roof with him. People are talking."

"I don't care."

"Don't you see? He does. Who do you think asked me to come on this trip? He's got his image to uphold. Only he's too scared to tell you."

"Scared?"

"Scared that you'll leave him. You've made him completely dependent upon you."

"I've made him? I only give him what he wants."

"And that's the problem, isn't it?"

Over from beneath the big cedar, Mr. Clemens caught Isabel's gaze. He beckoned to her from the center of his crowd. She shook her head, close to tears.

"We'd better go," said Reverend Twichell.

With a last glance at the grouper and his sycophant down in their turquoise hole, Isabel held up her chin and put on a smile.

Mr. Clemens was addressing the group. "So in closing, friends, remember that life is short. Break the rules. Forgive quickly, kiss SLOWLY. Love truly, laugh uncontrollably. And never, ever regret ANYTHING that makes you smile." The laughter of the crowd mixed with the balmy breeze.

When Isabel neared Mr. Clemens, he spread out his arm to her. "Here she is. My secretary. I have brought her here with me because she knows everything, and I find that I don't know anything. Every man needs a smart little secretary to keep him straight. Miss Lyon, take a bow."

23.

Later that January 1907
21 Fifth Avenue, New York

MR. CLEMENS'S DRAWL FLOWED as slowly as cold honey. "Who's in for another game of hearts?" He watched Isabel pour him another glass of Carnegie's whiskey, then signaled for her to pour one for their guest, Ralph Ashcroft, Mr. Clemens's new business manager. It had to be well past midnight. Isabel could feel the otherworldly stillness of the city outside parlor windows sealed against the piling snow. Oftentimes at this late hour, as she waited for Mr. Clemens to finish his endless billiards or played him at games of cards, she had the lonely sensation of their being the last living creatures on a planet that had died. But tonight, a week after their return from Bermuda, the ticking clock held no terrors. She attributed it to Mr. Ashcroft's jolly presence, or Mr. Carnegie's liquor.

"What is this now?" Ralph asked around his pipe stem. "Our one-hundred-twenty-second hand, or one-hundred-twenty-third? A person has not experienced cards until he has played with Samuel Clemens." His Liverpudlian accent, usually locked away when he was sober, had been liberated by drink, converting those lines into something like "A pearson has nought ex-pear-ienced cards until he has played with Samuel Claymons."

"We aren't done," growled Mr. Clemens, "until you bow to my superiority."

"Never." Ralph cocked a dark eyebrow. "Deal them, Miss Lyon, now there's a good girl."

Isabel scooped up the cards—a bit sloppily, she suspected. Carnegie's whiskey was hitting hard. She liked Ralph Ashcroft. Young, goateed, witty, as dark-haired as Mr. Clemens was light, he was the man who had conceived of the idea of turning Mark Twain into a company, forcing cigar merchants, toy manufacturers, playing-card makers, and the like, to pay Mr. Clemens for the use of his name. The rights to Mark Twain's image now flashing by on the cards she was shuffling had brought in enough money to invest in more Plasmon stock, making him the majority owner of the nutritional powder in America, and for three more white cashmere suits in which to do his investing, a fact that made Mr. Clemens more than a little gleeful. Indeed, Ralph Ashcroft was his newest obsession.

Isabel wondered how long it would last. In her years with Mr. Clemens, she had seen him pick up a new friend, charm him incessantly and dominate his life until, worn out from days on end of ten-hour billiard matches or twelve-hour card games, the boon pal slunk home, every ounce of platonic love wrung from him. Mr. Clemens would turn to fresh blood until his abandoned pal begged for his company and it started up again—or didn't start up, to the anguish and confusion of the formerly beloved. She'd seen Mr. Clemens use up the likes of Henry Rogers, William Dean Howells, Reverend Twichell, his priggish biographer Albert Paine, and several editors in this way, although they were the lucky ones who continued to enjoy renewed vogue when The King was good and ready for them. She'd heard of others not so lucky, like Bret Harte and Mr. Clemens's nephew Samuel Webster. Although she'd not seen it, she'd heard from Clara that no one could do as thorough a job of exorcising someone from his life as Samuel Clemens. Isabel hoped she'd never see it.

Mr. Ashcroft caught her looking at him. Smiling, he puffed on his pipe.

"No fair," she said, her brain furred from the whiskey. "I want to smoke a pipe."

"Do you now?" he said.

She grinned at the stupidity of her request. She hated smoke. She hated pipes.

Ralph took his pipe from his mouth, wiped the stem on his vest, and held it out. "Try it."

"No," growled Mr. Clemens.

"Why not?"

"Because she's a lady."

Be it from the drink or stubbornness or watching Mr. Clemens entertain college presidents, writers, and little girls in Bermuda for the remainder of their time there—anything but to be alone with her—Isabel told Ralph, "Here."

Elbows on the table, Ralph leaned toward her. "Put out your hand."

She did so. He placed the smooth wooden bowl in her palm. "Put it to your mouth."

When she obeyed, the stem was warm where his mouth had been. She closed her lips around it.

Ralph struck a match and cupped his hand under hers. Not taking his sights from her, he held the flame over the bowl. "Now suck it."

Mr. Clemens grasped the arms of his chair. "Wait a minute."

Isabel rolled her gaze up to him.

"You don't want a damn *used* pipe," he said slowly. He pushed himself up, ambled over to his bookshelf, and fetched a polished box. He dropped it on the table with a bang.

Isabel jumped.

"For you."

Ralph sat back as Isabel lifted the lid. Inside was a yellow-bowled meerschaum.

"I was waiting to give this to you at the right time."

Isabel was too dull with drink to question the truth of that. She threw her arms around him. He was slow to release her.

"Pack it, Ashcroft."

Isabel thought momentarily that he meant for Ralph to leave, until the younger man reached for the pouch of tobacco. Ralph loaded the bowl with tobacco and lit it.

"Draw in," Mr. Clemens growled, "but for Christ's sake, don't inhale it."

Isabel was puffing and laughing while resolutely not inhaling when Katy came in, wrapped in a pink robe.

Mr. Clemens sat back. "If it isn't Katherine the Librarian. You should have seen the job she did in arranging my books," he said to Mr. Ashcroft. "What the hell are you doing up?"

"I heard a bang, sir. I feared that an intruder had—" She broke off, her gaze on Isabel with the pipe in her mouth.

"Don't tell me that you want a pipe, too," said Mr. Clemens.

"Absolutely not, sir."

"Don't be jealous, Katy."

Katy sniffed. "I'm not. You gave me a much better gift, back in my day. A music box is much nicer than a pipe. No one is going to take that back from her."

When he stared at her, she said, "I don't deny Miss Lyon her pleasure. If a pipe makes her feel better, let her smoke. She's missed out on a lot in life."

Ralph burst out laughing.

"Good night, Katy," said Isabel, a little nauseous.

Mr. Clemens, puffing his own pipe, waved her out.

Katy stared at Isabel. "If I were you, I wouldn't laugh. You're lucky Mrs. Clemens isn't around."

"Oh," Isabel said lightly, "I know."

Katy smiled grimly, then, pulling her robe tighter, left.

"What was that about?" asked Ralph.

Isabel rose, too woozy to think. "We need some music."

"No," said Mr. Clemens. "Come here."

Ralph struggled to his feet. "I can do it."

"Play the Orchestrelle?" Isabel went to Mr. Clemens, who slung an arm around her waist. "Do you know how?"

"Nope." Ralph went over and sat down heavily on the bench. "Don't need to. The keys can work like a regular piano, yes?" He proceeded to play and sing. " 'Comin' through the rye, comin' through the rye—' "

"Sounds Scottish," Mr. Clemens called to him. He massaged Isabel's back. "I thought you were a limey."

"We limeys know the songs of all the countries we dominate."

"You haven't even dominated a puppy, Ashcroft."

"Nope." He sang louder, his gaze on Isabel.

Mr. Clemens grasped her tighter. She pulled from him, causing a surge of dizziness, and then broke the rest of the way free. Laughing, she waved her hand and foot in a Highland fling.

"Damn it, Lioness," said Mr. Clemens, "you're Scottish, too?"

Ralph picked up the tempo, whistling at Isabel as she danced.

"Nope!" She laughed and danced, head thrown back, and then jigged over to Mr. Clemens, glowering at the table. She pulled him from his seat, knocking the cards from his hands. Dozens of his images tumbled to the floor as she waved her hand in the fling. "My lord, will you dance with your humble subject?"

He grabbed her hand. She stopped dancing.

She was not afraid of him. "You are my King, you know. I'm going to call you that."

"Go ahead."

"Hail—to my King."

They stood face-to-face, Ashcroft's jaunty music ringing around them. Her gaze roamed his hard face, his tousled hair, his shining, intelligent eyes. She wanted to swim right into them.

The music stopped. Ralph stood up. "This is where I leave."

She was hardly aware of Ralph closing the door.

Tenderly, The King brushed a lock from her brow, then reeled her in until their bodies met. His heat, his solidness, made her cry out softly. He groaned when he kissed her.

He pulled back.

She pursued him greedily.

He took her hands from his face. "No."

"Why? Sam, I love you. I can hardly bear how much I love you."

"I can't."

"Why?"

"God, I wish I'd known you when I was young."

A loud thump shook the ceiling. "Ralph," she said absently. "He must have fallen."

"It wouldn't be much of a marriage."

"Marriage," she breathed.

"But if that's what you want."

"I didn't say that's what I wanted."

"Isn't that what all women want?"

"I just want you. And I want you to want me."

He kissed her deeply, then he took her hand. Through his scattered images staring up from the floor, he led her to the sofa.

"Well," he growled, "I do." He pulled her onto him.

24.

April 1907
21 Fifth Avenue, New York

ISABEL'S MOTHER LOOKED OUT the window of Mr. Clemens's parlor, took a drink of lemonade, repositioned the dress draped over her lap, then reattacked with her needle. Whoever thought that the former Georgiana Van Kleek would become such a little seamstress? Well, she enjoyed it. Producing the tiniest, most even stitches, shaping flat cloth into form, enhancing what needed to be enhanced on a woman's body while hiding what needed to be hidden—why, it was an art. Who knew that creating something could be so satisfying for the soul? The irony was when she had come upon her maid Poppy stitching away in her little attic room in Spring Side the evening she had dismissed her, she had actually looked down on her for sewing. Young, beautiful, dripping with five pounds of Van Kleek pearls and wedged within the vast bustled yardage of her brocade gown, she had dragged her peacock's tail upstairs to tell Poppy that she was discharged, and seeing the woman bent over her work, she'd felt an angry rush of superiority. *You, poking away with your little needle, dare to steal my husband from me, one of the Hartford Van Kleeks?* And to think now that the nimble-fingered woman might not have envied her as much as she had imagined.

Well, it didn't bear thinking about. Mrs. Lyon had a crisis on her hands. Her daughter was on the verge of netting a world-famous figure. There was no time to be crying over the past when Mrs. Lyon could be knitting the seine with which her daughter could catch him.

Take Mrs. Lyon's word for it: something wonderful was happening between them. Who would have thought it when Isabel had come back from Bermuda? In truth, one look at Isabel's glum face upon her return from the Happy Island, and Mrs. Lyon had flown into panic. Thirty-six more pincushions she had whipped up that evening, her hedge against imminent ruin.

And Mrs. Lyon had such high hopes for that trip! How her spirits were dashed when Isabel came home empty-handed, save for a gaudy yellow dress. Mrs. Lyon had promptly canceled her trip to Tarrytown. Why subject herself to the Garden Club when there was no good news to share?

But one never knew when one's luck would turn. Only one week later, Isabel was cheery and gay and asking Mrs. Lyon to help her sew a new wardrobe—Mr. Clemens wanted to see her in colored silks—and Mr. Clemens, for his part, couldn't keep his eyes off the girl.

If new clothes were what it took to snare the beast, then Mrs. Lyon would make them. She'd do anything short of ransoming a Vanderbilt if it would do the trick. Heaven knew that Isabel hadn't the time to put her hand to needle and thread, what with managing Mr. Clemens's affairs. Goodness, he was busy! Celebrities traipsed through his house as if it were Central Park. The man spoke at more dinners than Mr. Tiffany had lamps. He had even been invited to go to England this summer for a degree to be conferred on him by Oxford University, the English equivalent of Columbia. Let the Tarrytown crowd look down their noses all they wanted: *her* future son-in-law had been invited to take tea with the English king.

The front door opened. Mrs. Lyon could heard her daughter's and Mr. Clemens's voices in the hall. Isabel sounded happy, like she used to as a child. Mrs. Lyon's heart swelled at the memory. How sweet it had been to have little children in the house.

They were coming in her direction. "You really must stop leading Miss Johnson on," Isabel was saying. "She thinks she has a chance with you."

"You know better." It was Him.

Their footsteps stopped. Mrs. Lyon thought she heard kissing. She picked up her lemonade glass and put it down loudly. She thought she heard her daughter giggle. They resumed walking her way.

Mrs. Lyon scrambled to sink her needle into the cloth. She was pulling it through just as Isabel led Mr. Clemens into the parlor by the hand. "Mother, you're still working."

Mrs. Lyon nodded sedately at Mr. Clemens before turning to her daughter. "I finished a dress for you, dear. Go upstairs to your bedroom and see."

Mr. Clemens dropped down on the sofa. "Go on, Lioness. Try it on. Give me a show."

Mrs. Lyon raised her brows to let him know that she disapproved of vulgarity. But wait until he saw the dress. Mrs. Lyon had given it a particularly low décolleté. Isabel still had a good bust, and a woman should use every arrow in her quiver when hunting a man. "Yes. See how it fits."

Mr. Clemens sat back, then swung one leg over the other. "You can do the can-can for me in it. I ever tell you about the time I saw the can-can dancers in Paris?"

Isabel went over to him. "Me and everyone else who read *Innocents Abroad*. I got your dirty message that the dancers were naked underneath."

"So you're saying you'll dance the can-can for me?"

She tapped him on the cheek. "You are terrible!"

Mrs. Lyon didn't know how much more of this she could encourage. This was no Wild West saloon. "Go try on your dress."

When Isabel was gone, Mr. Clemens picked up the crystal paperweight given to him by the archduke of Austria and tossed it from hand to hand. "So, Mrs. Lyon, are you going with Isabel and Clara when I'm in England?"

"On their trip to Nova Scotia? No." She plunged the needle into the material with a satisfying pop. "I must leave them to get to know each other better, if they are to someday be . . ." She could not say related. She must not be too pushy, not before he had popped the question. Men had to think that everything was their own idea.

"I don't know, Isabel might need you there. Those two in a ship room might kill each other after a while. Clara can be a pistol."

"Isabel loves your daughter."

"I do, too, no matter what I say."

She tugged the thread taut. "You should tell her so."

"Clara? Do you tell Isabel?"

"Well, no. But she knows. We are as close as a hand in a glove."

"Huh. Clara and I get along like the same poles of a magnet, but she knows."

Mrs. Lyon looked at him over her glasses but said nothing.

He got out a pipe and packed it with tobacco. "Whoever thought I might be beating my grown daughters to the altar."

Mrs. Lyon's heart sang. But she must not act too eager. "You have to help them along. Encourage them to find nice men."

"It's repugnant to me. I think of them as little girls."

"Children do grow up, Mr. Clemens. They become people whom you must get to know fresh, as if meeting a new friend." She dipped her needle into the hem. "They are not the children you once knew. You have to relearn them."

He lit the bowl, sucking on the stem until the tobacco glowed orange. He waved out his match. "Yet doesn't that child stay forever hidden in the adult, animating the grown-up self with levers and tricks from behind the curtain?"

Mrs. Lyon was looking over her glasses at him, her needle stilled, when Isabel came out in a frosty pink silk that was dotted with black.

Mr. Clemens lounged against his pillows like a potentate, smoking his meerschaum and blowing gauzy rings. Isabel had taken to calling him her King, ridiculously enough, and at the moment he looked every inch of one.

"Do you like it?" Isabel swished this way and that, more like an ingenue than a forty-three-year-old woman. Something tugged at Mrs. Lyon's heart. She remembered when, early in their marriage, Charles had given her a new dress from a visit to the city. How she'd wanted to show it off for him when she'd opened the box and seen it. But flustered from the warmth that had come creeping up within her when she thought of him touching her, she had clamped down the lid. The disappointment on his face had flustered her even more, and before she could think of how to fix it, he walked away. Now a wave of regret washed over her so powerfully that she could hardly pull the thread through the cloth.

Mr. Clemens took his pipe from his teeth. "Now, that's what I call a dress," he growled. "You look like a succulent slice of watermelon. Come over here so I can eat you."

Isabel went to him, shy as a schoolgirl.

He pulled her to him, then, adoring her with his gaze, reached up to touch her face.

Mrs. Lyon rushed out to get some air. Children might even come from this, if only those two would hurry. She smiled at a pair of ladies strolling by, not noticing their too-short skirts and rouged lips. Visions of triumphant carriage rides with her daughter, her famous son-in-law, and their beribboned children were dancing in her head.

25.

July 1907
The *Rosalind*, Halifax, Nova Scotia

CLARA LEANED CLOSER TO the mirror to examine her face. "How cold is it outside?"

Isabel sat on the tufted satin bedspread, her knees almost brushing Clara's skirt as the other woman primped. Clara had insisted upon taking the most expensive room on the *Rosalind*, but the stateroom, although elegant with its glossy white walls and white panels edged with gold, was cramped, little more than a narrow galley along which the furniture was lined. Isabel thought it nice. A steamboat that ran between New York and Newfoundland could not be expected to be a luxury liner, like the one that Mr. Clemens and Ralph Ashcroft had just taken to London for Mr. Clemens to collect his honorary degree from Oxford. Clara, on the other hand, had greater expectations. Her room, the best on the boat, was too small, too musty, too noisy, too ugly. Already the steward ducked his head and wheeled in the other direction when he saw her coming, and they were only now sailing into Halifax, three days out from New York.

"I suppose it's in the low fifties, possibly cooler." Isabel ran her hand across the buttery satin spread. "The fog's as thick as pea soup. It put a chill in my bones when I was on deck."

Isabel had spent much of the first days of their two-week holiday wandering the ship while Clara stewed in the unsatisfactory cabin.

She had thought that the voyage would take her mind off her King while he was gone, but so far, it'd had the opposite effect. Without her heavy workload to occupy her, she had nothing to do but remember the amusing things he'd said to her, the brilliant things and the intimate, which would lead to her rehashing their most private moments and how she could have made them better. Was it her fault? Was there something more she could have done to please him? No amount of reassuring him that she loved him seemed to soothe him after his failures in lovemaking. Her understanding of his limitations only infuriated him. If only this trip to England, with all the adulation and pomp and press that went with it, could restore his animal confidence. His pride so desperately needed it.

At the cramped vanity table, Clara pinched color into her cheeks as she examined her eyes in the mirror. "Well, we asked for the cold, didn't we? It's better than staying home and melting in New York."

"July in the city is unbearable," Isabel agreed.

"What are you wearing when we go on shore?" Clara patted her hair.

"This." Isabel plucked at the woolen cape topping her simple shirtwaist, an outfit in which she was perspiring from having waited for Clara so long. Like a bride collecting her trousseau, Isabel was saving the new clothes that her mother had made until she was reunited with Mr. Clemens. She expected that they would be married when he returned, not that she cared two pins about what people thought of her. Having been shunned by her class for losing her family money, she couldn't be hurt any more than she already was. Nearly five years ago, when the woman from Bleecker Street had first learned that Isabel was working for Mark Twain's family, she had sent letters to Isabel, threatening to expose her affair with Isabel's father—from which a daughter had come—if Isabel didn't give her money. Isabel had laughed. In her circles, she was already an outcast; you couldn't ostracize someone already beyond the pale. But because this woman, "Poppy," was ill and could not provide for the child, Isabel regularly gave her money, Isabel's only stipulation being that Mrs.

Lyon wasn't told. Although Isabel had accepted her fall in status, her mother hadn't.

Even more than her mother, it was the Wild Humorist of the Pacific Slope who cared about appearances. He, the man who publicly took issue with the policies of the Belgian king, who wore white suits in the dead of winter, who, according to yesterday's paper, had walked across the street from his London hotel in his bathrobe, had been afraid of how it would look for her to accompany him to England before they were married.

Clara peered at her in the mirror. "How do you like my dress?"

Isabel glanced at the loud purple low-necked number. "Very nice."

Clara met her gaze in the mirror. "Will bought it for me."

"It's beautiful."

They watched each other's reflections. Will Wark had started accompanying Clara on piano soon after her American debut, and with his assistance at the keyboard, Clara's singing had bloomed, a forward move for her career. Accompanists did not often buy their soloists expensive dresses, however. Nor did the mere mention of their names make their soloists break into grins.

"All right, all right," said Clara, laughing, "it's true. We're in love."

"Clara, that's wonderful."

Clara threw herself into Isabel's arms. "I'm so happy!"

"I'm so happy for you."

Clara pulled back. "Do you know that I've never been in love before? I'm thirty-five years old and have never been truly in love." She blinked as if she realized that she was talking to a forty-three-year-old spinster, then, overwhelmed with her own joy, recovered from her momentary spate of sympathy. "It feels so wonderful."

Isabel was considering telling Clara that she understood and was experiencing her own kind of wonderful, when a knock came on the door. Clara looked at Isabel expectantly, their servant-employer relationship slipping into place.

The steward drew back warily when Isabel opened the door, then relaxed when he saw it wasn't Clara. He held out a slip of paper in his white-gloved hand. "Telegram for Miss Clemens."

Isabel gave it to Clara, then took money from her own purse to tip him—one less postcard for her mother.

Clara's mouth was hanging ajar when Isabel turned to her.

Isabel felt a stab of fear: Sam. "Is something wrong?"

"It's from Will." Clara didn't look up.

Isabel suppressed a sigh of relief. It wasn't Sam. "Is everything all right?"

Clara stared at the slip of paper, her freckles darkening.

"Clara?"

"Just go, would you?"

Isabel let herself out, too accustomed to Clara's rudeness to let it rattle her. The metal stairs rang out as she descended the flights to her cabin, third-class accommodations that shook from the roar of the nearby boiler room. Inside her room, she took off her cape and dropped down on the edge of her bed, her knees nearly brushing the white-painted metal of the opposite wall. She swung around to stretch out for a rest.

She had hardly settled when a hard jolt rocked her bed.

She sprang up. Aftershocks rumbled through her feet. Through the thin metal door, she heard the shouts of crewmen. If they'd had a collision, her deck would fill first. She glanced around, imagined her plain bed, her tiny desk, her opened leather case, floating. The clang of the alarm bell stung her into motion. She flung on her cape and dashed out into the hall.

Passengers were pouring from their cabins. Deafened by the clanging alarm, she helped a mother stuff her five children into life jackets and buckled them up. Leading them down the hall, she passed an open room in which stood a stooped elderly woman, her shaking hands folded at her chin.

She sent off the children with their mother.

"Let's go, dear." She collected the quaking woman, and murmuring reassurances drew her into the hall. Slowly, they mounted the stairs to the main deck, passengers hurrying past, until Isabel could deliver her to a crewman who was blowing his whistle, directing passengers.

Clara was huddled against the wall of her room when Isabel reached her. "Clara! What are you doing? You've got to go."

"I'm cursed." Clara put her head to her knees. Out in the hall, shouts rose over the clanging of the bell and the thundering of footsteps on the metal floor.

"Get up. Please. We've got to get to the lifeboats."

"Accidents follow me everywhere." Clara turned her cheek to her knee. "When I was a baby, Papa had one of his rages and kicked a rocking chair across the room. I went flying, just missing the stone hearth by an inch. He almost killed me. I wish he had."

Isabel snatched Clara's fur from her wardrobe, yanked Clara up, and shoved her arm into a sleeve.

Clara looked up at her, limp as a rag doll. "I should have known that I would die before I could be happy."

"You're not going to die, Clara. Please, help me here!"

"She won't give him a divorce."

Isabel stopped fastening the hooks and eyes of Clara's coat front. "Divorce? Who?"

"He doesn't love her. He's never loved her. He only married her because he had to—she trapped him with those twins."

"Who?"

"Will."

"Will? Will Wark? He's married?"

Clara's face contorted into a sob.

Isabel hustled her out onto the deck, where men, women, and children buckled into linen cocoons waited below boats being lowered by ropes and creaking pulleys. Moisture from the cloud through which they were drifting beaded upon the white-painted bulkhead, upon the life buoys clutched by the passengers, upon the railings over which Isabel peered. Lifeboats from the other ship began to appear through the fog.

"All safe!" a crewman bellowed through a megaphone. "Passengers, please return to your cabins!"

In the chaos that ensued as the shivering survivors from the other boat were being hauled on board while the *Rosalind*'s passengers were being urged to retreat, Clara grabbed a crewman rushing by with blankets. "Where's the captain? I demand to see the captain. Do you know who I am?"

The sweating crewman, whose face was as plain as a potato beneath the flat-topped sailor hat that had been knocked to the back of his head, squinted at Clara. He then glanced at Isabel, as if to reckon her ability to manage this madwoman.

"Tell him who I am!" Clara commanded Isabel.

"She's Clara Clemens."

"Yes, ma'am!" He started to push past.

"Mark Twain's daughter," said Clara. The sailor stopped. From within her bulky fur coat, she added icily, "I'd like to speak with the captain, please."

After a word with the harried captain and an apology—not Clara's—and the ship had docked and the passengers had flooded down the gangway with cries of relief, an exhausted Isabel found herself in an inn on the main thoroughfare of Halifax, drinking tea with Clara. Although it was July, a fire crackled in the fireplace, most welcome. Clara huddled next to it as if she'd fallen into the harbor like one of the unlucky passengers of the other ship, instead of harassing the crew of the *Rosalind* from within the depths of her raccoon coat.

Sunken within her furry collar, Clara didn't bother to look up from the telegram that she was composing. "When did the man at the ticket office say we would be arriving in Boston?"

"Tomorrow night." Isabel gazed outside the plate-glass window by their table. Across the street, a gigantic pair of eyes wearing golden spectacles hung from the three-story brick building, advertising the services of the optometrist in residence. The eyes seemed bemused, as if they recognized the humor in human frailties.

"I think I'll stay in Boston." Clara still wouldn't look up. "I want to see that strange collection of art that Isabella Gardner has put together. Will has seen it and says I mustn't miss it."

Isabel understood that Clara's telegram was to arrange a meeting with Will. She understood now, too, that Clara had gone on the trip only so Will could settle his affairs with his wife, and was now cutting it short since he'd failed to do so.

"Clara, you must know that I sympathize with you in whatever you try to do, but I hate to think what your father will say when he finds out that Will is married."

"Will is getting a divorce. He won't give up."

"But he is still married now, evidently. You must know that your father is very sensitive about matters like that. He canceled a benefit for the Russian revolutionary Gorky when he learned that Gorky was traveling in America with his mistress."

"Well, then don't tell him!"

"I don't plan to. But he will find out."

Clara lowered her head bullishly. "I don't see how Papa can say a word about me when he has kept you under his roof all this time without the benefit of marriage."

Isabel yearned to tell Clara of her father's tentative marriage proposal, but until firm plans were made, speaking of them made her nervous, as if she might make them disappear from wanting them too much.

"Here I was, worried about *his* reputation, trying to get you to live elsewhere to protect him."

"I am in your house because I work for him," Isabel objected.

"And Will works for me. See how nicely that plays out?" Clara laughed. "What's good for the gander is good for the gosling." She grew serious. "Really, Isabel, don't tell him. I've never been this happy in my life. Please don't ruin it for me."

Did Clara realize what she was asking? "I won't."

"Promise?"

"I promise."

She grasped Isabel's hand. "I'll never forget this. Thank you, Isabel."

Just then a man in worn corduroy plus fours approached them, a pad of paper in his hand. "Excuse me, ladies. I'm Sean Lynch, reporter for *The New York Herald.*"

"The *Herald*?" said Isabel. "Here?"

He grinned at her as if he held some knowledge over her.

"We're rather tired," Clara said with dramatic weariness. "We've been through a terrible ordeal."

"You should be tired, ma'am," he said to Clara. "I heard that you helped the passengers of the ship that sank."

"You did?" Clara blinked.

"I also heard that you went to the captain on their behalf."

Clara hesitated. "I did talk to him." She put on a pained expression. "They looked so cold. One woman was shivering so hard that I could hear her teeth chatter—an older woman. She made me think about my mother. I wanted her to have my coat."

"Mark Twain's daughter gave a victim her coat," he said, writing it down.

"Clara Clemens," she said testily.

"Thank you for your interest," Isabel said, "but I believe Miss Clemens is exhausted."

He crooked one side of his mouth. "So, Isabel Lyon, Mark's pretty little secretary: tell me about yourself."

The realization that the reporter might be here for her, and not Clara, dawned on Isabel—unless he had gotten wind of Clara's affair with Will Wark. Neither could be good.

Isabel stood. "Miss Clemens and I must be going."

"Traveling with Mark's daughter while he's in England—shopping for your trousseau together, are you? Does this mean there are wedding bells in the near future, Miss Lyon?"

Clara sat back in disbelief. "My father has no plans to get married."

"Is that true, Miss Lyon?"

Clara's gaze bore down on her.

"Mr. Clemens would be as pained as his secretary to hear of any such report."

Isabel regretted her words immediately. How would they sound to Sam? He'd feel publicly rejected. Even a less proud man would be humiliated, and Samuel Clemens, for all the fun he poked at himself, was the proudest man Isabel had ever met.

She smiled grimly. "Good day, Mr. Lynch."

She left as Clara gathered her things. How had the *Herald* known that she and Clara were in Halifax? All she could hope was that Mr. Clemens would never see whatever foolishness this reporter put in print clear over the sea in England.

• • •

Two days later, Isabel was entering the Fifth Avenue house alone, Clara having joined Will Wark in Boston, when she saw the *Herald* on the table in the hallway, folded open to reveal an article. Her cases still in her hands, she bent down to read it, wondering who had left it there.

A quick scan revealed that Mark Twain had been asked to comment on the report from Halifax that his secretary claimed they were not getting married. She read closer:

> *I have not known, and shall never know, anyone who could fill the place of the wife I have lost. I shall never marry again.*

Footsteps came from the parlor. Katy waltzed into the hall with her feather duster. Isabel's gaze wandered up from the print, which seemed to have scrambled into foreign symbols. She numbly registered a flash of brown turkey feathers as Katy swung the duster.

"Did you have a good trip?"

Isabel dropped a case, groped for the paper, and stuffed it into her coat pocket. She could read his hurt pride, his lashing out at her, between the lines. He had mistaken her deferment to his announcing their marriage and her avoidance of upsetting Clara for disinterest in marrying him. How wounded he must be, especially sensitive now that his manhood was in question. And forgiveness did not come easily to Samuel Clemens.

Katy smiled as Isabel fled up the stairs, her cases banging against her legs.

26.

September 1908
Stormfield, Redding, Connecticut

NO NUBILE ACTRESSES WERE scheduled to come today, no little girls wearing hair bows that were bigger than their pretty heads, no famous scientists, no robber barons, no editors, no reporters. Her Brownie camera in hand, Isabel strolled around the empty fountain at the end of the walkway that hung like a long pendant necklace from the back of the house. She was looking for deer. She loved to photograph them, the does especially, with their large eyes and wet black noses, although their meek, hunted expressions disturbed her. Wanting to bring them closer, she had put out a salt lick for them when she'd moved to Stormfield three months earlier, until a neighboring farmer thanked her for luring them in to shoot.

Pain shot through her fingertip. She snatched her hand from one of the cedars overhanging the fountain. Such deceptive trees—the feathery leaves hid hairy barbs that were as sharp as needles. She should have had them cut down but they gave the landscaping an Italian air. She tucked her camera under her arm and, sucking her invisible wound, gazed at the mansion rising from the series of terraces.

That house. For nearly a year, she had nurtured, coddled, and coaxed it into life, all by herself. The King hadn't even wanted to see the plans. He said he wanted a house outside of the city—its conception was up to her. The gestation period alone had nearly broken her.

How nauseated she'd been when she had come back from one of her several trips with The King to Bermuda—trips that featured more friends and drinking and less intimacy than the first—and found that the foundation was being dug on the wrong site. Her vision had actually swum as she waded through piles of dirt to get to the operator of the steam shovel to stop.

The dozens of subsequent train rides out to oversee the construction after a full day's work in New York hadn't done much for her constitution in the following months, nor had Clara's announcement that she wanted major changes. Only by sheer force of will had Isabel managed to keep the project on schedule, even when she'd arrived with a wagon train of furniture three days before the grand opening and found the place in chaos. With one last push, she'd cajoled the workers to stay past midnight, promising them Scotch, cigars, and a concert on the Orchestrelle. They delivered, she delivered; The King arrived in June of 1908 to find his new home serenely waiting for him, complete with his pipes hanging on their rack and a cat dozing on the porch.

All the suffering she had endured in its formation had been worth it. When The King first examined every inch of it, his eyes shone like those of a father wondering at his newborn child's perfect toes. How proud she had been. This house, her progeny, was a glorious example of what she could do for the man she loved, if he would only tell her what he wanted. She would do it all again—she would do anything—if he asked it of her. And yet it wasn't enough.

He had not given himself to her since she had sailed to Nova Scotia last year and made the innocent blunder of saying that she wouldn't marry him. He stayed away from her bed, keeping so busy that there was no time for intimacy. She'd thought the house in the country would draw them closer but it seemed to have the opposite effect. They hadn't had a moment to breathe since they'd moved in. The beautiful, the famous, and the rich flocked to this palace in the middle of nowhere, willing to take the two-and-a-half-hour pilgrimage from the city for a chat with The King—and for the inevitable write-up in the papers the next day. Isabel had hoped that out here in the wilds of Connecticut, The King could get off the endless, calliope-tootling carousel of appearances, speeches, and interviews that his life in New York had become. The world needed Samuel Clemens to eat fewer dinners and write more books. He needed to finish his autobiography, but he couldn't be bothered to sit still long enough to work on it. At an age when others were slowing down, her King was running faster, even out here in the country. It troubled Isabel to think what he might be running from. She feared that it might be her.

Some one hundred yards away, the door to the house opened. Ralph Ashcroft stepped out to the top of the terraces and waved.

She put the viewfinder of her camera to her eye to hide her smile. She didn't mean to like him so much.

He descended the steps to the next level of grassy terrace. "I saw you out here," he called. "Get any pictures?"

"Not yet."

"Then may I join you for a dip in the fountain?"

In the rush to get everything done at the house for the grand opening, the plumbing to the fountain had been put aside, as well as the selection of the statue for its center, and Isabel hadn't had a moment to attend to it. Knowing what a thorn in the side the unfinished waterworks were to her, Ralph teased her about it whenever given the chance. She didn't mind. He, of all people, appreciated how hard she worked.

"No, you may not take a dip," she said as he got closer. "You haven't a proper swimming costume."

"Don't mind these old clothes." He tugged at his shirtfront as he continued down the steps. "I was planning to take them off. All of them. You don't mind, do you?"

"No." She crossed her arms. "By all means. Off with them."

He descended the remaining two terraces, then he drew up before her—too close, but it was part of the joke. He smelled of clean flesh and of the starched cotton of his shirt. He grinned down at her. "I'll want some company, swanning around there in my birthday suit."

"You aren't getting it from me. Maybe one of Mr. Clemens's actresses will oblige you."

"You are much better company than any of them." He covered half of his mouth to whisper, "They're not as smart."

"Flatter me all you want, Mr. Ashcroft. I'm still not going to let you win at cards." The three of them played whenever he came.

He shrugged, the corners of his dark eyes crinkling. "I know. And I don't care."

They smiled at each other, affectionate compatriots. Isabel knew exactly what he was thinking: they could be more than friends if she would allow it. She was careful to pretend that she didn't know, although she wondered if her feigned ignorance fooled him.

She smelled cigar smoke. Up near the house, Mr. Clemens was leaning against a stone pillar on the top terrace, watching them and smoking, the wind flapping the hem of his crimson Oxford scholar's robe around the cuffs of his white suit.

Isabel stepped away from Ralph and shaded her eyes although it wasn't sunny. "Come join us," she shouted, then winced, remembering The King's gouty feet. "Wait. I'll come up there."

He blew out a cloud of smoke. "Stay," he called back. "I'll come. You two make such a pretty picture. I don't want to break you up."

A lone hawk wheeled in the sky as The King made his slow descent. Isabel could sense Ralph tensing next to her.

"Good afternoon, sir," he said when The King finally arrived at their level.

Their King ambled past them wordlessly and stepped onto the edge of the fountain, then onto the round cement platform in the middle, upon which a statue with water jets was supposed to be mounted. Languorously puffing on his cigar, he struck a pose with one arm cocked back, the other forward.

"Here's your snapshot, Lioness."

She aimed her camera.

Ralph glanced at Isabel. "Are we supposed to guess who you are?"

"You can't tell?" With the cool of a rajah, The King made as if to shoot an arrow.

"Robin Hood?" Ralph said.

The King snatched at his cigar. "I can hardly rob from the rich to give to the poor when I'm the rich one."

"True," said Ralph.

"No, damn it. You can't guess? I'm Cupid. What's wrong, am I too old for the role?" The King shot another imaginary arrow, the cigar between his fingers leaking smoke.

"Oh, now I can see it," said Ralph.

Isabel kept her mouth closed as she lowered her camera. She could see the cold fury in The King's eyes when he looked at her. She braced herself: he was in one of his moods.

"I thought," he drawled bitterly, "that you two needed a Cupid, the way you were making goo-goo eyes at each other."

Ralph laughed uncomfortably. "We were hardly making 'goo-goo eyes,' whatever those are."

The King sniffed his disagreement. "What were you two talking about?"

"If you must know," Isabel said, "about the actresses who come to see you."

He looked at her. "I don't give a damn about them."

She returned his stare. "You certainly invite them out here often for someone who doesn't care for their company."

"They make me feel young," he growled. "You don't do that."

She felt slapped, then ashamed that Ralph had seen the attack on her. For years, she'd seen The King act lovingly toward his family one minute, then turn on them the next, with all the unpredictability of a barn cat. Now, more and more, he was lashing out at her as well, only to be contrite a while later. She was embarrassed for others to see that she tolerated it, hoping that each episode would be his last. Something was eating at her King; this wasn't the man she loved.

"Well, she makes me feel young," said Ralph.

The King cut his eyes to him. "Easy to *feel* young when you *are* young. It's more of a challenge for those of us who are long in the tooth. Don't get me wrong, we're jealous of you young ones, the whole wrinkly ranks of us. As someone once said, 'It is better to be a young June-bug than an old bird of paradise.' "

"Pudd'nhead Wilson," Ralph said under his breath.

The King sniffed again. "That's right—the most truthful book I ever wrote. I blasted the sheer idiocy of defining someone by their skin color, the goddamn heartbreaking folly of it, and people took it as a farce. Why is it that when a person tells the truth, everyone thinks he is joking?" He gave a short laugh. "The humorist's lament."

The keening of the hawk cut through the uncomfortable silence.

Abruptly, Ralph said, "I have work to do." He strode up the terraces, taking the steps between the grassy levels two at a time.

The King turned to Isabel, then threw down his cigar. "Better go after your beau."

The words burst from her mouth. "Why do you feel you have to say that? You know that I'm committed to you. Though you won't take me in your bed anymore, though you throw young women in my face, though you reject me at every given chance, I'm committed to you, and I always have been. I have never given you a reason to think otherwise."

He ground his cigar under the toe of his boot. "You told the reporter that you wouldn't marry me."

"You're bringing that up again? That was last year! And I only said that because I didn't want to be too forward. I thought you'd think it was your place to announce our plans. I've told you that many, many times."

He looked up. "I think the truth slipped out. I think you're repulsed by an old man."

"You know that's not the truth. You're looking for an excuse to push me away. Why? Why do you push me away when we could be so happy?"

"I'm doing you a favor."

"A favor? Samuel, I love you. I want to be with you. How many times—how many ways—must I tell you this?"

He closed his eyes. When he opened them, he smiled sadly. "I'm just an old bird-of-paradise."

She touched his face. "You're a beautiful bird-of-paradise, extraordinary inside and out."

He kissed her hand, then put it down. "Thank you, my love, but if you only knew."

"I do know. I know you better than anyone."

"That's true. But you don't know everything."

"Sam, don't you see? I know the good in you. Test me all you want—I won't leave you."

The sound of voices up near the house pulled her gaze away from him. Clara, recently returned from a tour of England, was strolling on the uppermost terrace with Will Wark. Isabel paused, loath to end this moment, as if she and The King might finally get to the bottom of their troubles and start anew. Sighing, she waved when Clara saw her looking.

Clara said something to Will, who went into the house. The King heaved a showy sigh as Clara made her way down. "Damn lovebirds everywhere," he muttered. "Why doesn't he just marry her?"

Isabel skipped a breath. The papers had been full these last few weeks of the news of Clara's engagement to Wark. Isabel wondered where they got their information—Wark was still very much married. Isabel could not believe that this fact had not gotten out. Where was his wife? What must she think when she read about her husband's engagement? Surely she'd be coming after Clara.

Once upon the lowest terrace, Clara approached with her head lowered as if to ram her father. "Papa," she demanded, "please tell me that no one is coming here today."

"No one's coming. Today Miss Lyon and I have the place to

ourselves." He frowned. "Ashcroft is up there somewhere rooting around, too."

"Mr. Ashcroft has left," said Clara. "He was walking out as we came in. He is so rude! He hardly would say hello. I don't know why you keep him on."

"He makes me money," said The King, "the best character reference a fellow could have."

Isabel glanced away. She wished Ralph would hide his dislike for Clara. His scorn didn't help Isabel maintain her fragile balancing act within the house. Isabel never should have told him that Clara had made her promise not to inform The King that Will was married. Once he'd heard, Ralph's natural distrust of Clara had immediately tipped into contempt. He could not believe that she would ask such a thing of Isabel. Didn't Isabel realize that the longer Clara's secret went untold, the more furious The King would be?

Oh, yes, Isabel realized.

Clara frowned at Isabel. "What are you two doing out here?"

Isabel held up her camera. "Kodaking."

"Don't you have enough pictures of him already?"

The King shook his mane. "I'm a fascinating subject."

"Right. Will and I came here to practice. I hoped you didn't have any hangers-on around here—especially those awful little girls and their mothers. Papa, your infatuation with them looks so odd."

"There's nothing odd about it. It has been too long since my own little girls pattered around the house. I want granddaughters now, and since you haven't given me any, I went out and got my own."

Clara coughed in outrage. "It's a little difficult for me to marry and have children when you won't let me even talk to men."

"I know what's on their minds. I'm only trying to protect you. Give me some credit—I haven't chased off Will."

"Yes," she said testily. "Why the turnabout?"

"I trust him. I like his honest blue eyes."

Isabel could feel Clara daring Isabel to look at her. Honest, married Will kept an apartment next door to Clara's Stuyvesant Square flat, and although Mr. Clemens didn't know it, he was paying for both accommodations, not just Clara's. Clara swore Isabel to secrecy even as she asked Isabel to write the checks, swearing she'd return the favor someday. Not even Ralph knew about this further duplicity committed in the name of keeping Clara's affection, and Isabel was too miserable with guilt and fear to tell him.

"He's a very good friend," Clara said. "I'm glad you approve of him."

"When is he going to ask me if you can marry him?"

"Ask you?" Clara bit her thumbnail, then put down her hand. "I have decided never to marry. You know that, Papa."

True, thought Isabel. Clara had recently vowed never to marry. It was an easy pledge to keep when the man she loved would never be free.

"You'd think he'd want to make a respectable woman out of you," said The King.

She looked between him and Isabel. "Papa, do you ever hear yourself?"

"Too much for my liking."

"You can hardly talk about respectability when—"

He cocked his head coolly. "When what?"

Clara looked pointedly at Isabel, then glanced away, frowning, as if weighing whether it might be a poor idea to alienate the person who wrote the checks to finance her secret tryst. "I'm dressing for dinner. And please don't tell Will that ridiculous 'Golden Arm' story. It makes you look so crude."

"Ah, Susy's favorite."

Clara stared at him with disgust. "You completely broke her heart when you told that at her college after she'd specifically begged you not to. She never got over it. I don't know how you can joke about it."

He sighed, then fumbled in his pockets for another cigar. "That's the only thing I can do about it, Clärchen."

• • •

Isabel watched the young pair at dinner that night, side by side at the lace-covered table set with bone china. They were handsome together—Clara, with her thick auburn hair and her father's coiled energy, and Will Wark, with his workingman's affable charm and stocky build, his impressive nose, and those alert aquamarine eyes.

"I just loved England." Clara picked at an oyster with her fork. "The crowd was adorable at the Wigmore. It took them a moment to clap when I'd finished, as if the poor dears were still absorbing what they'd seen. I think my program took them by surprise."

Wark swallowed his oyster with a loud gulp.

"Thank you for securing the hall, Papa. I promise, next year I'll turn a profit on my tour."

"She will," said Wark, his clean-shaven square face earnest. "Her crowds get bigger every show."

"They do. There are barely any empty seats now."

As the person who controlled Mr. Clemens's personal expenses, Isabel had seen the receipts from the performances. The statements sent by Clara's new manager, Mr. Johnston, hardly indicated full venues. Isabel quietly speared her mollusk. She wasn't the one whom Clara and Wark were trying to convince.

Wark emptied another shell. "Next year," he said, chewing, "when we return to Europe, we'll sell Clara's appearances on shares. It won't cost you anything, Mr. Clemens. We'll *make* you money."

The King drew his attention from the window out which he'd been staring. "What? I don't care. Expenses are Isabel's department."

"I wish you could join us in Europe, Nana." Wark used the pet name he and Clara had given Isabel, as if she were their aging childhood nanny. "We kept seeing things that reminded us of you. Whenever we did, we said 'Nana would like this tea' or 'Nana would like this castle' or 'Nana would like these cakes.' " He glanced at Clara, who laughed. Isabel could well imagine how much of a joke what Nana liked had become between them.

As if sensing that Isabel was onto them, Clara quickly changed the subject. "Next time, Papa, I'm going to insist that Mr. Johnston book me in bigger halls in Europe."

The King kept his gaze out the window. "Conquer the little houses first. Being able to win over tough, small crowds—now, that's the mark of a real entertainer. It takes skill to bring a resistant group over to your camp."

An offended silence radiated from Clara's side of the table. The King, oblivious, kept his watch outside. Finally, she burst out, "What's so important out there? It's dark."

"Nothing. I thought I saw a comet." He looked at Isabel. "You don't think Halley's Comet could come early?"

"No. It's on a set orbit."

"Because you know that I'm going out with it."

"We were talking about me," said Clara. "For once."

Will chewed his shellfish, glancing at Clara, then smiled at Isabel as if to enlist her support. "Have you been to England, Nana?"

She had been when she was Millicent Dana's governess, a time in her life that she didn't particularly want to remember. "Not lately." She kept an eye on The King. He was upset about something.

"Well," said Will, "it gets a bit thick over there sometimes, having the Brits looking down their noses at Americans. I'm from Canada, but I'd see it when Clara and I went out. They'd hear our accents and they'd act differently toward us. They'd look at us with these snobby little smiles, as if we were trained monkeys there to make them laugh."

Isabel regarded him over her tiny trident fork. Although Wark's talent as a pianist had taken him far from his working-class roots in Ontario, he still had the laborer's chip on his shoulder. He clearly resented the privileged, even as he strove to be part of them. She wondered if, deep down, he resented Clara, with her European training and unlimited funds. She glanced at her King. No wonder he approved of Will. The King, too, was once a poor boy in pursuit of a rich man's daughter. How often patterns repeat themselves, or is it that we seek the comfort of familiarity?

"The Brits are the amusing ones," Wark said. "Every time a limey calls a 'sweater' a 'jumper,' I want to laugh. Somehow I picture kangaroos in woolens."

Clara's pout loosened. "Or when they call the hood of the automobile a 'bonnet,' " she said sulkily. "I see an Oldsmobile wearing a frilly hat." When Wark laughed, she thawed into a smile.

Wark was enjoying himself now. "How about when I told that waiter I was 'stuffed'? If you could have seen his face," he said to Mr. Clemens. He shifted to Isabel when it seemed The King wasn't listening. "I told the fellow, 'No thanks for dessert—I'm stuffed,' and the jackass coughed and turned away like he'd seen my sister's britches. How was I to know that the word had a dirty meaning over there?"

Clara threw her father a guilty glance. He took his gaze away from the window to look down on his plate, then seemed to see the oysters for the first time. Frowning, he jabbed at one.

"What's the matter with you, Papa? You haven't said two words."

"Just thinking about someone."

"Mamma?"

He looked at her blankly. "No."

"Who, then?"

"My father, as a matter of fact. Your grandfather."

Surprise registered in Clara's eyes. Isabel felt it, too. In her years with The King, he'd rarely spoken of his father, traumatized, she guessed, from witnessing his autopsy.

"Isabel," said Clara, "I understand that you have bought a great deal of gorse seed, with a plan to turn Papa's land into an English moor. Remember, Will, when we were riding the train to Yorkshire, all the yellow hills—"

"I never gave my father a chance. Wonder what I'd have made of him if he lived longer. As it was, I hated his guts." Finding everyone's stunned gaze upon him, The King put an oyster in his mouth, then spat it into his napkin. "These oysters look and taste like a fetus."

Clara whispered a strangled "Papa!"

Wark wiped his mouth on his napkin. "If that's what your dad thinks, he should be able to say it at his own table."

"Why must you be so crude?" Clara jumped up from the table and fled the room. Wark nodded at The King and went after her.

The King leaned back against his chair. "I seem to have that effect on people."

Isabel waited. From her years with The King, she knew it was best to be silent.

"My girls were fully grown before I realized how much they hated me. I thought I was their hero, but it turned out they couldn't stand to be around me. Could a person be more blind?"

"That's not true. They love you. They're terribly proud of you."

He nudged his plate away. "Susy was so ashamed of me that she didn't even want me to give the commencement speech at her college. She feared that I would tell 'The Golden Arm.' I swore to her that I wouldn't—who would tell that fool yarn at a commencement? But she knew. She knew! And sure enough, no sooner than I was given a chance, there I was, demanding of all those Bryn Mawr girls, 'Who's got my golden arm? Who's got my golden arm? Who's got my golden arm? YOU DO!' "

Isabel flinched.

He shook his head. "I don't know why I say the things I say. Livy's doctors knew I could freeze her blood with a single word and rightly kept me away from her. I so scalded Susy with my talk that she refused to come with us on that last tour. She stayed home, which exposed her to disease. If she had been with me in Europe, she wouldn't have gotten meningitis and died. And then there's what I did to Jennie."

She waited for him to explain about Jennie as he fumbled in his pocket for a cigar. He stopped. "You tell me if this is lucky or not: since my forties, I haven't been able to utter a single word without it enriching my pocketbook, and the gold rush is still gaining steam.

You've seen the reporters scrambling over the nuggets I drool. I can't observe the weather without them sifting it for ore. Yet it's this same cursed mine that spills the words that do my killing. Words! I kill the people I love with words." He shoved a cigar between his lips, lit it, then waved out his match. "I'm the King Midas of talk. Christ, I'm tired of it."

"It seems to me," she said quietly, "that you hurt yourself more than anyone."

He blew out smoke, then got up. "I can't eat anymore."

Isabel rose to go with him.

He waved her down. "I don't want to infest you with me right now."

As soon as he was gone, Isabel jumped up and went to the window. Above the silhouette of treetops, the full moon lit a sky hazy with stationary stars. All was quiet in the firmament. She sank back with relief.

• • •

After dinner, Isabel jotted in her daily reminder for a few minutes, then put on her cape to go see her mother, recently installed in the cottage on the grounds that The King called the Lobster Pot. Although the cottage was supposed to be Isabel's, she stayed nights in The King's house, in the bedroom adjoining his. He wanted her to be close, although she had not lain in his arms since before her trip to Nova Scotia last summer. His proximity, without being able to have him, was a torture to her.

As she fastened her cape, she heard singing coming from Clara's room upstairs. Isabel heard a tenor join her. Will was in her room?

When she'd gotten to the top of the stairs, she heard The King's whisper. "Isabel."

He came out of his room, dressed only in silk underdrawers. He was trim for a man his age, upright as a youth. "Guess what?"

"They sound heavenly." She pretended that he wasn't undressed.

"What they sound like is happy." He kept his gaze toward his daughter's suite. "Guess who just asked me if he could marry Clara?"

Isabel swallowed. "Wark?"

"I know it's surprising, as much of a handful as she can be, but yes, he did."

She needed to tell him about Will's marriage now, before this got past the point where she might hope for Mr. Clemens's forgiveness for not telling him.

He gathered her in. "Lioness, you make me happy, and you know I'm not an easy man to cheer. You have put up with a lot—with my terrible pride, my worse temper—and you're still around." He pressed her to him. "Why am I so lucky?"

She listened to his thumping heart, her mind snatching for words.

His voice rumbled in his chest. "Isabel, I can't give you what you need. I can't be a real man to you. It makes me ashamed."

She pulled back to look up at him. "Sam."

He put his finger to her lips. "I can't be a man in the way a woman like you needs. You saw how I was. I'm not likely to have improved."

Her heart ached for the boy whom she saw in his anxious eyes, and then for the tortured man. She could tell him about Wark another time. He needed her now. And she needed him.

Gently, as would one with a beloved child, she cradled his face. "Let me be the judge."

• • •

Through the panes of the window, a shaving of moon glowed high in the milky heavens. Isabel rolled onto her side and laid her hand on her King's chest as he stared up at the ceiling. "Thank you, Sam. That was just what I dreamed of."

He took away her hand. "Well, your dreams are what I call nightmares."

"Stop," she scolded. "It was wonderful for me."

He sighed tiredly. "Lioness, you can't lie to a liar."

"We were too excited. Next time—" She rolled onto her back, her hair, undone from its knot, tangling under her. She rested her arm across her forehead. "Maybe you didn't like me."

"Damn it, Isabel, I liked you too much."

She rolled back and kissed his chest.

He stroked her hair. "What am I going to do with you?"

"What you just did. Over and over until we get it right."

She kissed him, then got up and went naked to the open window, as if the moonlight might soothe her swollen flesh, still needing release.

A whip-poor-will's eerie call broke the calm of the night. Isabel thought of the legend that a whip-poor-will sang when a soul was departing—its song could capture the soul as it fled. She pictured souls, filmy, tattered, and urgent, sailing through the dark, pursued by the insistent cries of the bird. By the time its calling ceased, she had accepted her physical relationship with Sam for what it would be.

She returned to the bed and got under the covers. When she found his hand, he squeezed hers back before drifting into sleep.

• • •

A thump jilted her awake. She listened. There it was again: downstairs. In the kitchen. Was it the cats? They must be after a mouse.

She had closed her eyes, reminding herself to tell the butler, Claude, to look for holes in which the mice were entering, when she heard the door to the terrace open.

Probably it was Clara out for a midnight stroll with Will. Poor doomed pair, let them have their moment. She rolled over, then slid her foot until she touched the leg of her sleeping King.

A splintering crash sent her upright.

She looked down on her King. Still asleep. She got out of bed and peered out the window.

Her eyes could not make sense of it: out on the terrace, by the light of a lantern set on the stone wall, two men struggled to lift the partially smashed kitchen sideboard to waist-level, then unceremoniously dropped it on a step, where it broke open like an egg. A man delved into the gaping orifice, then held up something to the moonlight: Mrs. Clemens's silver teapot.

Isabel heard herself scream.

Sam sat up.

"Burglars!" She grabbed her dress.

"What?"

"Outside!" She struggled to put on her dress. "They broke in. Claude!" she screamed. "Claude, get your gun!"

Samuel was scooting to the edge of the bed when the door opened. A candle lit Katy's face, turning her ghostly. Claude and the other maids appeared behind her in the flickering light, their mouths straining open like those of baby birds.

"Burglars!" Isabel cried. "Help!" She clutched at her gaping dress and hobbled to the window then back. "They're running away!"

The sheets pulled around him, Mr. Clemens strode toward his robe on the chair. "Damn it!" He snatched up the robe and, with a flash of nakedness, wrapped it around himself. "Are you all just going to stand there? Claude—you gone soft? Call the sheriff!"

In Katy's light, the herd of servants bucked and turned in the hall, just as Will Wark thrust his head from Clara's door. He ducked back. Isabel glanced at her King. He had seen Will. Everyone had.

"Out! Out! All of you, get out!" cried The King. "Claude, what the hell are you waiting for?"

The maid Teresa burst into tears.

"What's the matter with her?" he exclaimed.

"She's scared," said Isabel.

"That's not it," Katy snapped. "She can't take the shock of it."

The King was breathing hard. "We're all shocked. Get the hell after them!"

"That's not what I mean," said Katy. She glanced at Isabel. "It's just that—it's shameful."

His glare dared Katy to criticize him. "What's shameful?"

"Mr. Wark is married," she said.

"Married?" The King roared. "They got married without me?"

"He's married," said Katy, "to someone else."

Time stopped. Or just Isabel's heart.

"Everyone knew?" The King gazed at the servants cowering in semidarkness. He looked down upon his robe for a moment, then up at Isabel. "You knew?"

"I had no choice," she whispered. She physically felt his trust receding. She knew she could never get it back.

PART FIVE

The New York Times, January 1909

TWAIN TALKS TO DOCTORS.

"Dr. Clemens" Describes Imaginary Medical School at His Country Home.

At the annual dinner of the Directors and Faculty of the New York Post Graduate Medical School and Hospital at Delmonico's last night Mark Twain, a member of the Post-Graduate Corporation, and appropriately introduced as Dr. Samuel L. Clemens, wore his now famous white suit of dinner clothes, and seemed to be comfortable in them. He talked at some length about his celebrated burglars. He declared that he had never lost anything through burglars; on the contrary, he had been a gainer, he declared, because the burglars had frightened away some undesirable servants.

27.

January 8, 1909
Stormfield, Redding, Connecticut

PAPA HAD MADE THESE past four months since the burglary a living hell. He'd given Clara no choice but to come down from New York and make her stand. Contrary to what everyone thought, she did not enjoy making scenes. She made them only when pushed to the absolute limit and she had no alternative but to go ahead and have a terrible tantrum. Did people think it felt *good* to injure her hands by tearing up books? Did they think she *liked* to wear herself down to a nub while breaking furniture, or to scream and scream until she was as hoarse as a crow? Clara tried not to crack, oh, dear God, she tried not to crack, and yet people kept pushing her and pushing her until she did.

She was a sweet person, a dutiful daughter, a dutiful sister, but she never got credit for it. Hadn't she sat in a chair next to her mother's bed for months—no, years—watching her own pretty face age in the bedroom mirror, watching her own trim body wither under the dumpy dresses that Papa had insisted she wear, listening all the while to her mother's breath rising and falling as that damn music box jingled—hurrah that Katy couldn't put it back together, try as if her life depended on it, little fool, after the Lioness stole it from Mamma and smashed it while in Italy. Susy never would have been able to have survived all Clara had borne. Susy wouldn't have lasted one day. And forget Jean. Nobody expected anything from her. She could run around saving animals while the rest of the house burned down.

But did Papa ever give Clara one speck of praise? No. Never. He was too busy sailing to Bermuda with the Lioness or lying to reporters or having tea parties with thirteen-year-old girls. Repulsive! Yet Clara was supposed to always give and give until there was nothing left to her but her name—and even that wasn't hers! Clara *Twain*! She would surely kill the next person who called her that.

Now it was her turn to take a nibble for herself, just the teeniest-tiniest corner of happiness. She wasn't hurting anyone, really, not anyone who didn't deserve it, and yet she was supposed to give up Will. Well, she wasn't. Not without a fight.

Look—there they were in Papa's precious billiards room, his precious *Aquarium*, the raggedy Lion and his Lioness, the pair of hypocrites who couldn't stand for her to be happy even though they themselves were doing exactly what they didn't want her to do. She threw her forty-two-pelt fox coat toward a chair and marched over to give them a piece of her mind. Halfway across the room, when the limp head of the fox on the collar was bouncing against the chair cushion with a *thunk*, she saw the trio huddled on the other side of the billiards table: company.

Damn it! Couldn't Papa live one single moment without company? The man had to have people telling him he was wonderful every moment of every day. Damn that farm boy of a butler for not warning her that they were there. Now she looked like a banshee in front of them.

The man in the group was staring at her. Hold the line. Look at *him*. Wasn't he just the candy? And about her age, too. She cocked her head to give herself more appeal and offered her gloved hand. Papa's little fishies weren't the only ones who could be adorable.

"Have we met?" Clara lowered her head to look up through her lashes.

"I don't believe so."

Nice voice. Educated. Oh, he was handsome. That chin. So aggressive and firm! Hadn't she heard something about how you could judge a man's equipment by his chin?

Her father pushed a billiards ball across the table to where a kitten was sitting in a pocket. That one was probably hers—Papa stole every cat that she had ever liked. It stuck out its paw and diverted the ball as Papa sauntered over.

"John Macy, this is my daughter Clara."

"His favorite daughter," she added. She saw the slight twitch at her father's mouth. *Ha. Got him.* As for the Lioness, she wasn't giving her the time of day. That drove her crazy, Clara knew.

Papa patted the dumpy woman next to Handsome as if she were something special and not just some little frump bursting the buttons of her shirtwaist. "This is Mrs. Macy."

My God, she was his wife? She was built like a gumdrop. She had to be at least a decade older than he was.

"And this—" Papa brought forward a young woman with the strangest look on her face. "This is Helen Keller, the Helen who makes Helen of Troy look as ugly as a mining-camp cook."

Oh, the famous blind girl, all grown up. Papa was always making a fuss over her. Evidently, that's what it took to get his sympathy—be deaf, dumb, and blind. Or just be Susy.

Now Gumdrop was galumphing over to Miss Keller's side to spell Papa's outrageous compliment into her hand. Clara's gaze went to the Angelfish pin on Miss Keller's blouse. Oh, dear God. Papa was at it again. He was going to get arrested if he didn't watch out.

Helen laughed. "I am hardly Helen of Troy."

Helen's unusual speech lifted Clara's gaze from the pin. She had never actually heard Helen Keller talk. It was more of a honk, wasn't it?

"Just don't go abducting our Helen like that fool Paris did to that lesser Helen," Papa said to Mr. Macy. "There would be hell to pay."

Mr. Macy snorted. "Ha. No, I won't."

Clara gave him a double look. Handsome was uncomfortable

about something. All those years of watching Mamma deal with Papa had given her a sixth sense about these things.

Helen Keller seemed unaware of the men's exchange; the Gumdrop did not relay it to her. "Poor Helen of Troy!" she exclaimed. "How must she have felt, being the cause of so many men's deaths?"

Oh, please—she actually believed Papa's bunk.

"I doubt if Helen of Troy cared," Handsome said lightly. "Not everyone has your sensitive nature. I have seen our Helen cry when I play the violin for her."

The Gumdrop's fingers, Clara noticed, stayed still.

"So nice to meet all of you," Clara lied. "Papa, I would like to borrow you for a moment, if I could, please."

"Being the cause of such trouble would have been a torture," said Helen. Her sigh was sort of a yodel. "I feel so much." She turned her empty face toward Papa. "Mark, do you think it is possible to feel too much? You're a writer—you must be a lightning rod for the emotions of those around you."

Oh my God. "Mark" was going to be insufferable. "I think my father might be more the lightning than the lightning rod."

Papa acted like he couldn't hear her, but Clara saw the corners of his mustache splay in a grimace. "If only I had your gift, dear," he said to Helen. "How much more clearly you see into other people's hearts than we sighted fools can, distracted with the lies our eyes and ears are telling us. You probably know what I'm feeling, clear across the room."

The Gumdrop spelled his words to Helen, making Helen smile. "I don't know about sensing it across the room, but if I could touch your face, I think that I might know what you're feeling."

"Come on over," Papa said. "Mrs. Macy, take away your hand so that you don't give her a clue." He settled back against the billiards table as Miss Keller approached. The Lioness was watching like a cat at a mouse hole—surely she wasn't believing this bunk. The Lioness was a lot of things, but she wasn't stupid.

Helen put her hands to his face and held her breath, as if to catch sensations from the great Mark Twain.

"What, then, dear?" he asked.

Clara wasn't waiting for any more of this hokum. "Papa, I do need to talk with you now."

"Impatient," Miss Keller announced. "You are feeling impatient."

Papa grasped the blind girl's fingers, then kissed them before putting them to his lips for her to read. "I don't know, Helen. I think you've got my wires crossed with my daughter's. Now tell us Mr. Macy's mood."

The Gumdrop turned an unhealthy red as Miss Keller searched her husband's face. When Helen took away her hands, Mr. Macy smiled at her as if she could see him. He kept that grin on his face just a little too long.

"Impatient," Helen said, "as well."

"Helen, dear, it seems your compass is stuck." Papa tried to act as if he couldn't see Clara. "How about your teacher? How about divining what she's feeling?"

Mr. Macy glanced at his scowling wife. He hesitated, then spelled the question into Helen's hand. She stared in that blank way of hers, then, sucking in her breath, went to Mrs. Macy. When she didn't immediately put her hand on Mrs. Macy's face, Mrs. Macy gripped her hand and put it to her lips herself. She glared at Helen as if demanding her to speak. Handsome turned toward the fireplace and made as if to warm himself.

This was obviously a strange situation. Well, Clara didn't have time for them to get ahold of themselves. "Papa, I really need to talk with you. Now."

Helen dropped her hand. Mrs. Macy returned Helen's hand to her face, her own pigeon breast heaving. Helen struggled to remove it, but Mrs. Macy wouldn't let her.

The Lioness's voice was too bright. "How is the weather outside, Clara? Maybe our guests would like a look around the grounds by torchlight. Stormfield is beautiful, even in the winter."

"It's cold," Clara said brusquely. She scooped the kitten from the billiards table pocket: hers. "I'm going downstairs. Papa, I will see you in the kitchen. Miss Keller, Mr. and Mrs. Macy, it was very nice to meet you."

Clara was halfway to the kitchen when she realized that she'd left her coat. Damn it. She'd have to send Katy up to get it before the Lioness stole it. She kissed the kitten on the head—it smelled like cigars—and went on.

28.

January 8, 1909
Stormfield, Redding, Connecticut

BRINGING MISS KELLER AND the unhappy Macys back down to the library for their tea was a bad move, Isabel realized. She should have kept them in the billiards room when The King left to squelch Clara's fireworks, letting them pet The King's cat Tammany, who'd crawled out from under a sofa when Clara made off with the kitten. Helen and Mr. Macy seemed awfully taken with the cat, stroking it together as Mrs. Macy stood by, plucking at a frizzy ringlet at her neck. Truth be told, Isabel hated the billiards room. She spent too much time in there already, watching The King teach his Angelfish to handle a cue (a waste of effort), or show off for actresses, or waiting for him to finish "one last game" with Ralph as he drank "one last sip of whiskey" when he could be taking her in his arms. Billiards were an obstruction that he threw between them, as were the Angelfish, the eternal round of visitors, the dictation of his autobiography—anything to keep her at arm's length. She understood why. It was payback for losing his trust by keeping Clara's secret, trust she had fought so hard to win. She wasn't sure how much more she could bear.

It was becoming painfully apparent that Horace was not going to respond to her summons to bring more tea. She would have to go into the lion's den with Clara to fetch the refreshments herself.

Mr. Macy didn't look up from signing into Helen's hand when Isabel picked up the tea tray and left for the kitchen.

The King and his daughter were beside the icebox, facing each other down, when Isabel entered.

Tammany's kitten pressed under her chin, Clara flicked a glance at Isabel. "Perfect timing."

Isabel put down the tray, ignoring Clara, although that never got one far. "Where is Horace? Our guests would like more tea."

"Horace is with all the other incompetents whom you hired: I just fired him."

Isabel glanced at The King for verification. Another poor move.

"Don't go crying to Papa, Isabel. It's over. Your whole outrageous pipe dream with Papa—done. I'm not giving up Will unless Papa gives up you."

Isabel absorbed the blow, then, holding herself as if made of glass, went to the stove and lit the burner under the teakettle. "If he wishes to get another secretary," she said carefully, "I would not stand in his way. He knows this."

"Stop it. I saw you two the night of the burglary. Everyone did. I'm not going to pretend anymore that I didn't. Why should I?"

"I saw you, too," said Isabel. "And Mr. Wark."

The King was breathing angrily. In her mind, she saw the jumble of the servants running away, heard the crack of splitting wood as The King kicked over a chair. He'd raised his hand to her and then, trembling, stormed from the room. Resurrecting that moment was an expensive defense.

Clara clenched her fists. "I don't care if you did see us. I love him. Did you think I would just go slinking off with my tail tucked between my legs because Papa demands it? I'm not giving up Will."

Isabel turned around as calmly as possible. "What does *Mrs.* Wark say about that?" She had seen an octopus once, while visiting the aquarium in Bermuda with The King. When The King had knocked on the glass, its eyes had looked murderous as its flesh pulsed from green to brown to black before it shot to the other side of the tank.

Now Clara's surprise, her fury, then her determination contorted her face in similar flashes of succession.

"Don't you lecture me! You of all people, the bitch who sniffed around Papa while Mamma lay dying."

"I have never done anything but my job."

"You are disgusting. The sad thing is that you can't even see how disgusting you are. And I thought you were my friend."

Isabel knew better than to glance at The King. He wouldn't defend her. That had always been part of their deal. She looked instead at the icebox next to Clara. The guests needed milk for their tea.

When The King spoke, it was in a leisurely drawl in spite of his heaving chest. "I am just trying to protect you, Clara. You haven't seemed to cotton on to this, but a person's good name is all they have."

"Says the person who made up his name." She snorted. "Don't make me laugh. You, protect me! That is rich. You made me Mamma's keeper until I fell apart, and when I tried to pick myself up and make something of myself, you turned me into a punch line for your jokes."

"That's not true."

"I asked you not to speak after my debut—I begged you—I didn't want you to come because I *knew* what you'd do! But no, you insisted on coming and did just what you promised you wouldn't: took the stage while they were applauding for me and turned it into a twenty-minute Mark Twain show. How they roared with laughter when you said I got my singing talent from you."

"I'm sorry, Clara. But you do see the humor in that."

"They forgot all about me, Papa. It wasn't even my concert anymore."

"All right, I shouldn't have done that. I told you I was sorry. How long are you going to hold this against me?"

"You can't even see how you break everyone's heart. You thought it was funny for me to believe as a child that a calf could be turned into a horse if I just groomed it and fed it carefully enough."

"Now, that was Patrick's joke, not mine. The coachman," he explained to Isabel, though she had known Patrick and heard this grievance a thousand times.

"He started it, but you went along with it," said Clara. "Oh, you went along with it, all right. You said nothing when he gave me new curry brushes that were 'sure to do the trick.' I babied that calf—Jumbo. Dear Jumbo! She was everything to me. Even when she grew up and had horns, you stood by when Patrick told me that if I only believed, she would turn into the horse of my dreams. And I believed it. I believed it because you agreed with him."

"Oh, are we listing all my mistakes now? Miss Lyon, get me a drink, because this is going to take a while."

"I still loved Jumbo," said Clara, "even after she had grown up and was obviously not going to be a horse. I didn't care. And then one day when I went out to the pasture to see her, she was gone. You let Patrick sell her."

"He did that without asking me."

"You could have bought her back."

"I did!"

"Not at first. I had to beg for her."

The King blew out a sigh. "She was just a cow, Clara."

"No, Papa. She was not just a cow. She was mine."

A knock sounded on the front door. They waited, silent, until Katy marched into the kitchen, her hair weeping from her flattened pompadour. She scanned Isabel with her usual look of contempt. "Mr. Gabrilowitsch is here, Miss Clara."

"Ossip?" Clara squinted at her father. "Why is Ossip here?"

The King crossed his arms, then, cocking his head, his mustache set in defiance, threw her a look. "He wants to see you."

Clara's mouth fell open. "You called him! You asked him to come."

"No, I didn't."

Isabel drew in a breath. That was true. The King hadn't called him. He'd made Isabel do it.

He felt in his coat for matches. "You ought to be flattered, Clara.

Didn't he have a concert last night in New York? And here he came all this way today to see you."

Clara drew in her breath as if filling her lungs with rage. With a little shriek, she snatched the ice bucket from the counter and threw it at her father before storming out of the room.

The hammered aluminum bucket rattled on the wooden floor as The King rubbed his head. He took away his hand to show his wound to Isabel. "She cut me?"

She went over and, frowning, rose on her toes to inspect his forehead.

"Isabel?"

She lowered her gaze to his eyes, then eased her heels to the floor. *Say it. Just say that you love me and I'll stay.*

He looked at her with those smart, wounded, defiant eyes, the eyes of a speared lion—losing blood but with plenty of fight before it went down—then touched his forehead. "Am I bleeding?"

"Not enough to kill you."

"You know that she's hell-bent on ruining my name, don't you?"

"Do you really think Mark Twain can be ruined?" She absentmindedly put down the silver creamer. "You once talked about wanting a submerged reputation, one so deep it can't be reached by sneers and slander."

He grimaced. "Your memory is too damn good."

"You said you wanted a reputation that was unassailable. Once beloved, always beloved. Once respected, always respected." She grasped his hand. "You *have* that kind of reputation, Sam. You're untouchable. Every person's best friend. No one can change that. Clara can live her life—you can live yours—and still your reputation will remain intact. You'll always be loved, no matter what."

He pulled away his hand. "Some things are unforgivable."

"Not in your case."

He laughed bitterly. "Do you really think that's true? I've been shaping Mark Twain since he was born in Nevada, making him ornery but respectable, irascible but kind. Livy understood this. She molded him as much as anybody, made him even more palatable, kept me in line when I was sick to death of him. She knew that Mark Twain was our bread and butter. After I'd run through her money, we needed him. I still need him. Why can't you get this simple fact?" His fingers went to his wound. He winced.

The pain in Isabel's chest ballooned into her throat, choking her. She stepped around him to get to the icebox. "I need milk for your guests' tea."

• • •

Now, loaded down with the tea tray, Isabel made her way back to the library and the Helen Keller party. She was crossing the hall when Ralph Ashcroft stepped out of her office. She was inordinately relieved by the concerned expression crumpling the skin above the bridge of his wire-rimmed glasses. Though she didn't know why Ralph should care for her so much, she was almost tearful with gratitude.

"Are you all right?" he asked in his British clip. "I heard your little Clara having a fit in the kitchen."

"I'm fine."

"You don't look fine."

"Thank you."

"You know what I mean. He shouldn't have made you do it, Isabel."

"Do what?"

"Darling, I wish you wouldn't be so defensive with me. You know what I mean—telephone poor Ossip."

She tried to look at him blankly.

"Isabel, don't let him bully you like that."

"He's not a bully."

He raised a brow.

How Isabel wished she could let the tray fall with a crash. She wanted to rest her head against Ralph's shoulder, to let someone else be the strong one for once.

"I have to take care of our guests." She started forward.

He grasped her forearm. "Do I need to come in there?"

"Why?"

"To take the pressure off of you."

"You, entertaining our guests? You know he wouldn't like that."

"Of course not. He always has to be the bloody cock of the walk. Has he shut down Miss Sullivan's husband yet? You know he will. Only one male lion is allowed in Mark Twain's pride."

She laughed in spite of herself.

He let go of her arm, then rubbed where he had gripped. "I wish you'd let me help you."

"You can't."

He lifted the sugar pot aimlessly from her tray, then put it back down. "I should be cruel to you, shouldn't I? Like he is. Then you'd want me."

The King wasn't always cruel. He could be sweet and boyish and kind. She'd seen it in Italy, before his wife had died. She'd seen it their first summer together, after Livy's death had set him free. But there was a side to him that was untamable, that made him capable of turning on his loved ones like a wounded animal, of turning on himself, chewing off his own leg like a fox caught in a trap.

"People want what they can't have," Ralph said. "I'll go away, then maybe you'll want me."

"Ralph." Her stomach lurched at the thought of losing him. So often since the night of the burglary, he was the only bright spot of her day. But she had no right to make him stay. Not when she was in love with another man. "The company is waiting."

"Yes. You had better go."

She couldn't bear the disappointment in his eyes. She continued down the hall, suspecting she'd done wrong.

• • •

Mr. Macy was spelling into Miss Keller's hand when Isabel entered the room. Miss Keller laughed loudly at her teacher's husband's words as Mrs. Macy glowered from the other side of the sofa. Isabel set down the tray. Poor Miss Keller could not modulate her laughter. What a disadvantage to not be able to keep oneself in check.

"Here we are," said Isabel. "Some nice tea."

"Perhaps you could moderate, Miss Lyon." Mr. Macy turned to her. "Helen says that women prefer men who challenge them. I say they prefer men who coddle them."

"I would agree with Miss Keller. May I refill your cup?"

He held up his cup and saucer, keeping his other hand in Miss Keller's to spell. "But it is in a man's nature to want to pamper the woman he loves."

"It is?" said Mrs. Macy.

Mr. Macy aimed his Harvard chin at his wife.

Miss Keller held herself still as if to hear. "What is it? Did somebody say something?"

"Annie," said Mr. Macy, "did you want more tea?"

His wife shot him a look of contempt that he did not see, busy as he was, spelling something into Miss Keller's hand.

The King shambled in and dropped into an armchair. He gazed around at his guests as if daring them to notice the small cut within the knot swelling above his eye, where the rim of the ice bucket had caught him.

Isabel raised the teapot. "Tea?"

The King waved her off.

"We were talking about whether women prefer to be coddled or challenged," said Mr. Macy. He gave one of his snorting laughs. "You would think I was asking whether they prefer to be burned at the stake or hanged, with the contempt for the question that I've been receiving."

The King patted his coat pockets for a cigar. "You want to know what I think?"

"Yes!" said Mr. Macy.

Isabel poured Mrs. Macy a fresh cup. Everyone clamored to hear The King's thoughts. She remembered disembarking from a journey abroad with The King and Clara, newspaper reporters swarming around them on the gangplank, shouting out their questions. He had happily obliged them, supplying quotes on everything from Theodore Roosevelt ("a showy charlatan") to the popular resort Newport, Rhode Island ("that breeding place—that stud farm, so to speak—of aristocracy of the American type"). Clara, who'd been trailing behind him with Isabel, had sunk into her fur collar and muttered, "What makes him the authority? He's just a humorist."

Now Isabel waited for The King's pronouncement as Mr. Macy struck a match and lit his host's cigar.

The end of The King's cigar sizzled quietly as he sucked. "What I think"—he blew out smoke, then sat back—"is that you're playing a fool's game, Macy. There is no understanding women. Ask me about cats, dogs, chinchillas, but not about women. Men and women, even man and wife, are foreigners. Each has territories that the other can never enter into, never understand."

Angry footsteps pounded up the stairs and into the hall, announcing Clara's return. She flounced into the room, then, putting on a pleasant expression, primly lowered herself into the chair opposite her father. "Did I miss anything?"

Mrs. Macy spelled the question for Miss Keller, who sniffed the air.

The King made an unhurried nod at the fox coat that Isabel had folded and laid on an ottoman next to him. "Not as much as these fellows miss their hides."

Clara made a face at him, then lowered her head at Mr. Macy. She lifted her eyes to gaze at him through her lashes.

Miss Keller smiled in Clara's direction, her sweet fleshy face a study in fondness. "We were discussing whether women prefer to be coddled or challenged."

Clara winced at Miss Keller's voice, then turned to her father. "What did you say, Papa? Let me guess: coddled. Because that is how he treated my mother," she explained to the guests. "He treasured her. He showered her with gifts. She was the only woman he ever loved—the love of his life." She flicked Isabel a triumphant look. "As everyone knows."

Isabel stirred her own tea.

The King puffed on his cigar. "Where's Gabrilowitsch?"

"I sent him off." Clara smiled at her father.

The King stared at her. "He left?"

"I made him."

"He really left? It's dark."

"I watched him go," she said sweetly.

Isabel could hear The King's furious breathing. She worried about the strain on his heart. He glanced at his guests. "Gabrilowitsch is a damn good pianist. You would like him. Isabel, go get him."

Clara pushed back a fallen lock of hair. "Yes, Isabel. Try. Try to get him."

29.

January 8, 1909
Stormfield, Redding, Connecticut

A LANTERN SWINGING IN HER hand, Isabel gained ground on the frail top-hatted figure striding down the road with his overcoat flapping. She regretted not taking the time to put on her galoshes before pursuing Mr. Gabrilowitsch. Snow was seeping into her pumps, and now her stockings would be wet while she entertained Miss Keller and the unhappy Macys, at least until she was released when they changed for dinner. However, it looked as if she might catch Mr. Gabrilowitsch. He hadn't gotten far—not even to the lighted carriage house. Like many men, he seemed incapable of the brisk pace that most women could achieve even while in the grips of a corset. Women were perpetually hobbled by long skirts, silly shoes, and steel-ribbed foundations, yet still they outran their men. Now that she thought about it, how appropriately "stays" were named—it was not just flesh that was to be kept in its place.

"Mr. Gabrilowitsch!" she called.

He looked over his shoulder.

"Mr. Gabrilowitsch, please!"

He walked on and then suddenly stopped. He put his black-gloved hand to his ear, knocking his hat askew.

She trotted to his side, then paused to gulp air that smelled of snow and cedar and cold earth. "Thank you for waiting."

There was something touchingly awkward about Mr. Gabrilowitsch, who was in his early thirties and boyishly small. Perhaps it was his formal hat and voluminous black overcoat, in which he seemed to be playing dress-up. Or it could have been his eyes. Although large and winsome in a mournful way, with their hooded lids, they were out of scale with the rest of his delicate person. They were contracting in the lantern light, as if their owner might be in pain.

He spoke with an accent that hinted of onion-domed churches and shearling hats. "I do not wait for you. I am ill and slow." He closed his eyes in misery.

"I'm so sorry. What is wrong?"

"You say Miss Clemens wishes to see me, but when I come, she tell me I must go."

"I didn't think she would react like that."

"So it was not her idea for me to come? It was you?"

"Not me." Although she was telling the truth, it was Twain-style truth—true and yet not true.

"You said it was opportune time to see her. Opportune! What does that mean?"

"It means it was an advantageous—"

"I know what 'opportune' means! I do not know why you say it when she does not want to see me."

I said it because The King commanded me to, and I am desperate enough to win him back to do anything. Forgive me. "She's been upset."

"Upset! Upset! She is always upset. Now it is my turn. I am upset!" He clutched at his ear.

Isabel drew a breath. "Are you unwell?"

"I have ache in my ear. It started last night at my concert."

"Come back to the house, Mr. Gabrilowitsch, please. I will call a doctor."

A cutter hung with lanterns crested the hill just ahead on the road. Isabel recognized a driver from the Redding train station; behind him were two men. When they saw Isabel, they half-stood and leaned out the sides of the sleigh. "Miss Lyon! Miss Lyon!"

Reporters. Who had alerted them? She took Mr. Gabrilowitsch's arm. "Please let me call a doctor for you. I can get you all fixed up."

Surely her stress was tipping her into paranoia. The reporters were probably just there to mine The King for more homespun wisdom, although it was rather late in the day. Surely after all The King's embroidering about Clara and Mr. Gabrilowitsch, the story about Clara and Wark was dead.

"Say!" cried one of the reporters. "Is that Mr. Gabrilowitsch?"

Mr. Gabrilowitsch turned around. "Yes? That is me."

Isabel tugged him in the direction of the house. "Which ear hurts—the left? I have some drops that I could heat for it. I have heard that blowing tobacco smoke into it helps, too." Isabel heard the jingle of the reins and the shish of the runners as the cutter grew closer.

"Mr. Gabrilowitsch!" shouted one of the reporters. "Are you still courting Miss Clemens? What do you think of the rumors about her and her accompanist?"

Mr. Gabrilowitsch stopped, and holding his ear, rounded his Russian forest-animal eyes at Isabel.

"Mr. Gabrilowitsch!" the other reporter called. "Is Miss Clemens your gal, or is she Mr. Wark's?"

Mr. Gabrilowitsch squeezed his eyes into a pained squint. "I do not understand. Miss Clemens is not my 'gal.' But I do not know why you say she can be gal for my friend Will Wark. Will Wark is married. I meet his wife."

In all of New York, perhaps only Ossip Gabrilowitsch, living in a dense musical reverie when not actually playing the piano, had not heard about Clara's affair with Wark. No wonder that after The King had gone into town in December and driven Clara out of their Stuyvesant Square apartment like the pharaoh forcing Moses out of Egypt, he had invited Ossip to Stormfield for a visit. Who else would have been naïve enough not to realize he was being manipulated?

Isabel steeled herself as the sleigh hissed to a stop and the reporters jumped out, the light from their lanterns careening into the trees.

She put on the smile that showed her delight in representing The King to the press, the one that made her look pleasant while she was dodging the truth and hating herself for it. "Gentlemen, may I ask you for your help?"

"And what about you?" said the one with the gap in his teeth. His cheekbones were the size and color of crabapples. "What about you, Miss Lyon? Are wedding bells still ringing for you and the chief?"

Isabel laughed even as the insides of her chest scorched. "I'm not even going to dignify that with an answer. But gentlemen, please, Mr. Gabrilowitsch and I could really use a hand."

• • •

Isabel returned to the living room, her stockings squishing in her shoes. She quietly took a chair across from Mrs. Macy, not wanting to disturb Clara, standing at the fireplace with a cup of tea, nor to disrupt the game of verbal one-upmanship being carried on by The King and Mr. Macy. Between them on the sofa sat Miss Keller, her hands on the lips of both men. Judging from the upward tilt of his patrician chin, Isabel guessed that Mr. Macy had not yet realized he was a beaten man.

Isabel was wincing under the new pain emanating like the war beat of tom-toms from the back of her skull when Miss Keller cried, "Miss Lyon—you're back!" She gave a single sniff. "You've gotten wet."

The men, arguing about which was the best of Shakespeare's plays, *Hamlet* or *King Lear*, weren't listening; nor, in fact, were the other women. Isabel was free to try to determine the extent of her own damp scent and, in doing so, became aware of the scents of the others in the smoky room: The King's smell of cinders and ash; the astringent mix of Mr. Macy's perspiration and hair tonic; Mrs. Macy's bready blend of stale skin and cloth; Clara's expensive perfume of jasmine and clove; Miss Keller's powdery sweetness—scents that were there all along but had been overshadowed by the information delivered by the eyes and ears. What other sensory cues might Miss Keller be receiving that the rest of the party was blunted to, even while she missed what they were seeing and hearing?

The King leaned away from Miss Keller. "Where's Ossip?"

Clara turned from the fireplace.

"I have him settled upstairs with a hot water bottle," said Isabel. "I'm afraid he has a terrible earache." She pictured the reporters, helping Mr. Gabrilowitsch into the house at her direction, then accepting a cup of coffee in the kitchen and the promise of an interview with Mark Twain in the morning as payment. When the morning came, she would have to concoct a reason why the famous humorist could not meet them.

"That's a pity," said The King. "I wanted Ossip to play for us tonight. How the man can take a block of wood, wire, and ivory and squeeze heavenly music out of it is beyond me. Go get him, Miss Lyon. My angel Helen is homesick for her native music."

Miss Keller laughed as Mr. Macy spelled The King's quip into her hand. The King smiled around the plug of his cigar, proud to have amused her.

Isabel tried to keep her voice pleasant. "I'm sorry, but I'm afraid that my pumping of the Orchestrelle is the only piano that will be playing tonight."

Clara sipped her tea. "You're so good at that. Such a good little pumper."

The King calmly pulled on his cigar.

Still clinging to Helen's hand, Mr. Macy edged forward on the sofa. "Miss Clemens, would you sing for us?"

"Yes, make her sing, Macy," said The King. "You won't regret it. She's quite the contralto."

"Bravo—I see you know now which voice I sing in, Papa. You introduced me as a mezzo-soprano the last time I played for your friends."

The King blew out smoke. "I'm a musical buffoon, Clärchen, dear, you know that. I don't know a tenor from a turnip. But you ought to sing for these nice people. I'm sure they'd love it."

"No," she said flatly. Then she added an unrepentant "Sorry."

Mr. Macy shifted back onto the sofa and glanced at his wife, but her cold stare gave him no quarter. He cleared his throat. "Returning to Shakespeare, what do you make, sir, of the new theory that the Bard of Avon was not really the actor William Shakespeare?"

Isabel grasped at a chance for unthreatening conversation. "Who might it have been?"

Mr. Macy turned to her. "Hm? Frances Bacon."

"Why Bacon?" growled The King.

Mr. Macy adjusted his chin as he assumed the role of scholar. "As you know, as Queen Elizabeth's chancellor, Bacon was a lawyer as well as a scholar and a scientist. He took interest in the theater, yes, but he was the queen's key man, so it was beneath him to write plays. He had to find a front man, and there, nice and handy, was the unknown actor Will Shakespeare. But perhaps Will Shakespeare was a poor choice if Bacon truly didn't want the credit. The plays are so full of history and law and the study of human nature, who could believe that their creator was a run-of-the-mill actor?"

The King rounded the ash off his cigar. "You might give Mr. Shakespeare more credit, Macy. We simple people have been known to make silk handbags from sows' ears from time to time. I'm the son of a failure with nothing to my name but sheer ambition and blind grit, yet damn it, I wrote *Huck Finn* and a few others. I'm proud of those damn books."

"Did you write them, Sam?" Clara dropped into a chair. "I thought Mark Twain did."

Eyeing his daughter, The King drew on his cigar. The tip of his cigar crackled and reddened, eaten by fire. Mr. Macy glanced at Miss Keller, who was sniffing the air like a rabbit. He shifted with discomfort until his gaze caught upon something across the room. His shoulders relaxed. "Hello."

Ossip Gabrilowitsch stood in the doorway, an ice bag to his ear.

The King waved Isabel back down onto her seat, then languidly tapped his cigar on his ashtray. "Ossip, get in here. What's wrong? You look like you just got spit out by a cyclone." Clara turned away, even as Miss Keller's party smiled at him expectantly.

Mr. Gabrilowitsch lowered the heavy lids that had protected his forebears' eyes against the winds howling across the steppes. "I have a ache-ear."

"Sorry to hear that. Miss Lyon, fetch the man a doctor."

Mr. Gabrilowitsch kept the bag pressed to his ear. "It is better I go home."

"Nonsense. Ossip, meet Helen Keller. She's blind and deaf, but don't let that fool you. This girl doesn't miss a trick."

Mr. Macy signed The King's remarks to Miss Keller, after which she got up and extended her hand.

"And this, Helen, is Mr. Gabrilowitsch, Clara's beau and a damn good pianist. Name sounds like 'Gabby Love-Itch,' but that's not how it's spelled, though 'Gabby Love-Itch' suits him to a T around Clara."

"Father. Stop it."

The King introduced Mr. Gabrilowitsch to the others. "We were just talking about Shakespeare, Ossip. Do you believe that Shakespeare was really a poor boy from Stratford who made good with his plays?"

"I do not know about Mr. Shakespeare."

"It's a charming picture." Mr. Macy spelled into Helen's hand as he spoke. "Will Shakespeare started out holding horses for patrons outside the Globe Theater, then worked his way into the playhouse and eventually became an actor, and then, well, we all know the rest of the story."

"He held their horses?" The King sagged and put his forehead on his hand, then, flinching at his wound, sat upright again. "I didn't know that."

"That's the legend," said Mr. Macy.

"He was just a poor boy who held rich people's horses," The King repeated.

"The poorest," said Mr. Macy.

"And they are trying to take his plays from him, saying the rich boy Bacon did them?"

"Well, it is more likely that Bacon wrote them, isn't it?"

"Are you a rich boy, Macy?"

Mr. Macy's signing hand went idle. Helen turned to him, questioning.

"Father," said Clara, "shut up."

A red spot appeared on each of The King's cheekbones as he calmly smoked.

"You speak disrespect to your father," said Mr. Gabrilowitsch. "You must apologize."

Clara burst out laughing.

Mr. Gabrilowitsch turned on his heel to leave.

"How kind of you to save Miss Clemens!" Helen called out.

Mr. Gabrilowitsch paused.

"The sleigh ride last month," said Helen. "When your sleigh nearly fell off the ridge at Redding Glen and you had to save Miss Clemens. Teacher read the article in the paper to me. We were so relieved that you saved The King's daughter."

Mr. Gabrilowitsch expelled a loud breath, his back still turned to them.

"He was a hero," said The King. "Now, don't be modest, Ossip." He took a slow draw from his cigar. "Tell them how you untangled Clara, who was being dragged by the horse on the edge of that ravine, and how you carried her to safety." He coolly smoked as the rims of Mr. Gabrilowitsch's ears turned crimson. Apparently, even Ossip had a glimmer of the outrageousness of the story.

Isabel had tried to convince The King of its implausibility when he had made it up to cover up Clara's affair with Wark. It was a miracle Ossip had gone along with it; he'd done so only because he'd thought that was what Clara wanted. Now, from across the room, it was clear that the slightly built pianist would have labored under Clara like an ant under a dead beetle. But The King refused to care how far-fetched his tale was, and he was right. Because it came from him, the reporters believed it. Helen and the Macys believed it. Even The King himself had come to believe it, as he so often did with the tales he'd made up.

Just then the doorbell jangled in the hall, causing Mr. Gabrilowitsch to rattle in his loose suit of clothes. Isabel remembered that there was no butler. The doorbell rang again as she rose.

"Excuse me." She paused to pick up the napkin that Miss Keller had dropped. She hadn't gotten to the library door when Ralph Ashcroft appeared.

"Visitor for Miss Clemens."

Clara sat up, blinking with energy. "Who is it?"

The King rose up and, radiating fury, stood over her, swaying until Isabel feared that he might fall.

Clara melted back.

"Stay there." He shambled to the door.

30.

January 8, 1909
Stormfield, Redding, Connecticut

RALPH ASHCROFT STEPPED INTO the room vacated by The King. Outside, the snow had resumed. It stuck to the windowpanes as Isabel went to his side, the burn in her digestive tract relocating itself to her heart muscle. His pointed Van Dyke beard grazed his high white shirt collar as he looked down at her; he put his hand to her lower back as they turned to face the guests. His simple gesture of support made tears sting her eyes.

She pulled herself together. "May I introduce you to Mr. Ralph Ashcroft, Mr. Clemens's business manager?"

Ralph saluted Mr. Gabrilowitsch, whom he already knew, then, after shaking hands with Mr. Macy, took Miss Keller's hand tenderly in his own.

"She won't break," said Mr. Macy.

Mr. Ashcroft smiled earnestly into Miss Keller's unseeing eyes. "Very pleased to meet you, ma'am."

Mrs. Macy spelled his words into Miss Keller's other palm.

Mr. Ashcroft kissed Miss Keller's hand, then put it down gently before turning to Mrs. Macy with a smile. "You must be Anne Sullivan."

"Mrs. Macy, chap," said her husband, correcting him.

"So this is the woman who delivered Helen Keller to the world. Madame, I thank you."

Mrs. Macy seemed to inflate slightly as she looked up at him.

"That you could find a way into her mind, when all of the usual channels were blocked, was nothing short of genius."

"Oh, Helen would have gotten out without me," Mrs. Macy said, spelling her words into Helen's hand. "She is more resourceful than you know."

Helen shook her head. "I needed you."

"Maybe not so much anymore," said Mrs. Macy.

Clara swung around in her chair, suddenly interested. "What was it like to be cut off from everything, Miss Keller? Did you make up a world of your own?"

Helen smiled upon receiving Clara's question from Mrs. Macy. "Don't we all make up our own worlds?"

"But weren't you let down by this tawdry old world, with all of its silly rules and small minds," asked Clara, "once Mrs. Macy brought you into it? I should think your imaginary universe was an improvement upon this disappointing one."

"I was just a child," said Helen.

"I do not know about you," said Mr. Gabrilowitsch, holding his ear, "but I like this world and all the beautiful music in it. Especially when I do not have the ache-ear."

Ralph sat forward. "It's interesting, when you think about it. From moment to moment, what I experience is different than what you experience. Here we are all together in Mr. Clemens's cozy library, with the fire crackling and the snow blowing against the windows, yet we are living in our separate worlds. You'd think we'd all be having the same experience, but we aren't. Mrs. Macy and Miss Keller"—he spread his hand out to encompass the entire group—"Mr. Macy, Miss Lyon, Miss Clemens, and I, all of us are thinking unique and private thoughts. Do you think we can ever truly glimpse what someone else is seeing?"

"Brazierres, I didn't think you had such poetry in you." The King strolled into the room, then, not bothering to say who'd been at the door, sat down heavily by the fire. "Aren't businessmen supposed to be all numbers and facts?"

"People don't stay in neat little boxes, Father," said Clara. "No matter how much you want them to."

The King opened his white cashmere jacket. Isabel willed his hand away from the cigars. He was taking in more smoke than air these days. Surely it would kill him. Perhaps that was precisely what he wanted.

"You're right, Clärchen. You should never think that you have pegged your fellow man. You get burned that way." He leaned to the side to pull matches from his pocket, glancing at Isabel.

Clara stroked her forearm as if it were a cat. "I've got a proposal. Miss Lyon, do you think you could outfit the pack of us in blindfolds and earplugs? I think we all ought to be forced into our own little universes, like Helen is in her world, just for a time. See how well we do."

Mrs. Macy's brows, thin as nail clippings, rumpled with disapproval as she signed the suggestion to Helen.

Helen squeezed Mrs. Macy's hand. "Unless you have someone like Teacher to guide you, you might find it frightfully lonely."

Clara shooed off Isabel. "Go see what you can do about rounding up those blindfolds, Miss Lyon." She twitched her mouth in a smile. "Please."

• • •

Upstairs, Isabel plucked monogrammed handkerchiefs from The King's chiffonier drawer, her gut knotting along its length with stress. She had bought the handkerchiefs for The King, as well as the bird's-eye-maple chiffonier. He had made fun of her for calling the piece of furniture by its proper name when she'd acquainted him with the house last June. While she was showing him the contents, he had made her repeat the word, *chiffonier*, then had said it himself with an affected lisp.

"What would you call it?" she had asked, more amused than exasperated.

"A cupboard." He had kissed her on the cheek with a tickle of mustache. "My little society girl."

At that moment she had realized: he had been sending her a message all these years. He knew she was not a society girl, no more than he was a society boy. They were two outsiders, looking through steamed windows at the party going on inside.

Now she heard footsteps in the hall—a woman, by the tap of her shoes. When Isabel turned around, Clara came to the door, the puffed tops of her mutton-leg sleeves nearly vibrating with her agitation. "What are you doing, going through Papa's things?"

"Getting the blindfolds that you requested."

Clara snorted scornfully. "Don't get one for me. I have more important things to do than grope around the furniture with Papa's friends."

"It was your idea." She would not let Clara rattle her. "Anyway, Mr. Gabrilowitsch seemed interested."

"Oh, him!"

Isabel lined up the edges of the thin linen handkerchiefs that had been so carefully ironed by Katy.

"I have been meaning to ask," said Clara. "Where did you get that necklace?"

Instantly, Isabel felt the weight of the strand of coral upon her neck. "Your father gave it to me. Years ago."

"It wasn't his to give. It was Mamma's."

"You're right," Isabel said evenly. "But it was too heavy for her to ever wear it."

"It was a gift to her from Papa."

Isabel had bought this gift on his behalf the first year she had worked for them, but she would not be provoked into saying that. She folded the pile of linen in half, then halved it again.

"She left that necklace to me."

"I didn't know that. I'll give it to you." She raised a hand to the clasp.

"I don't want it now."

"I'll put it in your room, then."

"You mean my 'Nightingale Cage'?" She laughed bitterly. "Was there ever a space more appropriately named? At last—Papa has finally built a cage for me."

Isabel would not respond. Last June, on his first tour of the house and grounds, The King had looked up and, seeing Clara's suite of rooms with its sleeping porch, dubbed it "Clara's Nightingale Cage." He had meant the name to please Clara, it being a nod to her profession as a singer, but it no more softened her disdain toward him than did his giving her money or singing lessons or an education in Europe. It occurred to Isabel that should he ever give Clara things which were inconsequential to him but important to her—her cow Jumbo, his approval of Will Wark, his favoritism over her sister Susy—*then*, he might reach her.

Clara lowered her voice. "Isabel, you've got to help me."

Isabel looked up.

"Papa is trying to force me to marry Ossip."

Isabel folded over the pile into a small square. "This is 1909. He can't force you to marry, Clara."

"He can't?" Clara sat on the edge of her father's great bed. "One time when I was a little girl, I ran into the kitchen to get a lump of sugar for Jumbo, and there was Papa, with our English maid Lizzie. She was leaning against him with her forehead tipped in to his chest, crying, like I would do if I'd stubbed my toe, yet somehow different. It was raining out, thundering, so they must not have heard me. I hid under the table where the cook made bread just as our mechanic, Willie Taylor, came in through the rear door. Before I could make sense of it, Papa grabbed Lizzie and pushed her into Willie Taylor's arms. He started verbally ripping into them in the way that my family did *anything* to avoid. Was there was ever a man born who could so demolish a person with words?" She folded her arms tightly. "I never saw Willie Taylor nor Lizzie again. Mamma told me that they left to get married." She looked at Isabel. "You knew about this, didn't you? He tells you everything."

Isabel closed the chiffonier drawer. "It's modern times. No one can force anyone to do something they don't want to."

Clara laughed. "You must be joking. It's medieval times here at Stormfield. King Twain rules from his throne. Don't you see? He can get away with anything. The world thinks he's a humorist, a clever champion for the downtrodden—"

"He *is* those things."

"He's also a tyrant and a bully at home, and you know it."

Isabel looked out the window, at the dark blue snowy fields, which dissolved into the black wall of the night. It seemed that she could hear her own isolation howling in her ears. "I'm sorry about Will, Clara, but you cannot blame your father for wanting you to part. Will is married."

"So is Papa."

Isabel gave an incredulous laugh. "No, he's not. Not anymore."

"You didn't let that stop you when he was married."

"You can't compare our situations. I never did anything improper when your mother was alive."

Even as she said them, her words rang false. No, she and her King had never physically sealed their love while Mrs. Clemens was alive, but Isabel had encouraged his attention. She had tried to make him love her as she loved him.

"Just don't let him make me marry Ossip. Please."

Isabel sighed, then shook her head. "How am I to help you?"

Clara threw her arms around Isabel. "You'll know how."

• • •

Ralph stood up when Isabel reentered the library, Clara trailing her with arms sulkily crossed. "Here we are, some blindfolds."

The King put out his cigar in his teacup. "Give me one for Mrs. Macy. Macy, you can put on your own. Clärchen, put one on your Gabby-Love-Itch."

As with children preparing to play a game, the mood lightened while all donned their blindfolds. "Should we play blindman's bluff?" said Ralph, securing his.

"What is that?" asked Ossip, his voice muffled. Clara had cruelly tied his handkerchief around both eyes and nose.

The King sat still for Helen to blindfold him, then Isabel, seeing that everyone was taken care of, put on her own. Her last sight was of Mr. Macy slipping his hand in Helen's.

"What are we supposed to do now?" snuffled Ossip.

"The exercise was to be able to experience the world as Miss Keller does," said Ralph, "not having vision or hearing to filter it through."

"But I can hear," said Ossip.

"Then count your blessings, boy," said The King.

There was a silence.

"Well," said Mr. Macy, "this is odd. What next?"

"This is Brazierres's damn game," said The King. "Brazierres, you tell us."

Isabel heard the swish of Ralph's jacket as he shrugged. "Let's just talk."

There was another silence, then several of them talked at once, followed by a subsequent strained silence.

"It seems," Ralph said after a further awkward collision of words, "that we rely on our sight to know when to speak. We need cues that we're not even aware of."

They sat quietly. Isabel could hear the soft hiss of fingers against a human palm—someone signing to Helen.

Across the room from the signing hands, Mrs. Macy spoke up. "I was essentially blind for most of my childhood, from six to eighteen, but I had been part of the seeing world long enough to know that I was missing an unspoken element of communication when I could no longer see. I knew I was missing *something* that my hearing and smelling, my touch, couldn't make up for, and it frightened me—although I'm afraid that my fear looked more like fury. Having lost her hearing and vision as a nineteen-month-old, Helen had never experienced these things when I came to her, and I have never been able to explain them. How do you explain something that has no words? Helen," she said stiffly, "Helen, I am sorry for failing you."

The hand that was spelling went still.

A quiet descended. Isabel became aware of every little sound—a ticking somewhere in the bowels of the furnace, The King's slow breathing. As she strained to listen, she felt something else: the reaching out of another person to her, not by movement of his body but with his very will.

Without speaking, she knew to take off her blindfold. Ralph was waiting for her, his brown eyes intense. *Marry me*, he mouthed.

She blinked with surprise.

Marry me, he repeated, and smiled.

The King pushed up his blindfold, uncovering one shining gray eye. It narrowed as it took in Isabel and Ralph.

Say something, Sam, she wanted to howl. *Fight for me.*

At that moment, Mr. Macy, still blinded, leaned in to Helen. He pressed his lips against her neck, then stayed there as a silent smile bloomed across her face.

Across the room, his wife sat with her hands in her lap and her eyes bound like Lady Justice, waiting for the game to end.

The King watched, crimson swarming over his face.

Mr. Macy drew back when he heard Ossip peeling off his handkerchief. Squinting with pain, the pianist held his ear as he scanned the library. "Where is Clara?"

31.

January 8, 1909
Stormfield, Redding, Connecticut

A SEARCH THROUGH THE HOUSE turned up nothing. Calls to the village were placed. Torches were lit. Tracks were examined in the snow around the mansion. Isabel summoned Giuseppe from the coach house for a report, and the rest of staff was questioned. No one had seen Clara, not even Katy, who would not look Isabel in the eye when she denied knowing anything about her disappearance.

Ralph, carrying a torch, caught up with Isabel when she was out on the terrace, coatless and scanning the rear grounds.

"Where do you think she went?" The flames groaned as he held up the torch, bathing the steps and the distant empty fountain, bereft of its Cupid, in its yellow light.

"I don't know." Isabel rubbed her arms against the cold. "She couldn't have gone far in this dark. She's probably holed up in the barn, enjoying the fuss being made over her."

Ralph's face looked young and earnest in the firelight. "Isabel, I was serious before. I do want you to marry me. It's no use pretending that I could just go away. I'm in love with you. I'll fight for you if that's what it takes."

She caught her breath. "You'd fight for me?"

"Of course I would." He laughed. "I *am* fighting for you. Every day—against that old lion in there, and damn it, he's winning. But I've got something on my side that he doesn't have: time."

"Oh, Ralph, don't say that."

"I'm sorry. But it's the truth. You need a full man, Isabel. You deserve one." He saw her wince.

He put his arm around her. "I'm sorry, darling. This is no way to win you over. It's freezing. Let's go in."

Reeling, Isabel returned to the library to apprise the guests of the situation. They listened, their faces pinched with apprehension, until The King lumbered in, his skin an increasingly frightening shade of red.

Mr. Macy stood. "I'm sorry about your concerns for your daughter, Mark. Unless there is some way in which we can help, I think we had better leave."

"You can't," The King said. "There's no train this late." He plunked down in his chair.

Mr. Macy ran his hand through his lank black hair. "Surely we can do something, then—go over to the village, ask around, see if—"

"Don't you think you've done enough harm, Macy?" The King said.

Mr. Macy held up his million-dollar chin. "And what harm is that?"

Sheltered within his private musical world and therefore unaware of The King's impending roar, Ossip jumped up from the edge of the chaise longue. "I am looking for her outside. No one is looking for her outside."

"I did," said Isabel. "With Mr. Ashcroft."

The King raised his shaggy head.

"Out back," she continued. "We didn't see any new tracks in the snow, although admittedly, it was hard to tell in the dark with all the various other footprints."

"She might take walk," said Ossip. "I told her an important thing. Maybe she need to think. But maybe she get lost and now is cold.

Now she is very frightened. And it is my fault." He pounded his fist on his hand. "I must find her. Now."

"It is possible that she went for a walk"—Ralph paused, acknowledging the ludicrousness of the thought—"and stopped in at one of the farmhouses around here when she got cold. Few of the farmers have phones to let us know."

Ossip's too-large pants unfurled around his legs as he strode for the door.

"Hold up!" bellowed The King. "Don't go off all cockeyed. I'm not losing two of you tonight. Isabel, ring Giuseppe to bring around the sleigh. We'll do this right."

Isabel went to the phone closet as the men in the party, save Mr. Macy, put on their overcoats and galoshes. Isabel was jamming herself into her wrap when Mrs. Macy stumped into the hall. "I'd like to come."

The red in The King's face intensified to purple as he bent down to buckle his boot. "You'd better stay."

"Do you have some galoshes I might borrow?" she asked Isabel.

The King straightened. "Annie. Dear. You've got to stay. I hate to tell you, but damn it, you've got a tiger by the tail in there."

Cold air swept in as Ossip opened the door and went out onto the porch. Ralph, pulling on his gloves, dashed after him, then banged the door closed with a whoosh of cold.

"I'd like to go," Mrs. Macy said firmly.

The King clapped on the Russian fur cap given to him by Ossip. It stood from his head like a crown. "Annie, I don't think you should leave those two alone."

She sighed deeply. "In some ways Helen is still a child."

Buttoning her coat, Isabel glanced at her King.

"She does not know when she does wrong." Mrs. Macy looked at Isabel. "I know what you're thinking: that John knows."

The King's icy words hung in the cold hall: "Want me to kill him?"

"I won't leave Helen. I won't. She's everything to me. As intensely as I hate her right now, I love her even more. But that doesn't mean that she won't leave me. I won't stop her if she wants to go."

He snorted as he helped her on with her coat. "So you do want me to kill him."

"No." She put an arm into a sleeve. "I want her to decide. Me or John." She slipped in her other arm, then shrugged into her coat. "And then, after that, I will decide if I can forgive her."

• • •

Soon they were huddled within the black leather shell of the sleigh, The King, Mrs. Macy, and Isabel sharing the buffalo robe, Ralph and Ossip holding lanterns, crouched on either side as Giuseppe drove through the bitter cold. The sleigh bells jingled, incongruously cheery in the frozen darkness. Golden lamplight melted over the trees, creating monster shadows that reared up and threatened, only to fall away with the retreat of the shishing sleigh. The stream revealed itself as a pane of sheer gold glass under which something trapped bubbled and thrashed.

When they broke from cover, the firelight spread over a snowy field stubbled with severed cornstalks, turning all a dark molten gold. A golden buck foraging in the snow raised its head, then bounded after two golden does fleeing.

Isabel asked Mrs. Macy, "Have you thought of leaving him?"

The night swallowed Mrs. Macy's short laugh. "Dozens of times."

Across the field, the lanterns illuminated Isabel's cedar-shingled saltbox house, where smoke was drifting from her chimney and lamplight flicked in the parlor window. What an expert her mother had become in making a fire, Isabel thought, she who'd had servants tending to them for half of her life. What it was like for her mother, a child of privilege, to be isolated in a cottage in the middle of the Connecticut countryside, having to cook and clean and do for herself, with nothing to keep her company but her frilly pincushions. How stifling life must be for her.

"Stop there," The King shouted to the coachman. "The old lady might have seen Clara."

When they drew nearer the house, Ossip leaped from the sleigh. He cried out in pain as he hit the snow. His lamp tumbled across the crust of white and went out.

The sleigh stopped. The rest of the party gathered around where he sat on the ground, his coattails splayed over the snow. He raised his trouser leg as Ralph held a light over him. Blood pooled in a dime-sized gouge.

"You must have hit a rock," said Isabel. "They're a hazard here—these hills are studded with them. Well, come inside. I can bandage you up."

She and Ralph were helping him up when the door swung open, sending out a yellow swath of light. "Isabel!" Mrs. Lyon bleated.

The group picked their way toward her down the path trampled in the snow.

"Isabel, what are you doing here?"

Isabel did not mention that it was her own house. "Mother, please get the bandages that I keep in the pantry. Mr. Gabrilowitsch has hurt himself."

"No!"

Isabel squinted at her mother, who was wringing her handkerchief. Her face was flushed, and the cameo pin on her collar had been knocked sideways. "Mother, are you ill?"

"No. Yes!" Mrs. Lyon put a hand to her belly. "My stomach."

"Go lie down, then." She gently pushed past her mother with Ralph and the limping pianist.

Mrs. Lyon trotted next to Isabel. "Put him on the davenport! Mr. Clemens, you sit right here." She patted the rocker turned to the fire.

The King was breathing hard—harder than the short walk up to the house should have provoked. "Damn it, Georgiana, we don't have time for social hour. Have you seen my daughter?"

She blinked at him. The fringe on the green velvet sofa shook as Ossip was eased onto it.

"I'll go get the bandages," said Isabel.

"No!" yelped Mrs. Lyon. "I've—I've moved them. I know where they are." She bustled from the room.

Isabel saw that beneath the upswept flaps of his fur crown, The King's face had turned the color of old ashes. Fine purple veins webbed his cheeks.

"Sam, sit down." She swept a batch of pincushions from an armchair into the mending basket.

The King lowered himself, panting. "You're still making pincushions?" he managed to say.

"Yes."

"I take care of you that badly," he stated, "that you still need to make pincushions." His crown listed when he laid his head on the back of the chair. "Is there anyone's life that I have not bungled?"

Mrs. Lyon trundled back in and shoved the paper box of bandages and a bottle of iodine at Isabel. "It's so late," she fretted. "Shouldn't all of you go back home? Isn't it time for dinner?"

The King rested, his eyes closed, as Giuseppe stood shedding snow by the doorway, blocked by Mrs. Lyon from retreating to the kitchen. Isabel cleaned and dressed Ossip's wound, assisted by Ralph, for whose silence she was grateful—the better that she could monitor the sound of The King's labored breathing. She was tying off the bandage when a thump came from the back bedroom. The King's eyes opened.

"Is someone here?" asked Ralph.

"Who would be here?" Mrs. Lyon clapped her hands. "Who would like cocoa?"

Isabel pulled Ossip's cuff over her handiwork. "Let me get it." She pushed up and strode toward the kitchen before anyone could stop her.

Mrs. Lyon bowled after her. "Isabel! Let me help!"

Isabel continued down the hall and flung open her mother's bedroom door. Upon the blue and cream field of Mrs. Lyon's coverlet, Clara leaned into the muscular embrace of Will Wark.

• • •

Isabel had the presence of mind to shut the door behind her. "What are you doing here?"

Mr. Wark spoke up first. "I came to the house but Sam turned me away." He tightened his hold on Clara. "We're getting married."

Isabel glanced at her mother, who smiled lopsidedly. "Did you get a divorce?"

"I'm working on it," said Mr. Wark. "Edith is being stubborn."

"Perhaps she's thinking of your two children."

"Aw, Nana. How can I be a good dad to them when my heart is with someone else?"

Isabel half-laughed. "Plenty of people have sacrificed their hearts for those who depend on them."

Clara lowered her head in defiance. "We don't care."

"Where do you plan to go? What do you plan to do? There's not a concert hall in America that would book a couple in your situation. I can promise you that your father will cut you off."

"Fine. Let him. I'll tell the world about you two. See how he likes that."

"Everyone already has their suspicions about you and Mr. Clemens," Will said. "You ought to hear them talk about it in town."

The door opened. The King towered and swayed in the entrance like a titan ready to topple.

Clara cringed against Wark. "Papa!"

The King stared mutely, his face a horrifying magenta-streaked yellow now, his skin papery, his eyes bulging beneath the lightning strokes of his brows.

Isabel rushed to him. "Sam!"

He flung her off.

"It's not what it looks like," Clara cried. "We have honorable intentions."

"Mr. Clemens—" Will began.

"You're trying to punish me," bit off The King. "You picked the worst possible man so you can bring me down. Your piano player! He's married! Soon as people find out, you'll be hated. I'll be hated. We'll be despised as scum. But you would do this to yourself, because the revenge will be so sweet."

"Papa! That's not true."

"I know about vengeance. I wrote the book! Didn't I tell upon my own father, hoping to get revenge?"

"Tell who?" Clara whispered. "Tell what?"

"But Jennie was the one who got hurt—I didn't think of that. It killed me enough to see my father whip her, but when Mother made Father sell her—" He forked his hand through his violence of hair. "They sold her to the worst slave dealer in town. The one who sold all his 'merchandise' to the death fields outside New Orleans. A house slave like Jennie wouldn't last a year! They sold her to her death." He dropped his hand. "See why I wrote so many stories in which the slave sold down the river was saved? Huck Finn, Pudd'nhead Wilson, Aunt Rachel, all of them—wishful thinking." The color drained from his face until it was the white of cooked bone. "My parents never got a penny for her. That dealer, the cheat, never paid them. She was sold to her death for nothing."

Isabel broke the horrified silence. "You were a boy. Whatever it is that you think you did, it wasn't your fault."

"The guests are waiting!" Mrs. Lyon cried.

The King stilled her with a look, then swung back, swaying, to Clara. "I got my revenge. By telling on my father, I made Mother hate him so badly that when he died five years later, she sold his body to the medical college. No families sell their loved ones to science. It's too shameful. Only unclaimed paupers and criminals become cadavers. But Mother sold him. And not just for the money. Oh, sure, we needed the cash—Father had a way of *repelling* money, Christ, we were broke!—but there were other ways to get it. I could go to work, my brother Orion could work, my sister, Pamela, could teach piano. No, it was because Mother hated him that badly. And she made me watch. Made little Sammy see it all. Every last knife cut, every slice into my father's flesh, I saw through the keyhole of his bedroom door." He laughed bitterly. "My mother knew a thing or two about revenge herself."

Clara hid her face in her hands.

His eyes reddened as he looked down upon his weeping daughter. "You've always been the most like me of all my girls. Always gave me the most trouble. Jean does whatever I want her to. Susy, high-spirited as she was, never gave me grief, either. If I asked her to put on a play for me, she whipped the whole neighborhood into the production. If I mentioned that no one had written my biography, she wrote one herself, though she was just thirteen. If I asked her to leave college at Bryn Mawr and swear off her lady friend, she packed up that day and went with me to Europe. She never saw that lady friend again, or any lady friend. I thought she did these things because she loved me. But no. It was because she was terrified of me." He let out a long, weary breath, his life force going with it. "Why didn't the girl ever fight me? I asked her to give up the love of her life, and she didn't even fight."

"No one can fight you, Papa."

"You do. Look at you. You're every bit as spiteful and mean and spoiling for revenge as I ever was."

A knock sounded on the door, then Ralph Ashcroft leaned in. He drew back when he saw the expressions in the room. Loud voices came from the parlor.

"Who's out there?" growled The King.

"Reporters. With Miss Keller."

"At night?"

"They got wind about Clara. Someone telephoned them. They went back to the house for a story, and Miss Keller told them you'd gone."

"Helen is with them?" Isabel asked.

"She insisted on coming with them to find her teacher. They

said she made an absolute fuss until they agreed to bring her, something about making a terrible mistake. She was pretty keen on leaving Mr. Macy, it appears." Ralph caught Isabel's arm. "Darling, you don't look well."

As slowly as a gashed lion near death, The King brought his gaze back to Clara. "Don't you see? I'm giving you a way out. People are ready to believe that you were never with a married man, that you were sweet on Ossip all along—and he actually does love you, God help him. He's got as miserable a life ahead of him as poor Livy had with me, but damn fool, he wants it. Take it, Clärchen. Take his love. Take everyone's love—take the whole world's. Because they will love you. They will love that damn Mark Twain and everything about him, including his daughter, as long as they believe he's real. Wallow in their love, Clärchen. I can tell you, it makes up for a lot." He sagged, his hand to his heart, then dragged his gaze to Isabel. "What are you waiting for? Go tell those damn reporters. Tell them Clara's marrying Ossip."

Clara stared at him, her face contorted with hatred. "It's too late. Your offer's no good anymore. Don't you hear what they're saying on the streets? You're living in sin with Isabel. Mark Twain's halo is in pieces."

Isabel looked into the drained yellow eyes of her dying Sam. She cherished him and all the parts of him—the boy, the man, the aging King. Her fellow outsider. She would not fail him.

"Mark Twain's halo is perfectly intact. How can he be living in sin with me when I am planning to marry Ralph? All I am"—she clung to his gaze, willing life into him—"is Mr. Clemens's secretary."

32.

May 1909
Stormfield, Redding, Connecticut

ISABEL SAT NEXT TO her husband in the train car. She had on the same velvet jacket she'd worn to her wedding two months earlier, the same broad-crowned boater tied down with a veil, the same ripe-plum dress. She looked at her hands in their netting gloves, then curled them closed.

Ralph, watching her, picked up a hand and kissed it. "Are you all right, darling?"

She soaked in the voice of her new husband, so earnest and so very young—he was only thirty-four. Already tall, he seemed to have shot up a few more inches since their marriage. Since proving himself in the marital bed, he strutted like an English Adonis. She smiled in spite of her straining nerves. That part of marriage was nice. "I'm fine."

He didn't seem convinced. "Are you sure you don't want me to take care of Mark myself? I don't have a good feeling about this meeting. God knows what Clara has put him up to. The little witch has gone off her nut—running to H. H. Rogers to have him audit the household accounts, accusing you of embezzling. She's spewing her venom all over town, you know, hinting of your crimes."

"I've not embezzled. There are no crimes. I've given that family every ounce of my devotion for the past seven years for fifty dollars a month and no more."

"I know, but—"

"How can she possibly hurt me when I have truth on my side? Surely people will see through her."

"Already she got him to fire us. We look like a couple of crooks."

"That's temporary. You'll see. He'll vindicate us."

His mouth tightened with doubt. He squeezed her hand.

She turned her face to the window as the train clattered through the rocky Connecticut woods. How had it come to this? Her destiny was entwined with her King; she'd known it from the start. She could no more pull away from him than could a river resist its surge to the sea.

Maybe that was why he'd called this meeting. He felt this, too. Maybe he wanted to fight for her. She drew in a breath. Could he finally want to fight for her? She didn't know what she'd do if he did. She was married now.

"I can't see what more Clara wants," said Ralph. "Why is she so determined to ruin you? Mark fired you; she gave up Wark. Everything is even."

"Clara likes things decidedly uneven—tipped in her favor."

He laughed grimly. "That's for certain."

"Deep down, she's not really after me. But I make a less dangerous target than her father."

"Well, she had better stop her antics soon." He pressed her hand once more. "No one is hurting my wife."

Grazing cows; farmyards where women hung up wash; new-leafed trees flashed by. Her hand still entrapped within Ralph's, Isabel's heart pounded at the thought of seeing her King. The last time she'd been with him was on her wedding day, in the city. What a windy day it had been, yet weirdly balmy for March. The sky above the redbrick city was blue, although the paving stones and sidewalks of Fifth Avenue were wet with rain when she'd left her hotel with her mother.

"Can you imagine?" her mother had said. The wind grabbed her skirt and shook it like a dog playing with a rag. She flogged it down.

"There wasn't going to be an organist! How can you have a wedding without music? It's odd enough that you are having the ceremony on a Thursday."

Automobiles shuddered by. It struck Isabel that there were no carriages. Where had all the horses gone? In the blink of an eye, they were obsolete and then they vanished, replaced by man-made steeds with steel hearts. The world had changed overnight.

Holding down her hat threatening to take off in spite of the veil tied under her chin, Isabel glanced at her mother. She was marching along with Isabel's bouquet of three gardenias as if she herself were going down the aisle. "It's just a small wedding, Mother."

"Not so small that I should not hire an organist. The man came highly recommended by the rector. Evidently, he's the best. Always go for the best."

"Thank you for getting him." What a disappointment she must be to her mother, having wed neither professor nor America's king. At least Mrs. Lyon seemed to enjoy the treat Ralph had given them in arranging for rooms at the exclusive Hôtel Brevoort, just down the street from the church. Her disillusionment had seemed momentarily eased when they had shared the elevator with the Turkish head of state.

Now the purse on Mrs. Lyon's arm rattled with bars of hotel soap as she batted down her skirt, lifted by a gust. They walked past Mr. Clemens's old house. How peculiar it seemed to Isabel to pass the steps she'd climbed hundreds of times and to look down through the basement windows and not see Mr. Clemens's billiards table. She was further disconcerted to do so while on her way to marry another man.

Two blocks up, Ralph waved to them from the wet steps of the Church of the Ascension, then, holding down his top hat by the brim, strode to meet them. He folded Isabel against him.

"It's bad luck to see the bride before the wedding!" cried Mrs. Lyon.

Ralph held Isabel tight. "We'll take our chances."

Mrs. Lyon strained to listen. "How is the organist?"

"I don't think one is in there. At least, I haven't heard music."

Mrs. Lyon gasped, pushed the gardenias at Isabel, and bustled inside.

Ralph pulled back to look down at his future bride. "You look gorgeous."

She glanced up at his top hat, shining in the sun, then down upon his crisp white shirt and tie, before settling on his grin, as comforting as ever. "So do you."

"Are you nervous?"

"No." She glanced anxiously over her shoulder. "Are the guests here?"

He nodded. "All six of them." He caught her gaze. "No Mr. Clemens."

She kept her face neutral. "He said he was coming."

"Change of heart, I suppose."

The pastor came out and, after shaking their hands, escorted Isabel to the vestry, a small room that smelled of candles and silver polish, and of the gluey scent of hymnals. She was to wait for her mother and then enter the sanctuary, whereupon the ceremony would begin.

She was pacing the stone floor when a knocking came on the door. *Tap-tap-tap-TAP.*

She melted with relief and let him in. "Sam. You came."

"Someone needs to give away the bride," he growled.

Her relief faded when she noticed his lack of color. The luster was gone from his eyes.

"Samuel?"

"Lioness, listen. You don't have to do this."

"But I do."

"Aren't you supposed to save those words for the ceremony?"

Tears surprised her.

"I didn't mean to make you cry."

She blinked at her bouquet, trying to compose herself.

He followed her gaze. "Here. Add to that mess." He swung his arm from behind his back. Three round flower heads bobbed from his hand.

"Hydrangeas!" She looked up at him. "Thank you."

"My favorite for my favorite. Closest thing to giving you a piece of me." He narrowed his eyes in a cagey squint. "In fact, go ahead and think of these as me. Then make sure you put them by your nuptial bed."

He could always make her laugh, even now. "Oh, but you are lovable and naughty and good."

"Now, now. Don't say anything I might regret."

She smiled in spite of her aching heart.

His voice became stiffly hopeful, like that of a boy talking himself out of being afraid of thunder. "These next few weeks are going to be tough, but we'll get through them. Remember, whatever I do is because of a promise I have made to Clara." His bravado lost steam. "God, this is a terrible thing."

She touched his hand. "Sam."

He shook his beautiful head. "I'm getting so weary of this nonsensical world. I wish that comet would come and take me away."

"Hush. Nobody's going anywhere."

He fixed her with his fierce gray eyes. "When it comes, I'm going to hop on its back and straddle it like a bronco. Everyone will tip their hats as I blaze on by."

"Yes. They'll say, 'There goes America's Sweetheart.' "

He snorted with disdain. "Only the grumpier ones will say, 'No, that's just that old bird-of-paradise, the Belle of New York.' "

They laughed, then, sobering, grasped each other in an embrace.

His voice rumbled in her ear, pressed to his chest. "God, I love you."

When she looked up at him, he kissed her tenderly.

Strains of organ music drifted in. He sighed. "That's my cue to go."

They let go of each other by degrees, until only their fingertips touched. "Goodbye, my Lioness. I'll see you on the other side."

• • •

Now Ralph was frowning at her as the train clanked over a trestle. "I really don't think you're all right, Isabel."

"I was just resting, thinking of our wedding."

He nodded. "This meeting is for the best. I reckon the old lion is trying to be a good sport. He wished us well enough after the wedding."

Isabel glanced away. When they had come outside the church after the ceremony to receive their guests, Sam had snarled, "The first one of you people who gets pregnant is going to get fired." The crudeness of his remark, its inert hostility, had stung her. Yet her husband had taken the same rude words as a compliment, a nod to his manhood for beating his rival.

She laid her head against Ralph's shoulder. Let him have his victory. He was good to her. She owed him some happiness.

• • •

An hour later, Isabel stood in her former office off the entrance hall of Stormfield, an exile in a room of her own making. How many times had she sat here and remarked in her journal of the wonders of the day? She had thought they could never end.

Controlling herself, she gazed out the small window onto the front porch. The chip had returned to the balustrade and had grown to the shape of Texas. The center of the exposed wood was darkening with rot. When had she first noticed that spot? It must have been the day of Helen Keller's visit, the day of the beginning of her end.

The weekend had not gone well for Helen and the Macys, either. After the crisis on that Friday night in January, which resulted in Giuseppe driving Wark to the village and presumably out of Clara's life, they'd stayed on through to Monday, but it had been an awkward visit, with Helen continually abandoning the Macys for time alone with The King. Each time Mr. Macy approached her, she unapologetically pushed him toward his wife, then scooped up the hand of The King. By Saturday night, The King, weary and distracted, had resorted to simply reading to the group from his work. He chose "Eve's Diary."

Isabel could see her King on his throne by the fire, the wooden cupids of the mantelpiece cavorting above him, the red-linen-covered book in his intelligent hands, his head bowed with exhaustion. He looked up at Isabel and Ralph, newly engaged and holding hands, as he turned the pages, then read on about Eve's mental and emotional quickness.

When he came to the ending, to the scene in which a desolate Adam stands at his beloved Eve's grave, The King paused to meet Isabel's eyes. The fire, snickering within its iron confines; Helen, eager for Mrs. Macy to spell into her hand; Mr. Macy, banished to the other side of the room, his champion chin upon his vest; all seemed to wait for his finish. Ralph squeezed Isabel's hand. How she yearned to shake it off.

The King had drawn a shattering breath, not letting go of her gaze. He did not need to consult the page when he spoke.

" 'Wheresoever she was, *there* was Eden.' "

• • •

Ralph's heels snapped on the tile of the hall. "Son of a bitch! I'm suing." Isabel stepped outside her former office to find her husband, strawberry-faced, fists balled. "He wants you now."

Rust and olive designs flashed beneath her feet as she ran over the carpet she'd so carefully chosen less than a year ago. Let this be a rapprochement. Even if he weren't calling her back to work for him, surely there was some role she could play in his life—a friend who knew him better than anyone. A confidante. Something! She just needed to be near him.

In the library, The King slouched in his chair under the playful mantel cupids like a Caesar sitting in judgment. An asp of smoke slithered from the cigar cocked between fingers resting on an armrest. Only the twitching flesh under his eyes broke his pose of nonchalant contempt.

She waited, hope pounding in her chest.

"Jean's back," he said at last.

She swallowed to quiet the noise in her ears. "I didn't see her."

"I assume she's out romping with her animals."

Isabel could not help herself. "I hope someone's with her."

He stared at her, then made a scoffing snort. "Still trying to paint a bad picture of her."

She held her breath, a creature suddenly aware of danger.

He spoke slowly and deliberately. "You hypocrite."

Isabel took the blow.

"Your one great crime—"

"Crime?"

"—the crime that I can't forgive you of, is keeping Jean from me. You exiled her to those depressing institutions, you kept her under lock and key, you made me listen to those goddamn quacks, when she could have been living here with me."

The thumping quickened in her ears. "She needed help. She tried to kill Katy. Repeatedly."

"Katy says you made that up. She says you made Jean look sicker than she was to get her out of your way. I could kick myself for not listening to her sooner."

"But Katy is the one who told *me* about the attacks. I never actually saw them." The implication of what Katy had done sank in. In what other ways had Katy sabotaged her? "It doesn't matter—I've only wanted the best for Jean. Dr. Peterson is the best specialist in epilepsy in the world. Jean got the care she desperately needed. Sam, no matter what Katy or anyone says, she can't be on her own."

"Show some respect!" he roared.

She drew back.

"You overstep your place like your bounder of a husband."

Icy fissures streaked through her bones.

He sucked down smoke. "Don't tell me you weren't there laughing over Brazierres's shoulder when he wrote that letter to me."

"What letter?"

"That nothing of a Liverpudlian sewer rat, that squalling baby who calls himself a man—*your juvenile husband*—thinks he's an equal of mine. He, a total nothing, writes to me, a figure in the world, and tells me what I should do. He mistakes me for a fellow bastard, born in the same stinking gutter."

Breathing hard now, the flesh above his bristling mustache ocher and purple, he paused to crush out his cigar. "He called Clara insane. Did you know that? He said her mind was 'diseased with envy, malice, and jealousy.' He said if I were a man, I would defend *you* and set the record straight." He gripped the arms of his chair and leaned forward, his face blackening with rage. "If I were a man. IF I WERE A MAN!"

"I'm sorry," she whispered.

"How you two must get a laugh out of the old man! What a toothless old lion you must think I am, so easily wrestled down by a pair of lascivious jackals." He snatched up a pile of papers next to him. "Your bastard of a husband has no inkling of what a real man does. A real man defends his flesh and blood. Do you really think I'd sell Clara down the river? Set the record straight!" He shook the pages. "I'll set the record straight. I'm documenting your whorish ways, down to all the times you stretched yourself out on my bed, your arm over your head and your legs open, where you would lie by the hour, enjoying the imaginary probabilities. Who did you think you were? The star of the harem waiting for the eunuch to fetch the sultan?"

Her knees buckled. She groped for the back of a chair.

"Here, let me read you a line: 'Miss Lyon is a liar, a forger, a thief, a hypocrite, a drunkard, a sneak, a humbug, a traitor, a conspirator, a filthy-minded and salacious slut pining for seduction, and always getting disappointed, poor child.' " He looked up, his face hideous with contempt. "What'd I miss?"

She shook her head, bile rising in her throat.

"Don't you *ever* question my manhood again."

Her voice cracked. "Sam."

"Get out."

"Sam, no."

"GET OUT!"

As she fled, she heard a cry of pain as the pages thudded to the floor. Only later did she realize that the cry, that of a heart being rent in two, had not been her own.

33.

July 1909
The Lobster Pot, Redding, Connecticut

WHITE SHEETS FLAPPED ON the clothesline strung across the yard as Isabel swiped her forehead with the sleeve of her cotton blouse, then plucked another tomato from the vine. She peered into the basket on her arm, sniffing in the fruit's tang of wormy dirt. It was her first crop at the Lobster Pot, her first full summer, and in spite of her inexperience, a decent haul. Inside the gray-shingled house, her mother was heating up water for canning—a new skill for both of them.

The crunch of stones and the whining of engines announced the approach of automobiles on her lane. She looked up as an automobile emblazoned with EDISON STUDIOS rumbled past, its dust billowing into the open touring car rolling behind it, in which sat the famous inventor himself. His notoriously grumpy expression and hayseed haircut were visible in the backseat. He and his crew must be making a motion picture of The King. How Mark Twain would like that. Now he might be captured on film, pontificating about her dishonesty, her whorishness, her penchant for stimulants and whiskey. She could only imagine the captions. She picked another tomato, a lovely specimen until she turned it over and found a gaping hole in the sugary coral flesh.

The summer had been brutal. Clara had graduated from a slanderous letter-writing campaign to mutual friends, to frequent conferences with the press in which she accused Isabel of thievery and drug addiction. Ralph had fought back, blithely exposing Clara's attachment to her married accompanist and the true nature of Jean's disease, which in turn goaded The King into publicly threatening to file suit against Isabel for theft. It had become a full-scale war of the ugliest kind. Isabel's head throbbed with the thought of it; she didn't sleep; and now Ralph was in England, rallying support for their cause. The next volley lobbed at her by the Clemenses she would have to handle alone.

She had taken her filled basket into the kitchen, where her mother was looking doubtfully upon the mason jars boiling in a pot on the stove, when someone knocked on the front door. Wiping her hands on her apron, Isabel went to answer it. Mr. Lark, The King's attorney, stood on the white-painted porch.

He thrust a document at her when she opened the door, then glanced away. In all these months since the burglary, she hadn't gotten used to the inability of men to look her in the eye.

"Hello, Mr. Lark."

"Don't bother to read it. I'll tell you the gist of it. Mr. Clemens has filed a complaint against you for stealing four thousand dollars from him, which he will press to the full extent of the law."

"His timing is quite clever, considering he knows my husband is out of the country and cannot help me."

Mrs. Lyon came to the door. "What is it, Isabel?"

"A big problem for your daughter." Mr. Lark turned to Isabel. "Mrs. Ashcroft, my client is a lenient man. He has offered to drop the charges under one condition."

"What?" bleated Mrs. Lyon.

"Mother, please."

Mr. Lark cleared his throat. "Mr. Clemens wishes for the return of this house."

The fruit of nearly seven years of work, of complete devotion, gone in an instant. "It's my house. I have the deed."

"It won't be much longer, unless you particularly enjoy a thorough dragging through the mud." He shrugged. "I understand he's got rather a lot on you."

"He can't do this!"

"Oh, but he can."

"Thank you, Mr. Lark." She shut the door.

She stalked up the stairs two at a time, then burst into the spare room, where she dropped to her knees and started pulling trunks from under the bed.

"Isabel! What are you doing?"

"Leaving. I won't be near that malevolent force another moment."

Mrs. Lyon's voice rose with her hysteria. "You're not just going to give him your house, are you?"

"No. I'm going to see our lawyer. I want to sell the place—I want to get away from that man—but I'm not giving it to anyone."

"Which lawyer? Not Mr. Hill in Tarrytown! Everyone there will know our troubles!"

"Everyone everywhere does know our troubles, Mother. I'm not going to take it anymore. I thought innocence was enough."

"Innocence is never enough!"

"Evidently not."

Isabel dragged a case onto the bed, then recognized it: she had taken this one to Bermuda. Tears boiled in her throat as she grabbed for a different one, one she didn't associate with her relationship with The King, one she hadn't used since Italy.

She popped the latches and flipped open the bag. In her violence, the cloth divider of the lid flopped loose, ripped open by the weight of a book behind it. Yellow pages fluttered out, along with crumbling remains of flowers too desiccated for anyone but her to identify, and the book. Isabel picked up the volume—Baedeker's *Florence*—then put it down. She recognized the smudged handwriting on the papers: hers. But they weren't her words. They were words that she'd forgotten.

She sat down and, accompanied by the shuffling sound of her

mother opening the wardrobe and transferring clothes in the next bedroom, began to read.

December 23, 1903

She liked flowers. Hydrangeas were her favorite. The boy hadn't known their name until he had brought them to her that first time. He had thought of them as snowballs, and strictly as fodder to chuck at his friends until bigger boys took over the game and the pack of them was finally chased off at broom-point by the owners of the bushes. He wasn't sure what had made him pick them for her that first time, and in Mrs. Quarles's yard, too, when he knew that Mrs. Quarles's black sausage of a terrier would bite him as soon as look at him.

But pick them, he did. Each snap of a stem sent a satisfying shiver through the parent plant as the boy plucked, spurring him to rip shoot after shoot from the resistant bush. He had accumulated a respectable bouquet, no, a church-altar-worthy bouquet, when the back door opened.

The dog shot out like an oily-haired cannonball. The boy pelted across the yard and flung himself over the fence, a mere tooth's breadth from a puncturing. He streaked toward town, posies in hand, his skin tingling from the piercing it nearly got. Cutting through the hot thick air that smelled like turtles—everything in that river town smelled like turtles—he flashed by a sow and piglets demolishing a watermelon shell, past two clerks slumped in rockers before a storefront, past the fragrant drunkard sleeping in the shade of some crates stacked and ready for the next steamboat. He ditched inside the general store, where he darted past Mrs. Holiday waiting for her coffee to be ground, dodged Old Man Breed fishing a pickle from the brine of the pickle crock, and skirted the lopsided wicker baby buggy containing the Robards' ninth child. He bounded up the sagging stairs, the stolen snowballs flopping against his freckled twig of an arm, to the rooms above, where his family uncomfortably lived.

Jennie was at the spinning wheel in the main room. She sang as she spun, her voice as sweet to him as fresh milk. " 'Go chain the lion down.' "

He waited, panting, as the wheel kept whining—the most beautiful sound in the world, the boy thought, like angels humming—until she had put a slender brown hand to it. The wheel stopped.

He held out the flowers.

"For your mama?" she said.

He swiped the back of his arm over his forehead, making his red bush of hair spring up. "No. You."

She sat back, the knobs of her knees making a tent of her yellow and brown calico skirt as she regarded the boy. He squirmed under her steady stare even as he drank it in.

She smiled. "Well, that is about the nicest thing anyone ever did for me."

His insides warmed with happiness.

"Those are my favorite flowers." She was missing an upper eyetooth, which only enhanced her beauty. He thought all women should have such a gap. "Did you know that?"

He shook his head.

"Hydrangeas. Your mama taught me that word: hydrangeas." She wiped her face on her sleeve, then got up. Though the air in the room was stifling, she moved with the light step of a doe. She had raised him up from a baby, all six and a half of his years—she'd been with his parents since they were married—and still she looked like a girl. The boy could watch her move all day, or listen to her talk or just breathe. In his household, with his mother's fury as ready to boil over as beans bubbling under a rattling lid—even more so since his brother Ben had died the month before—and with his father's cold stare, Jennie's presence was like cool water chuckling through a spring house. He thought he might marry her someday.

"I'll get you more."

"No. What my going to do with these?" She reached into a cupboard and brought out a tin cup. "We'll tell your mama they're for her."

She saw his face.

"Sammy."

He crossed his greenstick arms. "What?"

"Thank you."

And so his quest began to supply her with many hydrangeas. Neighbors soon found their bushes picked clean. Children had to turn to the spiky balls from sweet gum trees or the spongy pellets from sycamores for ammunition for their wars. He had even further unburdened Mrs. Quarles's bushes, allowing her shorthaired bullet of a beast several shots at cleaning its teeth on his ragged britches. Within a few days, mounds of drooping hydrangeas lay on the battered floor of the main room above the store, filling the air with a green tang as they wilted.

One afternoon his mother turned from the open window out which she'd been staring, her forefinger and thumb pressing her lips as if to seal in a scream. She looked down on the hydrangeas and scowled as if seeing them for the first time. Suddenly, she was in motion, her apron strings swinging, the locket around her neck thumping, the cords of her throat straining and white. She snatched up the limp snowballs and, one by one, hurled them out the window, little cream-colored fluttering petticoats that smashed on the street below.

September came and with it school. For a time, the boy forgot about hydrangeas. He liked school. He liked learning. He was good at it. It made him feel special. Smart.

One day, just past his seventh birthday in November, a day no one remembered but him and Jennie, who marked the occasion by putting maple syrup on his toast the way he liked it, he was walking home, reading his McGuffey's, when a soft tan blur caught his eye. There, in Mrs. Quarles's yard, shuddering in the wind that held the snaky breath of the Mississippi in it, was a single hydrangea head, faded to an airy wisp. How had he missed it?

With an eye on the door for the greasy black terror, he made his way to the shrub, his book clamped against his chest. Closing his hand around the speckled green stem, he yanked the survivor free.

The door banged open. The boy tumbled across the yard and over the fence, laughing, not only at beating the dog and its crooked yellow teeth but at picturing the surprise on Jennie's face.

He took the stairs to his family's lodgings at a happy hop. When he spilled into the room, Jennie was not there. She wasn't at her wheel, or tending the stove, or on her stool, mending cuffs or collars or socks.

His mother wasn't there, nor were his sister and his brothers. A steamboat had just docked, the tootling of its calliope audible clear across town as the passengers, God's privileged ones, trod down the gangplank to shore. Maybe the others were there. He knew that he would have been, had not his mission driven him home. He hated to miss a boat.

He noticed that the door to his parents' bedroom was closed. Sometimes when his mother had headaches, she shut herself in there. No children were allowed in if she was sleeping.

He listened. A muffled thumping came from behind the peeling door. Mother?

He crept forward, the pat of his bare soles swallowed by the stillness of the room. The shriveled hydrangea head trembling in one hand, he turned the glass knob.

They were against the wall, next to the picture of Jesus. His father sprang off her with a smack of wet flesh.

"Get out!" His father wiped his face on his arm.

The boy shrank into himself. He could not move.

"Sammy! What the hell are you doing?" His father stepped toward him.

Jennie touched his father's back.

The boy turned and trampled blindly down the stairs, mistaking the fear in his father's face for his own red-black rage.

PART SIX

The New York Times, April 22, 1910

MARK TWAIN IS DEAD AT 74

End Comes Peacefully at His New England Home After a Long Illness.

DANBURY, Conn., April 21.—Samuel Langhorne Clemens, "Mark Twain," died at 22 minutes after 6 tonight. Beside him on the bed lay a beloved book—it was Carlyle's "French Revolution"—and near the book his glasses, pushed away with a weary sigh a few hours before. Too weak to speak clearly, "Give me my glasses," he had written on a piece of paper.

The people of Redding, Bethel, and Danbury listened when they were told that the doctors said Mark Twain was dying of angina pectoris. But they say among themselves that he died of a broken heart. And this is the verdict not of popular sentiment alone. Albert Bigelow Paine, his biographer to be and literary executor, who has been constantly with him, said that for the past year at least Mr. Clemens had been weary of life.

The New York Times, April 23, 1910

MARK TWAIN AND HALLEY'S COMET.

To the Editor of The New York Times:

I wish to draw your attention to a peculiar coincidence.

- Mark Twain born, Nov. 30, 1835.
- Last perihelion of Halley's comet, Nov. 10, 1835.
- Mark Twain died, April 21, 1910.
- Perihelion of Halley's comet, April 20, 1910.

It so appears that the lifetime of the great humorist was nearly identical (the difference being exactly fifteen days) with the last long "year" of the great comet.

R. FRIDERICI.

Westchester, N. Y., April 22, 1910

34.

April 1910
Racine, Wisconsin

ISABEL'S MOTHER SNAPPED ON the light in the spare upstairs bedroom, disturbing the fringe of the lampshade. The rattling of katydids wafted through the open window, and the barking of neighborhood dogs. Somewhere out there in the dark, a baby cried. Mrs. Lyon never thought she'd live in Wisconsin. Wisconsin! In truth, she hadn't given the place much thought for most of her long life, until they'd moved there. While the climate might have been rather similar to Tarrytown's, it was worlds away in refinement and charm—although she did rather like the malted milk balls that were a specialty here.

She dabbed her nose with her handkerchief, then tucked it back up her sleeve. Though it was getting late, there was only one more of Isabel's boxes to unpack. Isabel really should thank her: *she* wasn't going to do it. She'd become such a funny little thing of late. So distant. Not her cheerful self at all. Vacantly tapping Beethoven's Fifth with her knuckle on the table when she thought no one was in the room—Mrs. Lyon couldn't understand it.

Mrs. Lyon picked up the box, immediately groaning from its effect on her hips. She had misjudged its weight. It was surprisingly heavy for its size: not that big, about the size of a department store hatbox. The side of the box was printed with FRESH TURKEY in red and green, with a sturdy red and green gobbler as illustration. She thought wildly that there might actually be a live turkey inside, heavy as the box was—an idea that gave her a chill, until she laughed at her delightful imagination. Mrs. Lyon wondered if the contents hadn't been disturbed since Isabel had packed to leave their Redding house last summer.

That had been a hurried move, being rushed along by a sheriff after Mr. Clemens had taken back Isabel's house, one of the most humiliating episodes in Mrs. Lyon's life. This was a different move altogether. Such a pretty house Mr. Ashcroft had bought Isabel here—not as nice as the house Charles had bought Mrs. Lyon, of course, but these were different times. Persons were flitting around in aeroplanes, for goodness' sake. Unsinkable luxury liners, big as a city block, were zipping people across the ocean. People were gaping at Frankenstein's monster on the silver screen instead of reading about it in Mary Shelley's book. Charles would not recognize the place. But Charles had not lived. She had.

You would think that Isabel would enjoy her little dollhouse more, fluff it up a bit, put up curtains in the breakfast nook, hang some ferns on the porch. She had planted some hydrangeas by the front door just after they'd moved in but had lost interest in gardening after that. There was no talk of putting in a nursery. Mrs. Lyon had resigned herself to what that meant.

Mrs. Lyon opened the box and removed a layer of balled-up newspaper. She uncrumpled one—*The New York Times*—then harrumphed. The *Times*! Traitors. After all the occasions when Isabel had treated the reporters so nicely on Mr. Clemens's behalf. The very fellows who had drunk Isabel's coffee over the years had fallen over themselves to print every foul lie Mr. Clemens and Clara said about her.

Mrs. Lyon took it personally. Hadn't she done those reporters a favor that night when Helen Keller had come to visit, walking through the cold and dark all the way from Isabel's house to call them on Mr. Clemens's telephone after Mr. Wark had come to her door near tears? She'd let the reporters know that Clara Clemens was considering marriage, that her swain was right in Mrs. Lyon's very house, and after finally convincing them that she was *not* crying wolf this time, they'd come. Regardless if they didn't get the story about Clara and Mr. Wark that Mrs. Lyon thought she was giving them, they got an even better one when the old man told them his daughter was marrying Gabrilowitsch. And look at the thanks Mrs. Lyon got!

She sniffed, stroking her high collar. Heavens, that had been a topsy-turvy evening. Mrs. Lyon had thought that after Clara's affair with Mr. Wark was exposed, Mr. Clemens would flee straight into Isabel's arms to save his good name. Isabel *was* living under his roof, and no matter what she said, it really did not look right. And the two were so much in love—why didn't they just go ahead and marry? All they needed was a little push, and Mrs. Lyon, as a good mother, gave it.

Yet when Mrs. Lyon essentially *delivered* him to Isabel, she wouldn't marry him. She went for Ralph. Why, you could have knocked Mrs. Lyon over with a buttonhook! In one stroke, her dreams of enlightening the Tarrytown ladies with talk of her daughter and famous son-in-law had fallen away. In one stroke, her vision of having tea with the English king had gone *poof*! Oh, the potential—wasted! Well, bad luck has a way of turning into good; it was a blessing that they didn't marry. For it turned out that Mrs. Lyon had been right from the start: the old man was just not nice.

Clutching her throat, she pawed through the wadded clippings to see if any were the articles with his foul accusations. Why, she'd shred them up! Isabel was the kindest, most caring girl in the world. Hadn't she made a lovely home for Mr. Clemens? Didn't she find the best doctors for poor Jean, who hadn't lasted a year without Isabel to watch over her? The girl had drowned in her own bathtub on Christmas Eve morning, eight months after Mr. Clemens had brought her home. Isabel had warned them that she couldn't be alone. Katy had found her dead—why didn't anyone wonder about that?

Mrs. Lyon sighed, feeling tired now as she sat among rafts of wrinkled newsprint floating upon her coverlet. At least Ralph had defended Isabel. For every accusation that the old liar and his daughter had come up with, Ralph had come back swinging with suits and countersuits. *He* wasn't afraid of the old bully. When he'd returned from England and found out that the rapscallion had forced her to sign away her *house*, he had the means to expose what a monster the brute was. Yet just when Ralph had the old villain against the wall, Isabel stopped him.

Mrs. Lyon could still see that day, clear as a bell—they were in the lobby of their hotel in New York, having lost the house. She'd begged Isabel to speak up. "Clear the air, child! Defend your name! Stand up for yourself!"

Mrs. Lyon could picture Ralph stalking to the telephone, then placing a call to the *Times*. Isabel had snatched the handset from him.

"Let Mr. Clemens keep his name," she'd said. "It means everything to him. I want him to have it."

"Why?" Ralph cried. "After all he's done to you!"

Oh, there'd been a row, out in public, too. But Isabel had held firm. She never defended herself, not even once.

Now the doorbell rang, giving Mrs. Lyon such a start that it rattled the clippings around her. She got up, gingerly straightened her sore hips, then tottered to the bedroom window just as the porch light came on and Isabel went out onto the front steps. Through the window screen, she could see Isabel receiving the reporters: two of them, one of them fat, the other one black-haired with a cowlick, like her son Charlie had. She found herself aching so sharply for Charlie, for young Isabel, for days she could never get back, that she could hardly breathe.

"He's died?" Mrs. Lyon heard Isabel say.

"Yep." This was the unruly-haired one who reminded her of Charlie. "This afternoon. Got it on the wire."

Suddenly, Isabel was brushing past them onto the walkway to look up at the sky.

"The maid says you killed him." The reporter flipped a page in his notepad. "A Katy Leary. She says he never got over your lying and stealing from him. Just mentioning your name would bring on a heart attack. She was there with him when he died."

Still shading her eyes, Isabel glanced at him as if at a fly, then lifted her face again to the dark. She hiccupped with laughter.

Mrs. Lyon saw the reporters look at each other. "Mrs. Ashcroft?"

The fat one tried again. "Is it true? Did he die of a broken heart? Or did Katy Leary have it wrong as to how you broke it? What I notice is that his health went downhill after you married Mr. Ashcroft. Weren't you and Mark Twain about to get married?"

Isabel jerked her gaze back down to them. "I have nothing to say."

"But what about you and him?"

Save for the buzzy tap of beetles against the screen, it was silent. When she finally spoke, Isabel's voice was thick. "Mark Twain was in love with his wife. Mark Twain was a family man who suffered from the loss of his children. I was his secretary. There was nothing between me and Mark Twain."

Mrs. Lyon listened, but Isabel would say no more. After the reporters left, she stayed out on the walkway. Mrs. Lyon was about to go down and bring her in when Isabel cried, "Sam, you didn't kill Jennie. Hear me? I forgive you. We all forgive you. We always have." Her sigh was that of a hurt animal, its injury deep and everlasting. "Oh, but you are lovable and naughty and good."

Mrs. Lyon's voice broke as she called through the screen. "Isabel!"

Her face still lifted to the heavens, Isabel raised her arms and whistled. "There goes America's Sweetheart." And then softer, almost inaudibly, "There goes my sweetheart."

Mrs. Lyon closed her eyes, then jumped when she heard the screen door bang. She dabbed her nose. What good did it do to dwell on the past? It couldn't bring them back: Charles or Charlie; her parents; nieces and nephews; friends she had loved. All you could do was to keep on going, no matter that your heart had broken.

She poked her handkerchief back up her sleeve thinking,

strangely, if she might trace Charles and Poppy's daughter. Had she little children? Were they smart, like Isabel? Would they like to learn to sew?

Taking a breath, she pressed her face to the window and looked up. Through the mesh, she saw it sailing over trees and rooftops, over the tip of the tallest steeple, over the glow of the restless city: a comet, searing its way through the velvet red-black night.

Author's Note

Even in a culture that encourages the rise of the self-made man, Samuel Clemens took his own creation to audacious heights. By the time Clemens was done fashioning himself into the humorist Mark Twain, his finished product bore little resemblance to the serious, often lonely and angry actual man. How did the son of a failed Virginian lawyer and his unloving wife go from a hardscrabble, traumatic childhood to an extravagant lifestyle in which he hobnobbed with kings and millionaires, the most widely known and beloved man in the world? Plenty of biographers have taken up the challenge of defining the man, but Clemens makes for a particularly slippery target in spite of his frequent talk about wanting to write the truth about himself. The truth is, Sam Clemens's fabled storytelling ability extended to the facts about his life.

It's telling that Clemens's "autobiography" is about Mark Twain, a made-up character. The autobiography of Samuel Clemens would be a different work altogether, and one that he never wrote. Yet the autobiography of the fictional Mark Twain got close enough to some of Clemens's true opinions that he insisted that it not be published for one hundred years after his death, thus putting a broad cushion between himself and his adoring public. One wonders what he felt that he needed to hide. As Thomas Edison said during Twain's lifetime, "An average American loves his family; if he has any love left over, he generally selects Mark Twain." Did Clemens fear that his adulation would be taken away if the man behind the curtain were discovered?

As much as the battle between Sam vs. Mark intrigued me as I considered writing about Mark Twain, the sand in the oyster that irritated me into layering a story around it was his treatment of his secretary of six-and-a-half years, Isabel Lyon. It bothered me that one month after Lyon married Clemens's business associate Ralph Ashcroft, Twain fired her. Over the course of the next few months, Clemens took away the house he'd deeded her, commenced a lawsuit against her, slammed her to reporters, and wrote damning letters to friends, including the infamous one to William Dean Howells in which he called her "a liar, a forger, a thief, a hypocrite, a drunkard, a sneak, a humbug, a traitor, a conspirator, a filthy-minded and salacious slut pining for seduction, and always getting disappointed, poor child." These letters became part of a 429-page manuscript exclusively devoted to destroying the reputations of Isabel and her husband. This stunningly ferocious vitriol was leveled against a woman who Clemens himself admitted knew him better than anyone. She intended to keep up her duties for Clemens after her marriage, for which she'd gotten his blessing, never imagining he would turn on her with a vengefulness that was breathtaking in its viciousness. To steal from Shakespeare, I thought the gentleman did protest too much.

Twain scholars have drawn up sides as to what caused this rift between Twain and the closest person in his life. One camp takes Twain's diatribe against Lyon at face value, believing that Lyon actually stole from him . . . when she wasn't trying to seduce him—unsuccessfully, according to the indignant Twain, who painted himself in an almost virginal light. The other position speculates that Clemens's daughter Clara was behind his abrupt betrayal of the most important woman in his life at the time. Twain approved of Isabel's sudden engagement to Ralph Ashcroft even as reporters were speculating about his own engagement to her; could Isabel's hurried wedding to another man have been part of a plan to cover up his daughter Clara's affair with her accompanist, Will Wark?

In this scenario, Twain had struck a deal with Clara: he would cease cohabitating with Isabel (who had an adjoining bedroom in his house) if Clara would give up the married Wark and let Ossip Gabrilowitsch make an honest woman of her, thus saving the reputations of both Clemens and his daughter. I believe that Clemens fully intended to keep Isabel as his secretary when she married Ralph, and fooled himself into believing that he could continue his close relationship with her after she was another man's wife. Interestingly, he told Isabel shortly after her marriage, "Remember, whatever I do is because of a promise I have made to Clara."

Meanwhile, Clara had started a letter-writing campaign against Isabel, as well as asking Standard Oil magnate H. H. Rogers to audit Isabel's accounts for possible embezzlement. On April 15, 1909, Clemens fired Isabel, yet he still had not made a public statement against her. The breaking point in Clemens's ability to go along with the scheme, it seems to me, was Ashcroft's letter sent two weeks after Clemens had fired Isabel, admonishing Clemens "to be a man" and defend Isabel against his daughter whose brain was "diseased with envy, malice, and jealousy." Already a prideful man, Clemens might have been especially sensitive to attacks on his virility, in particular from a man who was forty years his junior and had just married his beloved secretary. Twain hints in "Letters from Earth," written during that period, about disappointment in his own sexual capabilities:

> *[M]an is only briefly competent. . . . After fifty his performance is of poor quality; the intervals between are wide, and its satisfactions of no great quality to either party; whereas his great-grandmother is as good as new.*

In questioning Clemens's manhood, Ashcroft might have chosen the worst possible tack to rally Clemens behind him.

From this point on, Clemens's effort to distance himself from

Lyon took on the roar of a wounded beast, as if he were striking back after believing he had lost her to his virile young business associate.

To understand the relationship between Isabel Lyon and Sam Clemens, I had to understand the man. I went on pilgrimages to the places Clemens traveled or lived in while in the company of Isabel Lyon: New York City; Redding, Connecticut; Bermuda; and Florence, Italy. However, it was my stop at the Mark Twain House in Hartford, Connecticut, that altered the course of my book. The director there, Cindy Lovell, presented an overview of the two factions on the Lyon-Twain affair, then told me to go to the Mark Twain Papers in Berkeley, California, read Isabel Lyon's diary, and make up my mind for myself. I did so, and had my eyes opened.

From the pages of Lyon's daily reminder leapt a vibrant, intelligent, artistic woman who knew from the start that she was in a unique and historic position and was determined to make the best of it. From her first entry in 1903—"God does not put many such days into a woman's life"—she describes, over a six-year span, Clemens's actions and moods, the people who came to visit, and her own reactions. These observations became the road map for my story. Often I based the action on Isabel's entries, fleshing out the scenes with my imagination and nuggets from my research. In some cases, I used snippets of Lyon's and Clemens's own words. Clemens's incomparable gift for clever sayings was a novelist's dream; at times I plugged them into my characters' conversations, then embroidered around them.

As did the lion's share of events in *Twain's End*, the visit by Helen Keller, Anne Sullivan Macy, and John Macy actually happened. Isabel recorded that Helen was "plainly in love with Macy" and "he encourages this emotion and Helen not quite understanding it, makes no concealment of her feeling." Mrs. Macy seemed "distressed" by it, telling Isabel that "in some ways Helen was still a child." After reading hints in other sources about Helen's relationship with John Macy, I whooped out loud (in the very quiet Bancroft Library) when I came across this eyewitness account of its actuality in Isabel's diary. John Macy permanently left Anne Sullivan five years later, although she wouldn't grant him a divorce. He subsequently fell in love with a deaf woman, with whom he had a daughter.

Beyond Isabel's diary and Mark Twain's writings, *A Lifetime with Mark Twain: The Memories of Katy Leary, for Thirty Years His Faithful and Devoted Servant* by Mary Lawson, *Mark Twain, Family Man* by Caroline Thomas Harnsberger, and *My Father: Mark Twain* by Clara Clemens provided important insights into my characters, especially when read between the lines. *Mark Twain's Other Woman* by Laura Skandera Trombley and Karen Lystra's *Dangerous Intimacy: The Untold Story of Mark Twain's Final Years* were illuminating reading as well. The volumes of the *Autobiography of Mark Twain*, especially Volume 3, which contains the infamous "Ashcroft-Lyon Manuscript," informed my story greatly.

I first learned of one of the persons who I think greatly influenced the boy Sam Clemens in Ron Powers's *Mark Twain: A Life*. Jennie, the Clemens's house slave, was a character that I neither concocted for my book nor was her beating and subsequent sale "down the river" fictitious, although the story Clemens dictated to Isabel about Jennie came from my imagination. One has only to read Mark Twain's work to wonder what kind of mark his parents' treatment of someone so precious to him might have left upon him as a boy.

Isabel Lyon died at the age of ninety-four in New York City, working until her last few years as a secretary. She divorced Ashcroft after seventeen years of marriage. Actor Hal Holbrook consulted her in 1958 while developing his show, *Mark Twain Tonight*, recognizing her unmatched knowledge of Twain. She agreed to meet Holbrook on one condition: that he not repeat their conversation.

In the few months before she died, they met in her Greenwich Village basement apartment. There she would prop up her feet, pour herself a whiskey like she drank with Clemens, then talk of old times while puffing on the meerschaum pipe that Clemens had given her. She never did publicly speak out against Sam Clemens, nor would she address her character assassination at his hands. Perhaps she thought that innocence was enough.

Acknowledgments

WHEN I VISIT STUDENTS, I often address them in their school libraries. I tell the kids to look around at the books and imagine that behind each one is a person trying to speak to them. I realize now that I have understated the number. In reality, behind each book is a *crowd* of people, helping the author to get the story out.

In the front of the pack in the case of *Twain's End* is my agent, Emma Sweeney, who has stood with me since the book was just the wisp of an idea. Right with her is Karen Kosztolnyik, who has provided her patented kind-but-firm editorial encouragement and wisdom from the very start, and who has insisted, in her patient, dear way, that I give every last drop to the cause. I am thankful for their belief in me and my book.

I'm grateful as well for the tremendous support of the dream team at Gallery Books/Simon & Schuster: Carolyn Reidy, Louise Burke, Jen Bergstrom, Jennifer Robinson, Stephanie DeLuca, Liz Psaltis, Wendy Sheanin, Liz Perl, Michael Selleck, Lisa Litwack, and Becky Prager. This book would not be in your hands, friend-readers, without them.

I am indebted to the next group of people for making the staggering amount of field research necessary for this book an adventure and a pleasure: Cindy Lovell, executive director of the Mark Twain

House in Hartford; tour guide Daniel Sterner of the Mark Twain House; Neda Salem at the Mark Twain Papers at the University of California, Berkeley; Michael Wiertz and Carolyn Liv of Wave Hill, Riverdale, New York; Beatrice Simoni at the Pensione Bencistà in Fiesole, Italy; and Susan Boone Durkee, for the unforgettable day touring the Lobster Pot and the grounds of Stormfield, as well as for sharing her insights on Isabel Lyon and Twain and a chance to view the originals of her extraordinary portraits of the pair. I'm thankful for friends Ruth and Steve Berberich, Stephanie and Michael Connolly, and Stephanie Cowell, who were great helps and companions on various fact-finding missions. Thank you also to Diane Prucino and Tom Heyse for providing their mountain house as my writer's retreat.

Back home, I'm indebted to Karen Torghele, Jan Johnstone, and Thiery Goodman for their weekly infusions of support, and to Sue Edmonds, who not only is the most generous of cheerleaders, but the founder of this book. Thank you, Sue, for suggesting for the past few decades that Mark Twain would be a "really good subject." It took me awhile to get the hint, but I'm so glad that I took your advice.

Behind the crowd, giving me a lifelong push, are my sisters and brothers, Margaret Edison, Jeanne Wensits, Carolyn Browning, Howard Doughty, Arlene Eifrid, and David Doughty, and my wonderful nieces and nephews, in particular Linette Edison and Mary Streshly, who so often shelter their traveling aunt. But most of all I am indebted to my husband, Mike, for applying support on a daily basis, and to my daughters, Lauren, Megan, and Ali, whose love is the rock upon which I write.